ANASTACIA

Printed in Australia
Cover and internal design by Shawline Publishing Group Pty Ltd
First printing: February 2024

Shawline Publishing Group Pty Ltd
www.shawlinepublishing.com.au

Paperback ISBN 978-1-9231-0129-6
eBook ISBN 978-1-9231-0130-2

Distributed by Shawline Distribution and Lightning Source Global

A catalogue record for this
work is available from the
National Library of Australia

ANASTACIA

A HARRY BECKER MYSTERY

GORDON REID

Also by Gordon Reid

Evelyn Crowley

Becker

For June Maitland

Chapter 1

SHE SAT IN the car, watching the house. It was an ordinary sort of house, the sort you wouldn't notice driving along Swan Street. A small, red-brick cottage built in the nineteen twenties by the look of it. There was a lamp above the front door and three doorbells on a brass plate on a wall. No verandah, just a porch. On it stood two terracotta pots, one sporting a fuchsia bush and the other was what looked like a small cumquat.

Her name was Anastacia Babchuk. Her friends called her Chook, but not to her face.

She'd been waiting since before seven. One man had left soon after, walking down the road to a small supermarket. A family business that could afford to survive if you had another source of income. Especially income on which you paid no tax.

She checked her watch again. Ten past eight. The watch was encased in leather, for protection if things got rough. She'd once been a kick-boxer, a State champion. Didn't do much kicking now, just hitting when necessary. The car was a rented Holden. Nothing exceptional about that. Holdens were everywhere in Melbourne in 1996.

Something about the house puzzled her.

It had a scrubbed look, as if recently steam-cleaned. The garden was perfect. Real money must have been spent on this house, the kind of money that didn't like to talk about itself. Chook had seen enough. She moved on, parked about thirty yards past the house and used her mirrors. Waiting for the other son to appear.

She knew this area.

As a kid, she'd lived in the next suburb out, Burnley. In an old cottage, perhaps one of the originals. Just four rooms and a lean-to at the back for a kitchen and a laundry. No front verandah, not even a porch. There had been a verandah many years ago, but it'd become so rusty it had to be pulled down. Today you wouldn't have looked twice at the house if you'd been walking past, except perhaps to wonder who the hell would live in a dump like that? Just she and her father after her mother died. Until she could take it no longer, the silence. The not-speaking. Only a grunt now and then as he ate his *borsch*. Every night goddamned *borsch*.

He was a Ukrainian, who'd arrived in Australia in 1959. Got a job as a storeman in a warehouse in South Melbourne. Arrived with a wife, who worked as a cleaner at the Children's Hospital. They had a daughter in 1963. That daughter was now sitting in a rented car in Swan Street, Richmond, waiting to kill a man.

A tram went by. Then a police car crept up behind, silently and respectfully. She smiled to herself. A young bloke in uniform got out, walked up to her window, tapped on it. Slowly she rolled it down.

'Something wrong, Constable?'

'Would you mind telling me what you are doing here, sir?'

'Someone complain about a strange bloke sitting in a car? Outside their place? For over an hour?'

'Please answer the question, sir. What are you doing here?'

'That's none of your business.'

The local cop didn't like that. 'Would you mind getting out of the car, sir?'

Chook stared at him. 'You want me to get out of this car?'

'That's right, sir. If you don't mind?'

'What if I do mind?'

The cop tensed. He was a one-striper. Looked to be in his early twenties.

'Just get out of the car, please, sir.'

'And what if I don't?'

'I'm going to have to arrest you.'

'You're going to arrest me?'

'That's right.'

'Why?'

'Disobeying a lawful order.'

Chook smiled. She was enjoying this.

'Let me show you something.'

Slipped her left hand inside her jacket. The young cop jumped, his right hand dropping to his sidearm.

'Relax, sonny.' She pulled out her ID, complete with photo. Showed it to him. 'Ever seen one of these?'

He peered at it. 'Federal Police?'

'That's right.'

'You're an agent?'

'Right again.'

'Level three? What's that mean?'

'Sergeant to you.'

'You're a sergeant?'

'Do I look like some snotty-nosed probationer?'

'No, sir.'

'No, ma'am,' she said.

'What's that?'

'I'm a girl.'

'You're a girl?'

'You don't believe me?'

'They said a man.'

'You want me to get out and drop my pants? In the middle of Swan Street?'

'No, sir. I mean, No, ma'am.'

'Satisfied?'

'Sorry about that, Sarge.' He looked around. 'Doing a stakeout, are you?'

'None of your business.'

'Just trying to be helpful.'

'Piss off, sonny. You're spoiling my view.'

The young cop went back to his car, sat there for a while, no doubt reporting in. Then drove off, just as slowly as he'd arrived. Chook watch him go. Word would soon get around, about a big blond Federal bitch in an unmarked car watching a house in Richmond. She wasn't worried. No-one would know which was the target.

She relaxed, tapping the steering wheel. And waited.

In the old days, she'd walk all the way into the city, a skinny girl nudging six feet, looking in shop windows. Looking for a job. Never got one. Too tall, too ugly. She'd frighten the customers. Since then, Swan Street had been tarted up, old stores replaced by fashion shops and beauty salons and fast-food joints, but the buildings still had their Victorian corniches and their faded pride. Back in the gold-rush days, Melbourne had been the third biggest city in the Empire. Richmond now smelt worn-out, like an old shoe you should have got rid of years ago. Chook could still smell the Rosella factory, smell the tomato sauce and the pickle. And the poverty of all the years between.

One day, passing the White Swan pub on the way home, a short bloke, standing by a Harley Davidson and holding two glasses, had said: 'G'day, Lofty, feel like a beer?' He'd bought the spare for a mate, who'd vanished when the police had turned up. She'd never touched liquor in her life, but she'd accepted. Sipped slowly, glancing at the Harley.

'Nice bike,' she'd said.

'Yeah,' he'd said.

'That yours?'

'Yeah, wanta go for a burn?'

'I might,' she'd said. 'Then again, I mightn't.'

'Yeah? Really?' He thought about it, hopefully. 'Ever been rooted?'

'Not that I remember.'

His name was Stumpy Watson. Walked with one leg shorter than the other. Result of a car accident years ago. Not his fault, got a big payout. That's why he could afford a Harley. And that's how she'd started riding with bikies. And got into a lot of trouble, especially with the cops. The usual reasons— drugs, booze, common assault, habituating with known criminals. Things were different now. She was a cop herself, over six feet and a lot heavier. And a lot more decisive.

She was going to kill a man, if he were at home. His name was Salvatore Pisano.

If she did, no-one would give a damn. Just one Mafia boss rubbing out another Mafia boss, the local constabulary would say. Let them kill each other. Pisano was more than a boss. It was said he ran things in Victoria. If so, he was the boss of bosses.

Chook looked at her watch again. Twenty past eight.

This could go on all day. The other son might not come out. Maybe he was having a day off? Maybe doing the washing? Or the cleaning? For his father who was, according to local intelligence, seventy-nine and bedridden. His wife was seventy-one, Giuseppina her name. Back in Griffith she was called *La Donna*, the Lady. She did the talking, because her husband was—

Something was happening.

A car was backing out from a garage behind the cottage, an old but neat Fiat. Youngish man at the wheel. Not quite middle-aged, maybe early forties. Reversed onto the street, then turned the Fiat's nose around and drove off along Swan Street. Disappeared around a corner into Church Street.

She did a final check in her mirrors.

A hundred yards behind, an old man was walking a dog, the dog stopping every few yards to sniff and pee. The man was reading a newspaper folded into tight columns. Wearing thick glasses, looked as blind as a bat. On the other side of the street, two men were loading a van with two big words on its side: Move Yourself. They wouldn't be interested in her.

Chook patted the automatic under her left shoulder. Didn't expect to have to use it. Smothering should do the job. The Colt was just for show, in case anyone wanted to argue. She studied the house again, still worried about the three doorbells.

Some smelly, old Dago in there had ordered the hit on Evelyn Crowley. And Polly Politis had died trying to protect her. Chook had killed the hitman, and now she'd get rid of the bastard who'd sent him. But Pisano was close to death. She had to reach him before he croaked it. Had to have the satisfaction of killing him. No-one in this house was going to complain if she did. They knew the rules: You kill my brother, I kill yours. You rape my sister, I rape yours. No need to bring the police into this.

She got out and closed the door, waited for another tram to pass.

Then walked straight across to the gate.

Chapter 2

THERE WAS NO gate. Just a gap in a low brick wall about eighteen inches high. She walked up to the front door. The bell buttons still worried her. Then she realised—it was a safeguard. You had to know the combination. Which to press and in what order. She pressed the top one. Nothing happened. Pressed the second, the same. Then the third, no result. So, she pressed the first and the third together, which seemed to be the last thing any stranger would think of. Then she pressed the second. That was it. The door opened, just an inch or two. Held by a brass chain.

One eye looked out at him.

An old woman's eye, an inquisitive eye. A frightened eye.

'Oh, hi there,' Chook said. 'Salvatore? Is he at home by any chance?'

The eye blinked. 'Salvatore?'

'Yeah, Salvatore Pisano. Doesn't he live here?'

'What you want? I never see you before.'

'I want to see Salvatore. He told me the combination.'

'Salvatore, he tell you?'

'Yeah, I stuffed it up, as usual. Had to try them all.'

'Who you?'

'Liam,' she said. 'Liam from the old town, you know? Griffith? Up north? Used to work for him. Back when I was a kid.'

'You kid?'

'I was then, pickin' lemons. He used to call me Lemon Groves.'

'Lemon?'

'Lemon Groves, that's me. My real name's Liam Groves. It's sort of Irish. How is the old bastard?'

'*Bastardo*?'

'Yeah. Gee, I sure would like to see Sally again. Used to do jobs for him. You know what I mean?' She patted the Colt under the jacket.

'You want for to see Salvatore?'

'If that's no bother?'

'Salvatore, he sick.'

'Sick? Is he? Gee, that's bad. I'm sorry. Could I see him for just a minute?'

'No, no, no.'

'Just one minute?'

'He not here.'

'Salvatore's not at home?'

'He sick in hospital.'

'In hospital? Gee, which one?'

The old lady was trying to close the door. Chook had a hand on it.

'Which hospital?'

'You go now, please.'

'Gee, I've come all this way.'

'No, no, no—'

She stepped right back. Then hit the door with her full weight, fifteen stones.

The chain snapped. The door flew open, knocking the old lady flying.

'Your name Giuseppina?'

'*Si*,' she said.

Chook seized her by the neck. 'Where is Salvatore?'

'*Che*?'

Chook kicked the door shut. Shook her up. 'Your name Giuseppina Pisano?'

'*Che*?'

'Spikida Inglish?'

She nodded, terrified.

'Where is Salvatore Pisano?'

Afraid she was going to die. She had heart trouble, her blood pressure bad. Now going up and up, bang, bang, bang…

'Where is Salvatore?'

She tried to say, he sick, he no speak. Nothing much came out. Her eyes were wide with fear. Chook pulled out the Colt, poked her in the chest. 'I'm talkin' to you, stupid. Where is he? Where's your fucking husband?'

'Sal—Sal—'

'In bed? Don't give me no shit. You got him in here? Which room?'

She was choking.

'Come!' Chook said. Dragging the woman, almost lifting her off the floor.

Giuseppina Pisano had a screwed-up little face, wrinkled, lined, leathery, spotted with age, hook-nosed and hook-eyed, squinting up at her attacker. Frightened someone had squealed. Some deal gone wrong. What had she done? Salvatore had told her to make the decisions. Never say she made them. Nobody'd like that, a woman of her age, who's not the brightest and not good at being authoritative. Not good at sounding like Salvatore, even though he no longer speaks.

Every day she'd telephone Guido Terracini his shop in Chapel Street and ask him what she got to do and Guido say nothing. Guido, he just bookkeeper, he don't know nothing. But Guido, he's scared. He's plenty scared like her, like everyone in Melbourne. Who gonna be next *capo dei capi*? Who gonna get killed?

She was dragged from room to room, protesting.

'Salvatore? He no here. He in hospital.'

'What's wrong with him?'

'He sick, he got the stroke, he dying.'

'What hospital?'

The woman was wriggling and gasping. Rapidly changing colour, now red, now brown, now blue. Fear rattling her eyes.

'You don't know? You'd better know fuckin' well quick. Otherwise, I'm gonna have to make your eyes pop. You know what I mean?'

'Who you? Who you?'

Chook stuck the Colt under her chin. Looking in one room then the next.

'Who am I? I'm just a guy. I do jobs. Know what I mean? I do 'em quick. No fuckin' around. I should be out of here by now. Understand?'

'Somebody, he send you?'

'Yeah, somebody.'

'Who send you?'

'Who send me? Somebody you know, sweetheart.'

'Who I know?'

Chook lifted her by the neck, so her feet were almost off the floor. Only the toes touching. Held her close, almost nose to nose, stared into her eyes.

'Silvano,' she said.

'Silvano? Silvano?'

'Silvano Cosco.'

'Silvano? Angelo boy? Angelo, he dead.'

'Yeah, Angelo's boy. Silvano says Salvatore did it, killed his fuckin' father. Shot him sixteen times.'

'No, no, no. Salvatore, he no do that thing. He good man. Why? Why?'

'Don't ask me, lady. Not my problem. I'm just doin' a job. Already taken the money and I'm not givin' it back, understand? And I'm runnin' out of time. Where the fuck is Salvatore Pisano?'

'No, no, please!' She was spluttering something unintelligible.

'What's that?'

'He gone rally.'

'What?'

'He gone rally.'

'Rally? Rally? What's that mean?'

Her face grey now. She went down limply. Then passed out.

When she recovered, the madman had gone. Phoned her sons and tried to tell them, but they were not available. No-one was available except Renata on the desk. She was Stephano's wife. All Giuseppina could say was, you tell Stephano he got come home quick.

Eventually he did.

Then came the second son, Michaele, ten minutes later.

By then it was too late. Much too late.

Chook was crossing the road when it hit her. The old girl must have meant *Relais*, a place with a fancy name in Hawthorn, not far from Richmond. Just past Burnley, in fact. She knew it well enough. Her mother had died there of cancer, a year before she met Stumpy Watson. She got in the car and found the place on her mobile. Yes, they did have a Mr Pisano, but he was unable to speak. That did not matter, she said. Five minutes later she was out there.

It was a pleasant location, just off Hawthorn Road, in a side street that ran down to the river. One of the better by-ways of old Hawthorn—when it was home to bankers and owners of cash and carry stores and directors of co-operative building societies back in the nineteenth century, back before the big crash of 1893. The banks closing their doors, customers banging on doors, demanding their money. It was an old-money place, not the land of the rich, not Toorak, but it was middle-class, comfortable and nondescript. Now, new money was moving in, tradesmen's vans parked everywhere.

There was a large sign out front: *Le Relais*, which in French means relay station, a sort of halfway house back in the old coaching days. A place where you could rest before moving on. Half way to where? You didn't need much imagination to work that out. This place was a hospice, where you might go after a serious operation. Most likely you wouldn't recover. In the old days it had been a big family mansion, extended several times since then. Nothing especially smart or new or prosperous about it. Well-kept gardens, however.

Chook went to the reception desk. A woman in uniform smiled at her.

'Can I help you?'

'Mr Pisano, please. I rang a few minutes ago.'

'Oh, yes, Mr Pisano may be asleep.'

'At this hour? It's not yet nine.'

'He sleeps a lot. He doesn't speak, you know.'

'I know. Giuseppina told me he'd had a stroke.'

'Emphysema too. All those cigarettes.'

'Gee, the poor old bugger.'

'Are you one of the family?'

'Not exactly. I used to work for him years ago. In Griffith,' Chook added.

'Griffith?'

'New South Wales.'

'You'll have to sign in, I'm afraid.'

'Yes, of course.' Chook signed, giving Lemon Groves and a false address in Griffith.

'Lemon Groves?'

'Old Sally used to call me that.'

The receptionist smiled in the way receptionists do, both warmly and modestly.

'You'll find him down there on the left. Room six.'

'Thank you very much.'

Chook went in, not seeing a man at first, only a few rumpled humps in the bedclothes. Then she saw a head, rolled to one side, almost off the pillow. Mouth wide open, showing yellow teeth, some missing, a gold one to one side. His pillow was stained with pink dribble, the sheet too. Hair, thin and white. Quite handsome hair. In Chook's experience, most Italians had lovely hair, long and dark. They were good barbers too, tradesmen who knew their craft.

She went to him respectfully, bending as if to kiss him, the poor old bastard.

There was a smell in room. Not only the odours you would expect in a hospital—disinfectants and floor polish and drooping flowers. Not the smell of curtains or soft rubber soles on the polished floors. It was the smell of decrepitude. The smell of old age and old bodies and old teeth, badly cared for. All the cheese and garlic and olives and red wine. The food of the old days, the old ways. And the good times.

Pisano looked as though he'd been in Australia most of his life, probably arrived on a migrant ship soon after the war. Maybe a ship full of penniless hopefuls in the early fifties. Worked hard in a fruit shop or a grocery or on a farm and had made some money. But never enough. He'd want to be someone, have more money, have lots of children, everybody singing, everybody happy—in a country of easy pickings. No matter how much they had sent home to the old country, the old people in the crags and bluffs and the pines and rippling streams of the *Aspromonte* crags and peaks and pines and soaring eagle always wanted more.

Chook bent down close, examining that face, now at rest, breathing, choking, smelly. She'd expected to find a fat blob of a creature, but this man was not all that fat. Maybe he was not *the* fat man. But, if he'd been in bed for weeks or months, he could have wasted away. She didn't know. Perhaps Buster had been wrong. Perhaps the boss was not a fat man at all.

It didn't matter. Someone at his address had killed Polly, and that was all that mattered.

She looked as though she were going to kiss the old bastard, but she was checking his face. And his neck. There were indistinct blotches, like bruises which were not bruises but something else that comes with lying too long in bed, especially if you are old. It was a breakdown of capillaries. Large brown blotches that probably had started as red blotches. Here and there, random. As if his body didn't know where to start dying. In a few days, or weeks at most, the bodily functions would break down altogether. No matter how many times they turned him over, they could not stop the rot.

Chook was in luck. No nurse would notice any thumb prints.

She sat there, both thinking and not thinking about the job in hand.

This was the man who had ordered the hit on Evelyn Crowley, because she knew too much. The kid from Melbourne had got into the safe house in Canberra and shot first Polly because she was in the way and then Evelyn. Polly had been Anna Politis. Called herself Pollyanna, Polly for short. Anastacia was Chook, because no ignorant Australian could ever get her name right. It was Babchuk, pronounced Bab*chuck*, but everyone pronounced it Bab*chook*. Which drove her mad.

She'd spent weeks trying to find the hitman, some scrawny little creep on a big red dirt bike to Harry Becker's place, a farmhouse west of Wagga Wagga. Noticed the bike parked outside the gate. Had gone in and killed him. Now she was in Melbourne, sitting beside the man who'd sent him. An old man whose breath stank of decay. He was going to die soon, so what was the point of killing him?

None at all, except that she had sworn to the ghost and the spirit and the memory and the friendship of Polly Politis that she'd find him and kill him. Not only because she'd loved Polly, but because Polly had been the only woman who'd ever invited her into her own bed. Treated her like a fellow human being, a big bitch like her.

Chook didn't know what to do, so let her hands do what they liked to do.

Took his left hand in her right loosely, perhaps affectionately. Then slipped the left hand under the old man's cretaceous neck. If you happened to be passing, you might think his visitor was whispering to him. Which she was, but nothing complimentary. Nothing the dying creature would wish to hear, if he could hear at all. He must have been able to hear at home, when The Lady would pass on messages, asking for his decision. This old man was *lo capo dei capi*, the head of heads. The boss, who ran things in Melbourne.

Slowly, the hand under the scrawny neck closed, talons searching for the jugular each side. Then they went in. His eyes sprang open, not seeing but knowing. Something was going to happen. Chook watched the raddled face. It went red at first, swollen and stifled. Then blue. His mouth opened, his tongue moved, struggled. A brief cough came, like a fart from a fatalistic arse.

It took fifteen to twenty seconds. Then his face went soft and grey.

His heart had stopped.

Il capo dei capi delle famiglie era morto.

Chapter 3

SHE RETURNED THE Holden to the rental firm, picked up her Harley Davidson at the motel and reached Wagga Wagga early in the afternoon. Called at the office and talked to Laura Langley, who ran the office. Then rang Harry Becker, suggested they have a drink at the William Hovell. She sat in a corner, waiting. Sipping a middy of Hahn and thinking about Melbourne. It had taken a long time, but she done it. She'd killed the one who'd called the hit. Two women had died, Polly Politis and Evelyn Crowley, one good and one bad. Back in Canberra she and Polly used to watch Evelyn, sitting with or walking with Becker, chatting to her husband at home, or heard her on the phone.

Her house had been bugged. The police wanted to know what her husband was going to do—come in and tell them what was going on at the Royal Bank, or kill himself? A strange sort of woman, not so much mixed up as one who did not add up. At war with her criminal family, with her friends, her lovers and with herself. Not sure where she was going. Not really going anywhere, as far as they could see.

Quite likely, Evelyn was unknowable. A staged sort of woman, always looking good, always on the alert, watching reactions. Presenting herself without deliberately drawing eyes. A woman like Evelyn Crowley, perfectly sculptured, perfectly dressed, sitting like a model in a studio or a dignitary in a box at the opera? She was an image, not a real woman. She may have been flesh and blood, but she was not like Polly and not like Robyn. Real women who hurt and cried and yet laughed and sang, lovable for all their faults. Evelyn, it would seem, had been a highly composed woman, composed by herself. She was all image. No-one could know her, not even herself.

Becker walked into the William Hovell. He'd been badly injured when the house on his farm had blown up. A broken fibula. That was a month ago. Didn't need the canvas boot any more, and he could get by with a short crutch.

He sat slowly, awkwardly.

'How did it go?' he asked.

'No problems.' She told him about Pisano not being at home. Having to trace him to a hospice. Had to sit by him, watching him, eyes closed, breathing badly. Head almost under the cotton blanket. Gasping.

'Wish he'd been awake,' she said.

'If he was, he might have started yelling.'

She nodded. 'Would've loved to hear him screaming, but I had him by the throat.'

'You could have been arrested, if someone heard.'

'I don't give a stuff, mate.'

'You're crazy, Chook.'

Becker realised his mistake. He'd called her Chook. This time she didn't blow up. Just shrugged, pulled a face. Let it go.

'Yeah, crazy.'

'What happens now?'

'What happens? I've been recalled to Canberra. For a conference, they said.'

'A conference? For one?'

'Yeah, they reckon I'm too obvious.'

'Who says you are?'

'The bigwigs in Canberra.'

'Too obvious?'

'Yeah, a Federal cop is supposed to be invisible.'

'And you're not?'

'Ah, fuck 'em.'

'When did you learn this?'

'Laura told me when I got back.'

'When are you going?'

'When I finish this beer.'

Bruce came over, inquiringly.

'I'll have the same,' Becker said.

Bruce left. Bruce was one of those men who come and go, leaving no impression. Becker changed the subject.

'What did he look like, this Pisano?'

'Nothing at all.'

'Nothing?'

She thought about it, slumped and slumberous. It had been a long ride back.

'About eighty years old, with a face you wouldn't notice if he passed you in the street. Or, if you did, you'd forget it immediately. As ordinary as an unwashed potato. Dark brown eyes, tired eyes, tired of living eyes, like those of some dog that doesn't understand a word you say. And a broken tooth here and there and scabs and bruises. He'd been too long in bed. He was rotting. His skin breaking up. He stank. He couldn't speak. He was crap. Something you wouldn't want to find on the sole of your boot.'

'He was some sort of human being,' Becker said.

'So was Adolf Hitler.'

Bruce came back with the beer. And hesitated. 'Could I have a word with you, Stacey? Sometime?'

'Piss off, Bruce. I'm not in the mood.'

Bruce went away, softly and silently. If Bruce was hurt, he never showed it. Maybe he was one of those people used to being trodden on. Grateful for having a job. Doing the same thing every day, pulling beer. And being polite.

'So, what now?' Becker said.

'Life goes on, I suppose.'

'Barnes is dead. Did you know?'

'Barnes? Yeah?'

'Killed himself. Got up onto the hospital roof and jumped, head-first.'

'To make sure of it, eh? And Silvano Cosco—'

'He's still saying Pisano did it.'

Chook smirked. 'Perfect, that's perfect.'

She fell silent for a moment, then sighed. It was a long, drawn-out sigh.

'Before I left,' she said, 'I called in on my old man. Still at the old house in Burnley. It's a wreck now. Garden full of weeds. Good for nothing but the land. He was offered three-hundred-thousand just for the block, but refused. Said he was gonna stay there until he died.'

'How is he?'

'As uncommunicative as ever.'

'You've never talked about him.'

'What can I say? He doesn't tell me anything. Never forgiven me for clearing out when I was still a kid. Went riding with bikies.'

'What does he do?'

'He's on the age pension. That pays the bills.'

'Nothing all day?'

'Nothing as far as I can see.'

'And at night?'

'Has a part-time job.

'Doing what?'

Chook took a long time answering.

'Works in a crematorium. At night.'

'Jesus,' Becker said.

'Yeah, Jesus.'

They finished their beers and walked out.

It was late now, after four. The skies were dark. People were coming and going. Some shouting, calling across the street. They reached her bike.

'It's gonna rain,' Becker said.

'Only a couple of hours to Canberra.'

'You're gonna get wet.'

'I've been wet before.'

Becker was both relieved to be rid of her, and yet disappointed. Chook was a dangerous friend to have. On the other hand, he owed her a lot. 'When do you go?'

'Right now.' Chook looked at her wristwatch. 'Should make it in good time for dinner.'

Becker didn't know what to say. That he was sorry? That he was relieved?

'You didn't answer the question,' he said.

'What question?'

'Why did you do it?'

'Do what?'

'Go to all that trouble? Dispose of the bodies? Get your father to do it?'

Chook smiled as she got on the Harley, pressed a button, revved up. 'If you have to ask, you'll never know.'

She leaned over, put an arm about his neck. 'So long, mate.'

He did not respond.

'You're all right, Harry. Maybe some day—'

She didn't finish it, whatever it was.

Then she was gone again.

Becker stood on the footpath while people passed or skipped around him. It was dark, the clouds were heavy. Something big was bearing in from the west. Or north-west, hard to say. Might have come down from the north. Perhaps the tail end of a cyclone. They could come in off the Coral Sea, head into Queensland before turning south. Then plunge deep into New South, shut in by the Great Divide. Each day creeping farther south, everyone watching the TV news each night, wondering: Where is it going to hit? Chook might be caught in it. Or, she might not. Might beat it to Canberra, if it were going that way. Back over the mountains. The bank of roiling clouds very low now, blocking out the sun. Growling soundlessly.

He expected trouble. Lightning might hit at any moment.

People scurried, head down and eyes up, watching it.

Becker watched it for a moment, thinking he might do some business, now that he was in town. Might see Tommy Thompkins. Talk about getting in another two-dozen weaners, now that he'd decided to give farming a go again. After the disaster, the wrecking of the house, the death of his wife, the good wife. Robyn was a good human being. The kind you wanted to know. The more you saw of her, the more you wanted to see her, to live with her. Talk to her, hold her. Share a life with her. But she was dead.

They had a daughter, Roberta. He should go around to Railway Street, check on her. Muriel was doing a great job with her. Loved her, talked to her. Taught her. A miracle baby, saved by a surgeon at Wagga Wagga Base Hospital that day when the farm house blew up. Could not save Robyn. Her head smashed, her neck snapped.

But he didn't go.

He went home, anxious.

Drove a little too fast. Watching the tumbling black clouds. To one side over the river or perhaps closer than that, lightning struck. A safe flash, miles away. He waited for thunder, but didn't hear it. Windows closed.

Drove on and on. Hoping to reach home before the skies opened up.

Another flash, much closer.

Then one, only a few yards away. Hit a power line. Blue sparks came down in a pretty shower. A pretty awful shower. If one of those things hit the car...

It took three months to rebuild the house. Brand new, quite different to the old one and yet the same. Had the same layout, but new features. The old house had been traditional. Built in 1910, it had looked like any other cheap but practical farmhouse of that time. A central corridor straight down the middle with rooms each side. On the western side a living room, a kitchen, a bathroom and a laundry with a big cupboard in which you could lock away such things as guns. On the eastern side three bedrooms. Big rooms, airy.

The new house sat in exactly the same spot, had verandahs on all sides, including the back. The new house, built on brick piles to keep out the termites, and timber cladding. No corridor, it was open plan. On the western side, a wide sitting area led to a dining nook and then to a narrow kitchen behind a bar. Behind the kitchen was a laundry, and inside that was a strong locker—about the size of a walk-in pantry. On the eastern side three bedrooms as before, except that the master bedroom had an *ensuite* bathroom. Then a bathroom and toilet between the two remaining bedrooms, smaller. Kids' rooms, single beds.

Robyn had advised against a back verandah.

Facing due south, which meant it would always be in shade. Becker had insisted on a rear verandah. The house didn't look complete without it, he thought. Didn't look like an Australian homestead. The back verandah was gloomy in winter, not so bad in summer. Now it was early December 1996. It had taken almost four months to design and build the new house. It looked smart, green-grey Colorbond roof again and the cladding was lap and groove

22

hardwood, spotted gum painted pale green. The verandah decking was merbau, oiled and stained. It was a smart house.

Robyn would have been thrilled.

Chapter 4

THEY CAME BACK. They'd said they would. Becker didn't know until Bert knocked on the back door early one morning. Bert never came to the front door, being that sort of man. A man who knew his place, although he would never have thought of himself as a tradesman or a debt collector or even a funeral director. He had a lot of good farming land he did not cultivate. He'd let it go to wrack and ruin, and he had a dog named Blue. It was a good dog, savage if you got on the wrong side of it. A cattle dog, not so much big as broad and strong and fiercely loyal. And about twelve years of age. Now that Ray had gone, Blue was all Bert had.

He knocked again.

Becker was having breakfast when he heard.

It was a couple of weeks before Christmas, 1996. He'd d been in the new house less than two weeks. Alone, isolated in its newness, as spectacularly notorious as its owner. Three people killed, including his wife. Others injured, mainly by flying glass. All on his birthday back in August. He was now forty.

He opened the screen door.

'Them fellers,' Bert said.

'What fellers?'

'Been again.'

'What do you mean?'

'Them ones that tried to nick them weaners that night.'

Now Becker understood. 'The ones we shot at? And got away? And Blue went after them?'

'Yeah,' Bert said.

He was standing in his own peculiar way, wriggling. Not so much wriggling like a naughty schoolboy, but twisting and turning, like a washing machine that goes first this way and then that to get the clothes clean, swishingly. His feet still, his whole body otherwise swishing. And not looking at anything in particular, as was his custom. Or, habit. Bert was more a man of custom than habit, because he did it deliberately. Never looking you fair in the eye.

'How do you know?'

Becker came farther out, still holding the screen door.

It was cool and dark under the back roof. The paddocks were flooded with light. The sun was up and smiling like it was its birthday, grinning all over the world with freshness and fright. Because, if you didn't have the sun, you were stuffed. If you did have the sun, you were still stuffed, because that meant no rain. And, if you didn't have rain, the grass wouldn't grow. That meant you had no fodder for your stock. Which in turn meant you either bought in fodder and went broke or got rid of the stock and had no income. So you were stuffed both ways. If you had some money in the bank, it might see you through. If you didn't, you were stuffed three ways. Which is about as stuffed as a man on the land can get.

'Shot 'im,' Bert said.

'Shot who?'

'Blue.'

'Blue? Who shot him? The duffers?'

'Them all right.'

'How do you mean, shot him? Where? At your place?'

25

'Near the gate.'

'The front gate? Your front gate?'

It was a stupid question.

Bert had only one gate, while Becker had three—a main gate leading to the house, another gate opening from the cow paddock onto the highway and a third opening onto the lane. The duffers had had a truck and a ramp that night, or very early morning four months ago, a few days after the old house had been blown up. Becker had been living among the ruins on guard, the Winchester by his side. The duffers had had to leave the ramp in a hurry. Even so, the police still couldn't trace them. It looked like any commercial ramp, everyone had one. No-one claimed it.

'When?'

'Last night.'

'What time? Did you hear anything?'

'Nah, nothin'. Never can be sure, can yer? The flamin' 'ighway bein' there. And them trucks goin' all night.'

Becker recalled something.

When the fat man and Adams had killed Torrence by the lake that night in Canberra, they'd waited until a big truck with airbrakes got close enough on Morshead Drive, its brakes going *Tchiooh! Tchiooh!* Then Adams, whose real name was Adamo, had given Torrence one in the back and one in the head, or the other way around. It did not matter which. He was dead instantly. They'd been holding him, when they did it. Next thing, they'd pushed him into Lake Burley Griffin. Someone had done the same to Blue. Waited until something big and noisy had gone by, going down on the gears and producing a noise like one of those rockets taking off at Cape Canaveral. Then had pulled the trigger.

'Jesus,' Becker said.

He walked right out now, letting the screen door close. It didn't bang like the old screen in the old house had done, slamming *bang*! It did it quietly and latched itself gently, as if guided by a woman's hand. The architect had thought of everything.

'How many shots?'

'Two b'the look of 'im, the blood.'

'I'll come over,' Becker said.

He went back to the kitchen and turned off the water he was boiling for coffee. Put the milk back in the refrigerator but left the freshly opened Kellogg's on the bench. He always bought Just Right. He'd been eating it for breakfast for years, ever since he'd moved to Canberra. Ever since he'd moved to Wagga Wagga, ever since he'd bought the farm called *Nil Desperandum*. Ever since the explosion. Ever since Robyn had died. He was a man of habits now. Nothing changed, except each day got worse.

Becker walked back with Bert, through the narrow side-gate in the common fence on the western side and tramped across the weeds and Scotch thistles and dandelions and plantain and wheat stalks still surviving from the days when this had been a wheat farm. That was more than ten years ago, when Bert had given up. The bank was no longer prepared to finance him for seed to sow a crop. Nor to harvest it, if by chance he did grow any. Nor to pay for it to be trucked to market. Flat broke and ruined, Bert's block was the most neglected square mile of good red-loam country in this end of the Riverina. It was worth about three-hundred thousand dollars as it was, run-down and pestilent and impoverished. Good wheat country, but worthless if you couldn't get finance. Or, if you can't get up the energy to try again.

Blue was lying a few feet from the front fence, by the gate. Lying on his left side, his head stretched out, perhaps reaching for something, perhaps a bone or pat on the head. Eyes closed, the tip of his tongue sticking out. He looked asleep, and of course he was asleep. He would never waken. Never bark again, never bail you up and never snap and snarl at Nutty through the boundary fence. Nutty was right behind them. Normally, he was tied up at night, to stop him barking at Blue. Becker had untied him first thing and fed him on the back verandah. Then had forgotten him. He'd left the side-gate open, so Nutty had walked along behind them, sniffing, strangely quiet. He seemed to know what had happened.

'Two shots?' Becker could see only one, on the right shoulder. The bullet had probably entered at a high angle straight down, perhaps straight into the heart. Or near enough.

'On the other side too,' Bert said.

He bent down to turn over the big, grey, black and tan animal. A fierce animal. It would tear you to pieces, if you tried to give it any trouble. Blue had gone after the three blokes, who'd tried to load some of Becker's cattle up the ramp and into a rattly old truck that night, well after midnight. Bert had walked in, the old house being a wreck. At least blown out on one side. Walked across the shattered flooring, waving a torch. And had said: 'There's blokes—'

And Becker, who'd heard the footsteps on the rattling of the boards, had reached for the Winchester by the bed and been ready to fire.

Bert had said, 'Havin' a go at y'stock.'

Becker had pulled on some clothes and boots and followed Bert's torch and seen them across the other side of the creek, where there was a highway gate which was normally bolted and chained and padlocked. Had seen them silhouetted against the afterglow that encircled the horizon every night out there on the plains, moon or no moon.

They'd crept up, Blue deathly quiet, until Becker was close enough to shout: 'Hey, you! Get out of there!'

Some bloke had said, 'Jesus!'

And there was scuttling, weaners bleating, startled.

Blue had rushed them, barking. The blokes in the dark, not the cattle. He had more brains that. One ran for the truck, scrambled in and started it up. Another bloke said: 'Come on, Billy!' There had been running. Blue had gone for one of them, a young bloke by the sound of him. Had got a leg, sunk in his teeth. The boy had screamed. The truck began to move, the boy trying to scramble on. Blue was hanging onto his leg. Probably had got him by an ankle. Cattle dogs were like that, always went for a back ankle. Weren't called heelers for nothing. Then Blue had let go and came back, pleased with himself. He'd saved the cattle.

Now he was dead.

Nutty crept up to him delicately, both frightened and yet respectful. They had known each other for more than a year, the two dogs. Nutty was quite useless as a guard dog—a frustrated sheep dog with no sheep to round up. A good playmate for the kids. There were no kids now and Becker didn't know how he was going to get them back. Much preferred to live with their grandmother in town.

'The bastards,' Becker said.

'Good dog like that,' Bert said.

'You're sure they did it?'

'Did it all right. For revenge, didn't they? Said they'd be back.'

Bert was right. In Becker's letter box, three days after Blue had bitten the young bloke, there had been a note saying they'd be back. It must have been a bad injury, a torn and bleeding leg, possibly infected. Blue had had filthy yellow teeth. God knows what he was given to eat. Probably caught much of it, rabbits and chickens and birds and rats and scraps from the kitchen.

'What do you want to do with him?' Becker asked.

'Dig a hole.'

'I'll help you.'

'Ah, I'm right.'

'Where are you going to put him?'

'Ah, I dunno.'

'Under a tree by the house?'

'Ah, no—'

'Up the back somewhere?'

Bert thought about it, biting his lower lip, left hand on his head, fingers among his chaotic grey hair. Then he brushed his whole face down. It was a large and flat and worn hand, coming down from his head to his face and over his lower lip with a flutter and onto his chin, and finishing on his chest. It might have been on his heart. It was hard to know where anything was in a man like him. He seemed to have been roughly flung together by a God, Who had His mind on something else when He made him.

'I'll dig right here,' he said, blinking.

It could have been tears.

'Right here? By the fence?'

'That's where 'e died, didn't 'e?'

They stood there, looking at the animal. He was a friend, a bit rough and ready, but sturdy and ferociously loyal. A bit like his owner.

'I'll get a shovel,' Becker said.

He went back to his shed and got one. When he came back, Nutty was squatting by Blue, a respectful three feet away, watching him, head resting on his crossed legs.

'Out of the way, boy.'

Nutty got up and crept back, then resumed his squatting, front legs crossed again, chin resting on them, watching. The soil was soft and reddish brown, an ancient flood plain. Came up like chocolate cake. Good enough to eat.

'They must've thought he was my dog,' Becker said.

'Yeah,' Bert said, watching.

When the hole was deep enough, Bert picked him up and lay him down, getting down on his knees. Put him down as gently.

'Goodbye, mate,' he said.

They stood there, two men and a nut-brown dog with a white flash, watching a dead dog. 'If I ever catch up with them fuckin' bastards,' Bert said.

Becker did not reply. He knew all about revenge. Once you try that game you go down with the bastards. There was no way out. Revenge is never satisfied. It feeds on itself and never gets enough to eat. Anastacia had gone to Melbourne to kill a man, who had ordered the assassination of Evelyn Crowley. A good young woman had been killed trying to protect her. And what had she achieved? Sending that voiceless old man on his way. It had been like scraping something off the sole of your boot, she had said.

'You want me to fill in?' Becker asked.

'Nah, I'll do it.'

Bert filled in the hole, the rich brown clods going down until nothing much was showing, only the side of the dog's head and one hard, pointed, black ear and a patch of stiff, blue hair around his snout and neck.

'You want to keep his collar?' Becker asked.

Bert paused. 'Ah, no, 'e'd want to keep it. Have it with 'im. Wouldn't 'e?'

He shovelled in the last soil until he had a small, loose, cloddish heap by the front fence. Then he tamped it down with his shapeless and colourless boots. Never tied properly or neatly or tightly, always hanging open in some absent-minded way, the stuff of life. Or, if not life, then defiance.

'Yeah,' Bert said again, 'if I catch up with them bastards.'

Becker was going to say something like what Macbeth had said. He couldn't recall the exact words, though he thought he knew the meaning: Blood begets blood. He didn't say it. Somehow, he was in one of those tragedies, where blood always did beget blood. And there was nothing much he could do about it.

Chapter 5

HE DIDN'T HAVE to catch them. The police did. There was a knock on the front door a few days later. A gentle, slow and measured knock, much like the knock of authority. Becker was still bringing in things from the barn, as it was called. It never held stockfeed or animals, just two cars and a lock-up section, where he and his neighbours, and some he hadn't known well, had hopped in and helped him clear the old house, before the storm came months ago. And blew the wreckage away, the debris, the aftermath. Before it could damage someone or something. He'd been gradually re-outfitting the new house with the help of Hank and Anika on the farm next door. That is, on the eastern side of his property.

And thinking about where to put them—the pieces of furniture, the paintings, the framed photographs, even Robyn's dresses. He'd been tempted to put them in a wardrobe and pretend that she still lived there. He was thinking about that now, reluctantly. That sort of thing, he felt, was morbid. Pretending that she could still be alive and speaking to him and calling him 'dear' and shyly kissing him, saying she was the luckiest girl in the world and—

He opened the door, unsurprised.

It was authority in the shape of a young policeman.

They had met several months ago on the highway, going back to Wagga Wagga, when a Land Cruiser had sped past on the wrong side of the BMW and a shot had been fired. Buster had been killed, assassinated. And then Barnes had arrived almost immediately in a patrol car. Followed in time by another patrol car, Sergeant Jackson in it. His driver had been Max Kruger, a newcomer not long out of college and posted to Wagga Wagga and now given the highway job, Barnes having been suspended. It was worse than that. He'd killed himself.

Constable Kruger stood on the front verandah, the big red and blue-checked Holden with all the gear on top at the gate. He grinned like a fresh boy at a bush dance—happy to know you, hands politely clasped, head back and as approachable as a country pub after a hard day's work.

'Ah, g'day,' Becker said. 'Max, is it?'

'Yeah, Max, that's right.' He extended a hand. They shook.

'Didn't expect to see you again.'

'No, well, we met in strange circumstances, didn't we? I mean, gee, eh? I was expecting to have to pull my piece, when you and that bloke Barnes were having a barney and he put his hand on his weapon. Flipped the clip on his holster, I saw him. Standin' right behind him. Jesus, I thought, this is gettin' serious!'

'It was as close as that?'

'Yeah, Christ, mate, Jack was looking at me and I'm wondering what does he want me to do? Arrest Barnes or hold him? Or stick my weapon in his back and say: Sick up your hands? Jesus, I was nervous. Feared Jack'd give me the nod? The nod to do what? Shoot him? Shoot him where? In the middle of the back? In the head? Christ, I couldn't do that to a man. Could you?'

Becker ignored the question. 'I had my own weapon. I was holding it.'

'Yeah, but what if Barnes'd drawn fast, and plugged you?'

'Well, he didn't, did he? He went to pieces, collapsed.'

'Thank God for that. I don't mind telling you, mate. I was nearly crappin' myself with fear. Jesus, what if Jack'd given the nod?'

Becker had run out of patience. 'What can I do for you, Max?'

'Ah, yeah, that's what I came for. Got some news for you.'

'News?'

'Yeah, mate!'

'What kind of news?'

'We found who did it.'

'Did what?'

'Had a go at your stock.'

'Really? That was months ago. One night, it was. They didn't get away with any.'

'Yeah, I know, that's right. Guess how we found 'em.'

'Yeah?'

Becker had stepped right out now onto the verandah, it only being polite.

'I was tellin' my young sister there were real cattle rustlers in this district. Only a few months ago they tried it on at your place. And she's a nurse.'

'In Wagga?'

'No, the Goulburn Valley Base Hospital.'

'Where's that?'

'Shepparton, down in Vic. She'd come up with one of her friends to see me. Anyway, I said they wouldn't be back, because the farmer's dog had bitten one of them on the leg. She said that's funny, a young bloke was admitted a couple of weeks ago in terrific pain. He'd had a bad leg infection. It was so bad they'd had to amputate. She'd had to watch. Part of her training. She nearly fainted when all the pus burst out. More'n a cupful, she said.'

Becker couldn't see where this was leading.

'Anyway, she asked how this had happened, and the surgeon said dog bite.'

'Dog bite?'

'The young bloke must've been bitten pretty badly some time ago, maybe two or three months.'

'Where?'

'Eh?'

'Where had this happened?'

'Ah! That's the interesting bit. Apparently, the people with him said it'd happened out at Kyabram, north of Shepparton, not far south of the border. But we did some checkin' with all stations in the district to see if they knew of some kid who'd had a leg amputated lately. And guess what?'

'I'm sure you're going to tell me.'

'We found one, in Henty!'

He was full of enthusiasm, a young cop happy to be of service. Becker himself had been like that until he'd been posted to Kings Cross in Sydney and had had to walk down those mean streets on a crowded Saturday night. His hand not on but very close to his sidearm. You never knew what might happen. He was slightly amused.

'Henty?'

'Yeah, not far south of Wagga, is it?'

'I know where it is.'

'So do I! I was born there! Anyway, I told Jack and we pissed off down there in the car and called on 'em. Father and brother and son! Name's MacKinlay and they're famous for stealing anythin' that's not nailed down. Got a record as long as your arm.'

'You arrested them?'

'Only the father and the oldest son. Jack didn't have the heart to arrest the young one, only seventeen. Probably under the influence of his father. A family like that, born into crime. The older son'd lately come out of Beechworth.'

'Beechworth?'

'Prison. Yeah, he'd done time for brawlin' in the Beechworth pub. Not his first time, either.'

'What's to happen to them?'

'They come up before the local court in a couple of weeks.'

Becker had been standing with his arms crossed, occasionally looking at the gate, at the passing traffic, and at the patrol car, a souped-up Holden V8 pursuit car. Possibly the one Barnes had driven.

'They came back, you know,' he said.

'They came back here?'

'And shot the dog.'

The young cop was shocked. 'Ah, Christ!'

'Thought it was my dog. A few nights ago. We buried him next day.'

'Ah, Christ!'

'Old Bert's not the same now.'

That was not quite right.

Old Bert was much the same, only more so. Some days he didn't look like he could go on. That was it, the loneliness. Becker knew what it was like, loneliness. He'd rebuilt a house to look like the one destroyed. No-one else lived in it, probably no-one else would. No woman, anyway. Young Wendy would not, he knew. She seemed to blame him for everything. The boy, Terry, liked to visit, but would never be resident. He liked to visit a farm, muck around, do some shooting, then go home. Becker had a new daughter, a baby now four months old. She too was living with her grandmother in town. No-one wished to know him, except in a neighbourly way. The man who'd got blown up and lost his wife and nearly lost his new daughter. Little Roberta? What would become of her? He didn't like to think. Thinking was not good for the soul. He had some sort of soul, he knew. But it hurt and it was not the kind of soul he would've wished to have, if he'd ever had any choice.

'Well, there, Harry, thought I'd drop in and tell you the news.'

Becker stirred himself.

'Thanks for doing that. I'll tell Bert. He'll be glad. Said they'd come back. There was a note in the box, saying they'd come back.'

'And they did, eh? The bastards, shot a good dog only tryin' to do his job, protecting your cattle.'

'Thanks for calling in, Max.'

'See you around, Harry.'

Young Kruger had gone only a few paces, when he turned around. 'Jesus, I forgot to tell you!'

Becker waited. It was going to be something bad, he knew.

'Was having a beer with three blokes in a pub in Wagga the other day and one of 'em asked me if I knew a tall sheila called Stork.'

'Stork?'

'Yeah, Stork. Said she was also known as Streak.'

'Streak?'

'Yeah, and Lofty. Said he'd heard she was a cop.'

'Yeah?'

'She was a Federal cop, they reckon.'

'I wouldn't know anything about that.'

'He wanted to know where she was.'

'What did you say?'

'Hadn't seen her in ages.'

'Anything else?'

'No, that was all, I think. Only a casual enquiry. Said they used to ride with her down in Melbourne. Three bikies, they were.'

'Bikies?'

Becker was wary. 'Did he give a name?'

'One of his mates called him Shaft.'

'Shaft?'

'Yeah, thought you'd like to know. In case you run into her some time.'

'Thanks, Max.'

The young cop waved and grinned and clapped his hands. Or, looked as though he was going to clap. Instead, he clasped them like a man shaking hands with himself. And marched off, a happy young man, proud to be wearing the uniform. He should go far in the service. Becker had been like that once, when he was in Cootamundra, fresh out of the State police academy. Happy to be in the service in a good town, where everyone was friendly and some of the girls were more than just friendly.

That evening he called Chook in Canberra.

She was out on a job somewhere, he could tell. Background traffic noise. She was obviously driving, because she was faltering, keeping an eye on the traffic. The sound cut in and out. He could hear a siren, close enough to be hers.

'It's me, Harry.'

'Harry?'

He spoke slowly, almost shouting. 'Yeah, someone has been asking after you.'

'Who?'

'Some bikie who says he knew you down in Melbourne.'

'That was a long time ago.'

'He called you Stork.'

'Stork?'

'Yeah, and Streak.'

'Streak, eh?'

'And Lofty. You know him?'

There was no reply. The sound faded, then came back.

'Chook? Can you hear?'

'Yeah, but I'm driving. Just a minute.'

He waited. The traffic noise faded. Her intercom came on. She answered it. 'Said: I'm almost there.' Then came back to Becker.

'What did he look like?'

'The cop didn't say.'

'A fat bloke with a beard? Could have had a shaved head? And tattoos. On his cheek and neck?'

'No idea, but one of his mates called him Shaft.'

'Shaft?'

'You know him?'

She didn't answer. He thought he heard a sigh or a gasp or perhaps some sort of cry. She slowed right down; he could hear the revs dropping down to a purr.

'Chook?' Again, no answer. 'Stacey?'

She seemed to be struggling to get enough air.

'Anastacia?'

'Yeah, I'm here.'

'Are you okay?'

'Oh, Christ, he's out!'

'Who's out?'

There was a long silence, except for the traffic noise. He heard another siren go past her. Not loud, but loud enough. Something was happening in Canberra. Something big. Something that had every available car out on the road.

'You're busy?' he asked.

She didn't respond. Then she spoke hard and sharp and certainly. 'Something's happened at Parliament House. Just crossing the lake now. Got to go.'

She must have put her foot down. Her own siren began to scream again. She yelled above the noise, 'I'll call you tonight!'

Chapter 6

SHE DIDN'T RING until late. Or, late for him. He'd been going to bed early since the new house had been completed and he'd moved in. Or, moved back in, depending upon whether you think a house—that completely replaces an old house and looks like the old house from the outside but is structurally different on the inside and freshly bright and fitted with all the modern conveniences—is the original house reborn, or a completely new house. Although structurally different on the inside, it had been fitted out with the same furniture and pictures and crockery and cutlery and even some of his dead wife's clothes still hanging in a wardrobe. When was a house a new house? He did not know.

He once heard two philosophers arguing on late-night radio during one of his searches for late-night companionship back in Canberra. One said that if there were perceptible difference between two things then they were not identical. But, the other said, what about George Washington? The boy and the general were obviously different, yet they were obviously the same person. So, it would seem that even if two things are different, they can still be the same.

Becker seemed he was living in the same house but a different house.

Thus comforted, he'd tried to get some sleep. He had a small portable radio on a table by his head. Some orchestra he'd never heard of was playing Rimsky Korsakov. It was Scheherazade. He thought of Evelyn walking up the stairs at the Canberra Theatre, hanging onto arm of her scrubby little husband, the slinky green gown slipping this way and that across that beautiful female body.

The phone rang.

He picked it up, hesitantly. Shouldn't have told her someone was looking for her. Someone called Shaft.

'Yeah?' he said.

'Sorry I couldn't talk,' she said.

'That's okay.'

'Someone tried to kill the prime minister.'

'What!'

'As he was leaving Parliament House. With a sword.'

'Where was his detail?'

'One guy was outside, holding a door open for him. Two others in the crowd.'

'What crowd?'

'A demonstration, something about animal rights.'

'A bloke would kill for that?'

'No, no, he had nothing to do with chicken farms or horse racing or circus animals. He was on our radar, but we didn't think he was a risk. We stuffed up again.'

'Why?'

'Why what?'

'Why did he do it?'

'He was shouting something to do with Iraq.'

'Anyone hurt?'

'Two cops, one of them seriously.'

'And the bloke?'

'The third cop shot him.'

'Dead?'

'Straight through the back of the head. The bullet came out his right eye and hit a protester holding a placard. Nothing serious. The placard said: Chooks have feelings too.'

Becker laughed. He hadn't laughed in a long time.

'It's not funny,' she said.

'And the PM?'

'Not a scratch.'

'Were you involved?'

'No, it was all over by the time I got there.'

'Jesus, Chook.'

'Stop calling me Chook. I do have a name, you know.'

'Yeah, sure, Stacey.'

'That's not my real name. Say Anastacia.'

'Anastacia.'

'Say it again.'

He said it again.

'I love it when you say it slowly,' she said.

'It's too long.'

'Well, call me Anna.'

'That was Polly's name.'

'What's in a name?'

'Everything.'

'Yeah, suppose you are right.'

There was a pause. He thought he could hear her breathing. She seemed to open her mouth to say something, but did not speak.

'What are you going to do about it?' he said.

'About what?'

'That guy, Shaft?'

'That arsehole?'

'Bad news?'

'Yeah, really bad.'

'He was in jail?'

'For sixteen years. Must have got parole. It's only thirteen so far.'

'What did he go in for?'

'It's not what he went in for.'

'What do you mean?'

'It's what he did.'

'Who to?'

'Me.'

Becker was puzzled. 'You mean he didn't go in for what he did to you?'

'Yeah,' she said. 'I refused to testify.'

He wanted to ask, but couldn't. It was awful he knew, whatever it was. He could tell by her silence. By her breathing. By the tension. He was about to say, You don't have to tell me, but she cut in.

'He tried to fuck me to death with a broken broom handle. I told you this.'

'Oh, Christ, Chook.'

'There you go again, calling me Chook again.'

'Hell, I'm sorry.' He was flustered. Saying you were sorry to a woman who had been through such an ordeal was inexpressible. Whatever you said was an outrage in itself, the memories. He was still trying to find something adequate to say, when she said, quite out of the blue: 'How's the house?'

'It's finished. I've been in it for a week or more.'

She thought about it.

'I'd like to see it,' she said.

'It looks good.'

'I'm not working tomorrow.'

'Yeah?'

'Will you be at home?'

'Yeah, sure.'

'I might drop in to see you.'

'Great, please do.' He stumbled. 'You—you could stay for the night.'

'Really? Hey, you are a new widower, remember?'

'No-one would notice.'

'What about your children?'

'You mean Terry? He's here tonight. Came out on the bus today. He's gonna help me to spray the cattle tomorrow morning.'

'Spray them?'

'With insecticide. Filthy job. Has to be done every few months. Suggest you don't turn up until lunch time. The spray stinks.'

She thought about it. 'I might stay at the Hovell.'

'What if he's still in Wagga? This bloke called Shaft? You might run into him.'

You can't see a smirk on a phone, but he could hear one in a voice.

'That's exactly why I would stay there.'

'Don't be stupid, please.'

'I like being stupid.'

'Anna, don't pick a fight. He was with two mates.'

'All the better,' she said.

Chapter 7

NEXT DAY, BECKER and the boy started early. Terry was in his first year at high school. Loved the farm, came out from town every chance he got. Told all his friends that his father was a big rancher who bred cattle. Didn't say stepfather. That was wrong. Becker bought in weaners at about five-hundred dollars each and fattened them up and sold them at market for about a thousand each. He was a grazier, not a breeder. That didn't matter to the boy. Anything to do with a farm was heaven to him.

He and Nutty herded them, one at a time, towards the yards. Catching one was the problem. Nutty was not a cattle dog. He was a sheep dog and he didn't understand cows. He seemed to think they were big sheep without wool. He'd approach the wrong end of a young cow and the heifer would put her head down and challenge him, at the same time backing off. Probably the hardest thing in the world to do is to get a cow into a chute, or enclosure as it is sometimes called.

Old Bert had another cattle dog, also called Blue. Becker thought of borrowing him for a day. But he knew Bert would hesitate, afraid to let him go. He had nothing else. No-one ever called at his place. Unless it was the vermin inspector, to complain about the rabbits and the thistles and the refuse out the back.

So, they had to dispense with Nutty's services, select a heifer and walk her up to the chute, shooing her or whacking her on the backside with a whipstick. Then Becker had to climb up on a fence and with a spray gun and drench the beasts as best he could. This took at least ten minutes for each animal, the insecticide wafting in the unsteady air, now a breeze and now not a breeze.

They started a few minutes after eight and by noon they'd done the lot, twenty-five heifers. Then each had a shower, the house having two bathrooms. Then waited for Chook. Eventually, they gave up and had a bowl of mushroom soup each. With thick fresh bread and butter. They waited some more. Still, she didn't appear, so they had a chicken and leek pie.

They were sitting on the back verandah, in the shade, when they heard the footsteps. On the eastern side, heavy steps, certain steps, more like a marching gait.

They waited, listening.

You never knew with Anastacia. She was mannish in her step, drilled like a soldier on parade but after her own fashion. Had about her a certain smile. Not a friendly smile or a devilish smile or a scornful of smile, but a certain smile. She was a certain woman, certain in her certainty. She didn't give in.

This time, she was almost grinning.

'Anything left?' she said.

Terry jumped to his feet. 'Ah!'

'We thought you wouldn't make it,' Becker said.

'We drank all the soup,' Terry said.

'The meeting went on and on. How we failed yesterday. What if the prime minister had been killed? What went wrong? Whose head should fall? All the excuses in the world. That's all we had to offer, excuses, excuses. How can you know who will do a thing like that? You can't, can you?'

'You arrived in time?'

'No, I was a few minutes late. He was dead by then.'

'Who killed him?'

'One of the guards.'

'His driver?'

'No, a sergeant named Embury. Stepped out of the crowd and shot the poor bastard.'

'Why poor?'

'Embury could have challenged him. Told him to drop the sword, while the driver grabbed him from behind. That's what I would have done.'

'Did anyone ask Embury?'

'Yeah. Just said he thought it the best thing to do. In the circumstances.'

'In the circumstances?'

'Yeah, that's what he said. And smiled.'

'He smiled?'

'Just smiled? After killing a man?'

'Yeah, I know.'

Becker was on his feet now. He'd been about to continue, but Terry was entranced. So, he changed the subject.

'We're eating chicken and leek pie. Anika brought it over.'

'Any left?' She mussed Terry's hair. 'How are you, big boy?'

'Good!' he said.

'How old are you now?'

'Eleven!'

'Eleven? As much as that?'

'Yeah!'

'Still a dead shot with a rifle?'

'Yeah, we go all over the place, shooting rabbits and foxes and dingos and—'

'You have dingoes around here?'

'Not real dingoes,' Becker said. 'Crossbreeds with wild dogs. They're a pest.'

'Still going to be a soldier when you grow up?'

'Yeah!'

'Why do you want to be a soldier?'

'So I can go to war!'

'You're crazy. Any soldier who wants to go to war must be crazy.'

'Why be a soldier, if they won't let you go to war?'

'Better to be a policeman. They're always at war. They don't go to war— know why?'

'No?'

'It comes to them. It's always all around them.'

'Why?'

'Because they were born inside a war and they can never get out.'

The boy was puzzled. 'What do you mean?'

Becker intervened. 'Terry, take Anika's basket back to her.'

'Gee?'

'And the napkin. And thank her very much for the pies and the salad.'

'Yeah, I will.'

Any excuse to visit Anika. She was a pastry cook and always had special treats.

They watched him go. He scooted across the creek on the old wall of rocks John Kettle's men had made back in the 1830s to form a washpool, across the paddock by the heifers to the far gate on the lane between the two properties. The rocks served as a causeway and also a sort of weir. Water could run between the stones. They were biggish stones, real gibbers. The houses were almost a mile apart, so he would not be back for at least half an hour. He walked on and on into the day, the breeze having picked up a bit with the sun. The sun on his back and upon his steps—a jaunty, fast, almost hopping movement. Like a boy on the march. Like a hippity-hoppity soldier. Like a boy disappointed by not being allowed to go to war. Not to be a soldier. Puzzled by what she had said about the war being all around you. And there being no escape.

'I'll heat up a pie for you,' Becker said. 'You want two? They're quite small.'

'Sure.'

'You want a beer first?'

'That would be good.'

'I don't have Hahn. It's Carlsberg.'

'That's a girl's drink.'

'You're a girl.'

'If you say so.'

So, they had a Carlsberg while they waited for the pie. When it came, she ate quickly. One pie went in several quick bites. She was not greedy, just hungry.

'Want another?'

'No, no, that's enough. Are you inviting me to dinner tonight?'

'I'm not much of a cook.'

'Nor am I.'

'I thought you were going to stay at the Hovell?'

'I've been there, had a quick look.'

'Learn anything?'

'Not much. I asked Bruce. They didn't stay there.'

'Where did they go?'

'He didn't know. Said they asked about me.'

'What did he tell 'em?'

'That I was a cop.'

'They knew that already, I bet.'

'And that I was pretty tough.'

'That would impress Shaft?'

'No, he's out to kill me, no matter what it takes. Which would be perfect,' she added.

Becker jumped, although seated.

'You mean you want him to *try* to kill you?'

'Yep.'

'Are you serious?'

'Deadly serious. That's how I'll get away with it.'

Becker was going to say: Get away with what? But he realised.

'You're going to kill him, aren't you?'

She smirked. 'Why not?'

'You're crazy, Chook.'

She laughed. 'Okay, I'm crazy.'

'Why?'

She stopped laughing.

'Why? When I first got involved with the Gringos, it was a good gang, more like a social club. Nice blokes, most of them. Dependable. Vietnam vets and some odd bods, the usual drifters and idealists, who thought the life of the open road was the best they could do to clear their heads or freshen up their souls. Later, we got some disturbed kids, who'd become disturbed men, trying to hang onto some sort of self-respect. Get on a bike and go anywhere you like, see the country. There's a comradeship in it. That's what I wanted. I told you all about this, about my shitty life. I was all cracked up. In my head. I was rooting anything I fancied. And taking drugs. Started off whacking a ball in a gym, to build up some muscle. Got on opioids, started to get bloody awful constipation. Stumpy said to get off that, try some hash. Did that for a while, then got onto coke, just one a day, then got onto heroin. I told you all this.'

'Yeah, you did.'

'I had a boyfriend in the early days. Met him outside a pub, the White Swan in Swan Street, Richmond. He was called Stumpy.'

'Stumpy?'

'Stumpy Watson. Didn't I tell you about him? Had one leg shorter than the other. Stumpy was all right. Tried to stick up for me. Got into fights. Shaft fucked me one day when I was bombed out. Stumpy got worked up. Said I was a fuckin' whore.'

'What happened to him?'

'Cleared out. Don't know where he went.'

'And Red?'

'Red?'

'You said there was another guy, called Red.'

'Yeah, that was later, much later. Towards the end. I didn't ride with him, and he didn't fuck me. I think he was a cop, working undercover. Told me one day there was going to be a raid. Told me to get out quick. "You're a cop?" I said. He didn't answer. He said, "You know where they've got it stashed?" I didn't answer, but I must have nodded. He kept watching me, no doubt hoping I'd talk. But I did not, I was too scared. Didn't see him again. They killed him, I'm sure. For asking questions. I was sorry about Red; he was a nice guy, as bikies go. I think I was in love him by then, hopin' he'd get me out all that shit.'

'Where was this?'

'In a house not far out of Melbourne, up in the hills, the Dandenongs. An old weatherboard. The gang used to hang out there in summer. It had a few gardens, fruit trees and berries, mainly blackberries, and a few chooks. We ate well, on and off. Two or three other girls were there then. Molls, we were called. And molls we called ourselves. We did the cooking. It was not far from the Puffing Billy railway line. On weekends the train used to go by, rattling and whistling and steaming, loaded with kids and their parents, cheering and waving. We'd have to wave back.'

'So, you became this Shaft's girl?'

'No, he hated me. Used to call me Freak and Streak and Fuckwit and Shithead. I think the very look of me disgusted him.'

'So, the police were going to look for cash and drugs?'

'There was nothing much in the cottage, a few dollars and some hash.'

'But you knew where it was?'

'Yeah, sort of. Up the hill and in a cave, sort of hidden by blackberries.'

'So, there was a raid?'

'First thing next morning, before dawn. Hardly any daylight. They came crashing in. Three through the front door. It didn't open, it fell in. They stormed over it. They were at each window too. Someone was yelling, "Police! Armed police! Lie flat on the floor, arms stretched out!" That sort of thing. You see it in the movies now and it always looks comical, just a lot of actors trying to look like cops. We all cry with laughter now, when we see these action movies. Something always goes wrong.'

'Wrong?'

She laughed. 'Yeah, they shot one of the State blokes by mistake.'

'Yeah?'

'In the dark. With all those flashlights, criss-crossing. Someone thought he was holding a gun. Told him to drop it. He didn't drop it, because he was a cop.'

'So, they shot him?'

'In an operation like that, you can never be sure who's who or where or what they're holding.'

'So they found nothing?'

'Nothing much. They took everyone in for questioning, but no-one talked, including me at first.'

'They let you go?'

'No, they sent me to hospital. Fixed me up. I told you more than once.'

She stopped. Chook was sitting in her usual way, sprawled in a high-back wooden chair, an old chair, made of Murray pine. It had come with the house, when Becker had bought it. Sitting with her legs crossed, but not so much crossed as one leg over the other, neatly balanced, the boot almost touching Becker's leg, the left leg, almost touching his thigh, as if wishing to be closer to him. Without getting too intimate.

Her hands were folded across her belly.

Eyes closed, shut tight.

'So, what did you tell the police, when you were in hospital?'

'I said it was up a track, which ran by a creek. It was past an old property that had been a chicken farm. There was a long shed, rotten and stinking and fallen down. No-one had been there for years. But there was a notice on a post. It was a very old notice. The post was grey and splintery and bent like a scarecrow that knows there's no future in being a scarecrow. Not in a place like that.'

'What was on the notice?'

'Manure for Sale.'

'Manure?'

'Chicken shit. Apparently, it goes well on rhubarb.'

'So, the police found the money?'

'Yeah, and the guns and the dope.'

'And everyone was arrested?'

'Except me.'

'Why?'

'I don't know, but maybe Red had told them I might talk.'

'You mean, in court?'

'I think so.'

'And Shaft? What did he do when he found out Red was a cop? Before the raid?'

'He was raging, as I said. Started belting into everyone. They were scared to death. One of them tried to fight him. But he kicked him, kicked him and kicked him, in the guts. You could hear his belly squelching like the water in a sinking boat. And the cracking of the bones. Then he came to me. I was lying on my bed, dead scared.'

'He hit you?'

'No, he just said, "You told him, didn't you? You pathetic little cunt, you told Red." "No," I said. I tried lying my way out of it, but he was right and he was wrong. I mean, he was wrong what he did. He'd been wrong since the day he was born, that animal.'

Becker waited. He didn't want to hear it. But someone had to listen to her tale.

'He leaned down. I was sitting, but gradually sliding off the chair. I didn't know what was going to happen to me. I knew it would be bad. But somehow I didn't care. I'd been expecting this. I was so bad then, I wanted to die. But I didn't want my bones broken. His face was close. He was looking at me. He said, You know why they call me Shaft? No, I said, or did not say. I'm not sure. I couldn't hear myself speak when I spoke. He was poking a finger at me. He went on poking me, and asking. His finger went down and down. It went between my legs. I did not dare fight him. I'd been raped once, so I expected it again. Probably in front of everyone. No-one would come to my aid, I knew. They were all past it. Past any sort of human dignity or any other kind of dignity, if there is any kind of dignity to be found in this violent universe. His hand poked at me, not roughly. He didn't grab me. Then he said: I like shaftin' women.'

'What happened next?'

'Two of the molls held me, while he pulled my pants off. He said, Jesus, you stink. I did, I knew it then. I was sick, very sick. Sometimes I'd shit myself in my sleep.'

Becker blanched. 'Then what happened?'

'He told one of the molls to get the broom.'

Chapter 8

'I WENT TO my bed, curled up. He broke the broom handle in two, then stuck one bit up me. The broken end first. All I could do was lie there and cry. He tore me, he tore me so badly I bled and bled for days. Lying on the bed. Nothing to eat. Once, one of the girls came in and gave me water, but I pissed and shat it away. I felt so bad I wanted to die. I wanted someone to come and cut my throat. But they didn't. I could hear them talking, sometimes laughing. I'd hear a door banging. Or a bike starting up. Night went on and on. There was no day. Even if some daylight was getting into the room, I'd have my eyes shut. I couldn't open them. Once he came in and said: "She dead yet?" Someone must have said, "No." They went out. My life was going out with them. But it was going out within me. I hurt so badly. I was so torn and scratched and ripped and full of piss and shit and despair.'

'How long did this go on?'

'Three days.'

'Then the police came again?'

'Yeah.'

'And arrested some of them?'

'Yeah, but they were soon out on bail.'

'They had plenty of money?'

'Millions, they said.'

'But you went to hospital?'

'Yeah, as sick as a dog.'

'They fixed you up?'

'Not exactly. They stuffed me full of antibiotics. And fed me. Next day the police came and asked me to cooperate. If I did, no charges would be laid against me.'

'So, you spilled the beans?'

'Yeah, I did.'

'Told them where to look for the money and the drugs?'

'Yeah.'

'And the weapons?'

'The weapons too. They raided the place again that night. Went in with a bigger force, so I heard. Surrounded the place, used loud hailers. Grabbed the lot.'

'Found the loot?'

'No trouble at all.'

'What did they get? In court?'

'Various terms, but Shaft got sixteen years.'

'And now he's out?'

'Yeah, it looks like he got out in thirteen and a half on parole.'

'What'd he get for raping you?'

'Nothing.'

'Nothing?'

'He wasn't charged for that.'

'You wouldn't testify?'

'That's right.'

'I understand.'

Chook looked perfectly relaxed, slumped in the chair, legs crossed, or not crossed but cocked. Hands clasped or not clasped but held lightly, fingers to fingers on her belly. Like a woman telling a story. A tale told a hundred times, if only to herself.

'So, you then you had the operation?'

'The hysterectomy? Not for a week or two. They had to get rid of the infection first.'

'Yes, of course. You were very lucky, Anastacia.'

She smiled. 'I didn't think so at the time. But, after a while, when they cared for me, talked to me, gave me a job—'

'I think you need something. I don't have any Jack.'

'I don't need anything,' she said, 'except—'

He thought she was going to say, A little love. Or, some understanding. He stood up, waiting. She stood up too, a little shakily, he thought. She tried to smile, perhaps to smile way the past.

'I'd like to see what you've done.'

'To the house?'

'The house, the farm, everything. Show me around, Harry.'

'Well, starting with the house—'

Under her left shoulder he noticed the bulge and the butt of a weapon. He'd noticed it when she'd first sat down. She was loaded, he knew. Something told him it was different.

'What are you wearing?' he asked.

'Under my jacket?'

She drew it. It was not a large weapon. Rather, it was short and fat and boxy and ugly black. Not truly black, but a sooty sort of grey, sombre and dreary and cold-bloodedly awful. 'This is a Glock,' she said. 'Ever seen one?'

'Only in pictures. It looks heavy.'

'It's not really, mostly polymer. Most of the weight comes from the ammo. Fifteen rounds in the clip. Here, feel it. Feel the weight.'

He took it, a bit scared.

'Don't worry,' she said, 'it won't go off.'

'Where's the safety?'

'It doesn't have one.'

'What?' He almost dropped it.

She laughed. 'It's an internal mechanism. Each time after you fire a Glock, the safety stops it firing again until you pulled the small trigger. See, it has two triggers, one inside the other. If you pull the first trigger, the safety goes *off* and, if you keep pulling the second trigger it goes *bang*!'

'Where's the slide?'

She smiled. 'The whole top plate. Be careful, it's already cocked.'

'Already cocked? You mean you walk around with a cocked gun?'

'Yeah, it was designed for the military. Very fast, some say the fastest gun on earth.'

'Oh, Jesus,' he said.

She almost laughed. 'Jesus has nothing to do with it, mate. It's either you're fast enough or you're dead. The force is trying out the Glock. I'm one of a select few.'

'How fast are you?'

He was trying to hand it back to her, but she was not accepting.

'Oh, I practise at the police range every day or so. I've got my speed up. I can hit three bulls in half a second. *Bang, bang, bang!*'

'That's really fast.' He was still trying to return the horrible creation to her.

'Faster than Shane,' she said. 'You saw that movie?'

'A long time ago.'

'When he beat Jeb Wilson to the draw in the final shootout? I was watching that old flick when you called last night. Sipping a Jack and thinking of you.'

'Thinking of shooting me?'

She laughed. 'Never, never, never.'

'Here, take it, please.'

She smiled. 'Scared you, have I?'

But she took it, put it away under her left shoulder.

'Do you really need a weapon like that? All that firepower?'

She shrugged, glancing away at the paddocks to the east and at the creek in the middle of everything and at the bright summer light above the trees, the coolabahs and the wattles and the red box gums. And breathed in the rich air redolent of eucalyptus. A light breeze had come up. Just as well they had sprayed in the morning.

'All the better to kill him with,' she said.

He said nothing. She was going to do it, he knew. She had killed Pisano in Melbourne. She was going to kill Shafter, one way or another. And get away with it. Nothing would stop her. She had it all worked out. She knew the law and how to work it.

The boy came back, not so jaunty now. Head down, a bit miserable. It was a mile to the neighbour's house and back.

'I don't want to go home,' he said.

'You have to go home to look after Nan.'

'Wendy's there.'

'Wendy is not there. Wendy is at a swimming carnival today.'

'Then Anghie's there.'

'Angharad comes on Mondays and Fridays, you know that.' Angharad Thomas was a retired nurse. 'This is Saturday.'

'I want to stay and listen.'

'Do you?'

'I want to hear what she says.'

'Her name is Anastacia.'

'Anastacia, then.'

Chook was smiling. 'You can call me Anna, if you like.'

'Can I really? Thanks.'

'You have a responsibility to your grandmother,' she said. 'To look after her.'

'She's got the baby.'

'A baby can't look after her grandmother. What if your Nan has a bad turn?'

'What do you mean?'

'Suddenly feels sick. Who's going to get an ambulance for her?'

He growled and mumbled and backed himself into a corner.

'I tell you what,' Chook said, 'I have to go back now. How about you hop up back on my sickle? I'll take you back.'

He was astonished. 'On a police bike?'

'It's not a police bike. I own it. It's a Harley Davidson.'

'A real Harley?'

'Yeah, ever been on one?'

'Never!'

To Becker she said: 'I have to see some people.'

'Shaft?'

'If I can find him.'

'Ah, shit, Chook.'

'I told you not to call me Chook.'

'Sorry—'

She nudged the boy.

'Come on, Bronco Bill. Let's ride the big, black beast.'

Becker protested, 'What about a helmet for him?'

'He can wear mine.'

'What about you?'

She smiled.

'I'm a Fed.'

'A what?'

'A Federal cop. I can talk my way out of anything.'

Chapter 9

SHE CAME BACK late in the day and they had a scratch sort of dinner. All he had was some steak and onions and potatoes and cabbage and tomatoes, so she said she could cook that sort of meal. A workman's meal, she said. She'd often eaten that way with her father, who had no idea how to cook and left it to her. Her mother had taught her several recipes, but she had cooked only one, *borsch*. That was all he would eat. A tall, gangling, crafty and craggy man, he would eat like a horse, munching, the silence broken only by his munching and sniffing. And breathing. She'd got sick of it, eating nothing but *borsch*. Fucking *borsch*. So she'd run away.

That hadn't been the only reason.

She couldn't live with him any longer, could not live with his misery and his grumpiness and his silences. Except when he talked about the burning flesh, the smell of burning flesh. Human flesh. How they had stood them up against the walls in Odessa and shot them, then had burnt them. So that there would be nothing, not even their bones. That was just the start. In all, they rounded up more than 30,000 Jews and marched them off to Babi Yar in Kiev, and killed them. German and Rumanian troops. No more Jews in Odessa. Never again.

'Find everything?' he asked.

'It's amazing,' she said. 'You've kept everything she had in the old kitchen. Even her herbs.'

Becker sat at the kitchen bar, watching her.

It was that kind of kitchen, modern. You could sit at the bench and watch the cook as she worked. A glass of wine in your hand. Until she brought it to the ironbark table, sawn in the hills and the mills, the sawdust flying. And six matching chairs.

Anastacia was thrilled. 'Found dill,' she said. 'Now it'll be complete.'

She stirred dill into the pot. It had meat and eggs and everything needed for *borsch*, but not beet. He had no beet. But that didn't matter, she threw in diced tomatoes instead. He even had sour cream. He'd bought it fresh, because he was drinking too much coffee. It was burning his guts. For some reason, he thought that if he drank it with cream, it would not be so bitter. The fat in the cream might protect his guts. The flavour certainly improved, but the strength was still there. His heart still jumped. He had to cut down on coffee. He had problems, personal problems.

He didn't know what he would do about Wendy, who wouldn't speak to him. Blamed him for the death of her mother.

And Roberta, who'd not taken to him. Treated him as a stranger.

All she'd do was smile and blow bubbles and try to talk back to him. But she was not his girl. Roberta was her grandmother's girl. He was only someone who dropped in each week and asked how she was going. A pretty baby, you could see her mother in her, the soft brown hair like silk and the warm eyes, watching. And trying to say words, but it all came out garbled. Somehow you knew what she meant.

She was four months old, trying to speak to a man she didn't know was her father. He'd arrive with toys or flowers or money. Money to keep her going. And a nurse to check on her twice a week. A good little girl. Some day she'd be a big girl, and would want to know about her mother.

'It's ready,' Chook said.

She brought it to the table. He picked up some bread, new bread. Chunky bread and butter. It was steaming. The *borsch*, not the bread. Although that too had been heated. She'd thought of everything. Even if *borsch* was the only dish she could do, she had done it with care and hope.

They sat.

'How is it?' she asked.

'It's good.'

'Just good?'

'Yeah, sure.'

She was disappointed. She had tried, but hadn't expected much more.

He was a simple man; she could see that. A simple man with a lot of money and a lot of memories. Someone had tried to kill him in Sydney. Then someone else, it would seem, had tried to kill him in Canberra, the Mafia apparently. And then some punk kid had been about to kill him here in the old house. But she'd got there just in time. She'd killed the kid. Then, a year later he'd been blown up in this very house. Or not this house, but another house that looked like the original standing on this very spot.

They'd tried to kill him, but instead his wife had died in the blast. But his daughter had been saved.

He was like her own father, she could see.

Victor Babchuk was a simple man, but a prisoner of guilt and ravishment and despair, afraid to die. He couldn't stop seeing them, not only in his dreams but with his eyes wide open. Could not stop seeing the flames and the shrivelling corpses, at the wall. They'd had to douse them with oil, to make them burn. The Jews. The guards standing around, shouting *Loess! Loess!* Which, if you don't know German, means 'Go!' Or 'Quickly!' Or 'Hurry!' In other words, get it over with. So we can get out of here and go on and crush the fucking Ruskis! On towards the Volga. On towards the Caucasus and the oil. On towards victory. Heil Hitler!

'More bread?' she asked.

'Oh, I'm fine.'

He broke some.

'And butter.'

'Yes, of course.'

She watched him eating.

It was like a last supper. Someone was going to die. Shaft or her? She'd begun spread the word. Had called a dozen likely hotels in Wagga Wagga that afternoon. Had asked whether anyone named Shafter was staying? Asked whether they were asking about her. Making it clear she wanted to speak to him. Because she was going to kill him. Kill his mates too if it came to that.

She would make herself a target.

They would have to shoot. Or, if they did not, they were a pack of piss-weak defectives. So defective you almost felt sorry for them. Not everyone was born lucky. She wasn't born lucky, but somehow she was lucky now. She was a police sergeant. That made you something in this piss-weak world. She had cooked for a man she liked, a man who had invited her to dinner. The first man ever to do that for her. He'd said she could stay the night if she liked. Nervously, she'd thought. As if unsure what he was getting himself into, going to bed with a big bitch like her. Very fast with a very fast weapon.

'Okay?' she asked.

'You're a good cook, Anna.'

'Ha! You're calling me Anna?'

She waited for his reaction. 'Yeah?'

'One of them was Palfreyman,' she said. 'Remember that jerk?'

'I remember him.'

'You know what he is doing now?'

'No idea.'

'Teaching criminology at the college in Canberra. He should have been fired.'

'He was just doing his job,' Becker said.

'What? A drongo like him?'

'He wasn't a drongo. He just played it safe.'

She calmed down. 'Safe is right.'

He made a little speech about Palfreyman.

'He'd read all the books and obeyed all the rules. Some people are like that. They were born that way. That's how they get good jobs, for life, and a fat pension when they retire with nothing to look forward to but a game of bowls or a reunion somewhere or a Pacific cruise and then they die. No-one remembers them, when they've gone. Not even their own children. But they're not stupid. They have to play it cool. It's not their fault.'

Anastacia nodded.

He had, perhaps inadvertently, described himself. She was sorry. She'd made a mistake.

Harry Becker was an honest man, who didn't condemn anyone. He was lucky and he was unlucky. He lived and he died. There were men like him all over the world, she knew. They lived and they died. In the long run, they amounted to very little. No-one mourned them, no-one remembered them. A man has two deaths, someone had said. When his body dies and when the last man who remembers him dies.

She was watching him.

He was going to die, but not for some time, if she could help it.

This was one of the good moments of her life. She was sitting at a table, looking at a man. She had made a meal for him. He was eating it, he was satisfied, pleased. Pleased with her. She would like to be able to do that every day—make a good meal for a good man. She stopped eating, and watched him in the soft spotlight. The architect had thought of everything. If you are at a table talking with someone you know, someone you respect, you don't want floodlights. You want the face across the table. That face and no other.

'Harry?' she said.

'Yeah?'

'I like your house. It's—' She searched for a word. 'Smart and practical and—' She searched again. 'Friendly.'

'Friendly?'

'Yes, houses can be like that, can't they? You want to be with them all the time and in them.'

'Yeah?'

'It's like being in someone you like.'

'Really?'

She was watching him, holding her wineglass.

She'd almost finished her second red. She was thinking, he could see. She was going to say something very personal. He didn't know whether he was prepared for it, whatever it was. Her eyes were narrowed. For a moment in the soft light, she was all eyes. You could not escape them.

'Harry?'

'Would you do something for me?'

'What's that?'

'Would you fuck me?'

'Fuck you?'

'Please?' she added, almost shyly.

Her language was disgusting, but he understood. She was giving him a let-out, deliberately making it crude and repulsive. He could say 'No!' and no harm done.

He'd not long lost a loving wife. All because some creeps had wanted to kill him. But was that true? Was it the Mafia? Or was it someone else? If he'd not been the target, who was? Was it this woman, who was not a woman? Or really was some kind of a woman, who had been abused and battered almost beyond recall until, incredulously, the Feds had found her and helped her and got her going and made her a cop on a big, white bike with a siren and blue lights and a retractable aerial behind her. And a helmet with radio built in and thick gloves and jodhpurs and smile on a face you would not want to mess with if you had any self-regard.

'I'm a big, ugly bitch, I know,' she said. 'But I don't bleed and I can't get pregnant.'

She was waiting in the soft light. Hadn't finished eating. But had been thinking, about herself and what she was and what she was not. She was not a man and yet as a woman, she was a bit of a joke.

'If you don't want to,' she said, 'I'll understand.'

He finished chewing. Picked up his glass.

It was his second glass. It was not a Tarrango. He'd tried more than once to get it, but it was rare. The supermarkets rarely carried it. If he'd had a Tarrango, he would have been able to sit at a table and think of Evelyn. She'd asked him if she could tempt him. And he had said, 'Yes.' She had poured two glasses and handed one to him, and said: I like to drink it cold in summer. Then she'd begun to talk. About herself. A woman like that, you couldn't take your eyes off her, not if you were a man. Not if you were a woman too. That superb body, that slow smile, that mystery. Was she a good woman? How could a woman, who'd killed one man and planned to kill another, be good? It didn't matter. If you were with Evelyn Crowley, morality was only a word. It meant nothing. If she were opening her legs for you, you had to have her. Nothing much you could do about it, not if you were a man. Mother Nature saw to that.

He remembered something. Palfreyman had been interviewing him about the death of Torrence. They'd been talking about Evelyn. That smart-alec cop had given him some advice: 'Keep away from Mrs Crowley. That dame has dangerous friends.' She sure did. Evelyn had belonged to a Mafia family, but had wanted to get out. Before they killed her for talking to a cop.

He didn't feel like that with this kind of woman. She was more like a female warrior. With vengeance on her mind. A bit frightening, but he needed someone like Anastacia. They had tried to kill him twice, the bad people out there. They would try again.

'Am I so ugly?' she asked.

'You are not ugly.'

'I'm not attractive, am I?'

'You are attractive. People can't stop looking at you.'

'But not sexually attractive?'

'I've never thought about you that way.'

'Because I'm such a freak?'

'Stop that, Stacey.'

'I don't have any breasts, or hips. I don't have a good figure—'

'Stop it.'

'I'm all muscle.'

'That's better than fat.'

'I'm too tall and I'm bad-tempered and I hurt inside.'

'Hurt?'

'By the shame and misery and the hopelessness of it all.'

'What's hopeless about your life?'

'I can never have children.'

'I'm sorry,' he said.

'I can never have a someone to love me. Nor one I can love.'

'I'm sorry.'

'When I looked out the back window that day and saw Robyn playing with the kids and the dog, I thought how beautiful. If only something like that would happen to me.'

He didn't respond, eating slowly, thoughtfully.

'I couldn't make that call,' she said. 'To Canberra,' she added. 'Tell them what had happened. Ruin your lives for you.'

'Thank you.'

It seemed to be an empty thing to say, so commonplace.

He did feel sorry for her. She was unhappy in the way that the only rejected can feel unhappy. The ones who missed out on whatever it takes to be attractive. To him, women were simply female humans. You either liked one or you didn't. Going to bed with one was something you did only with a friend.

'Tall girls have feelings, you know.'

He thought she was going to say, 'Ugly girls too.' But she did not.

Becker didn't answer.

If he did what she wanted, he didn't know how he'd manage it.

No man would get randy standing next to her in a lift. Yet he understood her need. She'd been through a terrible ordeal many years ago. Most likely she'd never been loved, except perhaps by her mother, who'd died when she was fifteen. Anastacia would probably be nervous about sex. Afraid she'd fail, be rejected.

He owed her a lot. And she was some sort of friend.

He didn't have too many friends. He used to have friends when he was at school. Mucking around with a football, and trying to chat up girls. He did have a girlfriend once. She was the postmaster's daughter. Had black hair and blue eyes—typically Irish, she'd remarked. But her farther was posted somewhere else, and she'd disappeared.

He used to play his father's old guitar. Not well, but well enough to strum and even play a pretty tune here and there. One of them was the old Maurice Chevalier number: Louise. He was singing it to himself one day when a girl came into the hardware store, where he worked straight after finishing school. He'd not seen her waiting with a ratchet screwdriver in a and.

'That's my name,' she'd said.

'Oh? Sorry, what's your name?'

'Louise,' she'd said. 'Actually, it's Eloise.' They'd got chatting. She was a most polite, a girl with class. 'Please put it on our account,' she'd said.

'What name?' he'd asked. Then it came out; she was Eloise McNevin. He'd tried to chat her up, but she'd simply smiled, thanked him and walked out. He'd never seen her again. But, one day his daughter was to marry her son.

'Why do you want me to do it?' he asked.

'It's important to me.'

'Why?'

'It might help.'

She was both looking at him and not looking at him. As if shy and worried and humiliated by having to ask. Having to beg, a proud woman like that.

'Now?' he asked.

'When you've finished your wine.'

Chapter 10

THEY FINISHED BREAKFAST and prepared to leave. She was going back to Canberra. She had no luggage. Everything she needed was in the two saddlebags on her bike. He'd watched her dress after a shower. She had a long, lean, hard body, a boxer's body. Big in the shoulders and the arms. An up and down body, like a man's. She'd shown it off to him, strutting around. 'You like what you see?' she had said, 'Not much of a figure, is it? Makes you think you've shagged a man, doesn't it? But I don't have a prick, do I? So I've proven it, haven't I? I really am a woman.'

Then she'd pulled on her cotton knickers, no brassiere, of course. Then the shirt and jeans and sat down and pulled on black socks. Finally, the heavy, clunking boots. Dirty boots, but they were work boots. A motor-cop's boots. As of old, when she'd been on the beat in Canberra, riding a Kawasaki 750. With the wind in her hair and a smile on her face. Queen of the road.

He'd watched her slip on the harness.

It was a contraption with two leather loops—one went around the right shoulder, the other around the left. Both were held in place by a leather strap across her back. Nothing showed across her chest. From the left loop hung the holster on a short, thick strap. She picked up the Glock and cocked it, jacking a 9mm round into the breach. It was a fearful weapon. Ungainly, ugly, treacherous, likely to fire at any moment, it seemed to have a mind of its own. Nothing between it and death except the in-built safety system. You pull the small trigger and the safety goes off, she had said. Keep pulling and the damned thing goes *bang*!'

Finally, she slipped on the jacket.

She must have been hot in it most days. It was early summer, but still bearable first thing in the morning. Probably preferred heavy leather when riding a cycle. Just in case she came off. Never zipped up a jacket, not fully anyway. Maybe just the bottom inch or two, so she could get at the Glock any time, in a split-second. Or less.

They walked out to the Harley, parked under the old pepper tree. It had rained lightly during the night. And the seat was wet.

She opened a bag and pulled out a cloth, began wiping the seat.

'It's been great, Harry.'

She looked up, smiling.

Wiped the tank and handle grips. And the headlamp. Why she bothered about the headlamp, he didn't know. The wind and the sun would soon clear it. Perhaps it was no more than a housewifely action, a habit. Attacking the least speck of dust. Some women were like that—they wanted perfection.

She straightened up, kissed him.

'Thanks, Harry. I wish we'd met long ago.'

He was worried, thinking about it. He'd woken at dawn with the worry in mind. This woman was going to kill a man, perhaps three men in all. By inciting one man—the animal called Shaft, calling him out. Inciting him to have a go at her. With a rifle or a handgun or perhaps a knife or a broken bottle? He didn't know. It didn't matter what. As calmly as ice, she'd flip out the Glock and fill him full of lead. Then claim she was acting in self-defence.

That's how they did it in the old days in the west, the American West.

She must have seen a lot of westerns in her time, dreaming about it. Call the bastard out, standing at twenty paces and looking at each other. You always knew that the bad guy would draw first, because he had to. If not, he'd be humiliated in front of his pardners, in front of the crowd. In the main street, outside the saloon. The fastest gun always won. Mostly the good guy, but sometimes not.

'Anna?'

'Yeah?'

She was smiling in her own twisted and malformed and manly way. She had pretty ears, he noticed. Not the kind on which earrings would have looked right. Would not make her look feminine. Nothing would make her look feminine, but she had a certain steadiness about her. Perhaps that was the key to Anastacia. You always knew where you stood. She was either going to kill you or kiss you.

'Don't do it.'

'Don't kill a man?'

'You won't get away with it. The police will know you set him up. They'll hear you taunted him, made him a laughing-stock. Made him attack you.'

'So what?'

'That's murder.'

'Yeah, it's murder. But morally justified murder.'

'He didn't kill you.'

'He would have killed me, if the Feds hadn't arrived in time. I would have died of blood poisoning. All the crap and waste and filth that had been part of me for months, perhaps years, was leaking into my bloodstream.'

'But he did not *kill* you,' he insisted.

'Yeah? Listen, mate, he intended that I'd die. In my book that's murder.'

She got on the bike, started it.

The engine purred, like a machine already hot and itching to go. It had electric starting and a water jacket. It was quiet. Not a noisy Harley at all.

She was sitting astride, legs straight out, feet out. Steady as a rock, her face twisted into a smile of death and delight and destiny. She'd been thinking of this for more than thirteen years. The day had come. Or it hadn't come, depending upon whether Shaft had heard. Maybe he'd left town. Maybe he was scared to kill a cop. He might not show. Might be sick in his guts. Some mad sheila he had once shafted was going to shaft him with a Glock. And there was no way out.

She reached over, gripped an arm. Not tightly or firmly or affectionately, but like a friend who understands why you are worried.

'I'm going to do it, Harry. I'm going to draw him out.'

'In the main street of Wagga? In Baylis street?'

'Who knows? Thanks for everything,' she said.

Then, once more, she was gone.

He stood there, watching the gate. It was open, Nutty knew it was open. Nutty cried briefly, worried. The gate should be shut, he knew. Slowly Becker walked up and closed it. Before it shut, he peeped out, looked along the road towards the east. No sign of her. Not of a a woman on a big black bike. Nothing, gone. Vacating the landscape, the paddock, the trees and fences, the cattle and the wheat, the golden earth and the goodness of the day.

He recalled what Evelyn had said as she lay in his arms on that last night.

Thanks for everything, Harry.

Then they'd shot her. Straight through one temple and out the other. And he'd slept through the whole thing, in the depths of concussion and codeine and fear and longing.

Last night was not like that. They'd both been shy at first.

The sheets were cold, and both were incapable at first. So, for the first fifteen or twenty minutes they'd talked. About his plans for the farm and the three children, Wendy and Terry and little Robbie, as she was called, his daughter. He was going to do whatever he could for her. She would grow up to be a beautiful girl, smart and successful and happy. She'd win all the prizes and get a gold medal at Charles Sturt. He didn't know what she would study, but hoped it would be something to do with farming.

She would be a smiling girl, a proud girl, a popular girl, like her mother.

The kind of girl everyone wanted to know, not because she was rich or gorgeous or smart or the best root in town, but because she was good. Like her mother, Robyn the Good. A girl who could walk down Baylis Street, stopping every few yards because she knew everyone and everyone knew her. And wanted to chat to her or show their new baby or ask how she was going with her studies. She, being so smart, winning all the prizes. With a smile not only a happy smile, but a proud smile. A fulfilled smile. Fulfilled, because she knew what she was and what she could do. And she would do it.

That would be his daughter, when she grew up, Roberta Becker.

As he'd been speaking, Anastasia had propped herself up on an elbow, listening. With her free hand stroking him and making him big and hard for her. So that he hadn't noticed, thinking what the world would be like for Roberta. And whether he would ever see it. He didn't know how much longer he had. His mother was in an institution. Dying, not her body dying, but her brain. Being eaten away. It was the worst kind of death, not knowing that you were not knowing.

She kissed him on his lips. 'Thank you for telling me.'

Then she'd got on top of him.

It lasted ten minutes or more, as if she did not want sex but wanted only to experience it. Like smelling a good wine, so good it would be a sin to drink it. At first it was difficult for her. She flinched, then lowered herself very carefully, expecting more pain. Finally, she got right down, so that he was fully inside her. She was panting like a mountain climber who has reached the top. She was not exhausted, but relieved. Somehow, she had done it. It wasn't too painful and not too awful.

She'd got carried away, going at him as hard and fast and brutal as a man.

They came together.

She lay on him heavily, panting.

Flattening him. She was a heavy woman. Breathing hard, head turned, both looking at him and not looking. Her eyelids flicking now and then, her breath returning in shorter and shorter grunts until they became sweet little gasps.

'That was lovely,' she said, trembling.

For a moment, he thought she was crying.

Chapter 11

AFTER SHE'D GONE, he made the bed and cleaned up the kitchen and bathroom and did some vacuum cleaning, worked in the barn for a couple of hours. It was the original barn, not affected by the explosion. Nor had it been renovated by the previous owner, the dentist in Wagga. Its roof had been leaking and the gutters were choked. In some places they too had been leaking. The solder or cold solder, a kind of plastic glue, had worn away and the joins in the gutters were cracked. They were dirty, blackened and grubby. He'd had to take the guttering apart in a couple of spots and to file the metal clean and to rejoin with Bostick. And the electrical wiring, he was sure, was not good enough.

He shut it off and rewired it.

You were supposed to get a certified electrician, but it was an easy job. He wanted to replace the old filament globes with fluorescent lamps, to save money. All he had to do was pull out the old brackets and install new fluorescent ones. When he was sure he'd done a good job and the barn would not leak again, at least not for a long time, and the lighting would be brighter and clearer, he came up and got himself a coffee.

He was still putting cream in it, even though it was sour. He had to give up coffee altogether, he decided. It was burning his guts. He had to do something about it. See a doctor. He didn't know any doctor. He should ask around, get an opinion. He'd see someone next time he was in Wagga. It could be dyspepsia, or perhaps that trouble called reflux. His mother had it. She'd had it for year, even back in the days when she was not yet a widow. After that everything had gone wrong with her. Until two years ago, when she'd been admitted. It had been difficult to get her into a place.

She wasn't really aged, because she wasn't old at all. Only sixty-one, but a woman who felt that all the suffering in the world was visited upon her. Because her man had gone back to Vietnam, with all those Asians. Slopes, some people had called them. And got killed.

She was a born hypochondriac.

He hadn't known what a hypochondriac was until a few years later, perhaps when he'd been fourteen or fifteen. His aunt Erika was her sister and married to Smacker Barnes, who in turn had a brother, who had had a son named Barry, Harry Becker's second cousin.

Erika had cared about him. Had given him a twenty-first birthday party. He'd asked her why she was doing this. Because she will not think of it, Erika had said. What's wrong with Mum? Why is she like that? She won't talk to me now.'

Erika had taken her time answering. 'Your mother,' she said, 'did something.'

'Did what?'

'Said something.'

'What did she say? When?'

'Many years ago, when you were still a small boy.'

'What did she say? I don't remember anything.'

'She didn't say it to you, Harry.'

'Who then?'

'Someday, I'll tell you.'

Barnes was dead now. He'd popped himself. Or, more accurately, he'd dropped himself. Climbed to the top of the mental health unit building at Wagga Wagga Base Hospital in Edward Street and jumped. The building only two-storeys high, but that was high enough. He'd felt happy there. The staff were wonderful. The nurses and the paramedics had treated him like a valuable human being. Even the doctors had treated him as if he mattered, a perfect case. They used to bring students around to see him. It was a safe place, a place of peace. He hadn't wanted to leave, but the treatment was free for only eight weeks. After that, you had to pay.

It was not the money.

It was the thought of having to go home again, to that nagging bitch of a wife of his. Maria, the nagging voice, the humiliation. The achingly loneliness. The whole bloody banality of it all. He could have been something. He could have been a good cop, respected, praised. He could have been a sergeant by now, but he wasn't. Instead, he was the man who did not exist at Wagga Wagga police station.

Barry Barnes had been a man who added up to nothing. He had lived and he had died. He'd wanted be a cop, so he could say he was something, but he was not. He was just some ill-bred squirt, who'd hated his father. Who used to kick him, when he was down. Make fun of him. Make him cry. If he'd made it as a big cop, perhaps a sergeant, he would have grown up and shown the ugly bastard who was boss now. But that had not happened. He never made it as a top cop, he was a failure with a bitch of a wife at home. That's why the doctors brought the students to see him. When they looked at him, all they saw was a living corpse on the bed. He was dead, but his eyes moved. There was nothing else to him.

That's why he had jumped.

Becker was sitting on the front verandah, Nutty by him, watching the traffic go by. It never stopped, night and day. It went on and on, in the way that rivers go on and on, and time goes on and on. And life goes on and on. Except when it stops.

It might be serious, he was thinking. It might be cancer.

He didn't finish the coffee.

Usually, he drank it from a mug. This time, he'd drunk less than half. He stepped out to the edge and tipped it on the lavender and oregano, watching it pour out, gradually reducing to a dribble. Perhaps the answer lay in the mug, or its contents. It was like emptying the mug and finding something there in the dregs, the grains and the undissolved sugar. Some sort of sign, a glimmer of evidence, in which, if you were willing enough, you could see a simple explanation for his aches and pains. But there was nothing.

It had to be deep down.

Not coffee at all, but something that could mean trouble. Perhaps big trouble. He'd once known a cop, an old man who'd had pains. He'd eat a packet of Mylanta each day. Honestly, he did. He always had this gut ache.

The old cop collapsed one day on the job.

Becker and young Benson, the new bloke from Tenterfield, were patrolling the notorious Cross in Sydney. Strolling along Darlinghurst Road, their eyes flicking at anything that looked seedy or suspect or rotten or slimy or haunted in anyway, like the soul of the Cross itself. Where you could get a quick fuck for fifty dollars in the old days and a snort for twenty. Off the desperadoes, the ones who did it or handled it in parks or lanes or in corners of pubs or toilets and all the other rat holes of a city. Hungry rats. And a pair of rat eyes in the shady corners of the mind.

Yes, he thought.

He and Benson had been walking along and they'd seen a man in uniform. He was standing against a door, a glass door outside some peepshow where there were coloured lights running up the walls and women with the skirts up to their twats, and smiling enough to make you sick to look at them. They'd gone up to him. He was an old Senior. Not a senior citizen but a Senior Constable. Scruffy, his shirt wrinkled and his eyes gluey with age.

'You okay, mate?'

'Yeah, yeah,' he had said.

Becker had met him one or twice at the station, the old one on Taylor Square, next to the Supreme Court. He could have been the turnkey, or the man who made the tea for the detectives when they came back from a job.

'What's the matter?'

'Oh, Jesus, it's this pain.'

'Where?'

'In my guts.'

'I'll get an ambulance.'

'No, no, I'll be right.'

'What are you doing here?'

'Oh, I have to—I have to serve a notice on—Oh, Christ!'

'Call an ambulance,' Becker had said to Benson. 'Where's the pain, mate?'

'In my guts.'

'Yeah? This sounds serious.'

'Ah, no, it's this flamin' heartburn. I take a packet of My—My—'

'Mylanta? Look, mate, forget about tablets, you've got to go to hospital and get this looked at.'

'Ah, Christ, I can't go to hospital. I've gotter keep—' He'd cried out again. A small crowd had gathered. Everyone at the Cross loved to see a copper cry.

'This could be serious,' Becker had said again. Then to Benson: 'You got that ambulance yet?'

'They're coming.'

The old policeman began to slide. He was sweating. It was cold sweat. You know it's a cold sweat, more fear than agony, when you see the face go white and wrinkled, like slightly wet, wrinkled white tissue.

'You want to sit down, mate? Over here. Shit, where's that seat? Ah, yeah, down here. Can you walk this far? Only a few steps.'

A couple of kids were sitting on it. Becker told them to piss off.

'Ah, shut up,' one of them had said.

'Get off, I need this seat.'

'Ah, piss off.'

'Don't tell me to piss off.'

'Fuckin' cops, always havin' a go at yer.'

He tapped his sidearm. 'Get off or I'll stick this up your arse.'

'Eh? You can't talk to us like that.'

'You've got drugs on you, get off.'

'Eh? We ain't got no drugs, have we, love?'

The girl tried to speak, but failed. She had dead eyes.

Becker said: 'You will have when the drug squad arrive. Your pockets will be full of it.'

'Eh?'

'Get off!'

They got off. Becker got the old cop onto the seat. Eased him down. 'You want to lie down?' he'd asked.

'If I can stay here a few minutes—'

'If you're in pain—' The old man didn't want to lie down, on a seat in public. Everyone looking, and grinning. He tried to sit up. In his wretchedness, he still had some dignity.

'Shit, where's that ambulance?'

'They're coming, Harry. I can hear 'em.'

They'd stood by the old cop. He had white hair but not much of it. His forehead was a land of wrinkles and freckles and scars. A few blackheads on his nose and ears. The ambulance came across the junction with William Street. Benson was on the street, waving. When they got the old man into the vehicle, he buckled up. Crying with pain.

Then they were off.

At high speed to St Vincent's only a few blocks away on Old South Head Road. Where they operated immediately. They were too late. It was oesophageal cancer. Pretty bad. He seemed to be okay for a while. Then one day he was dead. What had killed him did not matter. As Benson had said in his bushwhacker's wisdom: Once you're dead you're dead. It don't matter what killed you.

In those days, Becker had been a good cop. Relatively young, married with three kids, one not his own. A good-natured cop with his whole life before him.

Now, he was not so sure.

A vehicle had pulled up at the gate. It was the big red Holden V8 with the lights and sirens on top. Kruger got out, the young cop, less than a year out of Goulburn. His first posting being Wagga Wagga. He'd copped it sweet for a Henty boy.

Got out efficiently, pulling up his belt. These days a cop carried a lot of gear.

Came stepping through the gate, as purposefully and firmly as a young and earnest cop could be. Grinning all the way, eyes fixed on Becker, then on Nutty, then on Becker again. Nutty had shot to his feet, eager, eyes wide, hopeful. Useless as a watchdog. Much too friendly.

'G'day, Harry.'

'Max.'

'How're you going?'

'Fair enough.'

Nutty shot down off the verandah. Kruger bent down, patting him. Ruffing him up.

'Look, mate, we've had a call.'

'What kind of call?'

'Tried to get you on your phone. Got no answer.'

'Ah, yeah, I put it down in the shed and forgot it.'

'Sorry to disturb you, but they asked me to call in and talk to you, you know?'

'What about?'

'That Federal officer, the tall one, the girl who looks like a—'

Something hit Becker in the heart. Something had happened. An accident? She'd been in a road smash? She was dead?

'Gee, mate, didn't mean to frighten you.'

'What's happened?'

'Nothing, but my boss, Jack— Remember him?'

'Yeah?'

'Asked me to look you up. See if you could help us. We're trying to contact her.'

'What about?'

'Yeah, well, I'm not sure. But some blokes have been asking about her.'

'Have they?'

'They seem to be the blokes I was telling you about, the ones in the pub. Jack thinks there might be trouble.'

'What kind of trouble?'

'Reckons these blokes are just out of jail.'

'Yeah?'

'So, we're trying to locate her. To tell her.'

'She knows about them. You told me and I told her.'

'Yeah, but that was a couple of weeks ago.'

'Tried ringing her?'

'Ringing her? We don't have any number for her.'

'Have you tried the Federal office back in town?'

'Yeah, we've tried that. No answer. You haven't got a number for her, have you?'

Becker was wary. He never gave out a cop's number to anyone, even to a fellow cop. You never knew who you could trust.

'No, I don't have a number.'

Immediately he changed his mind. 'It's on the phone, I left in the shed.'

'You couldn't find it for us, could you? It might be important. I mean, when someone fresh out of jail is asking about an officer—'

'Come around the back.'

'Ah, gee, good. Thanks, Harry.'

'How are you getting on?'

'What? Yeah, good, terrific. Christ, it's a great life, ain't it? Being a cop. Always wanted to be a cop.'

'Your dad a cop?'

'Ah, Christ, no. Had a shop in Henty, but that was long ago. Nothing much in Henty now. Not for a young bloke. Got to go where the jobs are, eh?'

'That's country life for you.'

They had reached the shed. Becker picked up his phone, pressed a few keys. Read out a number. 'That's her mobile,' he said.

Kruger relayed it. They walked back together. The young cop fascinated. 'By gee, you've made a good job of this place, haven't you? They reckon it's exactly the same place completely rebuilt.'

'Different on the inside,' Becker said.

'If I ever make it to sergeant, I'll have a place like this. Have a few cows, and a dog and a nice wife and some kids. Something to retire to. If I live that long, that is.'

'Got you worried?'

'Ah, yeah. I'm not sure I'm the right one for this highway job. I mean, I was chasing a bloke on a bike the other day—a dirt bike, you know them. The young bloke was tearing down the road at speed, so I took off after him. He went faster, I went faster till the turn off to Lockhart came up. You know it?'

'Yeah.'

'This truck came out from the left. Should have stopped for the sign. I thought the kid was gonna hit it. He speeded up, missed the truck by inches. I thought, Gee that was close! Then I realised! I was hurtling at the truck at one hundred and twenty k's an hour! There was no way I could stop in time! I was gonna die!'

'What happened?'

'I woke up.'

'You were asleep at the wheel?'

'No, I was in bed.'

'In bed?'

'Yeah, dreaming. Fast asleep, must have been all the worry. Have these dreams I'm gonna crash head-on into something that comes out of nowhere.'

He was laughing, striding along in his boots and good humour.

'You have dreams like that, mate?'

'I used to, in Sydney. And I wasn't driving. I was walking along a street. And faces were looking at me. And someone was calling me, calling. I'd look around, but never could see who was calling. Then I'd look in a window, at the reflection. I could see myself and myself was calling me. Calling to me. It yelled at me, "Look out, look out!" Then I'd wake up.'

'In the middle of a city street?'

'In the middle of a Kings Cross street. There's a difference.'

'Yeah, yeah, yeah.'

They reached the big, red, patrol wagon. Kruger shot out a hand. 'Gee, thanks, Harry. Good to see you again. You're a bit of a legend. Believe you took one in the shoulder one night. At the Cross, was it?'

'No, at home. Putting out the garbage.'

'Eh?'

'That's how it can end. While you're putting out the trash.'

Kruger was going to say something, but it stuck in his throat. They shook hands.

'Thanks for your help, Harry.'

Just then Becker's phone went off. It was Laura Langley.

'Harry, get back to town now!'

'What?'

'Chook's had a phone call. From someone named Shaft.'

'Shaft?'

'The one who's been asking after her. I was out, just got back. Dave says she took a call from him. Told Shaft she'd be in the Hovell if he wanted to chat.'

'Jesus, she'll kill him!'

'That's what I fear.'

'How long since she left?'

'About ten minutes, Dave says.'

'Call the police, then get up there yourself. Try to stop her.'

'You are the only one who can, Harry. She loves you.'

'I'm with a cop right now. We're on our way.'

He jumped in. The car took off. They reached about half way in five minutes. The intercom spluttered. The young cop took the call. Becker couldn't understand a word, just a blast of noise. Why the hell do they have to shout? he thought.

The driver had no trouble. 'Yeah? Yeah? What? I've got him right here. We're about ten k's out. What? Jesus. Yeah, right.' He stepped on the gas.

Becker had to shout above the screaming V8. 'What was that all about?'

'Your friend, Anastacia—'

'What about her?'

'She's having a beer at the Hovell.'

'So what?'

'A bloke holding a shotgun has just walked in.'

Chapter 12

WHEN SHAFTER HAD walked in, Chook was propping up the bar, a Jack Daniels in one hand. No ice. He'd walked in with two others, holding a shotgun. The other two were clean. He'd said: "There she is, the fuckin' bitch." Chook had turned slowly, leaned back, elbows on the bar. She put down the glass without taking her eyes off Shafter. Let the glass feel its own way. And stood there, arms spread, elbows back on the bar, except that the left hand, just the fingertips, was holding open that side of her jacket. Showing the Glock. It was like a scene from an old movie, a Western classic. A long and lean and half-starved gunfighter in a deadbeat saloon in Texas or Arizona, back when there were real gunfighters. Who settled their differences out on a street. Or even in a saloon with a Colt .45. To hell with the crockery.

She was truly pleased to see him.

'Good to see you again, Shaft. Or is it Graham Schaaf?'

He didn't reply. Just stood there with the gun, a sawn-off pump-action Remington 870.

'How was Barwon supermax? Did they shove it up you every night under the showers? Shafted you, did they? How'd you like that? Pretty good, was it? Little Miss Fuckwit Shaft.'

He was a tubby sort of man about fifty, a scruffy man. He'd been in jail for more than thirteen years. Looked like he didn't care now whether he lived or died.

His eyes were of a kind all their own.

Once blue, they had faded in the way that an oil painting fades if you expose it to too much light. Not cold eyes, but disinterested, switched-off. The kind that doesn't quite see things. Or, does see things, but not what you and I see. Another kind of brain behind small, poky and faded eyes. He was what he was, and there was no point in pretending he wasn't.

His eyes blinked.

Chook could have taken such a moment to fire and kill.

Or, merely wounded and disabled so the cops could leap in and grab him. Behind him were a few tables and chairs, pushed aside. Drinkers and gossips and idlers had jumped out of the way. Some crowded into a corner by the front windows. Others dragged outside by the police. Some idiots, glasses still in hand, were trying to look in. It was a bright, shiny day. Early December 1996.

Two cops stood at the front door. Others were inside. Two had come in from the back lane. Waiting now in the passage leading to the gaming room and the dining room and the kitchen. Everyone waiting for the first shot.

'Well, mate,' she said, 'what's it going to be? Are you going to be a good little boy and go with 'em or are you gonna use that thing? Remember how to use a pump-action? Been practising, have you?'

No response.

'Got nothing to say?'

Still no response, except another blink.

'What's it going to be, Shaft?'

Again, nothing. Just the unblinking stare.

Chook smiled in a kindly way. 'You know, I was sitting in a car outside a supermarket one day, when another car pulled up beside me. I was surprised by the noise coming from it. The doors were closed, but there was this horrible crying—'

The shotgun was pointing down.

Not actually pointing down, not down at the floor but casually, towards Chook's legs or perhaps to one side, almost inattentively. If fired now, it would probably hit an ankle or lower leg or a boot. Probably all of those, depending on the angle. No-one thought it would stay at that angle. Chook was still speaking—in a slow, casual way, there being not much to the story. Just the making of a monster.

'The driver's door opened, a woman got out. A big, brutish woman in sheer size and appearance, lumbering. A big, ugly, bitch of a woman. A bit like me, eh? Very angry, fed up. Had had enough. You know what she did?'

Shaft stared. For a moment he seemed to relax, you could hear his breath. He seemed to be listening, hooked by a simple story.

'Opened a back door. A child was inside, strapped in as required by law. But a fairly grown child. Four or five, I'd say. He was bawling, bawling his heart out. And yelling, with the anger of frustration and the humility and bewilderment. She told him to stop that crying. "Stop it," she said as she freed him from the harness.'

Shaft was afraid to blink. If he blinked, she'd kill him. If he did not blink, his eyes would become so dry and itchy that they would smart. Tears would run. He'd have to blink. Otherwise, he'd see only a tall, dark shape, leaning against the bar. There had been a whiskey glass on the bar, to the right of her right elbow. Now, it was a wishy-washy glass, empty, fuzzy.

Nothing much more happened for about fifteen minutes.

Chook went on chatting to him, sneering at him, taunting. Reminiscing about the orgies they'd had together and the cash and the booze and he drugs. And the degradation. Sounded chummy, as if she missed it all. The good times, the good for nothing times and the shagging. It went on and on. The whole pathetic brainlessness of it. The emptiness and the despair.

She asked him a question. 'What happened to Red?'

He blinked again. She could have killed him then. He wouldn't have seen it coming. But he'd lowered the gun.

His eyes opened a bit, as if surprised.

'Red? Remember Red? He was a cop, wasn't he? Told me to get out. There was going to be a raid. What did you do to him? Stick him down a well? Lots of wells in the hills, weren't there? There was one on the property, wasn't there? Up among the cherries and the satsumas. Or, did you take him out to sea? Dump him, weighted down with chains or rocks or what? You killed him, didn't you? He was a good cop. He cared about me. Tried to get me out. But I was too bombed out to move, wasn't I? Fucked half to death? By a dickhead like you.'

Still, he did not move. Still, the gun was half lowered.

His face twitched. Then it twitched again. He screwed up the whole side of his face as if trying to get rid of the itch by twitching it away. Like a fly crawling on your face when you've got your hands full.

He twitched again.

Didn't reply. He sniffed now and then, slowly and carefully. One sniff too much and she might kill him. He'd heard about her. Fast, very fast. Had been practising for years. The word was she could hit a bottle on a fence at one hundred yards. Had her own firing range up back. In the trees, by a creek. Firing away, day after day. Waiting for the chance to kill him.

Chook smiled. 'Got an itchy nose? Why don't you scratch it?'

Twitched again. The non-existent fly would not go way.

She almost laughed.

He grimaced, but that didn't move the fly. He looked sick. He was going to die, he knew. Should have plugged the ugly bitch when he walked in. Blown her to pieces and waited for the cops to blast him. Or, maybe he'd drop the weapon, like they said. Give in, go back to jail for the rest of his life, satisfied. Hang himself in jail. He didn't care now, but he wouldn't die at her hands. For thirteen years he'd been telling the world he was gonna kill her when he got out. Scatter her guts around in a fair fight. But she would not draw. She was a heartless bitch. Didn't play fair. She was making him pull first.

Worse than that, his guts were starting to rumble.

He might have to shit his pants soon. Maybe two or three minutes. He'd have to kill her before he exploded. It was the fear, the voracious fear. It was eating out his guts.

That was the situation, when Becker arrived. He followed Kruger in. Jack Jackson was already inside, a mobile to his mouth. Speaking softly, as if afraid to make anyone jump the wrong way. At the same nudging Kruger, pointing and nodding. Kruger caught on. Whispered to Becker: 'Say something. Talk her out of it.'

Becker didn't move. He'd frozen. Never had been in a firefight.

Didn't want to be here. He was trembling. Worse, he was shaking. Something had gone wrong with his legs. He tried to say, Chook. But it didn't come out. He stepped forward a few inches so that Kruger and Jackson were now behind him. Didn't know how he'd got his legs to move.

'Chook,' Becker said, not much more than a whisper.

She smiled. And nodded, an inch or so. Did not blink. 'It's okay, Harry,' she said. 'Everything's under control.'

'Chook, don't do it!' It came out as a great big whisper, useless.

'Do what? I'm having a friendly chat with an old mate, aren't I? Graham Shithead Shaft. Defective little cry-baby, Shaft.'

Shafter twitched. It was a ripple of pain. Must have had tremendous self-control. Did not blink. The shotgun still loose in his hands.

'Chook, leave it to the police!'

'We're just having a chat, aren't we, Shafty? Shifty little Shafty? Poor little piss-weak Shafty? Not got your mummy now? You know what that woman did? The one in the car? Pulled the kid out, held him still with one hand and whacked him on the backside, several times. Whack, whack, whack! He screamed. His little brain was screaming.'

Shaft blinked. Had to, vision blurring, eyeballs quivering. Had her fingers moved? Had her expression changed? Can you tell if they've made a decision?

A peripheral shape. A man creeping nearer? Trying to get around him?

'Drop your weapon,' someone said.

Must have been a cop. Sounded more nervous that anyone.

'Stop it,' Becker said. 'Stop it, Chook!'

She'd not finished the story.

'You know what happened? The big, fat woman dragged him by an arm across the road, like a piece of airport luggage. Dragged him into the shops, still screaming. Outraged and wretched.'

No-one said a word.

Shaft wavered. He raised the sawn-off a little, so it was now pointed, more or less, at Chook's thighs or groin or lower abdomen, or whatever.

'I sat in my car thinking about it. You ever heard a kid cry like that, dickhead? Ever heard a kid bawl his heart out? You know what? One day he was going to grow up, and he'd hate her. He'd want to get even. He'd want to beat the hell out of her. But he could not, could he? She's his mother and she's likely to give him another belting. A big boofhead like him. So, what'll he do? When he goes up? Take it out on another woman, won't he? And then another?'

Shaft blinked again. He peered, he really tried, but couldn't see the whiskey glass. If he could see it, he'd be able to see her right hand. Had it moved? It had, he was sure, closer to the jacket. The jacket was now wide open. The black butt of the Glock was sticking out like a lump of obscene coal. Right hand almost touching.

She was smiling.

'And he'll beat up more women, and girls, and stake them. All because his mummy had whacked him for crying. That's you, isn't it, little fuckwit?'

Shaft was trembling.

Someone on his right was moving, slow and carefully. A blue shape, must be a cop in uniform. He couldn't check. If he did, she'd whack him.

Becker tried again.

'Chook, don't do it. For Christ's sake, don't kill him. That's not the way. That's not what a cop would do.'

She ignored him. In the background, Jackson was still talking to someone. It sounded like a running commentary, very soft and low. A hand over his phone.

'So, shitless little Shifty, what's it going to be? Give in or get out?'

He shuddered. He was going, he knew. This was finality. Wasn't sure what the word meant. Nothing was final until it was finished. And when it was finished it was too late for definitions.

A young man said: 'Are you going to put that gun down?'

Kruger only three or four feet away, scared stiff. Guts icy cold. Smith and Wesson shaking. His hands gone white. Eyes closed, although he could still see. He could blink as much as he liked.

'Or, are you going to pull the trigger?'

Shaft quivered. He was going to blink, he knew. If he did, she'd kill him. Or, the cop would. Time had stopped.

He fired. Or, tried to fire.

The trigger moved, but too late. It was always too late.

The first 9mm slug hit him in the guts. The second hit him full in the chest, throwing him backwards. The shotgun jerking up so that when it did fire, it was pointing at the ceiling. The third slug went straight through his heart. There was no need for the third. Shafter was finished the moment he blinked. The third was purely personal.

The sound was terrific. Everyone gaped, frightened, shocked.

Something came down from the ceiling, bits and pieces of plaster, a light globe smashed. Shaft had been thrown back, crashing through tables and chairs. Glasses falling, smashing. He hit a wall. A framed photograph of William Hovell himself—taken late in life, with his winged collar and his long, white, mutton chops—hesitated for a moment, then fell. Someone cried: Oh, oh, oh—Like a woman, but no woman was in the room, except the one holding the Glock. It might have been Bruce. He had disappeared.

Police rushed in. Laura Langley too, dishevelled.

Followed the police in. An ambulance crew followed her. Max Kruger was standing over the body, too astonished to put his piece away. To uncock it. Jackson went over, took it from him. He was shaking so bad.

'Ah, Christ,' Max said.

'He's dead,' an ambo said.

The senior man came in. He was important, you could see, chief inspector no less. Everyone stepped aside. He looked at Chook and then at the body, then back at Chook.

'Hand over that weapon,' he said.

'I'm a Federal Agent,' she said.

'I said, hand over that weapon.'

Laura interceded. 'She doesn't have to.'

'And who are you, madam?'

'I'm a Federal Agent, and so is she.'

'That doesn't mean a thing to me. This woman is under arrest.'

'You can't arrest her. You have no authority over her.'

'Madam, get out of this room.'

'I'm also her lawyer.'

'Lawyer? I thought you said you are a Federal officer?'

'I am and I'm also an Army officer.'

'What's the Army got to do with this?'

'You see, I'm in the legal division of the Army and—'

'So, what are you doing here?'

'I am on secondment to—the Federal—the Federal—'

Her heart was going *bang, bang, bang*! The Army was never like this. She began to collapse. The big man caught her.

'Would someone get this woman out of here?'

A policewoman held her, but Laura refused to go. The very senior man had turned back to Chook. 'You're under arrest.'

'Yeah?'

'You deliberately taunted that man.'

'Who says?'

'I say.'

'You weren't in the room.'

'I was listening on my phone. I could hear what was said.'

'I was making an arrest.'

'What for?'

'Rape,' she said.

'Yes? Where and when did that take place?'

'Does it matter?'

'Are you going to do as I say? Hand over that weapon?'

She smiled at him, arms folded across her chest, covering the Glock under her left shoulder. Leaned forward, her nose not far from his. He had a soft, pink and pudgy nose—an Irish nose. A Jameson sort of nose.

'What's your name, Inspector?'

'Knowles, and I'm a chief inspector.'

'Well, you listen to me, Chief Inspector. The last man who tried to take my weapon off me is still rubbing his balls. Understand?'

She turned back to the bar, tapped on the bar with the empty glass. Bruce's head appeared. He'd been hiding behind it.

'I'll have another Jack,' she said.

Becker came over. He was shaking, but under control in a wobbly sort of way.

'Make that two,' he said.

'Make it three,' Laura Langley said.

Chapter 13

THEY TOOK HER to the station and charged her with discharging a firearm in a public place. It was just a holding charge, nothing to worry about. The issue was whether Chook had deliberately set a trap for the deceased, Graham Shafter. Despite repeated demands, she refused to hand over the Glock. When they threatened to take it from her, she'd said, 'Yeah? You want to fight me for it?' No-one accepted. Her point was that, as a Federal Police officer, she was authorised to carry a weapon. Also, she was under orders never to release it to another person unless ordered to do so by a superior officer.

'So, who is your superior officer?'

'She's sitting right here, Major Langley.'

'What's a major doing in a police force?'

Laura cut in. 'I'm on detachment to the Federal Police.'

'Then, order this officer here to hand over her weapon?'

'No.'

'I beg your pardon?'

'No, I will not.'

'Why not.'

'Because we don't take orders from the State police.'

His name was Knowles and he was frustrated.

'I'll have to see about that.'

Rubbed his nose on the bridge, as though his spectacles hurt up there. They watched as the spectacles jumped and flopped and fiddled and almost fell. He was an old man, thin his hair and pink his face. Looked like he'd had enough of police work. Just waiting to get out.

'All right,' he said quickly. Sighed, as he thought about his next words. 'Did you deliberately draw the deceased into a gunfight?'

'No,' she said. 'I didn't draw him into anything. He created the situation. He sought me out, he had a gun. He was going to kill me. You have his two mates, who knew he was going to kill me. They've made statements. They say he was crazy. He'd been crazy in stir. Kept saying that, when he got out, he was gonna get a shotgun and stick it up my cunt and pull the trigger. What don't you understand about that?'

'All right, all right.'

Knowles was beginning to perspire. He'd taken off his blue coat with all the bright silver buttons and hung it up over the back of his chair and sat down again. The room was bare except for a table and four chairs. Nothing on the walls, not even a calendar. Nor a picture of the Queen. Chook and Laura sat in two, the chief inspector and Jackson sat in the other two. A detective inspector leaned against a wall, arms folded. He was the one who had interviewed Becker in hospital, about the explosion. His name was Quinn or Quinlan. A dozy looking doozy with a sniffle. Probably catarrh. On the other hand, it could be happy dust.

His boss jumped his chair to get a bit closer, but still out of range. No-one knew exactly what he expected she might do. Perhaps kick him in the balls, if he didn't stop saying she'd set out to murder a man.

'All, right, given that Shafter had set out to kill *you*? How did he know you were in Wagga?'

'How would I know? Ask his mates. Ask Constable Kruger. He was having a beer with them in that very same hotel only a few days ago. According to him, he didn't say I was in town. But that, to a crim like Shafter, is a good as saying I was. I'm not blaming the young guy. He wasn't to know who they were. What Shafter intended.'

The chief wriggled in his chair, hands gripped between fat legs, like holding onto a saddle. He had a long, horsey sort of face, here and there fine networks of tiny red veins. He was sweating, but not because of the hot weather. He was facing an armed cop, who refused to give him the answers he wanted and refused to hand over her weapon. And who was likely to give him all the cheek in the world.

'I accept that you did not know Shafter would be in town. You did not know what his intentions were. You heard that he was looking for you. Who told you he was looking for you?'

'A fellow officer of the Federal Police.'

'Who exactly is that officer?'

Laura intervened. 'You don't have to answer that question, Stacey.'

'I will say this. He had received a phone call.'

'A phone call?'

'Yes, a phone call.'

'From whom?'

'He does not know.'

'And what did the caller say?'

'He had information for me and wanted to know where I was.'

'Just like that?'

'We get a lot of calls like that,' Laura said.

'What did this officer say to that?'

'If he'd leave a number, he'd let me know.'

'And he informed you? In your office?'

She nodded.

'What did he say?'

'What did who say?'

'What did the caller say to the officer?'

'Apparently said he was Shaft.'

'Shaft?'

She nodded again.

'Now revealed to be Graham Shafter?'

'So it seems.'

Knowles was getting used to this. He'd run into a brick wall, trying to get compliance out of these two Feds. They weren't exactly refusing to co-operate. They seemed to think some cop in a blue uniform in some out of the way town called Wagga Wagga did not amount to a hill of beans. And did not seem to think killing a man in an historic pub was anything to get excited about. These things happened in the bush.

'And what did you do?'

'I rang the number.'

'You rang the number?'

'That's what I just said.'

'What did you say? To him?'

'It was good to hear from him.'

'That's all you said?'

'That's about it.'

'What did he say?'

'He didn't say anything much. Did a lot of breathing, though. I think he was emotional.'

'Emotional?'

'You know how it is, when you get so emotional you're too emotional to speak. You want to speak, but you can't. Words no longer mean anything. Ever had that experience, Chief Inspector?'

He twitched. He'd often got that way. Only last week, he'd refused promotion for a senior constable, who'd given ten years of reliable service. But, he was not smart enough. Just another reliable flatfoot.

The man had gone home and thought about it. Had a couple of beers, and then shot himself. Up and under, like they do in the movies.

Knowles was still trying to get over that.

Anastacia was watching his face.

She leaned forward, the merest intimidation in her eyes. They were intensely blue. The kind you expected to sparkle, hurting your own. Electric eyes, penetrating eyes. She looked like some sort of mixture of Russian and Asiatic. Perhaps she was some sort of immigrant, who didn't know how to pay proper respect. And got a lot of fun out of telling you to get stuffed without using words.

'So, this fellow, Shafter, he said nothing at all?'

'That's right.'

'And what did you say?'

'I'd be in the William Hovell in a few minutes.'

'You told him where you'd meet him?'

'In effect.'

'What did he say to that?'

'He didn't say anything. He breathed, like he was going to die. You know that gasping sound, someone working themselves up to a climax? You don't know whether they are having a heart attack or jerking off. Ever received a call like that, chief inspector? Women get 'em all the time.'

The old man sat back. She was mocking him, he knew. Somehow, he was the one being interviewed. He looked at the other two. The detective was trying to suppressed a grin. His eyes were squinty, his arms still folded. Still leaning against the wall like he was having a treat, watching an old cop, clearly past his prime, getting a licking from a lanky sheila who looked like she'd spit in his eye if he got too heavy with her. Sergeant Jackson didn't express any emotion. He'd sat through a lot of interviews. He was here because he'd been on the inside during the drama. His name was not Jack at all but Cyril. He didn't like Cyril, had never liked it even as a kid at school. It had sounded sissy. So everyone had called him Jack, to which he could not object.

Jackson was a good sergeant. He played things by the rules, but he knew the rules themselves did not play by any rules. Nothing to do with human behaviour, human suffering.

'So...' The chief scratched his forehead. His skin was crusty below the hairline, insofar as there was a hairline. Odd hairs here and there.

'So what?'

Chook had relaxed, perfectly at ease.

Sprawled as usual in the chair in the interview room. Her long legs stuck out. She was leaning back, resting her head on a fist. A tolerant smile fluttering around her mouth and eyes and eyebrows and even her whole body. A female body sprawled before a fat cop, her legs wide open, taunting him. Not into lust or anything like that, but embarrassment. He knew she was telling him to get stuffed. He could question her all day and he'd get nowhere. Commonwealth law being superior to State.

'Did you say why you wanted to see him?'

'I said I wanted to talk about old times.'

'Old times?'

'When I was in his gang.'

'What kind of gang?'

'A cycle gang.'

'A motorcycle gang?'

'The Gringos, they didn't ride pushbikes to a bank hold up.'

'You robbed a bank?'

'No, they did. The molls, that's what they called us, we had to stay at home. Do the washing, look after the kid, that sort of thing.'

'What else did they do?'

'The boys? Handled hash and dope and smack and anything you wanted. They did a bit of money laundering, you know, playing the pokies. When bored they'd bash up rival gangs. Rearrange a few faces. You know what I mean?'

The big man sighed. 'God in heaven.'

'One day they poured petrol over a geezer giving them some shit. Then stood back and threw lighted matches at him. Most of the matches went out. But one did not. He went up in flame. I saw it. I was in a car outside. I didn't care what happened then. The more they killed each other, the better I felt.'

'I see.'

'And weapons,' she added.

'They sold weapons? What sort?'

She shrugged. 'Semi-automatics, handguns. Usually old Smith and Wessons, you know. Ex-police stuff, probably stolen. Or, perhaps sold to them by bad cops short of a fast buck. They even had a Kalashnikov.'

'God almighty,' the chief said.

'And a lot of cash.'

He nodded several times. It sounded like an old, old story.

'So,' he said, 'how long did this last?'

'Until the Feds raided the place.'

'The Federal Police? How many of them?'

'Only four.'

'Only four? Against an armed gang?'

'Plus half-a-dozen State police.'

'When was this?'

'Back in '83. The Feds were only four years old then. Didn't have a lot of resources.'

'Arrested everyone?'

'Not a soul.'

'Not a soul?'

She pulled a face. 'They found nothing.'

'So, what happened?'

'I told 'em.'

'You told the Federal Police?'

'I did.'

'Told them what?'

'Where it was.'

'Where was that?'

'In an old tin mine, up a bush track, behind a lot of blackberry bushes. Past an old chicken farm.'

'I see. And they went to jail, but you didn't?'

'That's right. I grassed on 'em.'

'You grassed on them?'

'That's right.' She clicked her tongue. 'I bore it right up them.'

'And the Federal Police made you one of them?'

'I'll always love 'em for that.'

Knowles almost smiled. 'So, now you are a Federal agent?'

'Grade three,' she said. 'Sergeant to you.'

'I see.' He shook his head, thought about it. 'Getting back to the incident this morning—Were going to talk about your betrayal? Talking to the police?'

'I wasn't betraying him. I was trying to escape from hell.'

'Yes, I understand that, but he would see it as betrayal.'

She snorted. 'He would see it as failure. He thought he had us all helpless and craven and at his service and worth kicking and hitting. You know what he did to me? When he found I was talking to a cop, an undercover cop, he got a broom and fucked me with that.'

The chief gasped.

She smiled. 'It's called staking.'

'Oh, my God!'

She went on. 'As if that wasn't bad enough, he broke the handle in two and shoved the rough end up my cunt and tore me. He tore me and tore me. He told the rest that anyone, who tried to help me, would get a flogging. And left me to die and—'

The chief jumped out of his chair. 'Oh! You poor child!'

He danced around, eyes closed, waving at nothing.

'No, no, I don't want to hear about that. Jesus, oh dear Jesus!'

He stamped around for a while, bumping into a wall more than once, a hand over his eyes.

They waited for him to calm down. It took a long time. The detective inspector and Jack Jackson simply watched, not showing any expression. You'd think it had nothing to do with them.

The chief had been a priest. Rumours had it he'd been kicked out for touching choir boys, but that was long ago. He had reformed, sworn to go straight. Talked to God about it and God had told him to put on a uniform and get out there and put the world to rights. He was a good man, weak now and then. Didn't have a stomach for horror. Especially stuff like this.

He sat down, meekly, waited a while, his head in his hands, thinking.

'So,' he said at last, 'did you report what he had done to you?'

'No.'

'You didn't wish to testify?'

'Not about that.'

'I understand, my dear.'

He shook his head, sat up straight, looked at the other two. They watched, stony-faced. It was some sort of test for him, he knew and they knew. He was the acting head of the local district, his superintendent being on sick leave. He had to make a moral decision without exactly challenging the law. The law, which was full of letters. And absolutely clear on some points, especially the one about not killing.

'Did you invite Shafter to go to the hotel with the intention to kill him?'

'No.'

'Did you realise that he might try to kill you.'

'I would have been surprised if he didn't.'

'Yes, of course. So would I.' He scratched behind his neck. His collar looked tight. A vein on his neck throbbed.

'You understood he would be angry with you? That he might seek revenge?'

'Yes, I did. But I didn't think he was going to arrive with a sawn-off shotgun. In a pub full of people.'

'No, of course. But you were concerned, when you saw him produce one?' Chook snorted. 'Wouldn't you be?'

'Did you provoke him? Knowing that he might kill you?'

'I gave him an honest to goodness opinion on what I thought of him.'

'Knowing that might provoke him? Provoke him enough him to shoot you?'

'It was possible.'

'You weren't concerned that other persons present might have been shot?'

'That did occur to me.'

'So, why did you provoke him?'

'I didn't provoke him. I wanted him, and the whole world, to know what sort of a creature he was.'

'Knowing that he might start firing?'

'There would be only one shot.'

'There were three shots.'

'I was never much good at sums at school.'

Knowles stared at her. 'This is no joke, Miss Babchook.'

'Babchuck.'

'What?'

'Babchuck. My name is Babchuck.'

'Chuck, then. I apologise. So, how did you know that?'

'Know what?'

'That there would be only one shot, as you claim.'

'I was a lot faster than he was.'

'You as good as killed him with the first shot, in the abdomen.'

'He could still have fired.'

'The shot to the chest finished him off, didn't it?'

'How was I to know that?'

'And the third was malicious, wasn't it? You made sure he was dead.'

She shrugged, then smiled. 'I was just saying goodbye.'

Knowles wasn't beaten yet. 'If he did fire, someone else might have been killed, apart from yourself.'

She smiled again. It was a mischievous smile. 'That's what happened, isn't it?'

'What do you mean?'

'You sent that boy, what's his name? Max? Sneaking along the wall, trying to get behind him. You had him point a gun at Shaft's head.'

'That was to shoot him, if he killed you. We didn't know whether Shafter would turn it into a massacre.'

'And what if he'd turned on Max first? Killed him, even if he knew I'd then kill him? You risked that boy's life.'

'It was an operational decision.'

'Your decision?'

Knowles stared at Chook a long time, biting his lips. Several times he began to speak, but could not do it. He sighed. 'I might have made the wrong decision. You can never know how it'll turn out. That—that was a terrible situation.'

He looked bad. Heart wouldn't stop jumping. Blood pressure was too high. Uncertainty wafted over him.

'You all right, Mr Knowles?'

'No, well—'

'Taking pills?'

He didn't answer.

'You're finished with me?'

The old man sighed, ran a hand across his brow. It was a theatrical gesture, he knew. He was beaten. Everyone could see he was beaten. No jury in the land would find her guilty.

'You can go,' he said, without looking at her. His face white now.

Quinn or Quinlan hadn't moved throughout the interview, except to scratch his nose now and then. Arms were folded and his brain was folded. He went along with whatever was decided. A company man, he had no opinion on anything, but he was pleased. Not because this bitch of a Federal cop had beaten poor old Mick Knowles, who should have retired years ago. But because Mick was an unreformed God-botherer, who believed in the essential goodness of humans—if you could get through to their hearts and show them the way of the Lord. Who should never have been allowed to put on a police uniform. She had made a fool of him.

As for Jackson, he had sat with his hands clasped until the end. His expression akin to admiration. He'd never seen anyone so cool. She had deliberately set it up, called out Shafter. Ridiculed him. Challenged him to shoot first. Knowing she was so fast that he'd be dead before he hit the floor. It was revenge, pure and simple. But no-one could ever prove it was not self-defence. And she had played with the boss, made him look stupid. But, not derided him. She'd been gentle, putting him down. Showing him she had some sort of grace and understanding.

Chook stood up.

'Thank you,' she said. 'It's been interesting.'

'Sergeant Jackson will show you out,' he said.

They walked out onto Sturt Street without saying a word. Becker was waiting for them. Immediately Laura's phone went off. She stepped away a few yards, head down. 'Yes, yes,' she said. 'Yes, she's out. Charges dropped...' She listened for a while. 'What's that? What? Who did you say?'

Chook tried to listen in, but Jackson had turned to her.

'How did you learn to shoot so fast?'

'Well... in my head.'

'In your head?'

'Yeah, in my head.'

'I don't believe anyone could learn to shoot like that in their head.'

'Nor did I.'

She looked around. Cars were going this way and that. It was soon after lunch. Two men getting out of a patrol vehicle saw her with Jackson. They stood, watching her. And watching him, looking for an answer: Had she been booked or not been booked?

Already she was the talk of the police network.

Becker came up. He was going to speak, ask her how it'd gone. She was speaking to Jackson. So, he listened in.

'Did you ever read a story called *A Game of Chess*?'

'I don't think.'

'It's by a German author. About a man who's sent to prison for many years. He's not been told why or how long. He's in solitary confinement. He has nothing. Nothing to look forward to, not even getting out of this place one day. Soon after he arrives, he's told to clean up his cell. He moves the bed aside to get at the accumulated dirt and finds a book lying there. It's a book on the rules of chess. Sure you've never read this?'

'I'm sure.'

'Well, he reads the book and in a few days he is playing chess against himself, in his head. There's nothing else to do. He has to hide the book from the guards. This goes on for years. Then, suddenly, there's a change of government and he is released. He starts to play chess for money. Enters tournaments, becomes a chess master. Becomes world famous. And very rich.'

'Where are you going with this?'

'That's what I did, in my head. Began when I was lying in bed in hospital after what that animal did to me. One of the nurses said, "You can't lie there all day, staring into space and feeling miserable. I'll bring you a book." She brought it and I read it. And you know what I did in my head? I learnt how to shoot. I became the fastest gun alive.'

'Never having touched a weapon before?'

'Yeah.'

'All in your head?'

'You don't believe me?'

He didn't answer the question. 'You did this so that one day you could kill a man without fear of failure? Without being caught?'

Chook smiled. It was more like a cheeky grin.

'What do you think, Jack?'

Chapter 14

THE CALL HAD been about her replacement. First, Laura had said she wanted a recall to Canberra, which was agreed. And she had recommended Chook as her replacement, but there had been objections. Chook was deemed to be too young to be a team leader, which was the equivalent of inspector in the uniformed world. Also, she was not greatly qualified. She was a good field officer, dedicated but a bit wild. Had a reputation for standover tactics. Not liked by the State police in Wagga Wagga. She was rude, grumpy, had a big chip on her shoulder. And another thing, she insisted on carrying a weapon always, even when off-duty or on leave, because she feared for her life. Which, from a bureaucratic point of view, is not a reasonable excuse.

Also, the shootout at the Hovell hadn't done anything for her career. Some people in Canberra thought she was too confident. A bit unsubtle for a force which largely did surveillance rather than a town sheriff's job. The Feds liked to leave all the crappy stuff, like stick-ups and murders and rapes and fraud and family feuds, to the State police. They were more interested in the big-time stuff, like organised crime and national security. She was now notorious, a newsworthy individual, who didn't wear a uniform and carried a weapon at all times. She was not good for the force's reputation. Also, she had a persecution complex, according to the brass up top. The killing of Shafter showed that she was fit and ready to kill. And would kill in the right, or the wrong, circumstances—depending upon your viewpoint.

No, Anastacia Babchuk would never make it to level 4, which was equal to inspector.

The really bad news was that Laura's replacement was to be Matthew Palfreyman.

He was the smug and smart and snitchy cop in Canberra, who'd tried to arrest Becker for the murder of Vincent Torrence, born Vincenzo Torrenza—a one-time Sydney cop, chauffer and con-man who thought he could squeeze a few more dollars out of the Mafia for screwing Evelyn Crowley in order to get information out of her. Was her husband going to talk about what was happening at the Royal Bank? Or was he not? Torrence had been found, floating face down, in Lake Burley Griffin early next day.

But Becker had not killed Torrence.

Those two cheeky birds, Polly Politis and Stacey Babchuk, had tailed Becker all night. At no time had he gone near the lake. He hadn't killed Torrence or anyone else.

They'd told Palfreyman to get stuffed.

For their impudence they'd been transferred to witness protection. That's when things had got serious. Evelyn had been killed. Simply because, being a member of a Mafia family, she'd known too much. She'd had to die. Lucky she'd not been forced to drink acid, like Concetta Cosco, the elder sister of Angelina Cosco, who...

Chook was ropeable. 'That birdbrain? Palfreyman?'

'He's been recommended.'

'Who recommended him?'

'His superiors in Canberra, it would seem.'

'To get rid of him, no doubt?'

'He can't be all that bad. After all, he is an inspector.'

'I heard they failed him.'

'He appealed and won.'

'Jesus, Palfreyman? He's stupid. Couldn't find his own dick on a dark night.'

Laura laughed, thrilled to be getting out of Wagga. She'd be back in the Army, at legal services. Possibly posted to Victoria Barracks in Sydney or Melbourne or some other place like that—old, traditional, quiet and professional. Everything going like clockwork. Writing briefs for courts-martial.

Police life was too scary.

What had happened this morning had scared the wits out of her.

That mad race to the Hovell, to stop Chook. She'd known immediately. Chook would do something stupid, crazy. As likely to kill Shaft as look at him.

When it was all over, she'd rushed in and said, 'I'm her lawyer,' and she'd lost control. Everything had gone wrong. She, a barrister at law, had lost control. Almost fainted.

The world of policing was too dangerous, unpredictable.

She was still shaking, just to think of it.

'You're crazy, Stacey. I mean, I can't work with you. I can't work here. I'm out of my bloody depth. I have nothing to contribute. I'm lost. I am sitting here and pretending to be a Social Security officer, reviewing pensions, while all the bloody time I am responsible for catching and nailing crims, who—'

She gave up, flopped in her chair.

Chook was already sprawled in another. Dave had been told to go for a walk. He didn't know what to do so he ambled around to the Hovell and had a geek. The police were still there. One of the staff was trying to clean the blood and guts off the wall, and being sick at the thought of it.

Patrons were still trying to get in.

The police were keeping them out, still gathering evidence, they said. Interviewing people. No-one knew when the William Hovell would reopen. Possibly not until tomorrow, Sunday. Then everyone would rush in and order a drink to see where it had occurred. The shootout at point-blank range. No mercy given. It was better than a western. Better than *Shane* or *High Noon*. It was local. Already people were saying they should make a movie based on it. Maybe get some big Hollywood stars. Lights, camera, action. Think of the publicity for Wagga. Think of the money rolling in…

'So,' Laura said, 'that's it. I'm getting out of here.'

'When?'

'Next Friday.'

'When will that dickhead be here?'

'On Monday.'

'Monday?'

'I'm sorry, Stacey.'

Chook didn't answer. Just sat there in front of Laura Langley and sulked.

'Look, I've argued and argued for you. You're a top cop, perhaps one of the best agents the force has had in many years. You go out there and catch them, but some people say you are too public— Oh, I forgot, I took a message while you were being interviewed, remember?'

'What was it?'

'I was busy, trying to save you from arrest. I said I'd call her back.'

'Her? What's the message?'

'She didn't say anything.'

'Name?'

'No, but—' Laura was fiddling with her phone, trying to find the call. 'All the caller said was, "Is that Anastacia?"'

'Sounds like someone who knows me.'

'Sounded young, very nervous.'

'What did she say?'

'Nothing much. I was too busy to talk. Advised her to phone again later.'

Just then Laura's phone buzzed again. She picked it up, listened.

'Oh, hullo?'

'Yes, hullo?'

'Is it possible to speak to Anastacia now, please?'

It was a soft, dignified, foreign voice, speaking hesitantly. As if keeping an eye on a door or a person or a dozing keeper.

'Yes, she is here.'

Chook took the phone.

'Angelina? Is that you?'

'*Si*, I am Angelina.'

'Where are you?'

'I am in a telephone box in—' She paused, as if looking around, afraid.

'In Wagga?'

'*Si*, I am not far.'

'Not far? How far? You ran away from the convent?'

'*Si*, they came.'

'Who came?'

She did not answer.

Chook put a hand over the mobile. 'Oh, shit,' she said to Laura, 'they've found her.'

'Found Angelina?'

'Where is she? We'll pick her up.'

'Angelina, where exactly are you?'

'Near a park—'

'What park?'

No answer.

'Is someone near?'

'*Si*, someone.'

'Who? Who is watching you?'

'I must go now,' she said.

'Angelina! What park? What town? What are your wearing?'

The line had gone dead. The phone was purring like a cat.

'She was in a phone box,' Chook said. 'Near a park.'

'What park?'

'She didn't say. I think she saw someone coming.'

'Give me that phone!'

Laura dialled a number. 'Give me operations. This is Laura Langley, Federal Police, at Wagga Wagga. I want a trace on the last call received on this phone. Yes, it's urgent. What? What? Yes, of course I'll wait.'

She put a hand over the phone.

'Let's hope it was a payphone. And not a phone in a shop.'

'She didn't want the State police.'

'She sounded scared? Of them?'

'Terrified.'

They waited. 'Yes, I'm still here,' she said to her phone. 'What? It's in New South Wales? Well, that's a big comfort, isn't it? I mean New South Wales is bloody pretty big, isn't it? —What? Please hurry! This girl is in danger. What? Of course I'll bloody well wait...'

She put a hand over the phone. 'They're getting closer and closer,' she said.

They waited.

Chook thought about Angelina, that lovely girl. About twenty-three, as straight and good as the Virgin Mary. Probably a virgin herself. Good Catholic girl, would never say boo to a goose. Love to marry a beautiful Italian boy one day and have lots of children. A brave girl, who had taken the cocaine and handed it to Maria Terracini so that they could trap that witless of a husband of hers, Barry Barnes. A corrupt cop who had—

'What?' Laura said. 'Here? In Wagga? Where did she call from? What?'

They waited again.

'It's a phone box? Where the hell? What? Oh, shit!' She put a hand over the phone again. 'They have to ask Telecom where the box is. Yeah, I'm holding. What? Where? Oh, God, that's just around the corner of—' She jumped up, grabbed her bag. 'Get in the car!'

'Where are we going?'

'That box is outside the Memorial Gardens. A few yards down Baylis Street.'

Chook had a better idea.

'They may have grabbed her already. Call the local cops. Call that chief inspector, I'll go down there.'

Laura fell back in her seat, picked up her phone again. 'Oh, Christ, what's their number?' Pushing back her hair. It was a mess. She felt like crying. It had been an awful day. Thank God she was getting out.

Chook was shouting something at her. 'What?'

'Call 000!'

'Oh, yeah, yeah, of course.'

Chook had gone.

Ten seconds later, she was on her bike. It was only two blocks to the gardens. There was a phone box on a corner. She pulled up, it looked empty. A woman was standing near, holding a small child. The child had an ice cream and a party hat. Must have been a birthday in the gardens.

'Did you see a girl?'

'A girl?'

'A young woman? Tall, slim, dark, Italian looking.'

'Italian?'

'In that box, on the phone?'

'We've just come out.'

'Did you see her running away?'

'There was a girl, tall, dark. She wasn't running.'

'Where was she going?'

'She was just walking.'

'Which way?'

'Through the gardens.'

'Did she look distressed in any way?'

'Distressed?'

'Frightened?'

'Oh, she looked as though she'd had some bad news. She—'

Chook didn't wait. She drove the Harley over the gutter and into the gardens, along a path at speed and yet, cautiously, searching this way and that. Almost calling. But that could have been a bad idea. If Angelina could hear her, then so could the others. She would not reply, not if she had any sense. She searched and searched every corner, even behind the bandstand. The girl might have been hiding there. But nowhere, nowhere at all. No sign of her. Maybe it was not Angelina.

She came out in Trail Street on the other side of the lagoon. Looked up and down. Saw a few cars, one or two kids on bikes. A man walking a dog. Otherwise, nothing. It was a bare street. At least, bare of Angelina.

Then she remembered the cathedral. A good Catholic would seek sanctuary.

She stopped by the man walking the dog.

'Have you seen a woman?' she said.

'A woman?'

'Yes, a young woman, dark hair—'

'Have you seen a woman?' he said to the dog.

It was then that she realised it was a guide dog. With a harness and a hoop above, to hold.

'I'm sorry,' she said.

She began to cruise on, gunning the engine, but not moving fast. Walking it along.

The man called without directly looking at her. 'We did hear someone, didn't we, Floss?'

Chook paused. 'You heard someone?'

'She was hurrying and crying.'

'Crying?'

'She wore a simple white dress.'

'How could you know that, if you are blind?'

'She was a postulant.'

'How could you know that?'

'She was crying and saying, they'll never have me now.'

'You mean she was on trial? In a convent?'

'Yes, yes. Postulants wear white. She was, wasn't she, Floss?'

The dog looked away, in the way that dogs look—here, there and everywhere else at high speed, her tongue hanging out. Yes, said Floss.

'There you are,' the man said.

'Was she hurrying?' Chook asked.

'Oh, she was, you could hear that.'

'Crying?'

'Crying? Was she crying, Floss? Did you see?'

The dog was a Labrador. The dog said, Yes. Panting.

'Heading for the cathedral?'

'We don't know, do we?'

'I'm sorry,' Chook said. 'We must find her.'

'She was wearing a crucifix.'

Chook was more puzzled. 'How could you see that?'

'Oh, one does not have to be sighted to see these things.'

'What was she saying?'

'Mother Mary, help me in my hour of need.'

'Thank you very much.'

Angelina was sitting in the third row from the front. At the end, near the aisle.

On the chancel a novice was preparing for a service. He had a box of candles. It was a beautiful box, perfectly cut and polished. Everything in the cathedral was beautifully cut and polished. Buckingham Palace could not have been cleaner. The novice had not looked up at her, when she'd slunk in. Not once did he look at her.

Praying, hoping to be saved. Or, if not saved, that she would find a kind word, an honest priest. The one who had come to the nunnery had been foreign. Not foreign in the sense of being from another country, but strange, inauthentic. She had sensed it at first glance. Sensed it in his footsteps. The mother superior had brought him in.

This is Father Quinlan, she had said.

Angelina had frozen. There was something about the eyes. They were friendly eyes. The eyes of a priest should not be friendly. Not friendly towards a woman, but inspiringly unsexy. This man had other eyes. Dirty eyes, shameful eyes. Not quite looking at you.

He was not a priest, she knew. Not now. He was a predator.

He had looked at her with lust. Not carnal lust, mind you. But the lust of death.

'Father Quinlan is here to select a novice of outstanding faith.'

What faith? They'd all asked themselves.

'You are fortunate,' Mother Superior had said. 'You have been chosen for service in the convent of St Columba in—'

She was shocked. She knew what that meant. St Columba was in Griffith. She was to be dragged back, dealt with. She had run. She had seen those eyes before. He was Father Ambrosio, a priest. When she had been a little girl, he had touched her. He had done awful things to her. She had told her mother and her mother had been horrified. Father Ambrosio would never do such a thing, she'd said. How could you say such an awful thing, child?

She had run out the front gate, her hair flying, in her simple white dress, her postulancy abandoned, and hailed a car. Jumped into it, said: Please, take me, take me, quickly! An old man was at the wheel. His wife was looking back at her. Why, girl, whatever is the matter? You look as though you have seen a...

Angelina prayed, not listening to herself.

Could hear the steps, coming closer and closer, behind her. They were a few rows back. Not loud, because of the thick, dull gold carpet. One long, straight and perfectly clean runner, right from the back of the cathedral down to the chancel. Not loud steps, actually no sound at all. The novice had looked up, looked at someone or something behind her. Then had gone on with his work. But now, he paused, poised, a candle in hand. Eyes following someone coming nearer and nearer—with each authoritative step.

The steps stopped. Fingers touched her right shoulder.

She flinched, waiting. Didn't look up. Afraid, thinking: Not even the Mafia would kill you in a church. Not in front of a priest even if he's only a novice.

'Angelina?' a voice said. 'I am Anastacia.'

Chapter 15

WHEN HE ARRIVED, they still hadn't decided what to do with her. Palfreyman had wanted to be picked up at the airport, shown around, taken on a Cook's tour. The first thing he's asked Dave was: Is that dame here? What dame? Dave had asked. That crazy blonde. Do you mean Stacey? Yeah, that bird. She's here, Dave had said. I thought she worked in Canberra. She does. She was here last weekend on personal business. And shot up the town? Not exactly the town, sir. She was trying to apprehend a suspect. What suspect? Some guy who'd raped her years ago. What? Palfreyman could not believe his ears. She was trying to arrest a man who had raped her? She's a Federal Agent, for Christ's sake. You can't be both the complainant and the arresting officer. What the hell does she think she is? The town marshal or something? Bring 'em in dead or alive? Gee-sus, what sort of place is this?

'This is Wagga,' Dave said, half apologetically. He didn't like to hear any place disparaged. He liked things to be as they are. With respect. They were driving slowly down Baylis Street. Palfreyman was not impressed.

'Yeah?'

'It means many crows.'

'Yeah? Sounds like a lot of ducks,' Palfreyman said. 'Wagga Wagga,' he said again, quacking. 'Or chooks.' He meant chickens.

'You'd better not call her Chook.'

'Yeah?'

'She doesn't like it.'

'That ugly bitch? Where is she now?'

'Stacey? Out at the farm.'

'What farm?'

'Harry's farm.'

Palfreyman had been chewing gum at the time. It nearly fell out of his mouth.

'You don't mean Harry bloody Becker?'

'Yes, Harry Becker.'

'That bloke? He's got a farm?'

They were passing the William Hoddle.

'That's the pub,' Dave said, indicating. 'She killed the man in there.'

'That dump there? They had a gunfight in that dump?'

'It wasn't a gunfight. All over in less than a second, they said.'

'Who said?'

'The local police.'

Palfreyman sat up straight, took his hands out of his pockets. He sighed, like a man who has seen everything. 'Why is she at Becker's farm?'

'She's staying there.'

'Chook is staying with Becker?'

'There's a reason.'

'Yeah? Why?'

'They've got someone in protective custody.'

'Who?'

'You'd better ask Laura,' Dave said.

He let the staff Mazda cruise along until it stopped outside a plain building in Tompson Street, one storey. Normally he'd park in the lot behind the building, but didn't think he should take a new boss in that way. A bit of an insult, trying to sneak him in without anyone seeing. The building was so plain you might walk right past it without seeing it. There were two or three plain, thin trees, doing nothing to adorn a plain, thin, building. There was nothing on the glass doors to say this building had anything to do with the government of Australia, not even a Commonwealth crest. It was modern commercial, reasonably functional but absolutely unimposing. Typically knock down and replaceable.

'This it?' Palfreyman said.

'This is it.'

'This the best the Commonwealth could do?'

He shook his head. They got out, walked in. Walked right down a long corridor to the back to a door, marked: Reviews.

'Reviews of what?' Palfreyman asked.

'Reviews of cases.'

'What kind of cases?'

'You'd better ask Laura.'

Dave opened the door and Palfreyman walked in.

'Ah, g'day,' he said.

He took a hand out of a pocket and put it out. Left the other hand in. Laura Langley rose slowly. She'd had her hair done on Saturday. It was much shorter, so much that she looked like a middle-aged schoolgirl. Or a schoolmistress. At a posh girls' school. It was straight and down to her neck, cut a fraction under the earlobes, where, if you looked closely, you might have noticed earrings. Opal earrings, a gift from her grandmother years ago, an heirloom. When she was twenty-one. She was a good-looking woman, not beautiful, but good to look at: a woman with a bemused smile.

Laura wore a blue suit that went with the blue in the opals. It was a mixture of colours which were both there and not there, constantly changing colour depending on the light, or the movement of the head, like opals themselves. And her complexion, it was perfect. Not a spot or any kind of blemish. Well looked after skin. She'd been unmarried for six years, had no children. She was still looking for a retired colonel with a fat bank account and a holiday house overlooking Palm Beach. No luck so far.

She looked at the offered hand. Made a split-second decision. Her first impulse was to refuse, but she had to do it. They shook. Her hand was soft and pliable, a lawyer's hand. His was thick and rough and hard, the kind you'd think about twice before touching.

'Had a good flight?' she asked.

'Bit bumpy coming over the hills.'

'Have a seat.'

He did so. Dave stood by the door, waiting to be asked.

'Coffee?' she said.

'Yeah, if you're having one.'

'Two coffees, Dave?'

'Sugar?' Dave asked.

'One,' Palfreyman said.

The door closed.

'You've got that bird here?'

'What bird is that?'

'Babchuk.'

'Only for a few days.'

'What's going on?'

'Witness protection.'

'Yeah?'

'We had a witness installed in a convent up north.'

'Where up north?'

She was not going to tell him, but she had to. 'Glen Innes. Someone showed up, a priest.'

'Yeah?'

'But he wasn't a priest, so she says. He *was* years ago, but got kicked out.'

'What for?'

'Interference.'

'With the girls?'

'And the boys.'

'So, why'd they let him in?'

'Into the convent? He was in full dress. The frock coat, even the *cappello romano*.'

'The what?'

'Little round hat.'

'Yeah?'

'He was trying to get her out of her convent. Take her to a cathedral, he said. She panicked, ran away, caught a lift with some people towing a caravan and ended up in Gilgandra.'

'Where the hell is that?'

'Up north, west of Tamworth. Then caught a bus to Narrandera. Where she got a taxi to here. She made a phone call. We picked her up.'

'And where is she now?'

She hesitated. She didn't know this man. But if he was to take over, he had a right to know.

'Staying out there, on the farm, with Harry Becker.'

'With Babchuk too?'

'Stacey is looking after her. We had to find accommodation, quick.'

'Babchuk's staying with Becker?'

'Only as a guard. The girl is under our protection.'

'Are they sleeping together?'

'Who?'

'Babchuk and Becker.'

'I have no idea.'

'Gee-sus,' Palfreyman said.

Laura was going to ask why? But let it slide. This man, in her opinion, was the most ungracious creature she had ever met. He was slumped in a chair, feet stuck out, hands in pockets again. And chewing on nothing in particular.

'She's a bad cop, from what I hear.'

'Do you?'

'Goes around killing people.'

'Not habitually. She's a good cop. I'd trust her with my life.'

'And Becker, he was a bad cop. You know that?'

'I know what happened to him.'

'He was corrupt. Taking bribes in Kings Cross.'

'I know all that.'

Palfreyman shook his head again. It was a peculiar shake, both sideways and at the same time lifting on one side. Simultaneously, on that side his mouth opened, or did not quite open, as he sucked in air. It was a confident sort of click of the tongue, that went wrong. A man, who was sure of everything. Leave it to him, he'd fix it. Or, unfix it. You never could tell. He lived in a world of things as they should be. Not as they were.

The door opened and Dave returned with three coffees, plus a biscuit for himself. He ate too much. Could never button up his coat, and the buttons on his shirts looked about to pop. He was a lonely man. And he was about to get a lot lonelier. He adored Laura. She was high-class. Or, what a former bank clerk from Tamworth thought was high-class. She dressed perfectly. Always smelled good, like a woman should and she had grace. She was a lady, as tough as a genuine lady could be. Sometimes looked as she would burst into tears. But she never did. Not when anyone was near.

'Ah, thanks,' she said.

Dave put them down. 'She's back,' he said.

'Chook, is she? Where?'

'Around the back, just rode in.'

'Well,' Laura said, reaching for her coffee. And settled back in her chair. 'Mr Palfreyman, you can tell her to her face.'

'Tell her what?'

There was no need to answer. The door opened and Chook walked in.

She saw the newcomer, paused, walked around him. Behind him, to another chair.

'So, Mr Palfreyman has arrived?' she said.

He did not bother to rise. 'How are you, mate?'

Chook did not reply. Slowly she sat, not lounging back as usual, but leaning forward, thumbs tucked into her belt. Staring at him.

'How's country life treating you?'

Chook didn't answer.

'Been shooting up the place, I hear?'

Again, no answer.

Laura was getting worried. There might be an explosion at any minute.

Dave was leaning against a wall. He had the rare ability to drink coffee while breathing out. He'd once played trumpet in a brass band. The trick with the trumpet was to fill your cheeks with air, then let it flutter your lips against the brass. So that, in effect, you could both breathe in and out at the same time. All brass players can do that. Dave could drink a whole cup of coffee slowly, without breathing. At the same time watching you, or whoever was speaking, with full, undivided attention. His eyes were a simple sort of grey with a hint of red. A faded cornelian glaze. Old eyes, that had never been fully mature. He was a faithful dog. Had no real future with the Federal Police, but he'd do anything for you.

'Hey, I'm talking to you,' Palfreyman said.

Still, Chook didn't answer.

You could feel the tension. It was like that interval between a lightning strike and waiting for the thunder, the resounding crack. Splitting the world wide open.

'How is she?' Laura said.

'Okay.'

'Still nervous?'

'Who wouldn't be?'

Laura said to Palfreyman, 'The girl comes from Griffith. But she cannot stay with any relations. Her father killed her sister.'

'Gee-sus, what happened to the old man?'

'Killed by his son. He went crazy. Shot him, didn't he, Dave?'

'Emptied a whole Tanfoglio 16 into him.'

'Never heard of it.'

'Italian, sixteen rounds.'

'Gee-sus, the girl saw this?'

'No, she saw her sister after they'd made her drink hydrochloric acid.'

'Yeah?' Palfreyman's body shook, so did his self-confidence. He had to cross his legs. Then uncross them. He didn't seem to know what to do with them, a leggy man like him.

'What sort of people would do a thing like that?'

'The Mafia,' Laura said.

'She's on the run from the fucking Mafia?'

Laura nodded.

'So why the hell did she come back here?'

'Her brother's in hospital here in Wagga, in the psych ward. They're trying to move him off to somewhere permanent, like Kenmore.'

'Kenmore, in Goulburn?'

She nodded again.

'So, why does the sister want to see him?'

'To help him. She's a committed Catholic. She intends to save him. Take him away somewhere to live together. She would look after him. She's promised God.'

Palfreyman laughed. 'God? Yeah? And what does God think of that?'

'He's psychotic.'

'Yeah? God or the brother?'

'The brother.'

'Where is she now?'

Laura glanced at Chook, now sitting with her elbows on her knees, hands clasped. Staring, her eyes flicked to Laura, but you could see where her mind was. That is, if Chook had a mind at all. You had to wonder about her. Anyone who could kill a man from a standing start in less a second was not natural, everyone said so.

'This minute? Harry's looking after her.'

'Harry Becker's looking after her? At his farm?' Palfreyman shook his head again.

'Is she okay, Stacey?'

Chook had been staring at Palfreyman with an intensity not exactly loathing but the kind of curiosity that might grip you if you saw a tarantula crawling up a wall, only inches from your head.

'She's calming down,' she said. 'No-one's gonna hurt her there.'

'How do you know?'

'Because I said so.'

Palfreyman backed down. 'How does she feel about Harry?'

'She trusts him.'

'Becker alone? Looking after her?'

'He's got help. A patrolman, a good young fellow, drops in. A neighbour, an old man with a shotgun, helps out.'

'Doesn't sound too secure to me.'

'It's temporary.'

'If the Mafia's gonna kill you, they're gonna kill yer,' Palfreyman said.

He shouldn't have said that.

Instantly, he realised his mistake, but it was too late. Chook flew at him. Sprang forward, would have strangled him if Dave hadn't dropped his coffee, and thrown himself between them.

Chook was furious.

'You disgusting little creep!'

'Hey, hey, cut it out! What the hell—'

Chook had raised a fist. She was going to hit him, but Dave was in the way. Laura, had jumped up. 'Stop it!'

Chook was seething. 'You killed her!'

Palfreyman jumped up, astonished. 'What?'

'You killed Polly!'

'What?'

'You incompetent dickhead! You let them get at her.'

'Hey, hey, easy there!'

'You had a Mafia killer working in your team. You were supposed to be protecting her.'

'Her? Her? We were protecting Mrs Crowley.'

'But, not Polly?'

'She was a cop. She was supposed to be protecting the target.'

'How could she, when some creep of a hitman was able to come in the back way and kill her, then Evelyn Crowley?'

'Why did she let him in?'

'She didn't let him in! He was inside before she knew. He must have had a key!'

Laura jumped up. 'Stop it, you two!'

'Ah, Christ, mate, come off it! No-one can think of everything.'

'How did he have a key to a safe house?'

'Ah, gee, cut it out. Anyone can get a skeleton key. Any crook locksmith will give you one.'

'You had two uniformed men out front in a car, playing tiddly winks. One of them should have been inside with Polly!'

Laura had run around her desk. 'Break it up, you two!'

'I didn't start it.'

She turned on Palfreyman.

He was a big man, taller than Chook but possibly not so heavy. A fit man, in the way a good athlete is still looks good for a few years after he starts to go to the dogs. Palfreyman was on the way out. An outcast, he'd come off badly in the inquiry in Canberra. Too stupid to see he'd had an informant in his team. Too blind to see a killer right under his nose. Adams was not the hit man. He'd chickened out, so someone in Melbourne had ordered the hit. Even so, Adams had been a part of it. He was in jail. He'd be there for life. But Palfreyman was on the outside. Been given a second chance, his last chance. Sent to the bush to get rid of him. He couldn't take it. Never could take the blame. Never could say sorry.

He was a stupid cop, who could have been something. But he wasn't.

'If you two don't settle down, I'm going to recommend that you be sent back to Canberra. Have I made that clear, Mr Palfreyman?'

'Eh? Me? I don't go around shooting blokes in bars in front of people. How many did she kill?'

'Just the one.'

'Why?'

'The animal came looking for her.'

'If you say so.'

'I do say. Now sit down.'

'You can't tell me to sit down.'

'Don't tell me what I cannot do. I'm still in charge here for the next couple of days.'

He sat. So did Chook. Dave had cleaned up the fallen cup.

Laura sat again and watched them, or not watched them. Her eyes were flicking from one to the other, thinking of something else.

'What are we going to do about it?'

'About what?'

'We have to look after her.'

'Get her out of the State,' Palfreyman said. 'Send her to Queensland or somewhere.'

'As I just said, she will not go without her brother! But the brother is insane. Not all the time. We took her to him, in hospital. He was astonished. He smiled, lovingly. Reached for her, pulled her down beside him. She put her arms about him, kissed him. He was safe at last. All cares gone.'

'What's the plan, then?'

'To get him released to the care of his sister. But someone is sure to kill her.'

'For?'

'Telling us what her father made him do to their sister.'

'Gee-sus. How is Becker going to protect her? He has to sleep.'

'Stacey will be there at night. Some of the day too.'

'I'll take my turn,' Palfreyman said.

'So will I,' Dave said.

'Weapons?'

'Don't you have one?'

'Had to hand it in when I left.'

'Dave?'

Dave opened a drawer in a steel cabinet, pulled out a Smith and Wesson .32, similar to the weapon Laura carried in her bag. Plus, a box of rounds. Then he produced a register and made Palfreyman sign for it. He had to stand to do that. He signed with an angry flourish, then stood back.

'Becker? Is he armed?'

'Has a Smith and Wesson .38 and a Winchester rifle.'

'Yeah? How's he going to fire a .38 and a rifle at the same time?'

'He has his boy.'

'His boy?'

'Stepson. They say he's a crack shot with a Winchester.'

'How old is this boy?'

'Eleven, going on twelve.'

Palfreyman shook his head again. 'Gee-sus.'

Chapter 16

ANASTACIA WAS TO remain in Wagga until the police completed their investigation of the outrage in the William Hovell. Obviously, she could not stay at the hotel. She was the centre of all attraction. The press tried to interview her. Even chased her with cameras and recorders. She had to get out of town and still hang around to assist. So, she stayed with Becker at the farm, taking her turns at guarding Angelina. Watched each night until twelve, when Becker took over until four. Then Bert took over. He sat on the back verandah, his old Hollis across his knees and two dogs, one each side. Today, Anastacia was in Wagga, bidden to attend a meeting with people from Canberra. People who'd decide what to do with her.

As for Angelina, she was uneasy, being so close to Griffith. And in an unknown place, but at least she was closer to Wagga Wagga and to her brother. Thrilled to see him, thrilled to be with him. She could talk to him about what had happened. Chook took her into Wagga Wagga for an hour or so at the hospital, driving the BMW. Sometimes they had a police escort, sometimes not.

Silvano was beginning to improve.

They talked about getting him out, but no-one in authority encouraged them. The medical staff thought he was irretrievable. Too far gone ever to recover. He had killed the father he'd loved, almost worshipped. He was calm enough with his sister, quite sensible. But could not live away from institutional care. So, it was thought.

Every now and then the young cop, Max Kruger, would turn up. Would walk in grinning. Trying to act normal after the Hovell. A simple country boy from Henty, full of enthusiasm. Told himself that he'd made it. He wasn't dead. Perhaps he'd made it as a real cop. This was real life. He'd crept up to a man backed up against a wall in a pub under instruction to fire if the man fired. He didn't have to. The man had not fired. That big woman who looked like a man had fired. Three shots, so fast all he heard was one echoing shot. Nearly jumped out of his skin. Gee, he used to say to anyone who'd listen, I was dead scared. Nearly pissing my pants. Hell, the blood, the blood. Caught some in the eye...'

'Is he a good man?' Angelina asked Becker.

She'd been watching him through the front window of the living room as he was chatting. Now he was walking back to the big red patrol car. He knew what she was thinking. The Mafia had killed her sister; her own father had done it. Or, had made her brother do it. Made her drink sulphuric acid. Concetta had gone to the Griffith police, reported what had happened.

She'd spoken to the wrong cop behind the counter. Word had soon got around.

'He's okay,' Becker had said.

'What is his age, please?'

'Max? I don't know, maybe twenty-five.'

'Oh,' she'd said, still watching. 'What is his religion?'

'Lutheran, I think.'

'Lutheran?'

'Most of them are, the old German stock.'

'Is he in the Federal Police?'

'No, he's in the State.'

'Oh,' she said, thoughtfully.

He was watching her side-on. A virtuous girl, said her prayers every night. Had wanted be a nun. Now, she was on the run from the church and the Mafia. They would kill her if they caught her, just like they'd killed her sister.

'How old are you, Angelina?'

'Oh, I—I am twenty-three.'

'Thinking of marrying a cop, are you?'

She'd jumped, caught out. 'Oh, no, I cannot do that. I am married already.'

'You are?'

'I told you, in the motel, to my lord, *Gesù Cristo*.'

'You hope to go back to a convent?'

Her hands moved into the simple gesture of belief. And of peace.

'Perhaps some day,' she said.

It was three days now. Three days since she'd moved in. It was a good, clean, fresh, mechanised house. Everything brand-new, everything worked beautifully. She had a room to herself and shared a bathroom with Anastacia, who wore a pistol, even when cooking. She was a good cook but her food was plain, almost tasteless to an Italian. She'd cooked last night for all four of them, even Bert. Cooked *pollo cacciatore* in red wine, with a big bowl of spaghetti and another of salad. They'd finished the bottle of red, a glass each for three of them. Bert would not dine with them. He didn't like wine.

Becker changed the subject. 'Is that the only dress you have?'

He knew it was. Angelina had fled the convent, a candidate for holy orders. Had been there only six months, sure she would be accepted—that soon she would wear the habit of a novice, black with a white veil. Now she had nothing, not even her own toothbrush.

'Yes,' she said.

She was still standing at the window. The patrol car had disappeared. The curtain was of a heavy cotton lace. She could see through a gap in the drapes. No-one outside would have seen her.

'My wife left some clothes,' he said.

She turned, startled. 'Your wife?'

'She died, in an explosion,' he said. 'Some months ago. If you like, you could try something on—'

'Her clothes?'

'Yes, they are hanging in—'

He went to the main bedroom, opened a wardrobe, took the first dress he saw and hauled it out on its hanger. Went back, held it up. It was a floral dress, very much a summery dress, short sleeves. Also sorts of flowers in red and green and white. A waisted dress, flared skirt. The sort of thing Robyn would have worn down Baylis Street, arms full of shopping and smiling, stopping and starting, having a word here and word there. Happy, everyone saying what a happy girl she was now that she'd married that fellow. They didn't particularly like her new husband, but they were glad for her. He was too quiet, always considering things. If you asked him a question, you could see the pause in his eyes, weighing it up. Trying to work out whether something would happen.

He hadn't worked out that she was going to be blown off a verandah, rushed to hospital, her neck broken. They'd saved the baby, a darling little girl, now living with her grandmother. Poor Muriel, the troubles she'd seen…

'What do you think?' he asked.

She was startled. 'Your wife's dress? What would people think?'

'No-one will see you out here. You look about the same height. Perhaps an inch taller. That shouldn't matter.'

She blushed. 'Oh, I think that is much too bright for me.'

Becker saw what troubled her.

Angelina was in mourning. Mourning for her father, who was dead, killed by her brother in revenge for the killing of her sister, Concetta. In mourning for her brother, who was in a mental institution, confined. Locked away inside himself. Not so much in his own skin, but in his imagination and his fear. He'd been charged with murder, and his case would come up at the next sitting of the Supreme Court. But everyone agreed, it was a foregone conclusion: not guilty on the grounds of insanity.

'Yes, of course, I'm sorry.'

He returned with the dress, threw on his bed, the double bed.

'Think about it,' he said. 'Would you like coffee? Tea?'

'Oh, yes. I would like—I will get it.'

'No, no, I'll get it. There are other dresses there, in the wardrobe. Think about it.'

He walked out, went to the kitchen, which was not a room but a bar at the end of the living room, beyond the dining table. Made coffee, thinking he'd make it for her too. But when he turned around, she had disappeared.

Becker took a cup and saucer and spoon and went out back, onto the verandah and the easy chairs sitting there. Always in shade, it was the best place to sit on a bright day about to become a warm day. You could sit there and look at the tall gums and black wattles spread along the creek. He was looking at the creek, now almost empty of water, and thinking: If anyone were going to approach this place, either by night or by day, that would be the way to come. You could slip from tree to tree. Nutty would be the main problem for an intruder. He slept on the back verandah in a big basket. His ears would prick up. He'd sniff the air, listening. Then he'd begin to growl. A warning growl. If he smelt a stranger, he'd bark. He was a good dog. Not very bright, but a good friend.

Becker heard footsteps.

She came out, wearing a dark dress. Not bright, not summery, but a wintery dress, not flared. Long sleeves. High collar. The kind you could wrap around your ears and neck in a cold wind. She was wearing other shoes too—Robyn's black shoes, high heels, heel straps, open toes. Angelina was not tall, but looked tall. Her walk was diffident, anxious. Uncertain.

'Is this good?'

He sat up, almost rose. 'You will be hot in that.'

'It is cool out here.'

He didn't argue. She was wearing a dark dress.

'I will get the coffee now,' she said. She meant for herself.

'There are biscuits in the tin on the bench.'

She went inside, at the same slow, careful pace. Considering.

He thought of underwear. He'd not retained any of Robyn's. This woman must still be wearing what she'd fled in, three days ago. He didn't know how to approach the subject. He should call Chook, ask her to pick up some before she returned.

Angelina reappeared.

Sat slowly, knees and ankles together. The dress was slightly too short for her. Came down to knees, not below and not above. As she sat, she tried pull down the hem. Slowly it crept back up. She sat and straight proper, holding the saucer, the cup raised. On the saucer was a biscuit, an *amaretto*. He knew the Italian word, because it was printed on the packet and he had bought the packet, last time he was in Wagga. She sat, taking one bite. Chewed thoughtfully. The *amaretto* is crunchy, coated with sliced almonds. And icing sugar.

'This is Italian,' she said.

'Yes.'

'You like Italian biscuits?'

'I like the almonds,' he said.

'*Biscotti*,' she said, chewing. Gazing thoughtfully for some time, gazing at the farmland, the buildings, the creek, the fences and the plains. Looking towards the distant hills in the east, bluish in the morning haze. At the same time, pulling down the skirt again.

'It is nice here,' she said. 'The smell of the trees.'

'Yes,' he said. Or, he thought he said.

It was good, the smell of the Australian bush—the eucalypts in summer, giving off their oil, their flammable oil, furious. If a fire swept in from the south or the south-west on a hot and windy day, the trees would become a line of leaping flames, an express train of fire, heading straight for the house.

Nutty stirred, looked up at the strange woman sipping coffee. Looked worried, as though he smelt Robyn in the dress. But it was not Robyn. A different shape and sound, a different manner. Very prim. No laughter, no tummy tickles for a good dog.

'How long will I be here?' she asked.

'Until some arrangement can be made.'

'I will not leave him.'

'Silvano?'

'He is lost—' she said, still nibbling. Took a sip of coffee, very poised. Like Evelyn Crowley. Dark eyes like Evelyn's, heavily lidded. Both women from the south, both Calabrians. He'd never been sure whether he could trust Evelyn. She'd killed one man, and was planning to kill another, her husband.

'Lost without me,' she added. 'I am lost without him.'

'Is there no-one else?'

'In my family?' She thought about that too. 'No, no-one.'

'Because of what he did?'

'Because of what I did too.'

'You did not kill your father.'

Angelina chewed for a moment, her thoughts far away. Or, not far away. Griffith was just over one hundred miles. Too close for comfort.

'I wrote the letter,' she said.

'No-one knows about that. It has not been published. The Federal Police have not used it to indict anyone. And the State police don't have a copy.'

'It is *tradimento*, betrayal. I never should have written it.'

'You did a good thing, a brave thing.'

'They will never forgive me.'

'Maybe one day.'

'No, never. You can never go against the family.'

'You should think of going way. Start a new life.'

'I tried that. I thought—I thought I was safe in a convent, but they found me. The church soon finds you. It is everywhere. Like God,' she added.

Like the Mafia, he thought.

Angelina had stopped chewing, the cup still raised before her lips. Her eyes wide. She pulled down the hem once more. It crept back up.

'You know,' she said absently, 'that man. They not say a word about who killed him.'

'What man?'

'That man, who was campaigning. Against the drugs. Many years ago. I was baby then, only three.'

'Campaigning about what?'

'The police doing nothing.'

'In Griffith?' He had to think. 'You mean Donald Mackay?'

'*Si*, Donald Mackay. They killed him.'

'To shut him up? Yeah, I heard about that.'

'Outside the supermarket one evening,' she said.

'He was going to his car, I heard.'

'Yes, and someone stepped out and shot him, twice. *Mamma* told me years ago, when I was sixteen. "Keep your tongue in your head," she said.'

'Did they ever catch him?'

'No, not him.'

'Who was he? The guy who did it?'

She drained her cup, then held it on her lap.

'I do not know,' she said. 'Everyone knows who made the order.'

'Everyone in Griffith?'

'*Si*, everyone.'

Becker had never had anything to do with that. He wasn't even a policeman then, merely a kid working for Tommy Thomkins—and thinking of joining the police. He'd been as enthusiastic as Max Kruger. And just as *naïve*.

'Do you know, Angelina?'

'*Si*, I know. Everyone knows.'

'Was it your father?'

'No, not him.'

'Someone he knew?'

'They all know the man.'

'Is he still in Griffith?'

'Oh, yes, he is there. He is very well respected.'

'By the Italian community?'

'By the church, everyone. When he dies, everyone will be there. They will be crying. Such a good man, they will say. The priest will be there in his robes, the *stola viola* over his neck. He will say the *ultimi riti* and ask God to receive this soul, *Signore* so and so, into his loving care. And they will all say, "Yes! Yes, go in peace and love, *Papà*! Go, go, son of the people!" Or something like that. They will cry. The women wail. It will be a big funeral, a beautiful casket, covered with wreaths. Six young men to carry it, on their shoulders. *Nessuna spesa risparmiata*. Italians love a funeral. They love death. It is the great romance, death. Isn't it? I have heard them say that. Every Italian wants to die. So they can go to heaven.'

Becker didn't know what to say. The hem was now up. Had been for a long time. She had given up. The skirt was too short. She must have known he was watching.

Slowly and carefully and tightly, she crossed her legs.

So, they sat there, admiring the perfect day.

Nutty stirred and scratched at a flea, then put his head down again.

Suddenly footsteps! Coming through the house. He jumped up, ran to the back door, the screen door. Barking and pleased as punch. Anastacia stepped out, loaded with bags. She'd been to Grace Brothers, you could see. Opened one bag, held out several packages, almost pushed them at Angelina.

'Four knickers, four singlets. I didn't know your bra size, but if you wash yours today—'

Angelina had risen, surprised.

'Oh, thank you, thank you.'

Becker was surprised. 'You went shopping? Didn't everyone recognise you?'

'No, no, Laura went shopping. Slipped the stuff to me after the meeting.'

'She didn't attend?'

Shook her head. 'Nor did Dave.'

'How did it go?'

'They're gonna punish me.'

'The sack?'

'Recalled to Canberra, I bet.'

He felt sorry for her, sorry for himself too. He'd miss her.

Chook stood back, studied Angelina. 'Isn't that dress too hot?'

'She chose it.'

'It's nearly Christmas.'

'She's in mourning.'

Anastacia handed over the last of the packets, a small one. No doubt toiletries from a pharmacy. 'Why?' she asked.

'Why what?'

'Why mourning? Who for now?'

'She can never go back.'

'To her family? I see.'

Chook looked away at nothing, thinking. When she was thinking, the rest of the world went blank.

'Maybe she can,' she said. 'What's today?'

'Wednesday.'

'Time enough,' she said.

'Time enough for what?'

'Something I discussed with Laura.'

Chapter 17

IT WAS QUITE simple, really. All they had to do was show certain people a copy of the letter. It was not really a letter, more a statement, not addressed to anyone. But it was signed by Angelina Cosco and dated. It was not witnessed, but that didn't matter. She was still alive and available if the matter ever went to court. And if anyone asked: Is that your signature? It wasn't a statutory declaration, witnessed by a justice of the peace, but in Laura's opinion it was good enough. It should ensure that no-one came near Angelina except as a friend.

Palfreyman was all against the idea. You're taking a great risk, he said. Exposing her to retribution. Chook was all for it, unsurprisingly. It was her idea. Still, Laura Langley was of two minds. It was daring, but it could go very wrong. And it was not sanctioned by anyone in Canberra. Palfreyman wanted top-level approval. Laura, said: We're supposed to use our initiative. If we ask for approval, they will say, No. Dave didn't say anything. Dave never said anything much. Whatever Laura decided would be right with him.

'So, let me get this straight—' she said, tapping her desk with her fingernails. Polished, not painted. They were meeting in her office that night.

It was a Wednesday. Chook was smuggled in under darkness. Becker was at home with Angelina.

'You want to call a meeting of certain people in Griffith or nearby, who were at that conference, when it was decided that Concetta had to die.'

'Yes,' Chook said.

'How does Angelina know who was there?'

'Her brother told her.'

'Her brother, Silvano?'

'Yes.'

'Is he reliable?'

'He's become quite lucid and chatty, since Angelina turned up.'

'Was he at the meeting?'

'He was told to wait outside. When the meeting was over, his father came out and said she had to die and that he was to do it.'

'Kill his sister? Kill Concetta?'

'With the acid.'

'My God, how horrible!'

Laura had heard this story before, but was shocked again.

'Angelina never heard her father say that?'

'Apparently not.'

'And Silvano? He may be capable in his lucid moments, but what if he is asked whether what Angelina says is true?'

'He may deny it, that's possible.'

'I don't know. We won't have much to stand on, if this goes bad.'

'It's not going to go bad. We get them together, and we show them the statement.'

'A copy of the statement?'

'Yeah, there will be other copies spread around. We'll tell 'em that.'

'They already know what's in the statement. We gave a copy to Angelo, remember? He would have told some of them.'

'There's no harm in showing it to them again, let them see it. See Angelina's signature. See what will be in the papers. Let them think about it. The main Mafia families in Griffith exposed. With file pictures. Running for cover, when the press tries to interview them.'

'And who is going to get these people to attend the conference?'

'Angelina, in a front page advertisement in *The Area News* on Friday morning.'

'Does she know about this?'

'She will when I tell her.'

'God save us all.' Laura was frightened, but she stuck it out. 'So, essentially, what's the deal?'

'If anything happens to Angelina, her statement will be released to the news media.'

'In Griffith?'

'In Wagga, everywhere.'

'Is this going to frighten them off?'

'I think it will.'

'This is the Mafia we're talking about, Stacey. They don't frighten too easily.'

'Then I'll frighten them.'

'And how would you do that?'

'It's easy, I'll kill one or two.'

Palfreyman jolted in his chair. He didn't like this plan, but he went along with it. He wanted it to fail. Wanted Anastacia Babchuck to fail, so he could get rid of her. It had to done before Saturday, when he would be responsible.

Laura put her head in her hands.

This was too much. A few days ago Chook had killed a man in a country pub. She'd called him out. And killed him in cold blood, casually. Like swatting a fly. And got away with it. No jury would convict her. She might do it again.

'Please, Stacey, don't say things like that.'

'I wasn't joking. If they kill her, I'll kill them.'

Palfreyman asked, 'How are you going to do that? And get away with it?'

'You should have been here on Friday.'

He laughed. 'You think you can kill a dozen people and get away with it?'

'I'll kill 'em with words this time.'

She was lounging in a chair, left arm hanging down, her fingers almost tickling the carpet. The other was lying across her lap, a few inches from the Glock.

'You'll taunt them? To get you?'

'Why not?'

'You're crazy,' he said. 'I mean, you are stark staring crazy.'

'So what?'

'They'll kill you.'

'So what?'

Laura jumped in, waving a hand.

'No, no, Stacey, don't even think about it. I mean, oh Christ, at that interview in the chief inspector's office, you made it perfectly clear you wanted revenge. He had a case against you. That old copper in uniform, you played him for a sucker. He was an ex-priest. He's probably heard a lot of terrible confessions in his life. He let you off. Don't you understand? You won't get away with it next time.'

Chook shrugged. And smirked. Didn't seem to care.

'So, what do we do?' Palfreyman asked.

'Let's take a vote?' Laura asked. 'Those against the plan?'

Palfreyman raised a hand. He wanted it on the record that he was opposed. It was too dangerous.

Laura looked around. 'Dave?'

He was waiting to see how she voted.

'Those for it?'

Chook put up a hand, little more than an indolent flap.

'Dave?'

'I'm with you,' he said.

So, it was down to her. She sighed, scratched her head, bit on her pen and then, took a deep breath.

'Well,' she said, 'let's do it!'

So, that's what happened.

They put a big ad in the *Area News*, saying that Angelina Cosco, daughter of the late Angelo Cosco, would appreciate the attendance of the below-mentioned persons at a gathering at the family home, of such and such address, to mourn the passing of her late father at twelve noon today, Friday. There were twelve names. They managed to get a good spot on page three. Complete with a clear shot of Angelo. Head and shoulders and smiling.

Becker drove Angelina to Griffith late that morning. She'd been told that the meeting was to enable her to expose the killers of Concetta.

A public shaming, nothing more.

She was all for it.

They arrived well before twelve. The house was empty.

There was an annex at the back, where lived the housekeeper and the gardener, who kept an eye on the place. There had been a maid, but she'd gone. Angelina's mother, Isabella, had fled to the house of her father's young brother, Romero. Isabella had not returned for even one day. Even avoided looking at the house from the main road if passing. She'd close her eyes and burst into tears. The house itself hadn't been lived in for months, not since Angelo Cosco had died.

The scene had been so horrific, the blood everywhere, that no-one would enter the place, not even the housekeeper. Not even after professional cleaners had done their best to remove the blood from the walls and the furniture. They'd tried to get it all out of the carpets, but had failed. You could still see dark patches here and there, where Silvano had followed Angelo, firing away at him with the Tanfoglio, emptying the magazine into him, sixteen rounds.

He'd managed to crawl along, over furniture, against walls, knocking desks and flower stands and even a cabinet of photographs from the old country. One or two framed pictures had fallen from the walls. A trail of blood led into the kitchen.

That's where Angelo had died, but still Silvano had gone on shooting. Bullets shattering the floor tiles. Some had gone right through the body. Hit the beautiful tiles, imported all the way from Italy. If you looked carefully, you could still see the blood in the cracks and holes.

No-one had tried to replace them.

They walked across the *terraza* and up to the front door. It was a bold blue door with a cast-iron, lion's head knocker. Angelina had a key.

She inserted it.

The lock gave way, the door moved in a few centimetres. She pushed it, very slowly, entering cautiously. A musty smell welcomed her, the smell of abandoned habitation. Sneaked along a hall, glancing into empty rooms each side. Bits of furniture. Walked on, afraid to see blood, wreckage, images. She'd fled to the convent up north before this had happened. Did not see her father's body. But he was here for her, if not on a floor, then in her mind.

'Okay?' Becker said.

'Yes,' she said.

Took one step, then another. Afraid, but she persisted. Reached the end of the hall, looked into what seemed a large sunroom, a small room each side. Perhaps a kitchen and a maid's room. All enclosed by a glass wall, and a glass door through which you could see a paved area under a trellis, burdened with grapevines. Bunches hanging down. In the middle sat a big hardwood table, too heavy for one man to move. No seats, they would have been stacked away. And to one side a small fountain. It was not trickling.

The trellis stretched from one small building to another. Small, like two-room cabins. Perhaps one had been Primo's home in the old days, when struggling on thirty acres to make a living out of a few grapes, a few oranges and a patch of vegetables. Perhaps the other was where he'd set up his crude winery—a tub and a vat, and eventually a homemade press. Where he made his first plonk, selling it from the cellar door. Or, even from door to door. That was back in the forties and fifties. For decades since, the grapes had gone each harvest to one of the giant wineries farther out at Yenda.

Angelina stepped back quickly.

This was where it had happened, where Silvano had slaughtered his father.

She strode back to the living room. That's all she would need, one room, the living room up front. No-one would be staying for a meal or even coffee. Certainly not a glass of wine. There were a few chairs, some covered with sheets.

'We will need more,' she said.

'I'll get them,' Becker said.

'No, no, let them stand. Let them hurt.'

She sat primly and correctly on one. Angelina never crossed her legs. It would have been unseemly, a daughter of Angelo Cosco. She was wearing one of Robyn's summer dresses. No longer in mourning. The chair she had chosen was very old, ornate, carved arms and feet, a big cat's feet. She sat with her hands on the arms, fingers clenching the claws at the end. A leopard's claws perhaps. The back was padded with an old tapestry, the pattern indistinct now. On the top rail was a carved head. Not of a cat, but some sort of gargoyle, perhaps half cat and half man. Mouth open, about to snarl or cry or shout? It was not clear. It had been her grandfather's chair, an heirloom. Only the head of the house sat in that chair.

Primo Cosco had come to Griffith back in 1929.

In those days, you needed about three-hundred pounds to get started. He'd worked sixteen hours a day six days a week for ten shillings a day digging ditches. Somehow, he saved three hundred pounds, enough to buy a block of thirty acres in Yoogali. Began by planting oranges trees and growing vegetables, trying to live off the land. In 1935 he planted muscatels, sold them on the open market. Then in 1940, built a little winery, nothing more than a concrete tub, in which to squash the grapes, and a vat for fermenting the juice. Soon he had his first bottles—dark, sour, muddy stuff. No-one could drink it. They spat it out and laughed at him. So he switched to semillon.

Not much quality, a bit sharp on the tongue like lemon juice.

He got into volume sales, to shops and hotels and bars in Griffith and Leeton and Wagga and all the mall towns about the Riverina. It was plonk, everyone said so. But it was drinkable. He bought up contiguous blocks. Soon he had one hundred and twenty acres. By the seventies, he had made a small fortune. The best of it came from the cannabis.

Then, in 1981, Primo died, leaving behind Angelo and Romero. Angelo had married Isabella Terracini, who gave birth to Concetta, Angelina and—

'Someone's coming,' Becker said. He was at a window.

'Who is it?'

'I don't know. Blue car, nothing unusual about it.'

He'd expected something rich, like a massive four-wheel drive or an Alfa Romeo.

'It's coming up the drive,' he said.

'A blue car?' she asked.

'Quite small. I think—Yes, a Hyundai.'

'A Hyundai? I don't know who that could be.' She sounded afraid.

'Don't worry,' Becker said. 'They're not going to hurt you.'

'Perhaps not now. They will be so polite, wishing to shake my hand, the daughter of Angelo. They will tell me how sorry they are such a terrible thing has happened to such a distinguished family. They will look around. They will be looking for the signs.'

'Signs?'

'Of horror, of regret.'

A knock at the front door. Gentle, like a child playing with the knocker. Becker and Angelina waited. Waited for a louder knock. It came. 'I will go,' he said.

Went to the door, opened it. An old man stood there, bent. A young man and a woman were behind him, expectant and apprehensive. Ready to catch him if he stumbled.

'Good afternoon,' Becker said.

'Good afternoon,' the young man said. He looked about forty and had a shiny, olive scalp. He was shy and held a tall, soft, brown hat, curled up around the brim. In the band was stuck a small, black feather.

'Is Angelina here?'

'Yes, she is expecting you. Please come in.'

He handed them copies. Surprised, they took them.

They came in, almost edgeways, like penitents. Afraid to be rejected, sent begging.

The youngish man said, 'We are Pescii.'

'Pescii?'

'*La famiglia Pescii.*'

'I don't speak Italian. Angelina is in the front room, to the side, there.'

'Ah, yes, thank you.'

They came in sideways, politely, half-bowing, eyes fixed on Becker, a *straniero*. Not even Italian, by the look and sound of him. The old man shuffling and grinning. Idiotic in his demeanour. He was the wobbly old codger at the table in the Capriana, the one who'd been celebrated on arrival. They'd all stood for him, shook his hand, kissed his hand, embraced him. The children too. This was the one the families had consulted. What should be done with the Cosco girl?

They entered the living room, copies in hand. Not knowing what to expect. Angelina rose from her chair.

The old man said, '*Buona giournata, signora stimata.*'

He had extended a hand. She did not accept it.

'*Buono giornata, signore Mario. Serai seduto.*'

'*Molte gracie.*'

They helped him to a chair.

The bald young man with the hat said, 'How many are coming?'

'Only those who need to come.'

Becker caught her eye and nodded.

Distantly they heard a door slam. They waited, heard footsteps on the *terraza*. Hesitant, suspecting a trap. Not seeing any. No-one behind the belvederes each end. No-one behind the lemon trees in the garden. Nor the apricots and the crepe myrtle. And, here and there, a viburnum. Such a beautiful summer's day in a beautiful land. In the distance to the north was a low range of bald hills. There were trees up there, but poor, scruffy, struggling things with few leaves, stunted. When it rained, the water ran off. Nothing soaked in. It was a withered place, the hills. Beyond the hills was the airport. The land was better there, grazing land. Griffith was a good place, if you knew the right people. And if the water kept flowing.

Another knock at the door.

Becker opened it. A man in clerical grey stood there.

'Ah, good afternoon,' he said, beaming in the way that such men do. Not wearing the cloth of the church, nor the *cappello romano.* Instead, a soft grey Borsellino. Nothing at all to suggest he was a priest, except a small silver cross on a lapel. He had a wanting air about him, an air of wanting to be with you, to know you. To be your friend, your confessor. To solve all your problems.

He held out a hand, smilingly.

'I am Father Quinlan,' he said, 'Ambrose Quinlan.'

He had a beautiful smile.

Chapter 18

WHEN THEY WERE all there, Chook had walked in. That was part of the plan. She'd had to keep out of sight until they were all in. All that were coming, that is. If she'd been there when they'd entered, they might well have been alarmed and fled. They'd left Palfreyman at the office in Wagga Wagga. He didn't want to be involved. Things were going to go wrong, he knew. Or, thought he did. She and Laura were hiding in the Mazda across the main road, down a lane, behind the rows of vines on another property. Barely able to peer above them. Laura had had to use a pair of opera glasses. They'd counted twelve. That's how many were named in the statement. Everyone who'd been at the Pescii house, when the decision was made. They had the names, but something was wrong.

Two of the males were young men, perhaps teenagers. And one, tall, heavy, dumpy woman with an awful bouffant hairdo was there. Something out of the 1960s. Lacquered, you could be sure. She must have been one of Angelo's sisters, probably Rosalinda. No doubt she was a stand-in for someone who did not wish to face Angelina Cosco.

Laura started the Mazda and drove across the road and up the long white drive, more than one hundred yards, to the house, parked and waited. Letting the motor run, the air-conditioner. It was hot in the car. Now midsummer. Chook got out, but Laura stayed in.

'No more coming, I'd say,' she said.

'Okay,' Chook said.

'I don't like this.'

'Don't worry, boss. Everything will be fine. Trust me.'

'That's the part I don't like.'

When Chook walked in, most were still reading the copies of the letter. All turned to look at her. They saw a tall man, or perhaps a tall woman dressed as a man. Angelina had been speaking, explaining the letter.

'So,' she said, 'that is it.'

She was having trouble with her throat. It had dried up. She coughed again. Becker took her a glass. They all watched as she drank, just a ladylike sip.

'*Gracie*,' she said. 'This is Mr Becker. I have been staying with Mr Becker. He has been kind. And the one who has this minute walked in? He is Mr Grove. His name is Lemon Grove. Perhaps you have heard of him?' She switched to Italian for those not proficient, the old ones. '*E questo è Mr Lemon Grove. Probabilmente ne hai sentito parle. Era con Salvatore Pisano a Melbourne.*'

They gasped. Someone said: 'Salvatore Pisano?'

'*Nei soui ultimi momenti,*' she added. 'In his last moments.'

They gasped.

'*Signore Grove é della polizia nazionale—in altre parole, i carabinieri.*'

Someone gasped, a young boy. They stared at Chook, leaning against a wall, arms not crossed but open, the jacket open. They could see the Glock.

'*Come parte del suo lavoro, deve uccidere le persone,*' she said. 'A part of his job is to kill people. *Persone con anime nere.* People with black souls.'

One or two cried out. Even the priest.

'*Forse hai sentito parlare di lui?*'

She took a deep breath, hand to breast, lightly. Then sat back, tired, almost exhausted. It had been an ordeal.

'Is everything understood?'

They were too astonished to reply.

'As you entered, Mr Becker handed you a copy of a statement. I have signed it. If you harm me or anyone near to me, the statement will be released to the local press. Not to the local police,' she said pointedly. 'The local press.'

She let that sink in.

'Is that understood?'

No-one spoke.

'It is necessary,' she said. 'Either you do as I say or die of shame. Some of you will go to jail for life. What will you say to your children?'

They cried out. The woman and the boys began to cry.

The priest was whispering in Latin. Crossing himself.

A man jumped to his feet, began shouting at her in Italian. She held up a hand.

'English, please. For the sake of our visitors.' To them, she explained: 'This man is my Uncle Romero, my father's brother.'

'Angelina, you wrong. No-one agree any harm. It only discussion. Angelo, he say he want advice. We give him nothing, nothing at all.'

'Who suggested the acid?'

'Nobody.'

'Nobody, *zio* Romero?'

He was clutching his hat, crushing it. Head thrust out, as if hard of hearing. His eyes screwed up in outrage.

'Somebody say this and somebody say that. You know how is? We talkin', you know? Concetta, she done bad thing, goin' to police.'

'Back in the old country, if a woman talks, she must be punished. You know that.'

'*Si, si*, Angelina. Nobody say she have be killed.'

'*Who* suggested the acid?'

He wriggled. 'That one way. Many other ways to do. Maybe thrashin' or a drownin'. You know how is? Hold the head under water a few minutes. No harm done.'

'So, *who* suggested acid?'

'Who? I not know. I swear on my life, I not know.'

'Was it my father?'

'No, no, Angelo, he good man.'

'And yet he made Silvano do it.'

'Maybe somebody have a thought. You know how is.'

'Was it Don Mario?'

Angelina was referring to the grinning idiot sitting beside him. His eyes were rolling in his head, a hand to a cancerous ear. Saying, *Costa sta dicendo? Costa sta dicendo?*

She watched him for several seconds, her eyes crawling over his face.

'*Ha vissuto troppo a lungo,*' she said. He has lived too long.

Someone cried out. It may have been the stout woman with the bouffant. A young man jumped to his feet. 'Who are you? No-one respects you. Who are these goons? We do not need you.'

'*Siediti*, Bruno,' someone said.

He sat, angrily.

She shrugged. 'You will go to jail. Is that understood?'

Becker watched them. He didn't know what she'd said in Italian, nor did Chook. But it was pretty obvious. Nemesis was visited upon them. The daughter of Angelo Cosco had spoken. She was now *lo capo*, or to use the feminine, *la capa*. In Italian there is a subtle difference: *lo capo* means the boss, whereas *la capa* means the head Giuseppina Pisano hadn't been a true *capa*, just a stand-in for her speechless husband.

'*All* of you killed my sister, Concetta. All of you are guilty. If there is any more crime in this district, each one of you will be charged with the murder of my sister, Concetta Cosco. Is that understood?'

They glanced about, at each other, at Angelina, at Becker. At the mysterious figure leaning against a wall. Long, relaxed, indifferent. Unsurprised.

Angelina stood up.

'So now, you may leave. Mr Becker will see you out. There is no point in trying to kill me. There are many other copies.'

They began to shuffle and shift. Then they left.

Angelina did not move. Becker went to the front door, opened it. The priest was the last to leave. Looked as though he wanted to say something to her, to admonish her or to plead with her. He could not make up his mind. Could only hold his hat before his thin and ungodly chest.

'One minute, Father,' she said.

'Yes? What is it?'

'Not you, not yet.'

He dashed for the door, but Becker held up a hand. Chook left her wall.

'You frightened me a long time ago,' she said.

'Frightened you, Angelina?'

'You sickened me.'

He was afraid. 'My child, I don't understand—'

'I am not your child, thank God. How long have you known me?'

'Why, since you were born. I baptised you with the water of St Columba in—'

'You raped me, when I was only eight.'

He went white. His eyes popped.

'Raped you? Dear God, what are you saying? No, no, Angelina. No, I could never do such a thing. On my life, I swear by all that is holy—'

'With your finger,' she said.

'No, no, no—'

'In the church, in the sacristy.'

'No, no, I swear, you are wrong, dear Angelina. I loved you; I loved your sister and your brother. I admired your mother, dear Isabella. She was so aggrieved. She came to me and said, Father, what have they done?'

'To Connie?'

'Connie? Concetta? Yes, such an awful thing.'

'Did you go to the police?'

'The police?'

'Did you expose them?

'No, no, I could not. Your dear father came to me in the confessional. Opened his soul, not to me, you understand? But to God. Told the Almighty what he had done. I could not reveal what he had told God.'

'Did he tell God what they had done to Concetta?'

'Yes, he did. I was horrified. But what could I do, Angelina? It was the confessional. I am bound not to divulge—'

She walked up close to him.

Could have touched him, touched his quivering flesh, his jaundiced old eyes. But she did not. Becker stood behind Angelina. Chook blocked the exit.

'I detest you,' Angelina said. 'If my father had known what you did to me, he would have killed you. But first he would have asked you which finger you'd used. You understand what I am saying?'

He was shaking, close to tears.

'Please forgive me, dear, sweet, Angelina, the one with the face, the sweet face. The child saying her prayers, so devout, so trusting, in the front row. I saw you there. God, help me. I could not, I—'

She tapped him on his chest.

'Do you know what happens to men like you back in the old country?'

He blanched, stepped back. Bumped into something. It was Chook. The priest began to cry. 'I am not Italian. I mean, I am Irish, my mother was

Italian. I am not like that. Not the way they do things in Calabria. I, no, please—'

'You are a spider, aren't you, Father? You prey on children.'

'No, please, Angelina. I am so sorry. I should not have done it! These temptations of the flesh, you know. We are all weak. Oh, God in heaven, be merciful. Grant to this child the divine grace of mercy, the—'

'Get out!'

He jumped back. Chook grabbed him, encircled him. One hand went down and down.

'What have you got there, Father?' Chook said. Her lips were to his left ear. 'Something to play with? How would you like me to play with it?'

'No, no, please—'

'Like this?'

She squeezed it. His balls too. A whole handful, her thumb going in deep. Right in to the bladder, deeper and deeper. He tried to scream, but Chook's other hand was over his mouth.

He convulsed from the pain.

His eyes began to pop. His ears too. The pain, the pain! He was going limp, surrendering to the pain, excruciating. In a way, he welcomed it. He always knew he would go to hell. He didn't want to go to heaven. He'd have to explain himself to the Almighty. And he had no idea what he could possibly say.

Suddenly he was released.

Chook patted him. Pushed him. Steered him to the door. Becker was holding it open. The priest did not make it. He began to fall, but someone grabbed him. Helped him with a hand and an arm. Led him out, stumbling. Trying not to scream in public. You never knew who might hear.

'Can I help you to your car, Father?'

'No, no, I—'

'I think you need help.'

Together they made it to the car. It was an old Maserati, a gift from a grateful parishioner for keeping his mouth shut. Becker was holding him now.

'Are you okay?' he said.

'Yes, yes—'

Laura Langley appeared beside them.

'Everything go to plan?'

'Oh, yeah, perfectly.'

'What's wrong with him?'

'The priest? He's had a nervous attack. Thought he was going to die and go to heaven.'

'What's wrong with that?'

'It'd be worse than hell for him.'

Chapter 19

WHEN THEY TOLD Palfreyman, he said, 'You what?' He was sitting in Laura's chair, when they walked in, perhaps getting the feel of it. He didn't get up. She didn't fuss about it. She was going to quit in half an hour or so. Drive to Canberra before sundown. She had to report back on Monday for debriefing. She'd then take a couple of weeks' rest, before reporting at Victoria Barracks, Sydney.

'We left her there,' she said.

'Left her in the house? All alone?'

'She's not alone now.'

'Yeah? What do you mean?'

'She's going to stay there, in that big empty house.'

'All alone? They'll kill her.'

'I don't think so.'

Laura sat opposite him, legs crossed, leaning back, a hand to her face, one finger touching a corner of her mouth, not quite entering. She had a strange smile, sometimes there, twinkling. Like a distant light you might see at sea. She hadn't believed they would pull it off. Palfreyman liked to lounge back in a chair, uncommitted. He was an uncommitted sort of man. A great lounger. A leg cocked up, a look of being the boss, perfectly at ease. Tapping a hand on the desk. Dave was sitting at his desk, watching. Dave had pale eyebrows, either up or down. This time they were up, but you would not have known, they were blond. Like camouflage, they were both there and not there, depending upon how you looked at them. He had fat, pink cheeks and a wondering smile. This was going to be good.

'Why?'

'Why?'

'Yeah, why?'

'It's her house. She inherited it. Actually, Silvano did, but he was declared to be of unfit mind. Angelina had herself made his guardian, so in effect it's now her house.'

'Yeah, I know that.'

'She has them bluffed.'

'Christ, Laura, as I understand it, they sent some smelly priest to Glen Innes to drag her back to Griffith and she scoots from his clutches. She turns up here, where someone might be trying to grab her, maybe kill her. And now you tell me she wants to stay by herself in Griffith? You know that place is full of Italians. More than half the inhabitants are Italian or the kids of Italians. And a lot of them are Calabrians. Is she stupid or something?'

'Not now.'

'Why not now?'

'Things have changed.'

'How?'

'First, she will not be alone. There's a married couple, a gardener and a housekeeper. They've been there all along. So, she will have company. Second, she is going to get her mother to return home. And third, she introduced them to Mr Groves.'

'Who?'

'Mr Lemon Groves.'

'Who the hell is he?'

She wriggled and shifted and jigged and whistled to herself in her chair.

'She won't have any trouble from anyone in Griffith now.'

'Why?'

She laughed. Palfreyman was not in the mood for games. He was about to take over. He had an eye on the clock. In ten or fifteen minutes she would be gone.

'Angelina has appointed herself the *capo* in Griffith.'

'The what?'

'The boss, the lady boss.'

'What the hell are you talking about?'

'She's now running the Mafia in Griffith.'

He jumped. Laura chuckled. 'She has them all frightened.'

'Frightened?'

'Out of their wits.'

'How did she do that?'

'I just said. She's told them she is now the *capo*. Or, the *capa*, in her case I think.'

'You mean, she's now the boss of the Mafia in Griffith?'

'That's what I said. Her father was the previous boss.'

'So, she's going to run all the rackets, the drugs and the booze and the graft and corruption?'

'Not any of that.'

'Then how can she be a Mafia boss?'

'By destroying anyone who *does* do those things.'

'What?' He jumped again.

Then he sank. She laughed.

'Keep your hair on. She told us her brilliant plan before we went over there. She's going to expose them, if they kill anyone or break any arms or fix any deals or bribe any police or sell any drugs or run any brothels or lie to any courts or—'

He sank right down. 'I don't believe this.'

She studied him. He didn't like being studied.

'You know what this country needs, Mr Palfreyman?'

He didn't answer. It was going to be outrageous, he knew.

'Armed men with a conscience,' she said, looking at her watch. 'I'm meeting Harry and Stacey at the Hovell for a drink,' she said. 'You want to come along?'

'Ah, no,' he said. He looked bad.

He'd been sent to the bush, but the bush was another country. In the cities they wanted to make a motza. In the bush they simply wanted to survive with some sort of dignity. Palfreyman had been a great man for the rules. He had no initiative. No spirit, really. He was just filling in time until something happened. He didn't know what it was, but he knew it would happen. The way things were going, it had to happen.

'Dave? Coming along?'

'Yeah, right.'

He was on his feet already.

Dave didn't say much, but you could depend on him. He was sorry. They didn't make too many women like Laura. He'd been sitting next to her for a year. She was a self-contained sort of woman, amiable and yet unattainable. But she always smelled good. Always had about her a certain womanly air. It was a daily joy to sit near a woman with perfectly manicured hands, and a twinkle in her eyes. Not to mention the entertainment of her earrings, blue. Always blue. To go with her eyes.

'This Mr Groves—' Palfreyman said, fiddling with his hands.

His hands, she had noticed, seemed to have minds of their own. While speaking they'd creep up towards an inner breast pocket. Then, like naughty boys who'd been spotted, they'd scuttled back. He had something in there, she knew. But he was not her problem now.

'What about him?'

'Who is he?'

She paused at the door, almost winked.

'Who do you think?'

Chapter 20

IF YOU DRIVE into Griffith from the east, you enter though the industrial area. On each side you see big transport depots and garages and workshops and everything else that serves the huge trucks, which carry away the wine bottles and fruit and vegetables and anything else grown in the Irrigation Area. As you proceed, the shops and old houses and oil depots and cafes and fast-food joints gradually give way to a better class of shop until you come to an aircraft on a tall steel pole.

It is not a model. It is a real Fairey Firefly, of the kind that once flew from a small carrier off the coast of South Korea in bitter weather, the decks slippery with ice. And the wind cold enough to freeze the nuts off a brass monkey, as they used to say. It was a propeller-driven machine that had a crew of two: a pilot and an observer, who also looked after the weapons. It was both a fighter and a reconnaissance aircraft.

You might be surprised by the sight. It is in full naval colours and has RAN printed in black on each side. No doubt, a memorial to the men who flew it back in those days. In every Australian town there is a memorial like that. You don't often see an old warbird.

That's where they parked the car. And got out. Silvano was immediately obedient.

It was a week before Christmas, 1996.

After the meeting at the old house, Angelina had remained. Had cleaned it up and moved in. Got some takeaway food, found some bedclothes and stayed that very night. She was now the mistress of the house and her young brother's guardian. Next day she'd contacted the hospital in Wagga Wagga and said she wanted to bring her brother home. Just for a visit, to see his reaction. Sure that he'd be happier there than in hospital. He was now quite stable, she believed. He didn't remember what had happened early that year.

The doctors were not so sure. He might become agitated, frightened, as it all came back. Angelina was adamant. She knew her brother. If she could ease him back into Griffith, re-establish the familiar. If she could ease him back into the farm and then into the house—

Silvano was a slight man, not long out of his teens. Looked much younger, too youthful to be a man. A delicate man, very damaged. Thin and sallow and suspicious. Instead of glancing around at the main street, he glanced up at the aircraft.

His face lit up. He recognised it.

'Yes,' he said.

'Do you remember *lo velivolo*?'

'*Si, si, lo velivolo*. I wanted to fly away in that, didn't I?'

'You wanted to be a pilot, wanted to go to sea and fly off the deck. Off the heaving deck?'

'Yes, yes.' He looked around, seeing things. The arts centre diagonally opposite. Trees down the middle of Banna Avenue. Cars parked in the middle.

'You want to cross this side?'

'Huh?'

'*Caro*, do you want to walk down this side or the other?'

He moved, but almost fell, missed a step at the gutter. Chook grabbed him.

The doctor was right behind him, worried. The joint opinion back in Wagga Wagga was that he was not yet stable enough. Angelina had said he was not stable, because he was in the hospital. Or, in the grounds or locked up whenever he had a crying fit, restrained. Or, was being walked by someone, a hand on his arm. Hospitalisation, she argued, was holding him back. The staff did not agree.

'He's hiding away,' they'd said. 'Hiding from himself. It is unsafe to take him back to his home town, to his home. To the house and the blood.'

'There is no blood now,' Angelina had said. 'I have replaced the tiles. Not a speck anywhere.'

'He will see blood,' they said. 'In his head.'

You could see what they were getting at. He was too unstable. He might become violent. Fly off the handle, kill someone.

'No, no,' she'd said. 'He must go home to the farm, to the vines and the memories. He must get out of here. He cannot stay here. If he does much longer, he will die here.'

'We keep strict watch on our patients,' one of them had said.

That was the unit manager, a strong woman with a nervous tic. The doctor had said nothing. He looked deep in thought, his head on one side, his eyes closed. He was breathing. You could hear him breathing.

'You didn't keep strict watch on that man, Barnes, did you?' Angelina had said. 'I am going to take him back to Griffith. To see what happens.'

'I will come with you,' the doctor had said.

He was a short, thickset man with a serious face and rimless glasses. He wasn't sure they could control him, if he started screaming. What if he ran away? Ran down a street screaming, waving his arms and jumping around as he did when he was frustrated, afraid, startled.

'I will ask a friend to come with us. She is very strong.'

'A nurse?'

'No, a policeman.'

'She? A policeman?'

'Does it matter?'

Chook had borrowed the office Mazda and picked them up. She and the doctor in the front, Angelina and her brother in the back. Silvano opened a door, wanted to rush across to see the Firefly. He was happy, amazed. But Angelina had to grab him.

'Wait,' she said, 'there's a car.' They waited on Banna Avenue.

'I'm good,' Silvano said.

'You are doing well,' Chook said as they crossed.

The doctor said nothing, looked more anxious than the boy. Who was not a boy, but seemed to have reverted. Although, as had Angelina asserted, he was quite reasonable at times. Most of the time, in fact. He read the local paper each day and books from the hospital library. At present he was reading *Seven Years in Tibet*. He seemed to know all about Tibet. He had been smart at Geography and Physics and Chemistry at High School, but weak at sports. Fell each time he tried to play tennis. Too weak to swim across an Olympic pool. A spindly sort of youth, ungainly. And yet, he had a purpose. It may have been a delicate purpose—to go mountain climbing or to be an aviator or a romantic poet like D'Annunzio, who was also an aviator. And a fanatical poet and rabble-rouser. Always getting Mussolini into trouble with the neighbours.

Hard to say what would have become of him, if things had gone the other way. If he hadn't slaughtered his father with sixteen angry shots.

Now, his sister was trying to get him back to some sort of life with some sort of direction and a faint hope of achievement. He was a jumpy young man, his eyes never still. His smile simple at times. At other times, beneficent. Like a man with a secret destiny.

They crossed safely and began walking. He tended not to look where he was walking, so couples had to split around him. They passed a hairdressing salon. A woman sat in a chair with a dryer over her head. A permanent wave or a permanent headache. She didn't seem to be enjoying it.

'Silvano—' His sister pulled him away. He'd been staring. The woman had turned, got a glimpse of him. Gasped soundlessly. One eye on him. He'd smiled. It was the fat lady with the blue eyes. Smeary.

Soon she'd be on the phone.

'If we walk along here—' Angelina said.

They walked or ambled along Banna Avenue. Not seriously but sensibly, not bumping into others, but not caring if they did. Instead, walking as through a garden of infrequent humans. This way and that. In shadow, the sun being high.

'I remember that,' Silvano said.

He had stopped outside a newsagency. Apart from placards and magazines and posters advertising Lotto and a dwarf-like clown on a stand by the door with a hand and cap out, smiling. His funny cap had a tassel. There seemed to be nothing.

'What do you mean?'

'That?' he asked.

It was not clear what he meant. Perhaps nothing at all. Perhaps a bright colour on a glossy cover. Perhaps a lurid cover. Yes, something on metal legs was holding a bare-breasted maiden. And she was screaming at him, voicelessly.

'I saw that,' he said.

'You mean the movie?'

'Yes, the movie. With Archer Wiffen.'

'Archer Wiffen? That was when you were ten, Silvano. We had a tape and you played it over and over.'

'Yes,' he said, 'over and over.'

They walked on. Walked the length of the street, until they reached the circle, at the heart of Burley Griffin's plan. It was large, as large as State Circle in Canberra encompassing the Federal Parliament building. They paused. The circle looked green, despite the long dry. Must have been watered each day. No shortage of water in Griffith. The main canal went right around the town. There were a few buildings, the City Council Chambers to the right, the Regional Theatre to the left.

'You want to walk over there, Silvano?'

'I saw a play, once. When I was at school.'

'Yes, you did. It was Shakespeare, *Julius Caesar.*'

'They stabbed him, didn't they? All of them?'

Everyone stopped dead. Everyone knew what happened to Julius Caesar. The blood, the blood. Waiting to cross the circle, watching cars to their right. Most turned into Banna Avenue. They made it across, all four of them. The doctor walking in stops and starts, hands behind his back, eyes down, apprehensive. There would be images, he feared. There would be images.

'And what happened?' She was testing him. What would set him off? Chook was right behind, just in case.

'They stabbed him, again and again. And he fell down.'

'And what did Caesar say?'

'*Et tu, Brute?*'

'That's correct.'

'*Et tu, Brute?* Then fall, Caesar!'

They paused before the theatre. It was open. You could go in and look around if you wished. A woman at the door was smiling. Holding pamphlets. A nameplate on her lapel.

'And what happed to Caesar?'

'They let him lie there, on the ground.'

'Was he wounded?'

The doctor moved in. 'I really don't think this is a good idea.'

Angelina was determined.

'Wounded?'

'Yes, badly. I don't know how the kids do that. Have blood on them and still be alive and looking, like the kids you sit next to at school. He's lying on the ground, moaning and groaning and clutching—'

'Clutching what?'

They moved on. Angelina did not. She stood tall and straight and resolute and dark in her Mediterranean aspect. A hand to her lips, thinking.

'Clutching his chest. He took his hand away.'

'And what did you see?'

'His hand was covered in blood. I don't know how Bobby Marchiano could do that. Get stabbed to death and not be dead.'

'He was acting, you know.'

'Yes, but it was so real.' Then paused, his eyes not quite with us. 'All the blood,' he said.

The doctor was getting angry. Muttering through his teeth, sibilating as if his jaw were wired. 'Miss Cosco—' he said.

'The blood?'

'Miss Cosco—'

'I was shocked. Everyone was. Daniella was beside me.'

'Daniella Cosco, you mean? Sitting beside you, you mean?'

'Yes,' he said, nodding, thinking back. 'She was shocked, chewing her handkerchief. It was lace. I thought she was very pretty. I thought, if she was not my cousin, I'd kiss her. But you can't, can you?'

'So, Silvano, what happened then?'

'Oh, he got up?'

'Who got up?'

'Bobbie Marciano. But he was Caesar. He was dead, he couldn't get up, could he? Not until the curtain came down. Or someone carried him off.'

'Yes, but he was acting, wasn't he?'

'That's what I said to Daniella, it's only a story. He's not really dead.'

'Caesar, didn't get up, did he? He was dead. I mean, in the story.'

'Yes, but he wasn't really dead, was he? It wasn't real life.'

The doctor was alarmed. Something was sure to happen.

'Miss Cosco, I think it is dangerous to play on the distinction between—'

'If he can distinguish between the real and the unreal,' she said.

'I don't like this at all.'

They stood in a little group in the foyer, three wondering whether this poor creature had any sense of reality. On a poster inside the door were a young man's face and a lot of darkness and perhaps the outline of an old house on a windy hill and some big words: *Night Must Fall*. And something about it being a classic thriller. Angelina gave up. It was going to be difficult, she could see. The woman with the pamphlets came over.

'We're doing that next Friday and Saturday,' she said. 'Emlyn Williams,' she added.

No-one had heard of Emlyn Williams, but Angelina took a pamphlet.

'Had enough walking?' she asked.

'I'm still good. I can walk, you know? I can walk and if I take my medication—'

'Would you like to walk back now? To the car?'

'I don't mind.'

'Walking is all right?'

'I do a lot of walking. They have a dog, you know?'

'At the hospital.'

'He's called Rusty.'

'Rusty?' Chook asked.

'Yes, because he's all red.'

'I see.'

'So they can pat him,' he said. 'You know?'

'So they can.'

'Dogs are good for you.'

'Yes, I know.'

'All red dogs are called Rusty,' he said, simply.

They walked back on the other side of Banna Avenue.

Every few yards, people looked at them, surprised. Some stopped, or paused and walked on. Or, hurried on. A few stopped in their tracks. One or two opened their mouths to speak, but did not. More than one glanced at Chook and remembered Mr Groves, at the meeting. Or had heard of him, had a mental picture. And had heard about Salvatore Pisano. Whispers, you know. No-one was quite certain what had happened down in Melbourne at that hospice. But here was the very man. Angelina had said so. Some said he was police, the Federal Police.

They returned, step by step. Silvano eager, like a dog on a lead. Tending to get ahead of them. Not quite all there, but reliable, communicable. You could follow his thoughts, his concerns. He had no memory of the slaughter, repressed memory. Not even when you mentioned blood. They got back to the Firefly on the pole at the intersection, waited for the lights change.

In the middle of the zebra, a girl stood stock still, staring.

He was smiling at her. Chook was ready to grab him, but he didn't move. The lights changed and he stepped out, strode across. He walked right up to her, not seeming to know her. Smiling simply, like a monk at a passer-by. Thankful for what God might put his way.

'Silvano!' she said.

He smiled, a silly smile. But sweet, unsophisticated.

'You're back?' she said.

'Yes, yes.'

'With Angelina?'

'Yes, yes, she said I could see the old place.'

'The old place?' She was startled. She was a pleasant looking girl, an Italian girl. You could imagine her standing in a vineyard, a mole on her chin, a bandana on her head and a basket on a hip. 'You mean Griffith? The town?'

'Yes, the town. It—it hasn't changed, has it?'

'No, not in six months, has it?'

'Six months?'

He glanced at Angelina, her lips tight. 'Six months,' she agreed.

'You are looking good,' the girl said.

'We are going home,' he said.

'Home, to the house? Your house?'

'Yes,' Angelina said.

'Oh?'

She looked frightened.

'Daniella?' he said.

'Yes,' she said, 'I am Daniella. I will tell Mamma. She will be so pleased.'

'I was telling them about Caesar.'

'Caesar?'

'Julius. You were shocked. I was telling them about the blood.'

'The blood?'

She looked horrified. It was not Caesar's real blood, but it was blood to him. She could see it in his eyes. He'd had the same eyes, when the police had hauled him to his feet and said, 'Silvano Valentino Cosco, you are under arrest for the murder of —'

'It was only a story, I said.'

'So you did. Are you home to stay?'

Angelina cut in. 'Stay? Oh, I don't know. He may not like it. If he likes the look of it, the house, the vines, the workers—The harvest will begin in two months. That will be interesting for him. He might join in, picking.'

'The house?'

She was frightened, you could see.

'Nice to see you again, Daniella. We'd better keep moving.'

Angelina took her brother's arm.

'Goodbye.' The girl had changed colour. Like a woman who'd suddenly realised she'd left a cake in the oven at home and forgotten to turn it off.

She had to get home, immediately. Tell everyone about it. Not the cake, but Silvano Cosco. They've brought him home.

They went to the Mazda. Got in and began to depart. The doctor was not happy.

'You're going to—?'

'I think we should,' she said. 'What do you think, Anastacia?'

'I'm game.'

'Yes,' she said, 'let us see.'

So they turned off Banna Avenue and took a main road. Not a highway, but a neat, straight road. The house was not far out, no more than two or three miles. Turned into an avenue of lemon trees. To each side, the vines green and heavy. A few men were pruning here, pruning there. Normally done late in Spring. It was hot but not too hot. Cutting back hard, forcing the growth into the fruit, semillon and verdelho and some sauvignon blanc. It was a big vineyard, four contiguous blocks making 120 acres. Three months to go to the harvest.

The house rose up to greet them. Or, it did not exactly rise up, because it was on flat land. Yet it seemed to look up as they approached, like a dog lifting its head when it first senses you.

The car stopped.

'Where are we?' Silvano was grinning like an impatient child. Almost jigging in his seat.

'You remember this?' Angelina asked.

'Yes, I've been here. I'm sure I've been here!'

'You used to live here.'

They got out and walked up to the house. Stepped onto the *terraza* under its pergola, brushed by dangling wisteria, no longer in bloom.

It was the solid, deep-blue door. With its golden knocker, a lion's head, his mouth open, displeased. Imperial in his self-importance.

'Yes,' he said, 'I know this place. I used to live here.'

'You want to see it again?'

The doctor was clenching his fists.

Blood pressure high. Face full of flush and puffiness. And his rimless glasses, they were jittery with anticipation. He patted his breast pocket on the left. Normally, he carried his spectacles there, in a small snap-tight steel case. Inside it today were a syringe and two ampoules. In the event of one not being enough. Something was going to happen, he was sure.

'I have had it cleaned,' Angelina said, reaching into her bag.

She paused. They stood ready. If he started screaming, they knew what to do. They'd discussed it in detail. Dr Kuchner would never have agreed, if they'd not had a plan.

'Are you ready?' Angelina was holding up the key, but watching him with half a smile.

'Oh, yes,' Silvano said. 'I think I left something here.'

'What was it?'

'I, I don't remember.'

'Are you ready?'

'Yes, yes!'

She inserted the key.

'Well,' she said, 'here you are, home again.'

And turned the key.

Chapter 21

A FEW DAYS later, Chook was recalled to Canberra. For discussions, she was told. She knew what the decision would be: recall to her old stamping ground. Becker was now alone at the farm, except that old Bert seemed to turn up each day or night. Bert had nothing else to do, except to roam his own property steadily going to wrack and ruin. Occasionally popping away at something, night or day, with the old Hollis. He had a new dog, called Blue Two. It was a cattle dog, but much younger than Old Blue, which, or who, as you know, was killed by the cattle duffers. The boy, Terry, came to stay. He loved the farm, loved cattle, loved shooting anything that moved. They were out early one day, when they came across two men. Not on Becker's property but among low hills to the south, on the road to Culcairn, the road to Albury. The road to Melbourne, looking for rabbits. To give the boy some practice on how to kill living things.

They'd seen a few in the distance.

Terry had taken a shot at one, missed. Then another, bowled it over, but it had limped away. They'd sent Nutty after it. He'd bounded off, delighted. Something to play with. He was not a retriever, nor even a killer. Not in Old Blue's class. He'd nuzzled the crippled creature, possibly bit on a back leg, and played with it, with one paw—perhaps rolling it over to have a better look. But the rabbit had escaped. Had struggled down a hole, lost, wounded.

They gave up, walked around the next granite boulder and saw the men.

There were two of them. Tall, thin, unshaven men.

Hard, lean men, pastoral workers, one young, one old. Dirt-poor by the look of them. Born poor, they would die poor. Born and bred on the land, hard workers when they had to work. Or, when they felt like it. Often itinerant, going from here to there. Looking for a job, anything they could pick up. Now and then in trouble with the law. Or, if not the law, with someone who picked a fight, often outside a pub, occasionally inside. Over money or women or honour. Or sheer desperation, it being a challenge, knocking another bloke's teeth out. Or, sheer boredom. Boots and all.

Hungry eyes, small, narrow and sunburnt eyes.

Always squinting. One was holding an old BSA rifle, .22 calibre, good for shooting small game, like rabbits. Takes a bullet with a high velocity but low impact. Lethal enough in the right hands, especially at short range.

They stopped, watching Becker and the boy. Who didn't like the look of them.

The young one had no upper front teeth. The other was leaning forward with his eyes. Not just staring, but poking, like a man with a stick. One stick, because the other eye was white. Flat white.

'G'day,' Becker said.

He walked up steadily, followed by the boy. The boy was carrying the Winchester, a .30 centre fire. More power, more mass, automatic loading. Whereas the BSA was single shot.

'G'day,' Becker said.

Walking slowly. The boy too, stamping his feet. Lifting them like a pony ready to run. They were only ten yards away now.

'Doin' a bit of shootin'?' the young one said, the one with the rifle. It was a bolt-action weapon. One shot and that was it. No time to reload, if there was trouble.

'Yeah,' Becker said. The boy was following to one side, trying to hide. A tall boy now, all of twelve. Off to high school next year.

'Get anything?'

It was a stupid question. Obviously, they hadn't got anything, Becker and the boy. Weren't carrying a bag.

'Nice day for huntin'.'

'Nice day for a walk,' Becker said.

'Live 'round here, do yers?'

'Not far away.'

'Seen yer before, have we?'

'I don't think so.'

'This your block?'

'Of land? No, not mine.'

Becker and the boy were slowly passing them, tentatively like two dogs circling. Hackles up, but not barking or snarling. Just sniffing. Not Nutty, however. He'd walked up to the older man, sniffed him, looked up at him. Whether to say hullo or to have a squiz at his blind eye was not clear. An inquisitive dog was Nutty.

'This your dog?'

'Yeah. Not a bad dog, useless for hunting.'

'What'd yer bring him for, then?'

'Likes to walk, and meet people.'

'Yeah?' the young one said. 'Friendly, eh?'

'You blokes after rabbits?'

'Nah, not rabbits.'

Becker walked on, respectfully. Trying not to look like he was afraid. Which he was. He and the boy had gone only a few more steps, when the young one said, a bit louder: 'Boar 'round 'ere.'

'A boar?'

'They reck'n.'

'A boar?'

'Yeah.'

'You're after a boar? With a twenty-two?'

'Only if we see him first, like.'

'You haven't seen him?'

'Nah, might be down in the scrub there,' One-Eye said.

'Which scrub?'

'Down the hill.'

There was scrub on the other side of the road. Probably a small and dribbly sort of creek in there too. You never knew. And you never knew where a boar might be. Becker had never seen a boar, but he'd heard about them. His father and a few other men from Kapooka had been out on a boar hunt once. They'd shot a boar, a real tusker, a big one. Had been attacking cattle. That was down Henty way too. They'd hung it up from a tree by its hind legs and stood beside it, holding their rifles and grinning, and taken a photo. They'd been using heavy-calibre weapons, all .30 or heavier. One of them had had a .358 magnum, big enough to bring down a deer. There were still a few in the hills, especially in the high country. The picture had been in the Wagga Wagga newspaper, on the front page, in fact. Everyone had said they'd been very brave. If a boar got you, it was good night. It could tear your guts out. Then start eating them. While you were still alive.

'If we see it, we'll give you a hoy,' Becker said.

'Or a shot,' the old one said.

They stood there, leaning to one side like dead trees.

Becker was not sure of the relationship. The young one looked to be in his late twenties, although he was so untidy he could have been older. Unshaven. Or, he'd a had a shave but at least two or three weeks ago. Not long enough yet to be called a beard. The older one could have been a brother, but much older. Perhaps old enough to be a father or uncle. If they belonged to the same family, it must have been one of those families where almost everyone as related by blood to everyone else. Husbands and wives. Like hillbillies.

One-Eye spat, then he said, 'Live down the road a bit.'

'Oh, yeah?'

'By the creek.'

Becker understood what he meant: Yerong Creek.

Becker walked on, well past now. He had to turn and look back. Stepping badly, almost stumbling. Knots of yellow grass.

'This side of Henty,' the young one said.

'Don't think I've ever been there,' Becker said.

He had been there, two or three times when young, with his father.

Henty was south of Kapooka. His father had been a sergeant at Kapooka, a training sergeant. Knocking recruits into shape, back in the time of Vietnam. Once they'd climbed The Rock and soared up and up and up. So high you could touch the roof of the World. There was nothing up there beyond the end of your fingers, except the sun. Which didn't like you looking at him in all his glory, half-blinding you. Then they'd run down again, slipping and sliding and laughing. It having been great fun climbing with your own Dad. And running down, slipping and sliding.

Now they were some distance, thirty or forty yards. But not far enough.

'You're the one, ain't yer?' One-Eye said.

Becker looked back, stumbling. 'What?'

'With the dog, that bit Billy.'

'Billy?'

'Ain't yer?'

Becker looked back again. The older man had raised the rifle.

Even with one eye, he was probably a good shot.

Fifty yards now.

'I don't know what you're talking about.'

'Nearly bit 'is leg off.'

'What?'

'That ain't the dog, but,' the young one said. 'Much bigger.'

'Give me the rifle,' Becker said to the boy.

'Are they gonna shoot us, Harry?'

'It'll be all right, son.'

That's what his father had said to young Becker, when he went off to Vietnam. And never came back, or came back but in a bag, after they'd lifted him up from the swamp. By helicopter.

'It'll be all right,' he said again.

Thinking: the Winchester carries seven rounds, but they'd already fired two. That left five. The BSA was a single shot, but a practised man, with more rounds between his fingers, could probably clear and load and fire at the rate of one each two seconds. He wished Chook would appear, shout, 'Armed police! Drop your weapon!' But she was in Canberra, probably telling a committee of pen-pushers that she had shot a man in self-defence. But each time they said, 'Did you deliberately taunt him into shooting at you?' she was sure to smile and say, 'What do you think?' Cheeky bitch. Probably get herself fired. No longer having the Commissioner's confidence. That's what had happened to Becker himself back in Sydney, years ago. And he'd never given any cheek.

One-Eye shouted, 'He ain't got a fuckin' leg now!'

Becker didn't reply. Felt he should, was too angry. They'd tried to get some of his cattle. Not many, maybe no more than six. They were the criminals, not him.

He recognised the old man's voice now. The one who'd called in the dark, 'Get out, quick!' as Becker and Bert had come on them in the dark, firing at them or above their heads. And had said, 'Billy get on the truck, quick!' Old Blue had got him by an ankle, filthy teeth digging in.

'Never be the friggin' same!'

Becker walked on. Quickly descending, down to the bush track. The Nissan was about half a mile back.

'Nothin' below his knee!'

He patted the boy, pushing him on, longer steps.

'An' you've got us comin' up to a court!'

'What's he talking about, Harry?'

'Keep walking, don't run.'

Approaching a fence now. Gnarled old fence. Away to one side was a dam, not in a creek but in a paddock in a corner. Gathered there four or five sheep, grey, dirty, neglected. A dead one lying to one side, belly open, black and rotten and stinking. Something having got at it.

'We'll get yer!' the young one called, the one with no front uppers. Probably couldn't afford a denture. Not even a dentist.

They were about a hundred yards away.

Becker ignored them, or tried to ignore them.

They made it to the fence. Pretty safe now, he thought.

Climbed through a Cyclone, not barbed. Out onto the track, stony. Drab and friendless. A few bushes along both sides. Something to get behind. But a man holding a Winchester had no right to hide. He had to stand, and maybe fight.

'We right now, Harry?'

'Yeah, we're fine.'

They dropped back to a rambling walk. Like out for a day's stroll in the English countryside. There was nothing English about it. It was wide open and dry and hot and lonely. A man could be killed out there and no-one would know, not even a man passing in a utility, who might notice something in a paddock. A pack of dogs, perhaps eating something and snapping at each other.

They walked on and on at an easy pace. Occasionally looking back.

Reached the Nissan, unlocked it, got in, panting. They had a bottle of water, cool to warm now. Becker let the boy drink first.

'Where's Nutty?' the boy said.

'Nutty? Oh, Jesus!'

Both got out. Called, but nothing happened. They'd not heard a shot, so he'd not been shot or shot at.

'Nutty!'

'Nutty!' Becker called. 'Here, boy!'

Again nothing. On the rise they could see the rocks, but not the two men.

'Nutty? Where are you, boy?'

Still nothing. Then a roaring or rushing or screeching through the bush.

It was Nutty, gasping, tongue out. Wildly looking back or sideways. Something else was coming after him, at high speed, head down, tusks out. A wild boar.

Becker shouted: 'Get back in the car!'

He grabbed the Winchester. The boar was coming straight along the dirt track. Fifty yards away, forty, thirty. Yanked the lever down, snapped it up, all in one second, raised the rifle, sighted. Fired, one-two. Not sure he hit. The boar faltered.

It was now only fifteen yards away.

Slowed, hesitated, squealing. Not possible to see any blood. Maybe the sharp shots had frightened it? No, it rushed again. Straight at Nutty. Terry had the door open, trying to get him in.

'Close the door, close the door!'

The boar turned, ran at Becker.

He fired again. Three shots gone out of five. Too late to dive into the Nissan.

Jumped back. The boar came again, plunging. Mouth open wide. Huge tusks.

Becker fired yet again. Couldn't miss at that distance—five yards, straight into its skull.

The animal folded, slid across the dirt and stones and twigs and dust.

It rolled, thrashing and kicking, then stopped at Becker's feet. Bristles scratched a leg. He didn't know what to do. If he moved, the boar might bite. A wild boar could snap a leg bone. Massive jaws they had, fairly dripping with savagery. Better to wait, see whether it was dead. He waited, scared to move. The animal spasmed, right down to its back legs. Slowly stiffened, stretched out. Dead? Becker didn't know. To make sure, he put the barrel to an ear, pulled the trigger. Straight into the brain. It was the last round.

He moved his left leg, then the other. Got back into the Nissan. Nutty got in too. Becker secured the rifle. Was about to put it on the back seat with Nutty, when he saw the two men. Coming though bushes. Through a few scrubby dollar gums. And a wretched orange bush. Must have been blown there from somewhere—the seed, that is. Or spat out by someone passing years ago, when there was rain, rain and still more rain.

Becker waited, an arm back, touching the rifle.

They came through the fence, bending or lifting corroded wires like men who'd been scrambling through fences all their lives.

They straightened up, looked at the boar.

Then came over. The animal was lying about three yards from the right front tyre. Took a good look, even bent down and peered, like experts. Then straightened up.

The young one said: 'Good shootin'.'

One-Eye nodded. 'At that pace.'

'Razorback,' the young one said. He didn't look too bright, but he knew pigs.

'What the difference?' Becker said.

'Razor's got a ridge along 'is back.'

'Backbone,' One-Eye said.

'Yeah, half-starved. Sticks up.'

'Always 'ungry. Got long legs, sharp snout too.'

'Dangerous, are they?'

'Yeah, they'll eat you.'

'Eat you, all right,' One-Eye said.

'Is that so?'

'A razor ain't no man's friend.'

'Yeah?'

'If y'stumble, like.'

'Glad I got hm.'

'Yeah, good shot all right.'

'Lucky 'e was goin' f'y'dog.'

'Yeah,' Becker said.

Nutty poked his nose over Becker's shoulder, panting, curious, happy. He'd beaten the wild boar to safety, escaped with his life. Becker was relaxing. He withdrew his arm, put both hands on the steering wheel. The young one was bent down. Hands on knees, peering in.

'Goin' home, are y's?'

'Yeah, enough for one day,'

'After that, eh?'

Give y' bit of a fright?' One-Eye said.

Becker pressed the starter. The engine roared. He revved it up a bit, perhaps unnecessarily. But it was a sort of statement: I'm a reasonable man, but I don't take any shit from anyone. Especially cattle duffers.

Young one stepped back, looking in the back.

'That a Winchester?'

Becker was slowly turning the Nissan to go back.

'Yeah, it is.'

'How many'd they 'old?'

Becker was going to say ten, but that was not true. The old one probably knew that.

'Seven,' he said, working the clutch, the vehicle edging on the sand and stones. A few yards forward, a few back.

One-Eye said: 'That'd be two left, wouldn' it?'

'Yeah, two.' Becker had turned vehicle around, inchingly. He let out the clutch. It began to move off slowly. The other walked with him.

'Come up Thursdee,' he said, 'we do.'

'What do you mean?'

'In court.'

'Yeah.'

'Wagga Magistrates?'

'Two-thirty, they reckon.'

'I'll see what I can do.'

The young one opened his mouth to say something, but the older one said: 'Come on, Keith. He'll keep.'

When they'd gone a mile or two, the boy said: 'Gee that was close, eh?'

'What was close?'

'They was gonna shoot us, wasn't they?'

'Weren't they, you mean.'

'Yeah, weren't they?'

'They're not that stupid.'

'Gee...' the boy said. He thought about things for a while. 'His name was Keith.'

'I heard that.'

Another mile or so.

'You're a really good shot, Harry.'

'Oh, I don't know about that.'

'You got the boar. How many shots did you fire?'

'I think it was five.'

'Five? Wow!'

He was grinning, at the bush and the road and the sky.

It was a high pale-blue sky. An Australian sky, a hot sky. Sign of bad times to come. It would be a hot Christmas, a hot summer, no prospect of rain. Not any rain that'd be of any use, anyway. 'When I grow up, I'm gonna kill a boar too!'

'Better not, son. They're very dangerous.'

'I'm gonna join the Army. Then I'll do lots of shooting.'

'Only if you have to. You can't go around in the Army, taking shots at things.'

'No, I suppose...'

They went on and on until they reached Uranquinty and joined the bitumen for Wagga. The boy said, 'You said "son".'

'What? Did I?'

'Yeah, you did twice.'

'Well, that's good, isn't it?'

'Terrific,' he said.

Chapter 22

FIRST, THEY CALLED on Muriel. She was surprised to see Becker. He'd not rung. On the other hand, not surprised; he nearly always called on her when in town. If he had to do business, if not at the bank, then at Tommy Thomkins' office. Even if Tommy were not in, he liked to see him. Not being there was not an impediment. The place had the air and the memories and the casual intimacy of Tommy. Plus the gentlemanliness. His granddaughter, Thomasina, was there most times, behind the counter. And her father, Tommy Junior, in the office. Old Tommy didn't come in all that much these days, being well past seventy. Obviously running down. But if you happened to run into him in the street, he always had a cheery wave and a doffing of the hat, even to a youngish bloke like Becker. And the old-fashioned courtesy, his essence. A man like Tommy was a treasure. You didn't have to buy anything from him, he was your best friend even if you didn't.

But first he called on Muriel, left the boy there.

Terry protested. Didn't want to be left with all of the women—as he called all females of all ages, even his big sister, who was fourteen, and his baby sister, who was four months. That's why he'd moved out to the farm for the school holidays. He couldn't live in a house with three women—four when

Nurse Thomas was there. Muriel understood that. A boy needed a father, just as a man needed a woman.

'I'll be a while,' Becker said, checking his watch.

'I want to come with you.'

'You stay here with your grandmother and big sister and baby sister. Talk to them. Say nice things to them. I'll be back later.'

'When?'

'About an hour. It's just gone eleven.'

'Ah, gee—'

'You stay here with Nanna and look after her. I'm sure there are lots of things you can do for her about the house.'

'Come on,' Muriel said, 'I have lumberjack for you.'

'Ah, all right.'

They walked out with him. Not a sound from the baby. She was sleeping, so he assumed. She was a good child, ate well, slept well. When you picked her up, gave her a cuddle, she smiled. Never cried, never suffered colic. When you gave her a tickle, she laughed. Raised her hands and tried to grip a finger or a thumb or your glasses, if you were wearing them.

Everyone cooed over her. Muriel had several photos already, in an album.

Little Roberta was a delight. Picture perfect already.

They followed him out to the Nissan. He was driving it these days. The BMW was not a farm vehicle. Becker had stopped worrying about protection. He'd taken the old Smith and Wesson out of its cradle under the driver's seat and stowed it in the glove box of the Nissan. Now and then he thought he should sell the BMW, but each time he did nothing about it. He would miss the BMW, but it was losing its presence, the presence of Evelyn Crowley. Not so strong now. Her perfume long gone. The sense of her being physically *there*, of being behind the wheel with him, occupying the same space, was fading. One day she would be filed away in a place where old memories go. Never to return.

They stood by the Nissan.

'Harry—' Muriel said. He knew what she was going to say. 'What are you doing about Christmas?'

Becker tried to think. He had no ideas at all.

'Nothing, I guess.'

'You could come here,' she said.

She was begging with her eyes, hands clasped, head to one side.

Muriel was ageing. Her neck was stringy now, the backs of her hands furrowed and spotty, her gentle face drawn, as if sketched. Not quite there, details left out. Her eyes smaller, her mouth a little pinched. Almost seventy now. A good grandmother. Good for Wendy, good too for the boy who would join her in high school next year. He would be living again with her. Terry had protested that he could take the bus each day from the farm and into Wagga. Becker was adamant. He didn't want the boy at the farm. It had been embarrassing, having him there when Chook was likely to drop in and stay the night. Becker didn't want the boy to see that—so soon after his mother had died.

'I don't want you to go to a lot of trouble,' Becker said.

'It's no trouble,' she said. There was a fracture of pain about her eyes. 'No trouble at all. You—' She flinched, not with pain but embarrassment. She had a little speech ready.

He waited, knowing.

'You are a good man, so kind to look after me. I mean with the money and the nurse and the responsibility. Little Robbie, dear Wendy and now—' She glanced at the boy. 'Now, a boy to look after too. It is an honour. I—' She fumbled. 'I know you are a good man, Harry. Robyn, she used to say it over and over. She was so lucky to be married to you. The best thing that had ever happened to her. She—' Another fumble with her bony hands, her guarded words and even her crinkly English eyes. 'She adored you, you know. Adored you.'

Becker knew that. Robyn had made that clear, embarrassingly clear.

'Oh—'

He didn't know what to say, could barely look at her. She was trying to get something off her chest.

'I want to thank you, Harry, for making her happy, if for only a short while. After what she'd had to go through.'

'It's all right,' he said. 'I—' He was going to say he had loved Robyn, but that would have been untrue. He had not loved her but had liked her, liked her enormously. Respected her. Would have done anything for her. He didn't feel all that bad about it now. He would always remember her. And her sweet words: 'Harry, dear, would it be okay if I —'

'So, if you would like…' Muriel said.

'Yes, sure, I'd like. We'd both like that, wouldn't we, son?'

'Yeah!'

'Hey, you must learn to say, "Yes." You'll never get into the Army if you say, "Yeah." Especially to an officer.'

He grinned. Exploded with impatient news.

'Nanna, guess what we did this morning?'

'I can't imagine.'

'We shot a boar!'

'You shot a boar? A real boar? A big pig?'

'In the bush.'

Becker began to get into the Nissan.

But Muriel remembered. 'Harry, what about your friend?'

'Which one is that?'

'The tall one, the girl from Canberra?'

'Stacey?'

'What would she be doing? For Christmas, I mean?'

He caught on. Muriel was in effect saying, 'I know you have a new lady friend. It's only four months since Robyn died, but that's understandable. Men have a need.'

'Oh, she's been banned.'

'Banned? Banned from Wagga?'

'Yes, confined to barracks.'

'For what she did in that hotel?'

'Yes, ordered never to show her face here again.'

'Oh, dear, why?'

'She's notorious. A fast gun, who goes around looking for fights.'

'That's what they say?'

Becker nodded. He hadn't heard from her for two weeks. 'What a pity. I thought she was such an interesting girl.'

'She is, in more ways than one.'

He got into the vehicle, looked out. Muriel was hanging on, another question in her eyes.

'And Harry, I have been wondering. Is she really a woman? I mean, people say such awful things. That she is a man who, you know, likes to dress up.'

'Oh, she's a woman, but not quite all there.'

'Not quite all— Oh, dear.'

'Maybe she'll tell you all about it one day.'

'Oh, yes, well, Harry, it is so nice of you to call.'

'I'll be back in an hour.'

'I'll have tea for you.'

He drove away.

'Now, my boy,' she said, 'you must tell me all about the boar.'

Becker went to the retirement village. It was more than that. Most residents could look after themselves, but there was a residential block for those who could not. They were in care. Some were demented, but his mother was not.

She was afraid. He went into the office, pushed a bell. The manager came out.

'Ah, Mr Becker! How may I be of assistance?'

'How is she?'

'She?'

'My mother.'

'Your mother?'

'Yes, my mother.'

'How is your mother? Oh, yes, we—'

The manager was like that. He never got to the point, if he could avoid it.

An evasive sort of chap in a blue serge suit. A carnation buttonhole too. He looked more like a funeral director than the manager of a retirement village, Anglican. Never one to be pinned down. Strictly correct in all he did, very self-important, officious at times. He'd been born for a job like this, a man of purpose. He tended to declaim.

'Oh, let me see? Mrs Becker? Iris Becker? Yes! I did have a report only yesterday.'

He paused significantly. Becker waited, leaning on his knuckles on the counter. Sometimes he felt like hitting this clown.

'A report?'

'Not actually a written report, nor anything one would describe as official or disturbing, you understand? But it was intimated that—' The manager's eyes floated to the ceiling. From it hung Christmas decorations. It was a week to go. He was a great one for observances.

'Intimated?'

'Yes, indeed.' He sang it. No-one could do 'indeed' better than he. Not even Pavarotti. It had an operatic thrill to it. There was something disturbingly operatic about the manager. He sang in the local musical society. Recently they had put on *I Pagliacci*. He played Canio the clown, and brought the house down, his singing was so bad. 'Now, what was it? Oh yes!' His voice dropped a register. Face went serious, seriously red. Perhaps embarrassed. It was going to be one of those things gentlemen usually didn't mention.

'What is?'

'Well, she has become... How should I put it?'

'Incapable?'

'Not only incapable, but—'

'But, what?'

'Incontinent.'

'You mean she pisses her pants?'

'What? Oh, yes, but we have been able to cope with that for some time. With pads, as you might know, but—'

'But?'

'She has become, how shall I put it? She has become loose with her bowels.'

'She's shitting herself too?'

'If you must put it so crudely, yes. I have had several complaints from the staff. She, it seems, is unaware.'

'In her sleep, you mean?'

'Oh, no, while going to the bathroom. Or, while dressing. I mean, we do our best. We have carers. They understand that she is incapable of controlling—'

'You want to get rid of her?'

'Oh, no, spare the thought. No, no—'

'You want to put her into intensive care?'

'Not intensive, no, no. She is not physically ill, you know.'

'She's demented, isn't she? She does not know what she is doing? Like a baby? That's it, isn't it? She's gone right back?'

'Yes,' the manager said. 'I am *afraid* so.' Leaned forward, giving Becker the benefit of his eyes. He had very serious eyes, like a rooster about to peck. 'There are special places for such cases,' he said.

'You want to get rid of her?'

'Oh, no, no! We would never put it that way. Get rid of? Oh, God forbid that the church would wish to get rid of anyone. The way they *suffer*.'

The manager was a great user of emphasis.

Becker had feared this would happen. That she would be both mentally and physically incapable. His mother would be demented. He might well fear the same fate for himself.

'What do you want me to do?'

'Ah, yes, we *are* investigating the possibility of another place.'

'You mean away from here?'

'*If* we can find one.'

'Is there one in Wagga?'

'Not in a retirement village.'

'You want to put her in a place for the demented?'

'Oh, well—' He shrugged. 'It may mean more than that.'

'How much more?'

'Oh, you see there are certain places, where, if one becomes too far advanced—'

'What sort of places?'

'Hospices.' He almost shouted it.

'Hospices? Places where they go to die?'

'Not necessarily—'

'Is there one in Wagga?'

'There is Mary Potter. They accept those who need palliative care.'

'Isn't that a Catholic place?'

'It is.'

'She would never go there. She hates Catholics. At the sight of a nun, she'd start screaming.'

The manager stiffened. 'It's either the Catholics or no-one, I'm afraid. In Wagga, that is.'

'What are the chances there?'

'We could *try* for you.' He made trying sound like constipation.

'No, thanks. I'll do it myself. You want to get rid of her, don't you?'

The manager was startled. He was easily startled, readily shocked. It was all an act, of course. He was like someone out of Dickens, portly and puffy and self-important. Dickens would have loved him. Would have grabbed him by the neck and shoved him into a novel, kicking and screaming.

'I would not put it so *crudely*.'

'That's it, isn't it? She's an embarrassment? No-one wants to pick up her shit?'

'I would not put *that* so crudely.'

'Well, it is crude, isn't it? She's not sixty-five yet and yet she is demented. Lost control. Diminished but not dead. We can't bury her yet, can we? Or send her to the flames. What is it? Death? You can't accept death?'

'Of course, we accept death. We have residents passing on all the time.'

'But the undertakers look after them then, don't they? But here, they are still living. It's repulsive, isn't it?'

The manager was outraged. 'The church does all it can!'

'That's not enough, is it?'

'I beg your pardon?'

'You can't touch them. Can you?'

The manager threw himself up to his full height but turned slightly side on, looking back across a shoulder. Like a man threatened by a savage dog.

'There comes a time, my dear Mr Becker, when—'

Becker slammed a fist on the counter. 'Shut up! Just shut up!'

The manager hopped back, as if smitten by God.

'I'll take her,' Becker said.

'You'll take her? Take your mother? To your home? Where is it? A farm, I believe?'

'If need be, I'll look after her. Somehow, I will—' He didn't know what to say.

Becker stood, head down, knuckles white.

'Mr Crossley, my mother is mad, but she is my mother. I came out of her, like a fruit out of a flower forty years ago. I'll try the Catholics, but if she won't let the good sisters wipe her arse for her, I'll take her home. I'll look after her. I'll get someone, a retired nurse, or—'

He looked up, said nothing for a few seconds. Then gave up.

'Good day to you,' he said. And walked out.

He drove into town, found a spot in Baylis Street and went into the Hovell. Bruce was behind the counter. He was still feeling angry. Aged care, he felt, was not about care but about money. Just a business like any other business. If the aged and the incapable of any age become an embarrassment, turn them out. Get someone else. Get their money.

'Give me a Jack,' he said.

'With ice?'

'Yeah, with ice.'

Bruce got him a Jack Daniels. Becker said nothing, glancing around. He'd not been here since the shooting, two weeks ago. Everything looked normal. He looked at the wall, against which Chook had blasted Shaft with three fatal shots, *bang, bang, bang*! So fast that those present still swore they heard only one shot. He glanced around, saw nothing. No blood, anyway. Then, something caught his gaze. A framed array on the wall behind him— photographs cut from a recent newspaper. Shots of the hotel and the interior of this very bar. There was a screaming headline: *Shootout in Wagga Hotspot. Dozens flee for lives. Excusive report by—*

Becker peered closer.

'*Deloraine Dudley*,' it read.

Hell, he thought. That was quick. She was on the spot. He'd not seen her. Must have rushed in with the cops and the ambos. The newspaper office was only a few doors along the street. He looked back at Bruce. 'You told her all about it?'

'She got a scoop, she said. It was in all the papers.'

The gorgeous Miss Dudley had made it. Had scored a job on the *Bulletin*, even before she'd completed her degree course.

'I'll have another Jack,' he said, then corrected it. 'No, I'll have a chaser.'

'Hahn?'

Becker nodded.

When he came back, Bruce spoke quietly, intimately. 'We haven't seen Stacey for a while,' he said.

'No, and you won't.'

Bruce was disappointed. You could see it in his face. Chook used to stay at the Hovell when in town. Quite a figure, her height and presence. She was a feature, leaning on the bar sipping Jack. Or sprawled in a corner, a boot up on a chair, all by herself, watching. Her ears wide open. Listening, always listening. She was a Federal cop, everyone knew it. The management made sure they knew it. No-one dared throw a punch when she was watching, listening. Filing it all away for future reference.

'No,' Becker said. 'She's been forbidden to put a foot in Wagga again.'

'Forbidden?'

'Because of her outrageous behaviour.'

'In this bar?'

Becker nodded.

Bruce was going to protest, but did not. He was not the protesting kind. 'I'm sorry.'

He went away, but came back.

'If you see her, please tell her I've done it.'

'Done what?'

Becker knew what he meant. But he was still angry. Not in the mood for being understanding or sympathetic.

'Had the operation.'

'Oh, yeah.'

Becker was still regarding the photographic array.

Chook had stood at this very spot where he now stood. Leaning back against the bar, elbows on the counter. Arms out, a whiskey in one hand, the other holding open her jacket to show the Glock. And a madman was confronting her, holding a sawn-off shotgun, and cringing. And trying not to blink. Knowing that if he blinked, he'd be dead. She'd been counting his blinks, timing them. They were coming faster each time. Just one more blink and he'd not be able to see. For at least half a second.

Shafter had to blink. He was a blinky sort of creature. Always had been, even as a kid. Knew she knew he had to blink. He'd have to fire before the next blink. He could feel one coming. Couldn't stop it. Had to raise the gun now, or fire blind. But too late. It was always too late. Alive one second, fresh meat the next.

Chook had turned and said: 'I'll have another Jack, Bruce.'

Bruce lowered his voice. A couple of blokes in firefighters' boots were clumping in, the barroom door swinging. He didn't want the whole town to know.

'If you see her,' he said, 'tell her I'm a girl.'

'What do you mean, You're a girl?'

'I had the operation.'

'What operation?'

Bruce was disappointed. He'd expected sympathy and understanding.

At last Becker caught on. Or, he thought he did.

'You mean a change?'

Bruce nodded significantly. Normally, he didn't make significant looks. He wasn't camp or queer. But he was a new man. Or, a new woman.

'Got a new name?'

'Bettina,' Bruce said.

'Bettina?'

'My mother's second name.'

'You're not wearing a dress.'

'I—I'm going to do it. I will do it,' Bruce said. 'I'm still trying to get used to it.'

'Bettina, eh?'

'Yes, what do you think?'

Becker finished the beer.

'If she rings, I'll tell her.'

He went to the police station and asked to see Jack Jackson. Becker had to wait a while, thinking about it. Life and lifelessness.

Jackson came out. 'You wanted to see me?'

'Yeah, about those two blokes.'

Jackson recollected. 'Arrested for trying to nick your cattle?'

'I've decided to drop all charges.'

Jackson was surprised. 'You're dropping charges?'

'I don't want to proceed.'

'You don't want to give evidence against them?'

'That's right.'

Jackson thought about it. 'Any reason?'

'That kid has suffered enough. Without a leg, I mean.'

'You've seen him?'

'No, but I can imagine.'

Jackson didn't smile much, never did. A taciturn man, but a good man.

'Thanks for coming in,' he said.

Becker turned to leave, but noticed three men standing to one side, talking. A few minutes ago, they'd come out of an office, at least two had. The third was lingering, holding open the door. Or, about to close the door.

Yeah, yeah, the man was saying. A man you'd be struggling to describe. Neither young nor old, no remarkable features, except for his smile. It was a smug sort of smile, impish to a degree. Secretive and yet matey when it had to be. Not the sort of man you'd trust at first sight, although you'd not be sure why.

Becker said to Jackson: 'Who's that bloke?'

'The one holding the door?'

'I've seen him somewhere.'

'You don't remember him? He interviewed you in hospital. After the explosion.'

'So he did. I didn't catch his name.'

'Mick Quinn, Detective Inspector.'

'Not Quinlan?'

'No, why?'

'Any relation to Father Quinlan?'

'Not as far as I know.'

The inspector caught him watching. He smiled.

'Got something on your mind?' Jackson said.

'Ah, it doesn't matter.'

Chapter 23

BECKER WALKED INTO the *Bulletin* office and asked to see the editor. The woman behind the front counter seemed to be surprised, even apprehensive. She paused, thought about him, then said, 'Do you have an appointment?' He shook his head. 'Is it about advertising?' He shook his head. 'Some news item?'

'No,' he said.

'About an account?' No, again. 'He's usually very busy,' she said.

'I suppose he is.'

'Is it a complaint of some sort?'

'You could say that.'

'Perhaps you should put in writing,' she began to say. But he'd begun to move towards the door leading to the editorial rooms. She tried to block his way, but he reached for the handle, turned it. The door opened. The woman stepped back, offended. Opened her mouth to protest, but said nothing more. She knew who he was. Knew that Becker and Anastacia Babchuk were friends. More than just friends, some said.

He walked in, puzzled. Didn't know which way to the editor's office.

All he saw was a door marked Chief of Staff. People were working, heads down at computer screens. Telephones were ringing. There was an ambient vibration to the building. He could not so much hear it as feel it, a steady rum, as if a big machine somewhere at the back was working. The press was rolling. *The Riverina Bulletin* was a daily. It hit the streets early in the afternoon, each day except Sunday. It was one of the big provincials, still independent. Owned by local people, old families, farming families. Who went a long way back.

Staff glanced up at him.

Two men were sitting at a long table at the back. One thought he recognised Becker. Or, if not recognised him by name, then recognised the look on his face.

'Can I help you?'

The front office woman was watching from the door.

'He wants to see Phil,' she said. In a loud whisper, the way women do when they want to make a point without making a fuss.

The man rose, perhaps to show Becker the way. Held out a hand in greeting.

'Frank Penny,' he said.

Becker ignored him. 'The editor?' he said.

'Chief of staff. You want to see Phil? Phil McNevin?'

'Is that his name?'

'And your name?'

'Becker.'

'You mean Harry Becker?'

Becker didn't bother to answer. He was still angry.

Penny led him in long, loping strides to a door. It was in a glass wall, possibly so that the staff could be seen at a glance. He knocked. Then opened the door, also glass.

'Excuse me, Phil—' he said.

An oldish man looked up.

He had streaks of grey but was young in the sense that he was not old or bald. Becker thought him about sixty, a healthy sixty. His face was pink and perfectly shaven. Worked with his sleeves half rolled up. That is, to the elbows. He didn't wear an eyeshade, as in the old movies, but wore mauve-tinted glasses. The overhead light was bright. This man was not merely the editor; he was the managing editor. The name on his glass door said so in respectable gold. Becker knew very little about him. Only that he was related to the McNevin family, which seemed to own half of Wagga Wagga. Or, if they didn't, they'd like you think they did.

'This is Mr Becker.'

'Becker?'

'Harry Becker,' he said.

The editor stood up, reached out a manicured hand. They shook.

'Mr Becker? What can I do for you?'

'I have a complaint.'

'Have a seat, please. A complaint, eh? Here at the *Bulletin* we welcome complaints. That way we get to know our people better.'

Becker bristled. 'Your people?'

'Our readers.'

'I see.' Becker sat.

It was a very old swivel chair with a leather seat and leather arms. He'd last seen a chair like that in a Hollywood movie. He thought Humphrey Bogart had been sitting in it. The movie was about newspaper ethics, but it was a long time ago. When newspapers had ethics. Now, as far as Becker could see, they had accountants instead.

'What is your complaint?'

Becker took his time answering. 'You want to get somebody killed?'

McNevin was stunned.

'Who do you mean?'

'A woman.'

'What woman?'

'Anastacia Babchuk.'

McNevin almost jumped. He was seated but he jumped, not so much upwards as backwards. His chair hit a filing cabinet.

'Babchuk? What do you mean?'

'Every time you refer to her in your paper, you can't help slipping in that same old corny line, can you? The fastest gun in the west.'

'Well—'

'As if you don't want the world to forget.'

McNevin flinched. 'Well, Mr Becker, that's how she is known.'

'That's how she is known, because you won't let your readers forget.'

'Yes, well, that's how it is. People come to be known by some newsworthy event. Don Bradman is always referred to as The Don, because he was a genius with the bat. Still holds the record for the highest score in a—'

'Stop making bloody excuses!'

McNevin was startled. 'What?'

'There's a display on a wall in the front bar of the Hovell Hotel. It's full of your reports and photos of her. One of your staff, a young lady named Deloraine Duffy, wrote much of it.'

'She was there that day, that day when the gunfight occurred. She was first journalist in.'

'And your camera man wasn't far behind her.'

'Of course. Naturally, we wanted pictures.'

'And there's a follow-up story a few days later, a purported interview with Anastacia. It's just bits of history and gossip about her. It's a beat up, isn't it? It even refers to the day that girl rode with Anastacia on her Harley to a party at my place. The day my house blew up. My wife died in that blast.'

McNevin bowed his head, shook it in a sort of genuine regret. As though this was one of those little problems journalists have to deal with every day. You could never please every reader.

'I'm sorry,' he said.

'Anastacia has never talked to any journalist about that event at the Hovell.'

McNevin shrugged. 'Yes, well—'

'You invent news, don't you?'

'Invent? Look, we have to run with whatever we've got.' McNevin picked up a little courage. 'I mean, if she would give us a story, a personal interview, any misunderstandings could be sorted out. I mean, for Christ's sake, that woman is news. She walks around this town as though she's Wyatt Earp. They say she carries a weapon under her jacket.'

'Uniformed police walk around this town with Glocks swinging from their hips. Nobody complains about that.'

'Yes, but they are police. Everyone knows that. But she is not in uniform.'

'She's Federal. They don't wear uniforms.'

'Yes, but everyone talks about her. She is news, whatever she does.'

'You want her dead? That'd be news, wouldn't it?'

McNevin flinched again. He knew what Becker was getting at.

'Dead? No, no, Christ no, of course not.'

'Every boozer in the front bar at the Hovell reads it. Tourists want to know about her. You know what that could lead to?'

McNevin did know. 'Ah, now, look, we're not responsible for what the Hovell puts up.'

'You are responsible for what you publish.'

'Yes, but—'

'You want her dead?'

'God, no!'

'Well, that's what's going to happen one day, isn't it? Some drunk is going to challenge her.'

'Pull a gun on her, you mean?'

'Why not?'

'Good God, it's not as bad as that. Wagga is a quiet town.'

'Which could do with a bit of livening it up? Is that what you want?'

McNevin had no answer.

'If that happens you will be responsible.'

'No, no, look—'

'And I will see to it that you are closed down.'

'What?'

'For inciting murder.'

'What? You can't do that.'

Becker stood up. 'Can't I?'

He was bluffing but it was working.

He too was a mystery in the Wagga Wagga district. A former cop who'd had to get out of Sydney, after things went bad. A man who'd bought a beautiful farm with a pile of money he could not explain. Or, didn't want to explain. A man who didn't have to work. A man who, it was rumoured, slept with the formidable Anastacia Babchuk. A woman who could kill you faster than you could blink.

That's what had happened in the Hovell bar, so it was said. When the Police had interviewed her afterwards, they'd asked how she knew that Shafter was going to pull the trigger. She'd replied: I saw that he'd have to blink. He had sore eyes. And he'd known that if he did blink, she'd kill him. So, he had to kill her before he had to blink. But she had known that he had known that. Had known when he'd made the decision. And had shot him, three times. Spun him a round, making the shotgun in his hands go off, bringing down ceiling plaster. Thrown him back against a wall, everyone screaming. People often said there had to a movie. They wanted a replay, even if it were only a movie. If no movie, no-one would know why it had all been about. Movies brought truth to the unknowable.

Becker gave it to him as he saw it.

'As a result of the legend you have built up, she cannot return to this town. She is banned by her superiors in Canberra. She likes it here. I think she'd like to live here, but you—'

McNevin jumped to his feet.

'Is that true? She wants to live here? Permanently? But her bosses in Canberra won't let her? Because they're afraid someone'll kill her? Can I quote you on that?'

Becker had had enough.

'Shut up!'

'What?'

'Just shut up, will you?'

McNevin didn't seem to hear him.

Becker was leaving, he had no more to say.

He went to the glass door, which was open. The chatter and the tapping and phone calls and even the ringing in the newsroom, had stopped. Only the repressed and inaudible rumbling of the press went on and on. As though some great machine were thinking about it.

McNevin followed him out.

'I'm sorry,' he said.

'You're an idiot.'

Becker walked through the newsroom. Everything in the place seemed to have stopped.

'I'm sorry,' McNevin said, still on his heels. 'I wonder—'

'Forget it.'

'I wonder if we could have a chat sometime. I know how you feel. We have to print what we have and to hell with the consequences. Journalism is like that. We must have stories, every day. If we don't, they don't buy our papers.'

The woman who'd admitted him was still holding the door. As he approached, she stepped back, pulled in her stomach. She was a stout woman, blond with hair piled high. Pearl earrings and granny glasses on her nose. Smelt of face cream or something perhaps more personal.

When Evelyn Crowley had invited him in to talk about doing a little job for her, he'd noticed no perfume but almond oil. Shampoo, he had thought. This woman, who looked old enough to be Evelyn's mother smelt the same way. But there was no mystery about her. She was just a functionary holding open a door. A bit-player in a movie that never was.

One of the rumours about Becker was that he'd been mixed up in crooked dealings at Kings Cross in Sydney. A lot of dirty money had changed hands. That's why he'd been kicked out of the State force. He did have a lot of money, which had come from Evelyn. Her money was just as dirty. Mafia money.

'Forget it,' Becker said.

McNevin followed him onto the street.

'Honestly, we do not want to imperil anyone, especially someone who is well known and respected in the district. And who everyone admires. Miss Babchuk—'

Becker turned on him. People were coming and going. Some glanced at them. Especially at Becker. Everyone in town knew of him. He was so well known, because he was not known at all. A permanent stranger.

'Just shut up. Do not talk about Chook as if she's one of your—'

He realised his mistake. Her nickname was not well known. He was the only one who used it. People in the Federal Police knew it, but never used it to her face. She was likely to hit them if they did. But, for some reason, she didn't hit Becker. They seemed to need each other.

'Chook? Is that what you call her?'

McNevin tried to laugh. To make light of it. His mouth was open, but the sound got swallowed. He was on dangerous ground, he knew.

'What do you want, McNevin?'

'What?'

'Just tell me.'

'Do you want some drunken arsehole with a shotgun or a handgun or whatever to challenger her? Out here on Baylis Street? Everyone gathered 'round? Watching? Scared but hooked?'

'Of course not!'

'You want her to kill someone?'

'No, no!'

'That'd make a great story, wouldn't it? Or, maybe you'd prefer some freak with a grudge to shoot her in the back? While she's licking an ice cream or chatting to some kids in the park?'

'My God, no!'

'Well, that's what might happen if you go on calling her the fastest gun in the fucking west. And running her face in your pathetic little country rag.'

McNevin swallowed. 'That's the last thing we want.'

'You don't want it? But you hope it happens? Is that it?'

'What? Hell, no!'

'Have you ever taken a bullet?'

'A bullet? From a gun? God, no, never.'

'It hurts, mate. It frigging hurts.'

'What?'

'That'd give you something to write about.'

'Write about?'

Becker made to leave, but came back.

'Have you ever been to Vietnam?' The editor did not answer. 'My father died there.'

'I know.'

'What did you say?'

'I know he died there.'

'How do you know?'

'I was in Vietnam.'

'You were in Vietnam? Doing what?'

'Shooting film.'

'Shooting film? Is that all you did?'

McNevin did not answer.

'Be careful, mate. You kill her, there will be consequences. Understand?'

Chapter 24

BECKER FORGOT THE boy. He was half way home, when he remembered. He should have gone back, but he didn't. He'd phone when he got home. When he did arrive, he found Bert sitting on the front verandah, holding his old Hollis. Sitting beside him were Nutty and his new dog, Blue. A cattle dog about the same age as Nutty, who was three, more or less. They called him Blue Two, who got on well with Nutty. Being much younger than the original Blue, he was more active. Liked to go for a run now and then. They tended to sniff around together. Like good friends.

A cattle dog is, by nature and breeding, not a hunting dog. It is completely attached to its human owner. Never strays and never plays. It stands guard and, if it doesn't have cattle to round up, it simply sleeps at its master's feet or under a cart or sulky or utility or any other sort of vehicle it can find on the long drives across the plains of New South Wales. Or simply from farm to farm, or paddock to paddock. It was said that one man and a dog could run a spread of twenty-thousand acres. The man was lucky. The dog was happy to do all the work.

On the other chair sat a young woman.

She rose as Becker pulled up, got out. Nutty ran to him, wagging his tail. Blue Two simply sat up, looked hard. Then settled down again.

'Angelina?' he said.

'Yes,' she said, rising. 'It has been so peaceful to sit here. I have been talking with Mr Henshee.'

'Henschke,' he said.

'Oh, yes, Hensh-kee. We met when I was staying here. And his new dog. He is such a good dog. We looked at the cattle. They looked at him and they put their heads down, but he didn't attack them.'

'How long have you been here?'

'Oh, an hour I think.'

'I'm sorry that—'

'Oh, no, no. It is a pleasure. I have— I have returned—'

She picked up a large, soft parcel, wrapped only in tissue paper. Bound with long, thin, pink tape, tied with a bow, a large red bow, an overflowing bow. A spidery sort of bow. Pretty pink.

'Robyn's clothes?'

'*Si*, I mean yes. You were so kind to allow me to wear them. When I arrived with nothing. Only my simple white dress and my flat shoes and my bag. I had to grab it and run, you know. It was terrifying, when I saw Father Quin—Quinlan—' She stumbled over the name. 'Here I am. Thank you for looking after me. I thought I would die when I arrived. I thought they would kill me. Nothing would stop them. But you and Anastacia—'

'It was a pleasure to have you.'

She chuckled. 'When I told *Mamma* I had been staying with a man for five days, she was horrified!'

'Really? What did she say?'

Angelina blushed, put a hand to her face.

'Oh, I could not tell you!'

He smiled. She was funny in her embarrassment.

'Tell me in Italian.'

'Oh, no, no, no!'

'I will not understand it.'

'Oh, no, I would be too— No, I could not.'

He waited. It was delightful to see. A good, simple, Catholic girl. No sex before marriage. Evelyn had been like that, once upon a time. When she'd been young and gorgeous and easy pickings for a smart-talking lawyer determined to screw her. So modest and trusting, not knowing what she was walking into. She had killed him, when he'd told her he was not going to marry her, even though she was carrying his child. This young woman, Angelina—he was not sure of her age—she too was perfectly pure. Or, was she? At that meeting, the meeting she'd called at the house of wisteria and pretty tiles, she had made it clear. She was now the boss. Everyone present had known what that meant. They had directly or indirectly killed her sister. Angelo Cosco was dead. His daughter, the surviving daughter, was now the boss. There would be no argument. Not if you didn't want the letter, which was not a letter, to be published.

'Thank you for coming, Angelina.'

'Oh, there is something—'

She dived down, lifted another parcel, gift-wrapped.

'What is it?'

'For Christmas, for you. For being good to me.'

'A bottle?'

'I didn't know what to give you. I thought you have everything. It is Chianti.'

'You are kind.'

She trembled like a schoolgirl. Then she did it. She stepped forward, hands up but not quite touching his shoulders, and kissed him on a cheek. Like she had done in the motel, at the door. When he'd given her the half-pound of coke, to trap that smelly little cop, Barry Barnes, to make him talk. She'd been instructed to embrace him, press herself into him. So that he would smell of her and of her perfume, if anyone sniffed him. To make it look like a romance, when it had been anything but.

'*Gracie amico mio.*'

For a moment, she hesitated, standing very close.

She smelled good, not gorgeous or anything like that. He detected no perfume except that of her lipstick and perhaps face cream lightly applied. Nothing gaudy about her. It was the honest smell of a clean woman, plus another. The smell of new clothes. Even the smell of new shoes, warm in the sun. She was newly outfitted, in a simple brown suit with cream blouse, collar points elevated proudly. The blouse was slightly open. Indeed, the top button was undone. Between her breasts, he saw the cross.

She waited.

It was a clear invitation from a shy Italian girl.

If you are interested, she seemed to be saying, you only have to kiss me.

She was proposing in a roundabout way. Obviously, she wanted to be attached to him, possibly married to him, a former policeman. Might have thought he was attached to the Federal Police. They had special powers, like the *Carabinieri*. They had crushed the Mafia in Sicily. Now they were on top of the Honoured Society back home in Calabria. At least, everyone thought so.

He did nothing. He could not.

It was bad enough, sleeping with Chook. It being only four months, getting on for five, since Robyn's death. For which, in a roundabout way, he knew he was responsible. If he hadn't been a bad man, it would not have happened. No-one would have wanted to kill him. Not a nobody like him.

She stepped back.

'I told Mamma *va tutto bene*. Everything was proper. Is that the right word? Proper? No bad behaviour by anyone. Anyway, there was another woman present. I said, "*Una accompagnatrice*." "Ah," she said, "*una donna?*" "No,"

I said, "*una carabiniera*." "*Una carabiniera?*" she exclaimed. "You slept with a *carabiniera?*" "No, no," I said, "I didn't sleep with anyone." "So, who was the *carabiniera?*" she asked. "*Signore* Lemon Groves," I said. "Ah, yes," she said, "Lemon Grove."' They all knew about *Signore* Lemon Groves. Angelina was now the *capo*, or *capa*. She had all of Angelo's money and was using Mr Groves to enforce her will. A killer who could visit you in your sleep. There was nothing you could do about it. Mr Groves was a policeman, who did private jobs.

She smiled and shrugged and pulled an apologetic face.

'I did the wrong thing, you think?'

He avoided the question. 'So, you are now the boss, eh?'

'*La capa*? Oh, no, I do not wish to be that kind of boss. I would like to be the leader of the Italian community in Griffith. Show them the old ways are finished.' She looked at her watch. 'Oh, I must go. Silvano will be worried.'

'He is still living with you? In the house? In Yoogali?'

'Oh, yes, and *Mamma* too and Patrizia.'

'Who is Patrizia?'

'Oh, Patrizia, she is an old friend. We have had her all my life. She does the cooking and the cleaning.'

'A retainer?'

'Oh, she is more like a member of the family.'

'Good.'

'So—' she said, turning to Bert.

The old man had said not one word since Becker had arrived, but he nodded. Doing nothing else but sitting there, holding his shotgun. Perhaps he thought he was protecting her. He and two dogs. Probably made him feel good. Sitting with a gentle young woman and thinking perhaps of some moment years ago, when he was young, when...

'I am so happy to meet you again, Mr Hensh-kee.'

Bert almost smiled. They stepped off the verandah, walked to the gate.

'How is Silvano?' he asked.

'Oh, he is fine. He is quite well, although he finds things strange.'

'Strange, in his own home?'

'Yes, but he has always been a little shaky. Nervous, but willing to please. Desperate to please, I think. He was so frightened of *Papà*, you know.'

'No sign of a breakdown?'

'No, not at all. He does not recall anything.'

'Nothing at all?'

'Oh, he remembers *Mamma* and Uncle Romero and Daniella. He was in love with Daniella, you know. You met her.'

'Yes, in the street.'

'She comes and talks to him. They even went to a movie together. He wants to hold her hand, but she is his cousin.'

'It's not allowed in Italian families? To kiss a cousin?'

'Oh, it is allowed. But you must have permission first.'

'From the girl?'

'From her family, especially her father.'

'And, would they permit it?'

'No, no, I fear not, not with Silvano.'

She shook her head. Sorrowfully, Becker thought. No girl would ever be allowed to marry Silvano Cosco. He was too much an unknown factor.

They had reached the gate. He opened it for her.

Outside was a long, low Alfa Rome, possibly her father's car. Possibly brand-new. It looked expensive, but he remembered—Angelina Cosco was now a rich woman. The head of the family, her brother being deemed incapable. Not insane, but incapable.

'At Christmas?' she asked. 'Will you be with your family?'

'My family?' He was going to say he had no family. But he remembered: 'Yes, with my daughter and her grandmother and big sister and big brother.'

'Oh, yes—' She paused, carefully choosing her words. 'And Anastacia? Will she be here?'

'Anastacia has been confined to barracks.'

'Barracks?'

'She must stay in Canberra.'

'Oh? She has offended some people?'

'Too many, it seems.'

She thought about it. 'Anastacia is very brave, is she not?'

'Too brave for some people.'

'*Si, io comprendo.*'

He was surprised. Evelyn had said exactly the same words, when she'd heard that people in Melbourne were killing the whole Scarafini family. Because they knew too much. Talked too much. And Alfredo had told her on the phone that she had to get out of Canberra now. *Io comprendo*, she had said. She and Becker had made a run for it, but had failed.

He opened a door of the Alfa Romeo. Angelina got in, tucking under her skirt—the way Evelyn had done as she'd got into a taxi outside the National Library in Canberra. Angelina didn't have Evelyn's long, dreamy legs. But she smiled in a long, dreamy way.

'Goodbye, Harry.' She pressed the ignition, but hesitated. Something impish came over her. 'Do you wish to know what *Mamma* said?'

'I'm sure you are dying to tell me.'

'*Ti ha violato?*'

He guessed what it meant. Something about violation. 'What if I had?'

'You would have to marry me.'

She laughed, more a giggle than a laugh. And blushed.

Watching her drive away towards the west and into the lengthening distance, he thought: Yes, there were always consequences. If you did *this*, there would be consequences. If you do *that*, there would be other consequences. Everyone knew how to behave. If you didn't, it was too late to learn.

He wouldn't mind marrying Angelina in due course.

When things became clearer with Anastacia. He seemed to have drifted into a kind of affair with Chook. Didn't know how she would react if he fell for the Italian girl. He'd fallen for Evelyn Crowley, another Italian girl, and look what that had got him. People who wanted to kill him. He'd had to admit it to himself that he stuck with Chook because she was fearsome. But she was protective. The whole world knew she would kill. She had shown in the Hovell pub that she could kill and get away with it. Would she kill him? If she thought he'd crossed her? Dumped her?

Angelina was alluring, almost as alluring as Evelyn had been, but a lot more honest. Virginal in every way. Naïve, perhaps. But doomed.

The Mafia was not going to accept her.

No way.

Chapter 25

CHOOK ARRIVED ABOUT nine o'clock on Christmas night. That is, not on Christmas Eve. She missed that. She rang about six on the 25th of December and said, 'What are you doing?'

'Nothing much,' he'd said. 'Sleeping off Christmas lunch.'

'Have you eaten yet?' she'd asked.

'Eaten? I don't think I could eat a thing. Muriel was very generous. She'd been cooking for days.'

'Good lunch?'

'Yeah, good.'

'Lots of presents?'

'Yeah, I gave Terry an air rifle.'

'An air rifle?'

'Yeah, the Winchester is a bit too heavy for him. Also, he forgets to put on the safety. I don't want to be shot if he drops it.'

'An air rifle can be dangerous,' she said.

'Yeah, but it wouldn't go off if you drop it.'

'And what did you get Wendy?'

'Oh, a tennis racquet and a volleyball.'

'She's sporty?'

'Yes, a junior champion.'

'That's great.'

There was a silence.

'Where are you?' Becker asked.

'Oh, sitting here and downing a Jack. What are *you* doing?'

'Oh, I'm looking at a bottle of Chianti I was given and wondering if I should open it.'

'Who's given you the chianti?'

'Angelina.'

'Angelina?'

'I think she meant it as a thank you.'

'In that case, she has good manners.'

'She was very impressed with you.'

'So she should have been. I was taking a risk, a Federal officer escorting a whacko who, potentially, could do his block and kill someone.'

'He's not that bad.'

'Yeah? That doctor was plenty worried.'

Becker didn't reply. Angelina's little experiment, taking Silvano back home, getting him adjusted, was very risky. He didn't want to think about it.

'Where are you?' he asked.

'In Melbourne.'

'What are you doing there?'

'Pursuing a few leads.'

'Concerning a certain gentleman of broad proportions?'

'You could say that.' Another pause. 'Why don't I come up and see you?'

'Tonight?'

'Why not?'

'No reason at all. But you are forbidden to come to Wagga.'

'I wouldn't come anywhere near Wagga. There's a back road from The Rock to the Lockhart Road just south of you. I'll see you in about three hours.'

And she did.

Just walked in, in her usual confident way, opening the front door without knocking, and marching in. Becker hadn't heard the Harley, but then it was an almost silent machine. She was flushed, taking off the helmet. She was not wearing leather now, but instead a soft, light, gabardine coat which still hid the Glock. She had to keep it hidden. But she knew how to slip the zipper and let the jacket drift open when she felt like it.

'Ah, what a great night for riding,' she said. Then put down the helmet beside the sofa.

'Good ride?'

'Yeah, the stars were bright. The moon was full and so was I.'

'Full of what?'

'Pleasure, to be on my way back here again.'

'Have you eaten?'

'Only some savouries with the Jack.'

'How many have you had?'

'Jacks? Only the one. Have you eaten?'

'No, I'm full of Christmas cake. I can let you have a lot of leftover cold ham and turkey and potato salad. Muriel forced them into my hands. There's cheese and fresh bread.'

'Sounds terrific.'

Chook had taken off her boots. She wore cotton socks and had big feet. Big, manly feet. The more Becker saw of Chook the surer he was that she was some kind of man. Maybe a man in a female body. She acted like a man. Was built like a man. Must have been full of testosterone. He was surprised she didn't have a moustache. Maybe she did, but used defoliant or wax or electricity to get it off. Occasionally, relaxed with her feet up on a table, she was surprisingly feminine. Almost shy, like not knowing how to handle the situation, being with a man and having fun. A man and a woman together, relaxed and yarning and playing at being more than good friends.

She sat on the sofa and sprawled back.

'Ah, this is great.'

'Are you going to take off that holster?'

She shrugged.

'You aren't going to sleep in it?'

'Why not?'

Perhaps she would, she was so tired. Her eyes closed, she nodded.

He thought about her. What sort of future did she have? Soon, someone would challenge her. That's how it always went in the West.

There had been an old movie.

Glenn Ford was in it. He was a storekeeper in the usual clapboard town out in the usual worn-out wilderness of the West. His wife had been raped and killed by a gunslinger. Glenn Ford swore that one day he'd kill the bastard. But the gunslinger had been fast, too fast for Ford. No-one in the movie would challenge him. So, Ford had practised day after day, until he was pretty fast too. Shooting tin cans and bottles on posts. The gunslinger had come back one day. Glenn Ford challenged him to a fight. He had to, it being a matter of honour. There was no option. They fought out in the street, according to the rules of the West. You saw their guns blazing, then a graveside scene. Close up of a tombstone with the storekeeper's name on it. The camera pulls back and we see Glenn Ford himself standing among the mourners. How can this be? you ask. There is a simple answer. It has been bruited about that the new fast gun had been killed. There was no point in riding into town to challenge him. He is stone-cold dead in the ground, supposedly.

Becker was thinking. One day some man would challenge Chook. That man would not play by the rules. It would not be a confrontation in a dusty street or a raucous barroom according to the lore of the west. It would be a shot that came out of nowhere. Or, came out of somewhere—maybe from a gun shoved into her back in a crowd.

She was smiling at him.

'What're you thinking about?'

'Ah, nothing. You want to eat now?'

'How about a glass of that Chianti?'

'Chianti? Okay.'

Becker got up and went to a sideboard that served as a drinks' cabinet. The sideboard was one of Robyn's purchases. 'Harry,' she'd said, 'there's a lovely sideboard in Clauson's in Morgan Street. It would look really lovely there by the table.'

'Buy it,' he had said.

'But, dear, they want eight-hundred dollars for it.'

'That's okay,' he'd said.

'Harry, I don't want to do anything you might think extravagant, a waste of your money.'

'It's no problem,' he'd said. 'If you want it, buy it.'

'You're sure it's okay, dear?'

'Anything for you, Robbie,' he'd said.

He'd already opened the package, surprised. Had expected to see a bulbous bottle with a long neck in a straw basket. But it was a perfectly cylindrical bottle. *Chianti Classico Riseva*, the label said. All the words were in Italian. There was a vintner's name, but it meant nothing to him. He pulled the cork. It went pop. He poured two glasses and brought one to Chook. She was really relaxed, sprawled. Tired, but happy.

'Thank you,' she said.

'I'll get some bread and cheese. You want some chicken and salad?'

'If it's not a bother.'

When he came back, Chook was holding the bottle.

'This is very good, *sangiovese* grape. This is very good.'

Becker placed cold chicken pieces and potato salad and bread and butter before her on a coffee table. Chook was still studying the bottle.

'Angelina gave you this?'

'She was here five days, you know. She was very grateful.'

'I know, mate. I was here. Hey, I think the little lady is in love with you.'

Becker sat on a chair, surprised. 'What? Me? She's quite young. Very shy.'

'What's wrong with that?'

'I'm forty.'

'Some girls like an older man. Much more experience, more money, more protection. Maybe she's looking for a father-figure. I wouldn't blame her. Living with a bunch of crazy Catholics must be a strain on any girl.'

'She doesn't need any money from me and, besides, how would I protect her? I'm not a cop. You're a cop.'

'I'm a girl. I think the very strict Miss Cosco would be horrified if I made a pass at her. Anyway, she caught me shaving.'

'Shaving? You shaving?'

'Yeah, with a tiny electric model. Many girls have to do that.'

'Under the arms, down the legs, you mean?'

'No, no, my face.'

'What?'

'She caught me in the bathroom. Opened the door and there I was half naked, no tits to speak of and shaving my face.'

'Why?'

'Why what?'

'Why were you shaving your face?'

'Haven't you noticed? I have a beard.'

'No, you don't!'

'Yes, I do. I'm full of testosterone. Have a moustache and every few days I have to shave. Otherwise it will show, a fine, downy beard, blond. No-one sees it until it's a few days old.'

'You're not a freak, just a different—'

'Yeah, a mad woman overloaded with male hormones. I think it happened when I determined to turn myself into a fighter, with my hands and fists and feet and head and anything else I could use short of my teeth. All that pumping iron in gyms, it upsets the balance. And the bloody steroids. I was eating them like candy, to build up my muscles. Killed the oestrogen and allowed the testosterone to multiply. So, what am I? A man with a vagina? What a frigging defective.'

'Stop complaining, Chook.'

'Don't call me Chook! I'm not a chicken!'

'And stop swearing.'

'Sorry, sorry.'

She was eating heartily, talking and drinking and arguing and frowning and being all-round disagreeable. In her usual way, thoroughly pissed off with the world.

Becker changed the subject.

'What's wrong with the Catholics?'

'What?'

'You said crazy Catholics.'

'Aren't they? All that hellfire and brimstone.'

'They're willing to pick up my mother's shit.'

'What?' Chook coughed, spluttered.

'Sorry.'

'Do you have to say such a thing while I'm eating.'

'You're eating too fast.'

'I'm hungry. Had nothing since breakfast, except coffee.'

Becker took his time explaining. 'I have to get my mother out of the place she's in. She's lost control—of her bodily functions. The Little Sisters of Compassion have agreed to take her. They have a small place called Mary Potter. But she won't go to the Catholics.'

'I don't blame her. They'd beat the fear of God into her.'

Chook had devoured all of the ham and chicken and salad. 'You sure you won't have a biscuit and cheese?' she asked.

'No, I ate too much today.'

'More wine?'

'Okay.'

She poured. Somehow, she had appropriated the bottle. Becker waited, watching the glass fill. She raised it, lounging back.

'And?' she said.

'I don't know what to do. I can't think what to do with her.'

'Ah, hell.'

They said nothing for a while.

'Does she know they're Catholics?'

'Not yet.'

'Hmmm—'

'You're not thinking?'

'I'm trying to help.'

'Last time you tried to help, Addie ended up in jail.'

He was referring to his first wife, Adeline who had been Adeline Atkins when he'd married her. With two daughters who may or may not have been his. And had demanded sucker, as she had mispronounced it. She turned out to be a predatory bimbo and born liar.

'I wasn't responsible for that.'

'You planted a bag of weed on her.'

'I didn't plant anything on anyone, I told you—'

'You are a shameless fixer, Chook.'

'Ah, shit.'

Chook chewed biscuit and Mersey Valley spread and sipped a sip or two. 'Are we going to quarrel all night?'

'Okay, okay.'

'I'll think of something, mate.'

'Yeah, yeah, I know.'

'Christ, what a miserable end for a woman's life. Was she a good mother? What was her name?'

'My mother? Iris? Yeah, I suppose she was.'

'Yeah, that's about all you can say, isn't it? You never know, do you?'

'And your own?'

'A good mother? She tried, she tried. She used to sing to me, Tartar songs.'

'Tartar?'

'The people in the middle of Russia and in spots in the Ukraine. She had a beautiful voice, weak but tender, especially when she sang to me. She was illiterate, you know. Could not read or write her own name. They had a hard time in Odessa, in Istanbul, in Cyprus. In Australia. But they made it. Did I tell you all this?'

'Yes, you did.'

'They started to get somewhere, be someone, then she died.'

'How is your father?'

'I called on him on the way down to Melbourne.'

Becker waited. Guessed Chook didn't wish to mention her father, especially what he did for a living.

'He was uncommunicative as ever. You can say something to him, like "How are you?" Or, "when are you going to retire?" But he shrugs and changes the subject.'

'Is he going to retire?'

'I don't think so.'

'Is he old enough?'

'Oh, yeah, he's old enough. He's gone sixty-five.'

'Why won't he retire?'

'You know why.'

'Because he works in a crematorium?'

'Don't make me sick, thinking about it.'

'I'm sorry, Chook.'

'Can't you for once call me Anastacia? I'm mean, that's my bloody name.'

'I'm sorry, Anastacia.'

Chook's eyes had closed again. Her mouth had twisted. She'd slumped back in the sofa, the wineglass held loosely, dangerously tipping.

'Here,' Becker said, 'I'll take that.'

'It's all right.'

'It's going to spill.'

'I am all right, I told you!' A long pause. 'Shut up for a minute, will you, Harry?'

Becker waited, watching. Gradually she relaxed, her breathing improved, but her fierce, blue eyes remained closed.

They remained like that for some time. Chook lounging in some sort of private torture, Becker trying to think what he should do. Get up and sit beside her, take her in his arms. But he didn't. It was better, he knew, not to go near her, not to touch her, when she was like that. Bitter, beaten, unable to fight her way back through the past.

'You're looking at my eyes, aren't you?'

'What?'

'My eyes, my squinty Asiatic eyes.'

'Asiatic?'

She nodded. 'Central Asian. My mother was a Tartar.'

'You said that.'

'Not Tartar as in cream of tartar. But Tartar from Turkmenistan.'

Becker wasn't too sure where that was.

'East of the Caspian Sea,' she said. 'They have beautiful dresses, national costumes and they sing and dance. That ballet guy, Nureyev, he was a Tartar.'

'I thought they lived in Southern Russia.'

'They do.'

'So why did they leave Turkmenistan?'

'They had to, eight-hundred years ago. To get away Genghis Kahn and his fucking Golden Horde. They were riding east, coming on fast on their short, stocky steeds, waving their scimitars and axes. The Tartars had to flee for their lives. Some reached as far as Ukie. Some didn't make it. Cut down, hacked to death. Some were raped and yet survived. I wouldn't be surprised if I had some Mongol blood in me.' She sighed. 'Might have one of those tests one day.'

'What tests?'

'Genetic, they're all the rage now. Everyone wants to know who really were their ancestors.'

Becker was impressed. She really did look like something out of Central Asia, riding at high speed, waving a scimitar.

'And your father?'

'Half Russian, half Ukie.'

'Quite a mixture.'

'Yeah, all mixed up.' She sighed again. 'Over the years.'

'You want coffee?'

'No thanks. What's the time?'

'Nearly ten.'

Becker stood up, reached out a hand. 'Come on, get to bed.'

She rose, stumbling. Becker caught her, led her to the main bedroom. She sat on the bed, pulled off her boots, then flopped back. Becker tried to get the Glock off her, ease it out of the shoulder holster.

'It's not cocked,' she mumbled.

Suddenly, Chook was asleep. It was like flipping a switch.

'Sleep well, Anastasia.'

He was about to turn off the light, when she mumbled something else. It sounded like 'fat man'.

'What was that?'

'I know who the fat man is.'

Chapter 26

WHEN HE AWOKE, Chook was propped up on one elbow, regarding him. Looked as fresh as a daisy. She must have taken off the cotton jacket and her pants during the night.

'What's the matter?' he asked.

'Why should anything be the matter?'

'Why are you looking at me like that?'

'Can't a cat look at a king?'

Becker laughed. 'Where did you hear that?'

'I don't know. Somewhere along the trail of childhood, I suppose. It must have been at kindergarten. We had a lovely kindergarten teacher, Miss Mauberley. She read beautifully from big picture books. I think she was related to Mr Mauberley. Who was Mr Mauberley? I don't know, but I think Mr Eliot knew him well. Who was Eliot? I think he wrote poems about cats.'

'Did you sleep well?' Becker asked.

'Like a top. I've never slept so well. It must have been Angelina's lovely Chianti. Yes, it was good, wasn't it?'

'What day is it?' he asked.

Chook was still regarding him. 'Did we have sex last night?'

'I don't think so.'

'You didn't do anything?'

'No, you were fast asleep.'

'Was I really? Do you want to have sex now?'

'I'm not fussy.'

She began to feel him. 'Boy, that's interesting.'

'I think it's just piss-proud,' he said.

'Piss-proud?' She laughed. 'I've never heard that expression.'

They laughed together. She bent down and kissed him on the lips. 'You want me to do you?'

'Oh, all right, hop on board.'

She laughed. Laughed all the time she was doing it.

'Why are you laughing?'

'I don't know. I must be happy.'

'You weren't too happy last night.'

'No, I get angry about things too easily, don't I?'

'You have a lot on your mind.'

'Yeah, well, at present I have only one thing on my mind.'

At breakfast, she said: 'I was having a strange dream.'

'When you woke?'

'I dreamed I was in Russia.'

'Not in winter, I hope?'

'No, no, but there was snow. I didn't feel cold. I was very warm. It was an old movie.'

'What old movie?'

'I don't know. It must have been *War and Peace*, although it started off with Lara in the snow.'

'Lara?'

'Doctor Zhivago, but I was speaking to Natasha at one stage.'

'Natasha?'

'In *War and Peace*. We were dancing in the ballroom.'

'You and Natasha were dancing?'

'No, no, the others were. I think General Kutuzov was there.'

'Kutuzov?'

'Yeah, wasn't he the one who beat Napoleon? At Borodino?'

'Yes, he was there.'

'At Borodino?'

'No, at the ball. Sorry, want more toast?'

'No, I'm right.'

'Coffee?'

'No, only one a day.' He was looking at a window, at the pepper trees, at the blistering sun. It was going to be a hot day.

'I think it was an old movie,' she said. 'Audrey Hepburn was in it.'

'So she was.'

'And Akim Tamiroff, he was the general?'

'What general?'

'The one who beat Napoleon at Borodino.'

'No, he wasn't. I saw that movie a million years ago. The actor was Oscar Homolka.'

'What a memory you have.' Pause. 'Stacey?'

She was staring into space, a cup a few inches from her lips. Her eyes were wide and far way, perhaps in the cornfields of the Ukraine.

'Stacey?'

'That's it!' she said. 'That was the name, Akim not Hakim.'

'What name?'

'The name the old man was saying. The one in Chapel Street, in the shop. I was holding him, shaking him. He lent his card to a man called Akim. So Akim would not appear on the flight manifest, if anyone asked.'

'So, who is the fat man? Akim who?'

'Nekrasoff. And he's a Ukie.'

'Sure of this?'

'Yeah, it all fits. He was picked up many years ago, in respect of a car crash not far out of Melbourne. A truck came out of nowhere at an intersection. The driver was a man called Neckaroff. But the local cops found his real name was Nekrasoff.'

'So?'

'It was all staged.'

'Yeah? What happened?'

'He got off, played the ignorant migrant moron. Swore he didn't see the stop sign. He was looking in his rear-view mirror. Swore someone was following him. No-one could prove he was not telling the truth.'

'What happened to him?'

'Lost his licence.'

'Is that all?'

'The court believed him. But since then, Mr Nekaroff, as he called himself, has flitted in and out of the country.'

'You gonna pick him up?'

'What with, an arrest warrant? What charge? The guy happens to look like Nekrasoff?'

He's probably got half-a-dozen passports with different names now.'

'Where can I see a picture of this guy?'

'You think he was the man beside you in Canberra? Drinking Turkish coffee in Manuka?'

'He might be.'

'I'll get a picture of Nekrasoff.'

At that moment a phone rang. It was Becker's.

'Oh, hullo, *bongiorno, signore* Harry.'

'Angelina?'

'*Si*, it is Angelina.'

'This is a surprise, Angelina.' He emphasised her name so that Chook would hear.

'Oh, you liked the Chianti?'

'Yes, I did. So did Stacey.'

'Stacey?'

'She likes to be called Stacey. Anastacia is too long for her.'

She laughed. 'Oh, Anastacia is a beautiful name.'

'We both drank the Chianti last night. Most of it.'

'I am so happy.'

There was a pause. She coughed.

'How is Silvano?'

'Silvano? He is very happy. He received lovely presents this morning.'

'This morning, Boxing Day?'

'What kind of presents?'

'Oh, books and videos and chocolates and a camera.'

'A camera? Today?'

'Oh, yes, in Italy presents are given on the next day. Not Christmas Day.'

'I see.'

'He is very keen for photographs. He wants to take one of Daniella.'

'Daniella, eh? Any hope of that?'

'Oh, yes, she gave him the camera. He is so excited.'

'I meant, he's in love with her, isn't he?'

Angelina laughed again. She had a beautiful laugh. 'Oh, I don't know. I hope so, we hope so.'

'You and your mother hope so?'

'*Si, Mamma*—' Another pause, another slight cough. She was going to ask him something, he could rear it. '*Mamma*, she asks if you would like to come to us for a meal? A luncheon, perhaps?'

'A luncheon? Today? Boxing Day?'

'*Si, all'aperto*. Under the *traliccio*, the grapes. By the well. The fountain will be playing. It is so cool there.'

'I would like to, Angelina, but, you see, Anastacia is staying with me, and—'

'Oh, bring Anastacia with you! I would love to see her again. *Mamma* would like to see you both.'

'What time?'

'Oh, I think twelve o'clock, before it gets too hot.'

'Twelve o'clock, then?'

'Yes!'

'What's twelve o'clock in Italian?'

'*Mezzogiorno.*'

'See you then, Angelina.'

'*Che Dio vada con te*, Harry.'

He hung up, or pressed the red button.

'We are invited to lunch under the trellis,' he said. 'By the trickling fountain.'

Chook sniffed. 'She's trying to take you from me, isn't she?'

'So what?'

'I'll kill her if she does.'

'I hope you are joking.'

Chapter 27

BEFORE THEY ARRIVED they could see lights flashing in the distance, well in from the road. Hoped it was not at the *casa splendida*. At the gate they could see a patrol car, one of the big red highway machines. They slowed right down. At least two more cars were at the house, not patrol cars but white vehicles with the blue-check stripe along the side and the big, blue word: Police. And on top the flashing lights. Normal town cruisers. As they pulled into the gate, an officer stepped out and put up a hand. It was Max Kruger. They crawled to a stop. He bent down to get a better look. Chook had wound the window down.

'What the hell, Max?'

'Ah, Jesus,' he said, 'ah, Jesus.'

'Something bad?'

'Yeah, real bad.'

'What?'

'Dunno, haven't been up there yet. Told me to stay here and keep everyone out.'

'When did it happen?'

'When? Ah, dunno exactly. I was heading along the highway, had almost reached Narrandera and about to turn back to Wagga, when I got the call. It was all cars. They wanted anyone available to go to Griffith immediately.'

'What did they say?'

'Ah, nothin' really. Only that they needed more cars.'

He was frightened, you could see. Repeating himself.

'How many hurt?'

'Dunno, they won't tell me. One ambulance up there.'

'Anyone dead?'

'One woman, they reckon.'

'Is it Angelina?'

'What? Ah, shit, I dunno. I met her at your place, when I called in. She was a lovely girl. You were lookin' after her, remember? Asked me if I liked being a policeman. She was good, sweet, decent.' He shook. 'Ah, Christ, I mean, why?'

'Is it really Angelina?'

'I dunno, I just dunno! Ah, gee, I hope they don't call me up there. I don't want to have to look at her, not if it's really her. Not a lovely girl like that. Ah, gee.'

He looked shaky. Ashamed too that he looked shaky.

Chook reached out. 'Come here.'

'What?'

'Come here!'

He did so, cautiously. She patted him on a shoulder, gripped an arm.

'Hang in there, mate. You'll be all right.'

They drove up the lane, slowly. The lemon trees heavy with fruit each side. The perfume piquant, almost inviting. No-one working in the rows of vines, not on a day like this, Boxing Day. When people should be out calling on friends, family. Anyone who was anyone in their world, to say: What did you get for Christmas? Or, what a hot day it is? Or, are you going away for a spell? Perhaps to the coast? To get away from the heat?

As well as two police cars, there were two or three other vehicles. Only one ambulance, its lights flashing. Two men on the terrace. Becker and Chook got out. One man was in uniform.

'Relatives?' he asked.

Chook pulled out her card. 'Federal Police,' she said.

'What have you got to do with this?'

'You don't need to know.'

'Eh?'

The plainclothes man was grinning. It was Quinn. 'Little miss Annie Oakley herself, eh?' he said.

'What are you doing here?' Chook asked.

'What am I doing here?' He laughed.

'You work in Wagga,' she said.

'I'm on leave.'

'What are you doing at a crime scene?'

'Thought I might help.'

Giggling now, his guts shaking. You could see it. It was like watching a pot boil. You know it's going to boil over soon, if you don't keep an eye on it.

'You in charge here?'

'The boss's inside,' he said.

'Is that all you can say?'

Chook looked at the uniformed man. 'This dickhead a mate of yours?' No answer.

'He grinned all through my interview, when I was telling them how I was raped with a broom handle years ago.' She poked a finger at Quinn. 'Isn't that so, funny boy? What would you have used? A broken bottle?'

Quinn stopped smiling. Fear flickered.

'Who's the boss?'

'Chief Inspector Torcelli.'

'Torcelli?'

'That's right.'

'That's right, ma'am.'

'Eh?'

'You're lookin' at a sergeant, kiddo.'

'Yes, ma'am.'

They walked in, slowly. Checking this way and that.

Nothing in the living room, prepared for visitors, pictures on the walls. Then along a hall, past a few doors and into the sunroom with its glass wall. Under the trellis outside, the table had been set. Bowls of fruit, nuts, preserves, cutlery, napkins already. The fountain was trickling. Someone was crying in a room to one side, the door almost closed. It was a woman saying and over: '*Hanno detto che andrebbe tutto bene...*' Another woman seemed to be crooning words of comfort. So softly that, even if you were Italian, you may not have understood.

In one corner of the sunroom, someone was taking photographs.

Two or three uniformed cops were standing around, looking useless. Plus two ambulance men. Everybody seemed to be waiting. Not only for the man with the camera to finish, but for something inexplicably patent. At first sight, the man with the camera looked like a cop. He was wearing dark blue coveralls. But something was missing. 'Police' didn't appear on his back. He was not snapping the body but marks on walls, bloody smears. On the tiles and on the legs of a long settee. Even some on the cushions, if you looked carefully. And what appeared to be fine red specks on a wall, where someone might have coughed blood.

Chook walked over. She was going to speak to him, but a tall man in uniform intervened.

'Who are you?'

'Federal agent Babchuk,' she said.

'Federal agent?'

'Sergeant to you.'

'Who says you are?'

'Ask your man at the door.'

She ignored him. He was not so much big as lanky and awkward. His jaw was long and his eyes small, like currents stuck on a loaf of bread. Didn't like her disrespect. There was an uncertainty about him, as if unsure of himself. Unsure whether anyone respected him. When the man with the camera stepped back, Chook walked forward. The body was lying twisted under a sheet.

She pulled it back.

'Don't touch,' the tall man said.

'Don't tell me what to do.'

She pulled back the sheet right to the knees. It was horrific.

Angelina was lying on her back, more on the right shoulder than on the left, her head turned to the left as if looking back at a pursuer. Eyes seemed to be staring at these people, the bystanders. You could still see the fear in her green eyes.

'How did it happen?' Becker said.

The boss said, 'And who the hell are you?'

'Becker,' he said. 'We were invited to lunch.'

'Then get out of here.'

'He stays,' Chook said, still squatting.

The uniformed man at the front door had followed them in. 'That's Agent Babchuk,' he said. 'Federal Police.'

'What the hell is the Federal Police doing here?'

'This is a federal case,' Chook said.

'What's federal about it?'

Chook didn't answer. She was looking at the stab wounds. Must have been at least a dozen, the blood too awful.

'Who did this?' Becker asked.

'Him, in there.'

'In where?'

'In the room behind you! Can't you hear it?'

Becker didn't know exactly which he meant. Perhaps the room the crying was coming from. He stood around, uselessly. Quinn had come in, hands in his pockets, wriggling. Eyes going everywhere except to the body on the floor tiles. Majolica ceramic on the stone-cold tiles, beautiful tiles. You never saw such beautiful tiles, imported all the way from Italy at great expense back in eighties. When young Angelo Cosco had decided to plaster the old red-brick cottage with stucco, turning it into a *casa splendida*. Complete with belvederes. Back when his father was dead and business was better than ever.

Chook replaced the sheet, was about to put it over the face, but hesitated. Eyes were still open, accusingly. She stared deep into them. Got right down close, her own only a few inches from them.

'Who did it, Angelina?'

Becker was surprised. It was obvious who did it.

There was another sobbing, much lighter. Also coming from the room, where the woman was saying: '*Hanno detto che andrebbe...*' A different kind of sob. Not really a sob at all, more like a mournful whimper. Like someone talking to himself.

Becker went to the door, partly open. Saw two women, one consoling the other.

Then, beyond them, a boy sitting in a corner, hugging his knees, talking to himself. Holding a knife. It looked like a kitchen knife, no doubt one of a set hanging on a wall. Long, about eight-inches. The blade was not shining.

A hand fell on Becker's shoulder. He stepped back.

Chook pushed the door wide enough to slip in. Looked first at the two women, then went to the corner. Becker pushed it wider. The tall man was standing behind him, apprehensive. Becker could hear it in his breathing. 'What the hell is she doing?' he asked.

Chook squatted before the boy. Sat there for some time, looking at him. Like you have to do when you go up to a nervous horse that doesn't trust you. Didn't speak, just looked at him, although her lips were moving. The door was wider now. Others were trying to peep in, including the boss. 'What the hell is she doing?'

'Whispering,' Becker said.

'Whispering?'

'Yeah, whispering.'

So, they waited. There was no alternative. The boy had the knife. His head was bowed on his arms, folded across his knees. Now and then Chook would say something quietly and he would mumble an answer. They could not follow it at all. Then suddenly they could.

Chook was speaking.

'—when we walked across the road and there she was! Standing stock still in the middle of the road, so surprised to see you! You remember that?'

Silvano nodded.

'Couldn't believe her eyes, could she? It was you, her handsome cousin! Then she stepped forward, smiling and said...'

They lost her next words. He nodded again.

'Pleased to see you?'

Another nod. Without looking up.

'She said we could see a movie, a video at her place. You'd like to see that, wouldn't you? She's got *Waldo Pepper*. Would you like to see *Waldo Pepper*?'

He nodded.

'How about brushing up a bit, washing your hands?'

'Yes,' he said.

'She's a very pretty girl.'

'She gave me the camera.'

'She gave you a camera? What camera?'

'Wanted me to take photos.'

'Of you and her? Together?'

'Yes.'

'Did she come with the camera? I mean, personally? Today? Yesterday?'

'She left it.' His voice was stronger now. Well above a whisper.

'She just left it? Where did she leave it?'

'Gave it to Patrizia.'

'Who's Patrizia? Is she the lady with *Mamma*? Talking to her?'

'Yes.'

'What did Patrizia do with it?'

'Put it on the table with all the other things.'

'You mean by the Christmas tree?' There was a small tree on a small table in a corner of the sunroom. 'And you opened the box and there it was, the camera? With a card from Daniella?'

'Yes.'

'And now you can take a lot of photos of her?'

'She didn't bring any,' Silvano said.

'What do you mean? Any photos of herself? The camera was in a gift box, gift-wrapped wasn't it?'

He nodded again and again. Like a hammer going up and down, mechanically.

'So, what photos do you mean? Old photos?'

'I saw them.'

'You saw them?' He didn't answer. 'Where are they now?'

He looked up, must have seen the faces at the door. Refused to answer.

'Okay,' Chook said, standing slowly. 'Let's go and see her.'

He grunted something.

She had a hand under one shoulder, prompting him. He began to rise, still buckled over, head down. The knife only a few inches from her ribs.

'Where's the bathroom? This way? Next door?'

'If you turn left—'

'We'll find it.'

'Two bathrooms.'

'You have two bathrooms? In this house?'

'Yes.'

'Really? Hey, you want me to take that knife? While you brush up?'

'Yes.'

Everyone stepped back. 'I'll take him now,' the boss said.

Chook ignored him. As they passed into the sunroom, she handed the knife to Becker. It was still sticky with blood.

'This way,' she said. Instead of handing him over, she steered the boy to the middle of the room. 'Where did you see the photos?'

He looked around, eyes caught on the shape under the sheet. Began to whimper again.

'Okay,' she said. 'We'll talk about them later.'

She looked at the tall man. 'I'm handing him over to you, for custody. Temporary custody,' she added.

'What do you mean, temporary? He's killed his sister and he's going into custody for as long as I say so. This is murder. And who the hell are you to tell me what to do?'

'He's all yours,' she said.

'Take him away,' he said. Two men in uniform took him. He turned on Chook. 'Who are you to tell me?'

'This is a Federal case.'

'Federal?'

Chook spoke very slowly.

'Someone has killed the daughter of a Mafia boss. The Mafia is involved in organised crime. That's our province. So that makes it a Federal case, understand?'

Torcelli was unhappy. 'You can't come waltzing in here and take over.'

'She—' Chook nodded towards the body. 'She was under Federal Police protection and—'

'Some sort of protection. You release a psycho into the community and he kills his sister. Hacks her to death.'

She stared at him. 'Where are the photos?'

'What photos? I haven't seen any—' He shrugged. 'Has anyone seen any photos?'

They all looked blank. She tried to explain. 'He saw some photos and that's what set him off.'

'I don't know what you mean.'

She looked around, spotted Quinn.

'You see any photos?'

'I dunno what y're talkin' about.'

'When did you get here?' Chook asked.

'Me? When did I get here?'

Quinn tried to look amazed, but she persisted. 'Answer the question.'

The boss intervened. 'This officer does not have to answer any questions from you.'

'But he will, won't you?'

'What?'

'He'll answer, if I take him to court.'

'What?' Quinn was amazed. Or, affected amazement.

'Answer the question,' Torcelli said.

'Eh? Hell, I heard all the sirens, so I rang Operations an' said, "What's going on?" An' they said, "Trouble at the Cosco place." "What's sort of trouble?" I said. "Big trouble," they said. So I came over to see if I c'd help.'

Chook said: 'You'd better be telling the truth, Mr Quinn.'

'Yeah?'

'Seen your uncle lately?'

'Who d'y'mean?'

'The priest.'

'Father Quinlan?'

'Yeah. Tell me, why are you Quinn and he is Quinlan.'

'Just a difference in spelling. It happens in families.'

'That all?'

'Hey, what is this?'

'Maybe someone in your family didn't like to be called Quinlan?'

'What are you getting at?'

'How close are you related to him?'

'What's that got to do with anything?'

'Just answer the question.'

Torcelli cut in. 'What are you getting at?'

Chook ignored him. She waited. Quinn was frightened, you could see.

'He's my uncle.'

'Your uncle? Is that right?'

The boss tried again. 'What's going on here?'

'Why don't you ask him, Chief Inspector?'

'Don't tell me what to do.'

Chook smiled at him. 'And what's your name?'

'My name? Didn't they tell you? It's Torcelli.'

'Your first name?'

'Why?'

'I'm trying to be friendly.'

'It's Pietro.'

'Mind if I call you Pete?' Torcelli didn't answer. 'Let's take a walk.'

She led him outside and stood him under the grapes. As tall as he was, she was taller. 'It looks as though you have a problem.'

'What kind of problem?'

'Someone showed him pictures of Cosco, taken when he was found shot to pieces by his son. That's what set Silvano off, made him frantic, horrified. That's why he killed his sister, in a mad frenzy. Now who would have done that?'

'I have no idea.'

'Who would have such pictures?'

Torcelli was startled. 'Why, no-one, except of course—'

'Police pictures?'

'Are you saying that—'

'Where's the camera?'

'What camera?'

'He received a camera as a present this morning.'

'What's a camera got to do with it?'

'He saw his father's body and went mad.'

'It must have been a flashback.'

'Maybe.'

Torcelli was flummoxed. 'I knew it was a bad idea, bringing that boy back here. He was sure to remember one day.'

'Look, Pete—' She patted him on a shoulder. 'I'm gonna have people down here tomorrow, by chopper. They're going to ask questions, aren't they? This looks like a Mafia killing. Maybe someone decided she knew too much. They killed a Federal witness. You'd better have the right answers when they arrive.'

'You're telling me? I am a chief inspector in the—'

'Otherwise,' she continued, 'somebody in Canberra will be asking somebody in Sydney about the quality of policing in this town. Understand what I'm saying?'

One of the ambulance men stepped in. 'Can we take her now?'

'What? Yeah, yeah, get her out of here.'

They went back, watched them lifting the body. Then strapping it down on the stretcher.

'I don't know anything about this,' Torcelli said.

'That's the problem, isn't it? Why don't you know?'

'*Dolce Gesù*, what are you accusing me of?'

'I'm just telling you, as one cop to another, what it could look like.'

'You have no right to talk that way to me.'

She stared at him. 'I'm a Federal cop. And I don't take any shit from no-one. Understand?'

Torcelli jolted, then gave in. 'You're saying someone showed police photos to that young bloke?'

'Who would have them?'

'I don't know.'

'Why don't you know?'

He did not answer.

'Check them for fingerprints.'

'Yes, yes I will.'

'Who has the negatives?'

'Why are you asking?'

'I won't ask again.'

He gave in. We do.'

'Did a cop take them?'

'A cop? The negatives? Why, we don't have an official photographer. We use the services of a—of a private man.'

'That one? Who is he?'

The photographer was packing up. Torcelli looked worried.

'What's his name?'

'That man? He would never do such a thing.'

'Why wouldn't he?'

'Because he's my son.'

Chook searched his eyes. Torcelli had worn-out eyes, old brown eyes with golden specks. And piled-up curly brown hair, which should have been his crowning glory, but wasn't. It was clumpy, irregular. He was frightened, anyone could see.

She produced a card, poked it into his top pocket.

'Call me on this number when you have something for me.'

'You're telling me what to do?'

'I'm telling you for your own good.'

The ambos were wheeling her out. Chook followed with her eyes.

'Goodbye, Angelina,' she said.

Chapter 28

BECKER WANDERED AROUND. Sometimes listened in on what Chook had to say. Otherwise he wandered about the house. Went into the side room again. It looked like a parlour, or private sitting room. There were lots of family photos in oval mounts on the walls and on cabinets and even on top of an ancient traymobile with big, rubber wheels. One showed a woman in a deep chair, more a lounging chair than a lounge chair. Tilted right back, so it was more like a bed than a chair. She was well dressed, ready to receive visitors. Even some white lace at her throat. Not so old, could have been a very young bride thirty years ago. Before the disasters began. Before Concetta Cisco went to the local police and told her story. And spoke to the wrong man. The very wrong man.

And they'd had to kill her. It being the old way.

The other woman was still with Angelina's mother, head on her chest. Both seemed to be asleep. Chook took a few steps, stopped. The housekeeper looked up.

'Are you Patrizia?' Chook asked.

The woman nodded.

'Did Daniella give you the camera, this morning?'

She shook her head.

'When did Daniella call?'

Another shake.

'You didn't see Daniella?'

'No, no.'

'Who gave you the camera to give to Silvano?'

'Nobody give me. I find at fron' door when I go out, maybe nine, maybe just after. I go out for to sweep.'

'It was just sitting out there on the patio?'

'*Si*, by the door.'

'All wrapped up with the card?'

'*Si*, a card you say.'

Someone said: 'Is this what you're looking for?'

Quinn was at the door, holding it.

'Where did you find that?'

'In the front room, sitting on a cabinet.'

'Who put it there?'

'How would I know?'

Chook stood up, took the camera. It was a Sony digital. Not a lot of digital cameras around in 1997, but they were available. This one looked brand-new.

'How do you work these things?'

'I don't know,' Quinn said.

She went out, caught the photographer about to leave. 'How do these things work?'

He took it, peering at it. Scrutinising it.

'Quite simple,' he said.

'Show me?'

'You want me to show you how to use it?'

'I want to know if it has been used.'

'Okay.'

He pushed some buttons. A picture showed on the back screen.

'What is that?'

'Well, it just seems to be the floor. That seems to be the leg of a chair. And that's a toe of a shoe.'

'What floor?'

'I don't know, maybe this floor.'

'Any more shots?'

He pressed the button again. Another picture showed, meaningless. Several more, perhaps of the sunroom. The furniture looked familiar. Then, suddenly, Angelina's face appeared, laughing. Reaching for the camera. Then there was another, just an ear and the back of her head.

'Jesus,' the photographer said.

'He's playing with it, isn't he? Trying to get used to it?'

'Yeah.'

Now a better shot of Angelina, standing back, posing unwillingly. Then yet another with Patrizia in the background. There were twenty or thirty of the sunroom and the back garden and the table set for lunch and the overhanging grapes. Then another of Angelina, very close, and laughing. Both arms out.

Then, suddenly nothing.

'Is that all?'

'Looks like it.'

'Is there any way to tell whether there were other shots that may have been erased?'

'Not as far as I know.'

'Does this camera have a number? Can it be traced?'

'Yeah, the retailer can be traced. He would have noted the model and date of sale.'

'And the buyer's name?'

'Not if they paid cash.'

'Did you sell this camera?'

'No, I did not.'

'Are you sure?'

'I don't sell Canon. I sell Nikon.'

This was back before every cop on the beat had an iPhone and could take whatever shots he or she needed.

'What's your name?'

'Paul, Paul Torcelli.'

'Is that your father out there?'

'Yeah, that's right.'

'Did you take the original police photos? Of Angelo? Dead?'

'Yes, I did. They don't have their own forensics unit here. Not fully equipped, anyway. They're still using film and they don't have their own lab.'

'Got any idea who would have access to those photos?'

'Practically any cop who was interested.'

'And who's got the negatives?'

He began to answer, but bristled. 'Are you accusing me of anything?'

'At this stage I'm not accusing anyone of anything.'

Chook went back to the old woman. She was sitting up now, head in hands. Patrizia was standing beside her. 'Donna Isabella,' Chook said, respectfully. It was a whisper. Neither woman seemed to hear.

'Donna Isabella,' she whispered again. 'You had a lovely daughter…'

The Nissan was purring along. Becker was driving, while Chook was using her phone, talking to people. Otherwise, she was unusually quiet. They were going through Narrandera, said nothing until they came out the other side. At Narrandera there are two bridges over the one river. Or, that's what it seems to be, the one river. You drive over one then another. But one is the great canal, which takes the water off, upstream from the town, and carries it down and down and out and out over the flat plains of the west, through more and more channels. Which feed the huge irrigation scheme, the huge food bowl.

They crossed the main canal, then the river. Then they turned left and set off along the Sturt Highway. They were on their way home to *Nil Desperandum*. It was an easy run.

They hadn't gone far, when Chook said: 'It's too neat, isn't?'

'What's too neat?'

'Someone shows Silvano some photos. They reveal something awful. At a guess, I'd say they are police photos, taken at the scene, where he killed his father. He starts screaming. Angelina rushes to him, tries to calm him down. He goes wild. Stabs her several times. Straight into the guts. The staff rush in. He stabs two of them. Then he starts crying, sits in the corner, waits for the police. Like he did after his killed his father. They come and try to grab him. He won't hand over the knife. They're too scared to take it from him. There are two women in the room with him, his mother and the housekeeper. We turn up and we talk him down. Why did he do it? The photos, is all he can say. But what photos? No-one can find any photos. Then out of the blue Quinn produces a camera, a digital camera. You press a button and it lights up. You touch the screen and the pictures change. But all of the pictures were taken by Silvano. Nothing bad in them. Nothing to make him start screaming. Going berserk. He must have seen some other pictures, too horrible for him to look at. And another thing, Quinn found the camera on a cabinet in the main living room. So, why did no-one notice the camera, when they first went in?'

'No-one was looking for a camera then. You were the first to mention a camera.'

'No, Silvano was the first.'

'You suspect Quinn?'

'Yeah, I suspect him.'

'You've got no evidence that there were any such shots on the camera. Also, if there were, no evidence that Quinn removed any.'

'Yeah, mate, but Quinn could have a reason.'

'For what? Stealing police photos? Copy them on a new-fangled digital camera? Let Silvano see them on the same camera? Then wipe them before the camera is found? That sounds like a long shot to me.'

'He was holding the camera. All he had to do was press a button to wipe the file photos. Then hand it over.'

'Death by camera? That sounds like something out of Agatha Christie.'

'He's not that smart.'

'Then, who is?'

She didn't answer. They were halfway home, when her phone rang. 'Yeah?' she said. She listened for some time, then said: 'Thank you for doing that.'

'Interesting?' Becker said.

'That was a mate in Canberra.'

'Yeah?'

'I asked her to check on Quinn.'

'And?'

'He was born in Griffith in April 1963.'

'So?'

'According to the records, his father was Joseph Ambrose Quinlan.'

'Uncle Ambrose?'

'Not his uncle at all, is he?'

Chapter 29

SHE WAS TRYING to teach Becker to make a Ukrainian omelette when Torcelli rang. They'd checked their files and no pictures were missing. They'd even got fingerprints off the pics of Angelo. There were one or two strange handprints that could not be explained, but none belonging to Quinn. They'd got some of his from a glass he'd used for drinking. No resemblance whatever. Torcelli was sure the prints had not been out of his office. Chook was bamboozled.

'We found Daniella,' Torcelli added.

'And?'

'She says she did not give Silvano a camera.'

'Did not? Then who did?'

'She doesn't know.'

'How was it wrapped?'

'Wrapped? We found the wrapping. And the box it came in. And the card. We showed the card to Daniella.'

'And?'

'It's not her handwriting.'

'Quinn's, then?'

'No resemblance.'

'Maybe he was trying to disguise it?'

'I've seen many disguised hands. They all look pretty stiff. Nothing stiff about this one. Looks quite natural.'

'Did Quinn come into your station?'

'Yeah, he did, several times.'

'Who did he talk to?'

'Almost everyone.'

'What did he want?'

'To say hullo at first. One day he asked to see the files on a case we'd run a few years ago. We were both involved, Griffith and Wagga.'

'And he was left alone with the files in a private area?'

'It looks like it.'

Torcelli sounded bad. Really worried. 'Why would Quinn do a thing like this?'

'He has a problem. Or, I should say, his father has a problem.'

'His father?'

'Yeah, his father is Father Quinlan.'

'What?'

'Big secret.'

'How do you know this?'

'Angelina said so at the meeting she called of people she said approved the killing of her sister, Concetta. The priest liked to touch up pretty little girls. He did it to Angelina when she was eight. In the sacristy. At the meeting, she implied that she might expose him.'

'Who to?'

'The families.'

'What families?'

'The Mafia.'

'Oh, Jesus!'

'That's how it looks, Pete.'

Torcelli was breathing hard on the other end. You could imagine him holding the phone with one hand, holding his head with the other, possibly scratching it. Torcelli's forehead had looked like it'd had a lot of scratching over the years. He seemed about to cry. He was that kind of man. A real trier, but never would quite make it.

'So, the real target was Angelina?'

'That's about it.'

'You know about Angelina, don't you? She was a Mafia boss's daughter.'

'Yeah, we knew that.'

Anastacia turned to Becker. 'Now, heat the pan... Sorry, Pete, we're making pancakes here.'

Torcelli was moaning. 'Oh, *caro Crista, che cosa succederà?*'

'I'm sorry, Pete.'

'Oh, hell—'

Chook did some thinking.

'I'll tell you what you can do. Arrest Quinn on some holding charge, like interference with police records.'

'We don't have any evidence that he did.'

'You don't need evidence. You can hold him for twenty-four hours without charging him. Grab him about six tomorrow morning. Put him in a cell. If you want me, I'll be there about eight. I'll have a quiet chat with him. Quinn will confess to taking the shots, making sure Silvano saw them by sending him a belated Christmas present, a camera. Why? To send him crazy. To kill Angelina. Why? To stop her exposing his father, the priest. Or, if that failed, give her such a shock she'd never again dare open her mouth.'

'You think that's it?'

'No, I don't. But it will sound authentic to a man like Quinn.'

'Oh, *dolce Gesù!*'

'Wait a minute—now drop in the butter. Sorry, I'm talking to Harry.'

'What if Quinn won't talk?'

'I'll be there early tomorrow morning. I'll make him talk.'

'What if he won't talk then?'

'I'll tell him what the Mafia does to men who finger little girls.'

'His father?'

'Yeah, his father.'

'What do they do?'

'They cut off their fingers.'

'All of them?'

'Yeah, all of them. *Ciao*, Pete. Thanks for calling.'

Chook hung up. Becker was still stirring. The butter had melted.

'Now tip it into the pan.'

He did so, slowly.

'Do I keep stirring?'

'No, just spread it to the edges.'

'Like this?'

'Yes.'

'And now what happens?'

'Wait until it's done on one side, then flip it over.'

'I meant, what's going to happen? In Griffith?'

Chook leaned against the bench, arms folded, still holding her phone and watching Becker and the omelette. She'd already made the salad. 'Now flip it over.'

He did so. 'You think Quinn is behind it?'

'I think it's the other way 'round.'

'You don't think Quinn did it?'

'I think Quinn has been set up.'

'Really?'

'Yeah, he's the fall guy, as they used to say in the old black and whites.'

'Why?'

'Yeah, why? It's starting to burn, you know.'

'Sorry!' He lifted the two halves out.

'You got any wine?' she asked.

'Enough for a two glasses of Angelina's chianti.'

They ate. It was late, after eight o'clock. Yet the sun hadn't gone down. They ate out on the eastern verandah in the shade. It was still a hot day. Summer had set in. They used a small table and two chairs. There was no need for candles or anything romantic. The smell of the bush on a hot day was enough.

'How's the pancake?' Chook asked.

'Great.'

'Let's drink to Angelina.'

They raised their glasses. 'To Angelina.'

Chapter 30

CHOOK GOT THERE about eight. Quinn was bleary-eyed and confused and stupid and protesting his innocence. They didn't tell him what he was accused of, apart from interfering with police records. Not exactly a criminal offence, but an internal misdemeanour, which could get him the sack. He was confused, not sure what was going on—exactly what they wanted him to say so early in the morning. Behaving like a man who knows he is guilty, but can't work out what he is guilty of. Because they won't tell him. Chook was in the best of moods when she arrived on the Harley.

Torcelli had the suspect in an interview room. He said over and over, 'Why did you do it?'

'Why did I do what?' Quinn would reply. This went on and on.

Finally, Chook spoke: 'It's not copying official files. It's being part of a conspiracy to commit murder.'

'What?'

'You heard me.'

'What conspiracy?'

'To kill Angelina Cosco.'

'What?'

'Because she was about to expose your father, Ambrose Quinlan.'

'Father Quinlan? He's not my father.'

'According to the records held by the Registrar of Births, Deaths and Marriages in Sydney he is. You changed your name, didn't you? Just the spelling?'

'Ah, shit, is that all?'

'You conspired to kill her.'

'Conspired with who?'

'We're not too sure yet, but that doesn't help you.'

'What the hell are you talking about?'

'You copied official photographs of the body of Angelo Cosco after he was murdered by his son, Silvano Cosco.'

'No, I never did!'

'You used that Sony digital camera to do it.'

'No, I never did.'

'Then you wrapped it up in Christmas paper and attached a card, saying it came from Daniella.'

'What?'

'Then you left it at the front door of the house out there, left it overnight.'

'No!'

'In the morning. Patrizia the old maid, picks it up, shows the package to Silvano. He opens it, delighted to have a Christmas card from his beloved Daniella. Plays around with it. Starts using it. But what comes up first? Not pictures of what he has just taken, but police file pictures of the slaughter of his father.'

'Eh? Ah, hell no, no!'

'Ah, hell, yes!'

'I can't take any more of this!'

Quinn was beginning to break down. Going to pieces. Close to crying.

Anastacia was ruthless. She had no proof, but she was relentless. They had to get him to confess within twenty-four hours or they'd have to release him. Torcelli was not happy. Quinn was being bulldozed into a confession.

This was not the way to treat a fellow officer.

Chook went on.

'What were the first shots to come up? Shots of his father, slaughtered. Blood all over him, all over the walls, the furniture, on the floor. Shots of himself, slumped beside his father's body, embracing it. Silvano crying. Other shots of him being taken into custody? Am I right?'

She was guessing all this. She'd not seen the official prints.

'No, no, no!'

'Then, when you arrived on the house, you picked up the camera and erased them, didn't you? The official shots? No-one would have seen any significance in the digital camera at that stage, would they?'

'Ah, Jesus—'

'Then you hid the camera until you supposedly found it. Where did you hide it?'

'I didn't hide it. I just noticed it sitting at the foot of the Christmas tree, unwrapped. Thought that funny. Who puts a gift back under the tree after opening it?'

'You erased the official pictures? Then put it back?'

Quinn didn't answer. He was shaking his head, holding it. Tears had begun to drop.

'Look at me,' Chook, said.

'What?'

'Look in my eyes.'

'Why would I look in your fuckin' eyes?'

'Because you are a piece of shit, aren't you? You knew Silvano would go berserk if he saw such pictures.'

'No, I didn't!'

'Why did you think he would kill Angelina?'

'I didn't! How could I know what he'd do?'

Chook had to agree. Quinn couldn't know. There was a big hole in her theory.

She changed tack. 'A good Christian, are you?'

Quinn didn't answer.

'Like your father, are you?'

'What?'

'A good Christian does not finger young girls. Not in church, anyway.'

'Ah, shit, I don't have to listen to this.'

'You're going to listen. Because you're like him, aren't you?'

'No, I ain't!'

'So, you know what I'm talking about? How did he have a son like you? He was a priest, for Christ's sake. They're supposed to be celibate? How did he produce you? How old was your mother? Thirteen? Fourteen? Fifteen?'

'Don't talk about my mother like tha! Like she was a whore.'

'Your father was a whore. And you're like him, aren't you?'

'Jesus, I want a lawyer.'

'You'd better get one. You're going to need one, Sport.'

He was crying now. 'Don't call me Sport!'

'Is that what it was? A bit of sport?'

'I want a lawyer!'

'No lawyer is going to save you, Quinn.'

'I never did it!'

'Who asked you to do it?'

He didn't answer.

'So, who are you protecting? Not just your father, is it.'

Quinn said nothing, frightened in his eyes and teeth and hands. His hands were tearing holes in themselves. Liked rats trying to hide.

Chook leaned closer.

'Your father? Ambrose Quinlan, will be disgraced, won't he? Defrocked. Sent out into the angry world? A disgraced priest. Did you do it to save your father from revelation? You Catholics like revelation, don't you? Not when you are on the receiving end of it, I bet.'

Quinn sobbed.

'You killed Angelina Cosco. The daughter of Angelo Cosco, who was the Mafia heavy in Griffith? What fuckwit would do that? I mean, in a town full of Italians?'

Quinn looked up, not at Chook or Torcelli, but at nothing at all.

'Ah, shit, I dunno.'

'You dunno? You're stupid or something?'

'Eh?'

'You know what'll happen next?'

Quinn shook his head. He did know, but didn't want to think about it.

'They'll kill you, won't they?'

Quinn gasped, just a squeak.

'Did you hear me?'

Shook his head.

'You know what they do to men who finger their daughters?'

Quinn moaned. He'd given up.

'They kill them.'

'What they do if you fuck their daughters?'

Quinn shook.

'They stick a red-hot poker up their arses, don't they?'

'Ah, shit! I haven't fucked any of their daughters.'

'But you killed one, didn't you?'

'The poor bastards scream and scream, don't they?'

'Stop't!'

'But no-one hears them, do they?'

'You know why? They tape them up, so no-one can hear them, don't they?'

Torcelli had had enough. 'Stop! Please stop it.'

Chook was relentless. 'Black binding tape. It might go on for days!'

Quinn squealed. Torcelli cut in again.

'You are torturing him!'

Anastacia ceased, sat back. She was happy.

'That's nothing compared with what they'll do with him.'

Torcelli tried to be reasonable. Tried the fatherly approach. 'If you didn't do it, Quinn, who did?'

'I can't tell you.'

'Why can't you tell us?'

Chook was delighted. 'So you know? Why can't you tell us?'

Quinn was shaking, crying still, in great gulps. 'They made me do't,' he said.

Torcelli asked, 'Who made you do it?'

Quinn looked away. At the blank walls. At the nothingness of an interview room. At the Queen on the wall, in her smiling blue sash.

'Someone.'

'Does this someone have a name?'

Looked everywhere, fear written all over his face.

'How did it start?'

'What d'you mean?'

'Did someone say to you, Angelina Cosco is going to name your father? Father Quinlan?'

He nodded.

Quinn seemed unable to speak. His face and throat were bloated, like he was going to vomit. Not food or beer or anything as substantial, but his whole soul.

'Who said that?'

He didn't answer. Chook cut in.

'Look, stupid, Angelina told me about your father, what he did to her in the sacristy. When she was eight.'

Quinn looked up, straight at her.

'She was going to kill him. She was the head of the Mafia now.'

'No, no, she was not the head.'

'She said she was, they told me.'

'No, no, that was just a dream on her part. They would never have accepted a woman.'

Chook reached out, patted the desk. 'Angelina was not going to do anything about your father. She accused him after the meeting, when everyone else had gone. I know, I was there. I heard her. So did Harry Becker. He was there too. You can ask him. Angelina would not have made a public accusation against your father. She was a strict Catholic. She loved the church. She'd do nothing to hurt the Church as such. She just didn't like him. Understand?'

Quinn almost nodded.

'So it was someone else, wasn't it?'

He suddenly spoke. 'That's all they said.'

'That your father was about to be get busted for child molestation?'

He nodded.

Torcelli said, 'For the tape, Inspector Quinn nodded. Now, it would seem that person was *not* a friend trying to warn you, was he? It was a man? A man who was at the meeting? He was trying to recruit you? Am I right?'

Quinn nodded.

'Again, for the tape, Inspector Quinn nodded.'

'A well-known person?'

Quinn hesitated. 'Yeah.'

'Was he a member of the Cosco family?'

He jumped. At least his eyes jumped, his shoulders too. But he did not answer.

'A prominent member of the Cosco family?'

Tried to look as though the question meant nothing to him.

'Let me try some names. Was it Romero Cosco?'

His eyes seemed to sink back in fright.

'It *was* Romero Cosco?'

Quinn didn't answer. His breathing was bad. So tight he was going blue.

Chook cut in: 'Who is Romero?'

Torcelli answered for him.

'Romero Cosco is, or was, Angelo's young brother, about ten years younger. There were four of them, two sons and two daughters, Angelo, Rosita, Marina and Romero. Angelo married one of the Terracini girls.'

'Isabella?'

'Yes, and they had Concetta and Angelina and Silvano.'

'And who is Daniella?'

'Romero's daughter.'

'Okay, I get it now,' Chook said. 'Romero was angry because Angelina was made Silvano's guardian. He thought he should instead, being the next male in line. So, he thought up a cute way to send Silvano back to the padded cell. Just drive him crazy again. With pictures. That would show that Angelina was not competent as his guardian, eh? She couldn't handle him in a crisis? So, he could then go to court and claim he would be the better guardian? Until he could take over the property one day? Was that it?'

Quinn was staring now. Scared half to death, by the look of it.

'I dunno, I suppose so.'

Torcelli finished the picture for him.

'As luck would have it, Angelina was there when he saw the file pictures. And he attacked her, his beloved sister. Just lashed out at the nearest figure. And now she's dead. And, the Lord be praised! Romero can get himself appointed guardian! A lot sooner than he thought!'

They watched Quinn. Shaking so badly the table was shaking.

'Was it Romero Cosco?'

He did not speak. Seemed to have stopped breathing. Looked as though his breath was going to burst through his eyes.

'Was it Romero Cosco?' Torcelli asked again. 'For the tape, the subject refuses to answer.'

Chook hopped in. 'Did he say why he wanted you to take photos?'

No answer at first, then Quinn began to stumble. 'Said that'd stop her talking.'

'About your father?'

He nodded. He felt wrecked but relieved.

'But that was not the reason at all, was it?'

He was surprised. 'What d'you mean?'

'They wanted to get rid of Angelina. She was going to be a problem, wipe out the bad elements?'

'I don't know anythin' about that.'

Chook nodded. 'They would not have told you. You were conned, weren't you?'

'What do you mean?'

'They weren't interested in what Angelina planned to do to your father. They were worried about what she'd threatened to do to them.'

Quinn was bleary-eyed, stunned. He'd been used.

'Who gave you the camera?'

'What?'

'The camera? It wasn't your idea, was it?'

He clammed up.

'Are you protecting someone? Was it Romero? Now, what's your first name?'

'Michael.'

'Michael?'

'Yes.'

'They call you Mick?'

'Sometimes.'

'Mind if I call you Mick?'

He didn't answer.

'So, Mick, here's the deal—'

Chook waited for Torcelli to agree, but he chief inspector said nothing. Not even a nod.

'You tell us everything, but we keep it quiet. You know what I mean? It's an old technique. You've probably used it yourself over the years. You make a statement, telling us exactly what happened, but we don't use the statement. We don't charge you. We keep the statement, as an investment in your future. You get it?'

Quinn nodded, Torcelli was surprised. He and Chook hadn't discussed a deal.

'Also, we do not mention your father. He will not be arrested. Provided that he behaves himself. You know what I mean?'

He nodded.

'For the tape, the subject nodded,' Torcelli said.

'In return, you will tell us all about the Mafia.'

He protested. 'I don't know anythin' about the fuckin' Mafia!'

'Maybe you can find out?'

'What? How c'n I do that?' His voice had become slurred. He was beaten.

'You might have a chat with Romero Cosco.'

'Christ, he'd kill me!'

'It's as bad as that?'

'They kill y'if y'talk, y'know that!'

Chook patted the table again. 'Not nice people, I know, Mick, but you're not family. You're from Ireland? Aren't you? Or, your father was, wasn't he? You're a cop. They won't kill a cop. Don't want dozens of uniformed people snooping around, going through their houses, their drawers, their sheds and their trucks and their drains, do they? Digging up their vines, looking for bodies, do they?'

Quinn began to droop, head to one side, eyes half-closed, watery. He could have had a good career once, but not now. He was a weakling. Terrified someone would find out one day he was the bastard son of a priest, who liked to touch up choir girls.

They watched him.

He seemed about to spill the beans, so to speak. But he did not. They had a feeling he was holding something back. Perhaps something they'd not thought to ask.

'What do you think, Mick?'

'They'll kill me.'

'All we want to know is this: Who gave the order to kill her?'

'What? Shit, why'd they tell me?'

'Because, if they don't, you are going to talk to the local cops.'

'I've already talked to you.'

'I'm not local. I'm federal.'

'I just don't know why they wanted her dead.'

'Well, *we* know. And you tell him *we* know. Tell Romero the police have it all worked out. It was a simple plan to get rid of Angelina, but not only that. The narrow objective was the farm, more than a hundred acres of prime vineyards. Hundreds of thousands of dollars coming in each year. You tell him the cops are wise to him and his little plan. And they are about to arrest him.'

'What for?'

'Murder, pure and simple.'

'Eh?'

'Tell him he's in serious trouble. Tell him the Feds are moving in.'

'The Feds?'

'Yeah, in the person of me and some pals from out of town.'

280

Quinlan thought about it. Or, didn't think about it. His brain didn't seem to be working.

'So, what do you think, Mick?'

He was leaning forward, head in hands.

'Okay,' he said. Just okay.

Chapter 31

BECKER HAD COME out of Tommy Thomkins' office in Fitzmaurice Street, when he ran into Palfreyman. Again, Palfreyman had his hands in his pockets. Not just in them, but jammed into them. As if he were walking around, looking for a fight, but now wanting anyone to see them. Which they could, because they were in his pockets. But they bulged, the pockets. So, he had something else than mere fists. And grinning like a drunk who'd just got out of bed. Weaving a bit, not so much drunkenly as like a bloke just fooling around. Having a bit of fun at your expense.

'Jesus,' Becker said, 'it's you?'

'Yeah, mate, it's me.' Palfreyman was a tall man, as tall as Chook, but not so straight. Tended to bend in the wind. 'How're you going?' he asked.

'No complaints.'

'And how's your lady love?'

'Which lady love is that?'

Palfreyman laughed. 'Which lady love? That poofter you live with, when he's in town. That bitch, Miss smartarse Babchuk. Everyone knows what she is. A bloke without a dick, that's what.'

Becker rose to the occasion. Or, the hairs on the back of his neck rose, like those of a dog that has smelt something weird. 'What did you say?'

Palfreyman laughed again. 'That ugly bitch was told to stay out of Wagga,' he said.

'She wasn't in Wagga,' Becker replied.

'Yeah? I heard what she got up to in Griffith.'

'What did you hear?'

'Stitched up a deal with Quinn.'

'Yeah?'

'A deal that'll get Quinn killed.'

'She knows what she's doing.'

'Yeah? That bitch, she'll be responsible.'

'What for?'

'The death of poor bloody Quinn.'

'Quinn? Is he dead?'

'No, but he'll soon be.'

'How do you know?'

They were standing on the footpath. One or two pedestrians had dodged around them. Or, had stopped and gawked. Palfreyman was jigging, grinning like a schoolboy who thinks he knows everything.

Becker asked again: 'How do you know?'

'How do I know? How do I know?' Palfreyman laughed again. Sounded as though he was on something. There was a loopiness about him.

'Just answer the question.'

'Someone's gonna pop him, for sure.'

'Who's gonna pop him?'

'You know who.'

'Tell me!'

Palfreyman was slowing down. Frowning and looking away. Even at the pedestrians trying to get past. Possibly not seeing them.

'The Mafia,' he said. 'The fucking Mafia, that's who.'

'Why would the Mafia get involved?'

'Involved in what? Some shonky copper being the illegitimate son of a priest? What's in it for the Mafia?'

'He's involved, you know that.'

'Involved in what?'

'He planted that camera.'

'We know that. How do you know it?'

'How do I know? Ah, everyone knows it. No secrets in the force, you know. Now he's talkin' to that mad bitch, Babchuk. Gee-Suss,' he added.

Palfreyman shook his head. Looking away towards the river, thoughtfully. As if something was going to happen. Had to happen so there was nothing he could do about it.

'So what?'

'She's set him up for murder, that's what.'

'Quinn set himself up the minute he did a deal with the Mafia.'

Becker was going to ask, what do *you* know about the Mafia? But he didn't. Something was seriously wrong with Palfreyman. He had changed. Back in Canberra, he'd been a self-confident fool. Hadn't realised he had a *mafioso* working in his team. No wonder the crims had such good intelligence, as Chook had said at the cemetery. When they'd buried Evelyn that cool day at the end of May last year.

Becker began to move off, but Palfreyman hadn't finished.

'If Quinn gets it, I'll see to it that bitch gets it too.'

'What do you mean?'

Palfreyman smiled. 'Walked right into it, didn't he?'

'Quinn? Into what?'

'A police trap, a verbal trap. You've got nothing on him, so you say his father will be exposed if he does not cooperate. That's it, ain't it?'

Becker didn't reply. Chook had told him, that was it exactly. A deal in which you lose, no matter what you say.

'He hasn't been arrested.'

'Of course not. He's runnin' around free, ain't he? And what's gonna happen to him? The fuckin' Mafia are gonna pop him, aren't they? To shut him up.'

Becker shrugged. There was no point in arguing with this man. A twisted man, Palfreyman.

'You see if I'm not right,' he said.

'See you around.'

Becker walked away, but bumped into a woman.

She'd been gawking. A small girl with her, perhaps ten or eleven. The woman jumped back, then smiled. As if he were her long-lost brother.

'Harry, it is you! Harry Becker!'

He blinked at her.

'I thought so. Remember me? It's Rose!' He could not place her. 'Rose in Coota!'

Rose? Cootamundra? he thought.

'Rose?'

'Yes, of course!'

She stepped forward. 'You haven't forgotten, have you? Oh, gee, it was a long time ago, wasn't it? How many years? Must be fifteen, eh? Oh, you must remember our little chats in the tea rooms, the Rose Tearooms. I got the job because my name was Rose. Not actually Rose, but Rosemary.'

She was close now, the girl moving in too, smiling.

The girl was quite pretty, in a substantial way. Like her mother, if the woman were her mother. This woman, this Rose, this girl from the tearooms in Coota, as she called it, was heavier now. She hadn't been exactly a slim waif when he'd known her, in those first weeks of his first posting. To Cootamundra of all places, something like Wagga had been fifty years before. Wide street, huge old hotels, soaring and spreading and dark and empty. In the main street, where often nothing had moved except a dog scratching an ear.

'Ah, yeah,' he said, 'vaguely.'

Palfreyman was still there, hands in pockets, grinning, shaking his head.

'You remember me? Rose O'Hare?'

'Yes, now I do.'

Then walked off, still shaking his head. And grinning insensibly.

'How are you, Harry? Gee, it's good to see you.'

She had all the gushing openness of a simple country girl.

She said to the girl: 'This is Harry, love. He used to be a policeman in Coota. I knew him there. What a lovely young man, he was in his policeman's uniform. Everyone thought he looked marvellous. Nice manners too. All the girls were mad about him.'

She went on and on.

Not too bright and a bit too heavy now, Rose O'Hare. But your best friend for life, if you'd let her. Wearing a cheap cotton, short sleeves, freckled arms and a rose pattern on her bosom. It was an ample bosom, well packed. Still had a good figure. Could have been a bathing beauty years ago in a local pool, when the world was young and the summers were long and languorous.

'What are you doing here?' he asked.

The girl was smiling at him, perhaps hoping he was her long-lost father.

'Ah! Looking for a job,' Rose said.

As honest as a new penny, open-hearted and perhaps not too bright.

The girl had a few freckles and wore sandals. They looked like old sandals, perhaps homemade. One or two teeth missing, not unusual at her age. Reddish freckles and green eyes. He recalled the girl in Canberra, Christine. Evelyn's daughter. She too had had green eyes and auburn hair. Coppertop, she'd described herself. And she'd been shot. *One, two!* The first bullet had missed. But that hadn't mattered from the assassin's point of view.

The second had gone straight though her brain, leaving a neat, red dot in the middle of her forehead.

'What kind of job?'

'Ah, well, I was in nursing, you see.'

'Where?'

'Where? All over the place—Where were we, love?' She was addressing the girl. 'Oh, I am sorry. Oh, I chatter on, don't I? *This*,' she said with motherly pride, 'is Prilly. April,' she explained. 'She was born in April. Oh, don't worry—' She mouthed the next words: She's not yours.

'Where?'

'What's that?'

'Where did you work?'

'Oh, in Narrandera and Hay and Deniliquin and even up north in Gilgandra. Got around, didn't we, love? Started with my training in Coota, after you left. Got really sick of serving teas and scones with jam and Devonshire cream that never comes from Devonshire, does it? I started at Coota hospital.'

'And became a nurse?'

'Yes, well, not quite a nurse, not a registered nurse. You have to do three years for that. And even go to university these days, don't you? No, I was a nursing assistant.'

'So, where did you last work?'

Becker was starting to form an idea.

He'd been given two more weeks to find a place for his mother. Otherwise, the staff at the retirement home would go on strike. But the only places that would take Iris Becker in Wagga were both Catholic. And Iris, in her madness, hated Catholics.

'Oh, at Narrandera, weren't we, love?'

The girl nodded. She had a pretty smile, affectionate. Rose turned to him. 'She's deaf, you know.'

The girl smiled at him. It was a smile of angelic belief.

'What happened there?'

'Oh, you know, the usual thing. The matron, she was a real—' She mouthed 'bitch'. 'Always at me. Pick up this, pick up that. Get a move on. We don't you pay you to sit around yarning with the patients. It's not easy to work fast, when you're carrying a bit of weight, is it? And some of the patients, you know, they were—' She mouthed: '*non compos mentis*'.

'You've worked with that kind of patient?'

'Yes, everywhere. They seem to think an assistant nurse's fit for no better than cleaning up after those who, you know, can't think too straight. Can't even recognise their own relatives. And need to be washed and cleaned up after they've—'

'Are you looking for a job?'

'Here in Wagga? Oh, I tried the hospital and they said they didn't have anything.'

'How about Mary Potter? It's run by the Catholics.'

'Do you mean—'

'Dementia cases? Yes, unable to control themselves. In fact,' he said, 'it's a hospice.'

'Hospice? You mean, they go in there and don't come out?'

'Many of them don't. Have you done that kind of work?'

'All the time. Someone's got to do it, haven't they?' The light went out of her face. 'And the laying out.'

'Laying out?'

'In a shroud. It does happen, you know. The poor things. Finished and got to be disposed of. Some relatives are callous, aren't they, Harry?'

He didn't answer. She was not acting, he sensed. She really had done that kind of job. Cleaning up the shit and laying out the dead.

He thought about it.

'Do you think the Catholics would have something?' she said.

'They're always asking for staff.'

She thought about it. 'Someone's got to do it? Haven't they? Someone?'

He made up his mind. 'Rosemary—'

'Oh, Rose, please!'

'Rose, would you like a job?'

'You mean at this Mary Potter?'

'No, I was thinking of a live-in sort of job.'

'In a house?'

'Yes.'

'Here in Wagga?'

'A sort of carer's job.'

'Caring for someone, you mean?'

'Yes, my mother.'

'Oh,' she said, 'the saints be praised!'

Chapter 32

HE DID NOT move his mother to the farm. It would have been too complicated for him and too dismaying for her. Iris in a strange house would feel she'd been abducted. Enclosed as she had been within an institution for three or four years. Would probably be frightened by the wide open spaces, the cattle, the dogs. Better to make her feel she was still enclosed in Wagga, but less tightly. So, he rented a two-room flat at the bottom of Docker Street, close to the Lagoon. In an old house that had been divided. The owner lived in the other. It had a rose garden and lilies in a pond and vines hanging across the verandah and up posts, jasmine and honeysuckle.

They moved in there, Iris in one room and Rose and her daughter in the next. Rose proved to be a gem, everything she claimed to be. She was devoted, a workaholic. Never too tired to do a bit more. Iris was disturbed at first, asking for Dot and Mavis and Cleo, who she'd known at the church home, but soon accepted that she was out. She could walk down the main street and look in the windows of shops in Fitzmaurice Street, and if they went far enough, into the Memorial Gardens. It was a daily amazement to Iris.

Becker knew he had failed his mother for years. He'd allowed her to be shut away in a place with only walls to gaze at and the same dishes every day on the table and the television set, often dead to the world. Like the residents. Lopsided in their chairs, asleep.

Young April went to school in the public school around the corner in Simmonds Street. She was in sixth class. She wasn't totally deaf. Had a hearing aid, but the battery had gone flat. Becker soon fixed that. At twelve, she was a bit behind with her studies. But that was understandable, given that she and Rose had moved around. Becker wondered about Rose. She was the one, who'd asked him to take her to a dance back in Cootamundra fifteen years ago. He'd done so but, when they were half way there, she'd said she didn't want to go to the dance. She wanted him to have sex with her. And she'd produce a condom from her bag. Which, she'd said, she'd borrowed from her sister... You've probably heard the story.

He was not sure about her movements from place to place. Had she been sacked? Had she been incompetent. Or, had been competent, but no-one could stand her nonstop chatter? Or, was she in effect on the run? On the run from what? He gave her the benefit of the doubt. Iris loved her. Sure, that Rose was her cousin, Roseanne Brinsley from Uranquinty. And she loved to see the television going. Especially as Rose told her what was going on and who Mr Howard was. He was the new prime minister and always looked very important on television. Rose was always asking her what she wanted to see. Would she like to have a rest now? Would she like another cup of tea? Coffee? Milo? Anything?

No-one could have been more attentive.

And if Iris accidentally and without knowledge made a mess of herself or on the floor while tottering to the toilet, Rose was full of compassion.

'Oh, dear, dear,' she'd say. 'How did we manage to do that?'

And, if Iris had turned and seen and somehow realised that she herself was responsible, Rose would say, 'Never mind, never mind, Rose is here, darling. It's not your fault.'

And they had visitors.

At least once a week Muriel and Angharad Thomas would call, often bringing the baby for her to see. Iris would coo over it, a marvel to see. Or, even without the baby, she having been left at home with Wendy, now fourteen going on fifteen, a reliable girl, a big sister who cared. A perfect little mother. A champion swimmer too, and played girls' cricket, and won a title. She had her own cap.

Terry came now and then and told them he had shot a red-bellied snake with the Winchester. He and Becker were walking up the creek at home to do some target shooting. They'd gone through a clump of Scotch thistles and something had moved. Harry had not seen it. The snake was only inches from his foot. Terry had yelled, 'Look out!'

Becker had jumped aside, astonished.

At the same time Terry had raised the rifle, sighted. And blasted the snake. It had writhed and writhed. Then had died, its head blown off. Well, not quite blown off, but skewered with blood and matted thistles and a thrashing tail.

And Harry said, 'Gee, that was close, mate! I didn't see it. It must have been heading for the creek.'

And I said, 'You nearly stepped on it.'

'That was some shooting,' he said.

'Yeah, I said. 'Pretty good shot, eh?'

'Nearly as fast as Chook,' he said.

'Who's Chook?' I said.

'That tall girl who comes to see me now and then.'

'Ah, yeah,' I said. 'The kids at school reckon she's faster than greased lightning.'

'Is that right?'

'Ah, Dad,' I said. Then I realised I said Dad. And he looked at me and kinda smiled and said, 'You want me to be your dad?'

'Yeah, if it's okay with you,' I said. 'Seein' I ain't got one.'

'Haven't got one,' he said. 'You'll never get into the Army if you keeping saying "ain't".'

He said nothing for a while, so I said, 'Are you gonna marry her?'

'Marry who?' he said.

'Chook,' I said.

'Why do you say that?' he said.

'She hops into bed with you, like Mum used to.'

'Yes, she does.'

'Are you going to marry her?' I said again.

'Oh, I don't know about that. I don't think she's the marrying kind.'

'Grandma says she is.'

'Is what? Going to marry me? Why does she think that?'

'By the way she looks at you, when you're not looking, she said.'

'Oh, did she?' he said.

'Anyway,' I said, 'Am I as fast as Chook?'

'Anastacia,' he said.

'Anastacia,' I said.

'Nobody's as fast as Chook,' he said. 'But you're pretty good for twelve.'

Everything went well through that hot and healthy and unworried summer until the last weekend in January. If it's hot, everyone in Wagga Wagga heads for the public swimming pool in Morgan Street or for the beach. Yes, they have a beach in Wagga. It's on a bend in the river at the bottom of Johnston Street. You have to park blocks away and walk down through a caravan park to the river. On this day, Becker dropped Muriel, Wendy, Terry and the baby at the park and then went off to find a spot for the Nissan. Iris and Rose and Prilly were already there, it being only a few blocks to walk from the bottom of Docker Street. Already hundreds in the water or on the sand or walking around.

They got Iris and Roberta settled in a shady spot under some trees and everyone, except Rose, went in for a dip. Rose said she would not leave dear Iris. And Iris smiled and looked like she was somehow conscious of where she was. Reminded of life some time ago, when she was young and a dip in the river was about the best fun for a kid. And Rose? Well, she was doing it, because Iris needed her. Rose was the kind of woman who wanted to be wanted.

Wendy was showing how she could dive, although there's nothing to dive from except a broken tree. And a horde of kids waiting their turn. She, Wendy, swam out and then dived like a porpoise, her legs straight up from a standing start. Then jack-knifed and went straight down.

She had a good figure. Robyn would have looked a bit like that at the same age. Not skinny, but well developed for a fourteen-year-old going on fifteen. A real female shape, dripping wet in her costume. Never one to wear a bikini, Miss Modesty herself. But strong, a champion swimmer.

Some of the others followed her in, Terry and young Prilly and Becker. They left the baby with Iris and Rose. Such a pretty girl, she was, Roberta. Now five months old and had the softest and smoothest hair you ever did touch, dark brown. Good enough to eat. Perfectly clean. Muriel was a good grandmother.

It was a lovely time, cool off the water. Fragrant off the trees.

Everyone yelling and cheering and laughing.

Wendy came up from a dive, a jackknife, her mouth wide open and gasping. Looking astonished, perhaps frightened. She began waving.

Everyone thought she had a cramp, but she did not. She was yelling for Becker. He stripped down to his shorts and waded out. Then, in the depths he paddled to her.

It was not far out, twenty or thirty yards. The river is not wide there, being about two-thousand sinuous miles upstream from South Australia and the everlasting sea.

Becker got near enough. 'What is it?'

'There's something,' she said. And spat more water.

'What do you mean?'

'It touched me,' she said.

'What touched you?'

'A thing,' she said. 'With a hand.'

He was right out to her now, more than halfway across. Deep there, only a few smart kids on the other side showing off and jumping. Bombing each other, they were.

'What sort of thing?'

She paddled and floated and flapped her arms, keeping herself up.

'It touched me,' she said.

'Let me see.'

Becker dived down. He was a long time gone. Once or twice, he bumped into her. She jumped or called out, but it was not the thing. She knew it was him. He put a hand on her, then rose up and apologised. 'Did you see it?' she said.

Everyone on shore was watching, puzzled.

'No,' he said, and went down again.

Came up again, shaking his head.

He did this three or four times, then he came up and said, 'Wendy, get out of the water!'

'Why?'

'Do as I say.'

A calm, sensible girl, she did so immediately.

He went down again and again. Then he came out, dripping and gasping.

'I'm gonna call someone,' he said.

'What is it?' they asked.

He ignored them, went up to his clothes and got his mobile and called someone. They waited a long time. At least ten minutes. Two cops in a patrol car nosed their way through the caravan park down to the water. Max Kruger was one of them. Max was still a one-striper then. They talked to Becker for a while, then the senior man got on his phone.

And they waited again.

Muriel said, 'Harry, what is it?'

'I don't know.'

But they knew he did. Or, if he didn't, he had a pretty good idea.

Then two more cops turned up in a big white four-wheel drive towing a tinny with an outboard motor. They were divers. They got into their gear, including goggles and flippers and went out in the tinny, about twelve feet long.

They searched down and around. Now and then, one of them would call: 'Here?' No, Becker would say, a bit to the left, in line with that big spotted gum behind you. And about two-thirds of the way across. Everybody watching, waiting. Everything had gone out of the day. Even the sun.

Then one of the divers raised an arm. And both men went down and pulled up something.

They pulled and pushed it to the shore, using the tinny to help. Slowly.

Everybody was watching, agape.

One of the divers went to the cops on the shore. Said something.

'All right,' the senior man said. 'Everybody leave this area immediately!'

Everyone yelled, 'Why?'

'Because I say so,' he said. 'This is a now a crime scene.'

They retreated reluctantly. Becker was not so reluctant. 'Get dressed and get out of here,' he said. So they did as he ordered.

They were walking back slowly through the caravan park, when the police dragged it out of the water. You could see a head and some hair and perhaps a hand poking out one side. The flesh was white, waterlogged white. The hand looked like it had been chewed by something. Perhaps by the Murray cod or, more likely, the crayfish.

'What is it?' Terry asked.

Becker was drying himself.

'I don't know,' he said. 'But I have a good idea.'

He got his family going, retreating. But held back, waiting to catch Max, shepherding the crowd back through the car park. 'Is it Quinn?' he said.

'Yeah, it looks like him all right.'

Chapter 33

CHOOK WAS IN hot water. She was to accompany her controller, a man named Breckenshaw, to Wagga Wagga. He didn't say why, but just that they were going. She was to drive. He was a slim sort of man, not tall and not short, a man with a pointy head, pointy nose and pointy ears as well as pointy shoes. A thoughtful man, Breckenshaw rode most of the way to Wagga with his arms folded and looking out the window to his left. If he looked to his right, he would have had to look at Chook.

She was puzzled. If, as she expected, she was to be banned from Wagga Wagga for life, why were they heading back there?

Occasionally, he would scratch an ear or played with his bottom lip, flicking it like strumming a guitar or a harp. He was, in fact, a harpist. He'd once performed in the school ensemble at Rugby, where he'd been little more than someone's fag. He was past that now. He'd been in the Met, but had risen to nothing in particular. Except one day, when things went very wrong. Something to do with Bermondsey.

He was a deep thinker. Drove Chook mad with his thinking.

If she'd ask a question relevant to the matter in hand such as, 'Am I going to be sacked?' He'd simply say, 'That remains to be seen.' Or, if she asked,

'Who are we going to see in Wagga?' He'd reply, 'Wait until we get there.' When she switched on the radio, seeking solace in music, any kind of music, he promptly switched it off. The Mazda was air-conditioned, but Chook was close to boiling point.

Central Office feared that, if she were on her own bike, God knows what mischief she might get up to. A wild card like her, brilliant everyone thought. A great operative, no doubt. Plenty of initiative, tending to run off the rails now and then. Not to mention frightening the good citizens of Wagga out of their wits with her gung-ho displays of firepower. There had been only one such display and only one volley—in self-defence, she kept saying. No-one who'd been there could argue with that.

They got into Wagga about noon a few days into February.

It was still hot, if not hotter.

The talk of the town was the discovery of the body of Detective Inspector Mick Quinn found floating in the Murrumbidgee River. Not on the surface, but at the feet of Miss Wendy Sheldrake, whose name hadn't been changed following her mother's marriage to Mr Henry Becker of *Nil Desperandum*, fifteen kilometres west of Wagga. Miss Sheldrake was one of the town's star performers. Champion of the high dive at the old swimming centre in Bolton Park. She was being thought of for the State titles. The police were saying nothing more, but rumour had it that drugs were involved.

Dave was waiting for them at the front door. Looked washed out, probably by the heat. Suit coat respectfully buttoned. It looked tighter than ever.

'I thought I'd better catch you first,' he said.

'This is Mr Breckenshaw,' Chook said.

'Inspector Breckenshaw,' that gentleman interposed. He firmly believed that if you didn't have a title, you were nothing.

'Jenkins, sir.'

'You look done in,' Chook said.

'It's not a pretty sight,' Dave said.

'What's not a pretty sight?'

'There's something wrong with him.'

'Who?'

'Agent Palfreyman.'

Being the junior officer, Dave worked weekends. He loved being useful. A naturally shy man, he hated having nothing to do. In return, he was given Mondays and Tuesday off. This was a Wednesday.

'What's happened?'

'He's at his desk.'

'Palfreyman? What do you mean?'

Breckenshaw said: 'Would you kindly tell me, Sergeant, what is going on?'

'Looks like something's happened,' Chook said.

'So it would seem.'

'You'd better go in,' Dave said.

'What's happened to him?'

'I think—' Dave said.

They walked along the passage, came to the door marked: Review. No reviews were done there, but that didn't matter. Reviewing claims for pensions was just a cover. Dave pushed it open, his head averted. The smell hit them. Stale food, bad breath, hard liquor and unwashed man. Palfreyman was sitting at the desk, one hand in a drawer.

He looked startled, as if caught in the act.

His eyes were open, but didn't seem to focus. Or, they did focus, but not on them. He must have been aware the door had opened and three figures had inserted themselves, if only their heads or noses, into the room. It was airless. Possibly the air-conditioning was not working. An empty bottle sat in the wastepaper basket.

'I think—' Dave said again.

'What?' Chook said.

'He's been like this for three days. Counting today.'

'What's wrong with him?' Breckenshaw asked.

'Stoned by the look of it, sir,' Chook said. Called him 'sir' to needle him.

'Palfreyman!' he said, commandingly but not loudly. Palfreyman looked like a man who is asleep with his eyes open. 'Can you hear me?'

'Eh?' He tried to focus, but could manage only a limpid smile.

'What's happened to you?'

It was pretty obvious. He was stoned, as Chook had said.

'Me? Oh, I…' His voice trailed off, his brain not far behind.

'What have you done to yourself, man?'

'What?'

'I said, What have you done to yourself?'

'What have I done?'

He tried to prop his eyes open. 'Oh, I—'

'Are you drunk?'

'Drunk? Ah, I don't know. Am I? Hard to say, isn't it? When is a man drunk? When he is plastered and under the influence of—'

'Drugs?'

'Drugs? What sort of drugs? You know—' He breathed deeply and suddenly, more like a hiccup than a breath. Whole body shook and heaved and then deflated. Except his eyes. They rolled up into his head, perhaps looking for his brain.

'I said, are—you—under—the influence of drugs?'

'Drugs? I don't know. Am I? Who are you, anyway? Who are you?'

'Breckenshaw,' he said. 'Head Office.'

'Breckenshaw? Breckenshaw? Don't think we've met, have we?'

'Yes, we have. I sent you here. Thought it would help you—'

'Help me? A few weeks in the country. Nice town, fresh air, no bullshit.'

'After what happened in Canberra.'

'Eh?'

'You went through a red light,' Breckenshaw said. 'And hit a car. The uniformed people arrested you. Under the influence at the wheel, they said.'

'Ah, that was nothing. That was—It was just one of those things.' He sang it, almost shouted it. 'No-one was hurt.'

'You were lucky. We had to talk to people to get you out of it. To give you one more chance—Sit up straight, man! And take your hand out of that drawer!' Breckenshaw snapped at him.

'Eh?'

'What do you have in there?'

'What do I have in here? In this drawer? Oh, I don't know. Might be a mouse or a cat or a gat or a piece of apple pie or—'

Breckenshaw looked at Chook. 'What's he been issued with?'

She didn't know. Dave said, 'A .32 automatic. It was Laura's Browning. I mean Major Langley. She was issued with it, but now she...'

Breckenshaw thought about it.

'Are you holding a weapon? A Browning automatic? In the drawer? In your hand?'

Then he said, 'Palfreyman! Sit up straight, get your brain into gear and tell me, in simple words, what has happened to you?'

Palfreyman looked surprised. 'A weapon? A weapon? I don't know. Am I? I don't think—' Ducked his head, had a quick look. 'No, I don't think it's a weapon.'

'What do you have there?'

'Oh, this—' He rattled or knocked something in the drawer. It sounded fairly heavy and solid, like metal. 'Nothing much, really. Just a friend.'

'A friend? Show it to me!'

'Oh, no, no, I don't think my friend wants to see you.'

Breckenshaw tensed, tried to use a gentle approach, almost sympathetic. 'What has happened to you, man?'

'What has happened? That what you're asking me?'

'Something's gone wrong, hasn't it?'

'Wrong? Ah, I dunno…'

Palfreyman was grinning like an idiot. And laughing.

'What a joke. I mean, you bastards wouldn't let me sit the inspector's exam. Said I was incompetent. You said I was a disgrace. And what'd you do to me? Sent me out to that college in Woden Creek to teach fresh-faced little farts from the bush some basic law? I mean, I know only one basic law and that, Mr Breckenshaw, is—protect your back! Always protect your back, because, if you don't, someone will stick it into you. Out in the cold. Mr Breck—Breckenshaw. Yeah, Breckenshaw. You pissed on me, didn't you? The whole pathetic lot of you. Pissed on me, and when I got a bit drunk and ran a light I had an accident. I didn't see the car on my right. I mean, you talk about law. Well, it's per—perfectly clear, isn't it? Mr Charles Breckenshaw, there is only one law in the whole fuckin' Federal Police force. And that is, stay on top or you'll be lyin' on a stone floor in some shitty little joint in some clapped-out part of some soulless city with a hole in your guts and you're thinking: Oh, Jesus, oh sweet Jesus, what's happened to me? And you thought you were gonna make a mark, didn't you? You took the bullet and no-one said thank you. Not one word of thanks. And you lie there, thinking why the hell? And someone is saying, Get an ambulance! And someone else is shouting into a phone: Officer down, officer down! Ah, you sent me here to fucking Wagga Wagga, and what do I find? That hard-faced bitch called Babchook. Or, whatever they call her here. And everyone's cheering and saying, Good on you, Calamity Jane. Good on you, Calamity…'

His voice trailed off. His eyes closed.

Breckenshaw crept closer, one or two steps. Couldn't make it out, what he had in the drawer. So he looked at Chook and nodded. She put a hand on the sidearm under her left shoulder.

'Palfreyman, are you under the influence?'

No answer, except for a piggish sort of grunt. Palfreyman leaned back and shook himself, flexing whatever muscles he still had under control. And tried to sit up straight.

'How long have you been like this?'

'Like this? Oh, I don't know.' He blinked hugely. 'Came in for a quiet smoke and a drink and a shot of something, you know.'

'When was that?'

'Oh, I don't know. Sunday, I think. Yeah, late Sunday. Dave was still here. Asked him to go and get me a bottle of White Horse and a pie with tomato sauce. He went off and took a long time. Eventually came back with the whiskey and said they didn't have any pies hot, it being so late on Sunday. Anyway, they were Friday's.'

'Then Agent Jenkins left?'

'Yeah, I think he did. You left, didn't you, Dave?'

Dave didn't answer.

'Palfreyman, I'm asking you, where is the pistol officially provided to you? A .32 Browning?'

'Do I have a Browning?'

'That's what I want to know.'

'Where is it? Oh, I remember now. Yeah! I threw it in the river.'

'In the river? Where did you throw it?'

'Where? Oh, any old place. Don't remember exactly.'

Chook cut in. 'Why did you throw it in the river?'

'Why?' Palfreyman, shook his head. 'I threw it in after him.'

'After who?'

'After Quin—Quin—'

'Quinn?'

'Yeah, that's the bloke.'

Breckenshaw asked: 'Who is this Quinn?'

'Eh?'

'You just said you threw it in after Quinn.'

Chook interceded. 'Inspector Quinn, State police.'

'State police? What happened to him? Quinn?'

'Eh?'

'Did you shoot him?'

'Eh?'

'Did you shoot this Quinn?'

'Ah, well, y'know, I had to, didn't I?'

'Why?'

'What?'

'Why did you have to shoot him?'

'Ah, Jesus, he was gonna talk, wasn't he? This crazy bitch here grilled him, told him a pack of lies. Said she was gonna let him off the hook if he talked. All about the fuckin' Mafia. I mean—'

He didn't seem to know what he meant.

Chook cut in again. 'Were you the one, the one who—'

'Let me handle this, Sergeant Babchuck.'

'Just a minute, sir. This is vital.'

'I am in charge here! What is he talking about?'

'Just shut up, sir! Now, Palfreyman, were you the one who worked it out? The one, who said you could frighten the wits out of Silvano Cosco by showing him the pictures? Use a digital camera to copy them, then send the camera to Silvano? As a Christmas present?'

'Eh?'

'Sergeant Babchuk—'

'Do I have to hit you, sir? Palfreyman, did you?'

'Did I what? Ah, yeah, I did. Pretty smart, I thought. So did Quin—Quin—'

'And he sold the idea to them? Who exactly? Was it Romero Cosco?'

'Eh? I don't know. I suppose I did. I didn't know crazy Silvano was gonna kill his own bloody sister, did I?'

'Sergeant, there will be serious consequences—'

Chook ignored him. 'And what did you get for this advice?'

'What'd I get? What'd I—Wow! What'd I get? Wow! Bow-wow-wow.'

He howled. Threw his head back and howled.

'They paid you, didn't they?'

He began gurgling wordlessly.

'What did you get?'

'What'd I get? Ah, Christ? I got what everyone wants. I got paradise!'

'You got money?'

No answer, just a mad smile.

'You got drugs?'

Still the mad smile.

'What've you got in the drawer?'

'What?'

'What have you got in that drawer?'

Breckenshaw slapped the desk. 'Is it a weapon?'

'What?'

'Are you holding a weapon?'

'A weapon in this drawer? Ah, Christ—'

'If you don't have a weapon, take your right hand out of the drawer.'

'This hand? The right hand?'

He was looking down inside the drawer. What he really did have in there, no-one knew. He was out of control.

'Palfreyman, I am ordering you. Take your hand out of the drawer!'

'This drawer?'

'Yes, that drawer.'

'This drawer? The one I've got my hand in? Why is everyone so interested in what I've got in this drawer? It's only a little—' He sat up. 'Who the hell are you to tell me what to do. Shit, I've been on raids where they kill you, if you don't know what you're doing. They kill you, if they're a bunch of starry-eyed crazies all doped up and don't give a shit if you kill 'em. Because, I know you, Mr arse-licking Pommy bastard from nowhere. I mean, when you were at the Met, you were a joke. You stuffed up that raid in Bermondsey, didn't you? They were waiting for you with an Armalite and an Uzi and Christ knows what else. You lost two good men and three wounded. All married men. Women and children cryin' at the funerals. On the BBC, I saw it when I was there. So, they sent you out here, to get rid of you. And—and—'

Palfreyman lost track. His eyes rolling. 'Oh, Jesus,' he said.

Lay back in the chair. It was the high-back chair Laura Langley had vacated only two months ago. Ran his free hand over his eyes, blinked again. His right hand was still in the open drawer. He was past it now, washed out, and stoned, they could see.

Drugs, most likely.

'This is the last warning, Palfreyman. If you have a weapon in your hand, drop the weapon. If you take your hand out and you are still holding a weapon, the sergeant here will shoot you. Do you understand? She will attempt to hit you in the hand or the arm. If that proves impossible, she is authorised to kill you. Do you understand? She is hereby authorised. No messing around. Straight through the heart. If need be.'

It was a tense moment. Palfreyman was grinning, leaning back, his head high. The free hand to his eyes, then to his forehead, about to yawn. Instead, he began to laugh. It was an end-of-the-world kind of laugh.

The right hand came out. Holding something small and dark grey, almost black. Hard and metallic.

Chook didn't attempt to hit it, or the arm. There was no time.

She went straight for the heart. No messing around. Everyone jumped, including Palfreyman. The 9mm bullet knocked him back in the chair on wheels. Struck the wall behind. The sound ear-splitting.

'Oh, Jesus,' Breckenshaw said.

'You said to kill him,' Chook said.

'My God, I didn't say you *had* to kill him.'

'You said, *if* he drew a weapon.'

Breckenshaw crept past Dave and looked. It was not a weapon of any kind. It was a small, hard, metallic box, hinged. 'Pick it up,' he said to Dave.

Dave opened it slowly. Then it snapped fully open, spring laden. One of those steel spectacles cases with a plastic cover outside and some sort of felt padding inside, perhaps fine soft cloth. 'What's in it?' Breckenshaw said.

Dave checked it for several seconds, then held up the box..

'Ampoules,' he said.

'Ampoules?'

'Five of them.'

'You mean, morphine? Is there a syringe?'

'Yes, sir, there is. Very small.'

'They paid him with morphine,' Chook said.

'God, the stupid bastard. What the hell am I going to tell—God, woman, why did you do it?'

'You said to fire *if* he pulls out a weapon. It looked like a .32.'

'I said if it *is* a weapon, not if it *looks* like a weapon.'

Chook didn't reply. Still holding the Glock.

'And I said to go for the weapon, or his hand, or his arm.'

'You said to kill him if I *thought* I had to.'

'But *only* if it was too late to—'

Voices outside. Someone was knocking on the door. Dave went to it, leaned against it. More knocking and a voice: 'Are you all right in there?'

'You said if I thought it was a weapon and it was too late to shoot it out of his hand—'

'No, no—'

'You said it was my call. Well, I *made* the call.'

'Has anything happened in there?'

They heard several voices now. Someone turned the handle, tried to open the door, but Dave was leaning against it.

'You are an idiot, Sergeant Babchuck. A dangerous idiot. No wonder people at Head Office are worried—'

'And you are a useless idiot, sir. There is a difference.'

'What am I going to tell these people?'

'Those outside? Say he shot himself.'

'Shot himself? But why?'

'We found him with drugs.'

'He didn't have a weapon.'

'They don't need to know that.' She was still holding the Glock.

'Either that or tell 'em you ordered me to kill him. Right, Dave?'

Dave was scared, but he nodded.

Someone was banging on the door. 'This is the manager! Has something happened in there? Please, open this door!'

'Let him in, Dave,' she said. 'Only the manager.'

'No, no, don't open the door!' Breckenshaw said. 'Don't let them see—'

He was a deflated man, begging for a way out. The disgrace, the—

'Open this door!' someone yelled.

Chook shouldered her weapon.

'Dave? Open the damned door.'

Chapter 34

AFTER THAT, THINGS became difficult in Wagga Wagga. The field post was closed down. The whole town knew why. Instead of harmless public servants poring over files in that secretive office in the Commonwealth building in Morrow Street, there were three or four Federal officers, all armed to the teeth or able to reach for weapons if they needed them. And a lot of difficult people were involved. Such as Detective Inspector Mick Quinn, who, it turned out, had been under surveillance for some time by his own people, the State police. It seems he was running a little business on the side, cannabis.

When Quinn told certain people in Griffith the Federal Police were going to arrest them for the murder of Angelina Cosco, a meeting was held. On the advice of the old godfather, Don Mario, supported by Angelina's young uncle, Romero Cosco, a decision was taken. Quinn had to be eliminated. He might talk, go Crown witness. So they made that policeman, Palfreyman, an offer. Kill Quinn and he could have all the morphine he wanted. It seems that they knew all about Palfreyman, and his habits.

As for Chook, she was relieved of all duties, but on full pay. Which showed a measure of understanding at the top and perhaps a little sympathy. After all, she was a star performer. She could have been someone. Maybe a chief inspector one day? Not bad for a girl who'd been a fucked-out junkie when a kid. She was stood down, inoperative. Told to keep away from Wagga, an instruction she interpreted literally. Did not go into Wagga, not once. Simply rode to Gundagai, then along a back road to Junee and then on to Coolamon, where all she had to do was turn southward and cross the Murrumbidgee at Old Man Creek.

Spent a lot of time at the farm, *Nil Desperandum*. Where she was happy, helping with the cattle. Doing odd jobs, such as fencing and felling and clearing and painting and spraying. She loved it, but regretted what had happened. Deeply regretted. As inadequate as he was as a cop, Palfreyman didn't deserve a hole in the heart. And sudden death. Gaping death.

The days were deepening sooner now; the heat had largely gone.

The creek was still dry. They hadn't seen any worthwhile rain for months. But everyone said there'd be rain in May. Becker wasn't too worried. He had the bore water for his stock. It was slightly smelly, humans would not drink it if they could get something else, like pure tank water. Tank water smells like galvanised iron, which is not too bad. Bore water can stink like rotten-egg gas, but west of Wagga it was not too bad. The cattle didn't object. And if they were happy, everyone was happy.

She was cooking chicken kiev one night late in March.

Chicken pieces stuffed with butter were already cooked and all she had to do was roll them in bread crumbs eggs and herbs and put them in the oven, already heated. Washed her hands and picked up the wine Becker had poured for her and sat on the lounge before the non-existent fire. The living area was air-conditioned.

He was setting the table.

'Harry?'

'Come here, will you? Please?'

Picked up his glass and went to her. 'What is it?'

'What's the matter?'

'I feel rotten.'

'Because of what happened to Palfreyman?'

'Yeah.'

'What's the problem?'

'I should not have shot him, should I?'

'You had to do it. You were told to do it.'

'No, I wasn't. I was told to use my judgement. If it looked as though he were holding a weapon, I could shoot him.'

'Well, that's what you did, didn't you?'

'I didn't use my judgement.'

'You didn't?'

'I shot him,' she said. 'I deliberately shot him.'

'Jesus Christ!' He spilt wine. It dribbled down the glass.

'It's true,' she said.

'No, it's not!'

'Yes, it is.'

Becker studied her. She was not looking at him, but looking as though she were watching dancing flames. There were no flames, of course.

'I was staring at him. I did not blink. Told myself I must not blink. In the moment of a blink, he could have whipped up a weapon, already pressing the trigger. And that smile on his face. Or, if not on his face, then in his eyes, a flicker of a smile. I knew he was going to do it: He was going to kill me. So, I shot him.'

'Yes, but there was no gun.'

'Harry, Harry, how was I to know?'

'Maybe he wanted you to shoot him.'

She was surprised.

'By the sound of it, he wanted you to think there was a gun. He was in a bad way, finished, fed up, no way out. He didn't have a gun. He'd thrown it in the river. So, he thought he'd use yours, get you to shoot him. Straight through the heart.'

'It was that bad?'

He didn't answer. She studied him. 'Have you ever felt that way?'

'Yes, once or twice?'

'Before you met Evelyn?'

'And after that. I failed her.'

'You are a good man,' she said.

'Thank you.'

They sat like that for some time. Now and then sipping and thinking. And looking into the non-existent fire.

'I don't have much to offer you,' she said.

'What you've got is good enough.'

'Really? It's not much, body-wise. I'm neither here nor there. I'm a woman without a uterus and without breasts. I can't give you children. If I could, I couldn't give them suck. On the other hand, I'm like a man without a prick. I have an ugly body. Every time I see myself naked in a bathroom mirror, I want to cry. I'm not a woman or what some would see as and would want in a woman. I am ugly and impulsive and hot-tempered and I swear like a Cossack, as my mother would have said. And I mess up almost everything I do. I want to be a woman. I would love to be a real woman. Wear gorgeous clothes and smell pretty. But I know that people would take one look at me and laugh. I have been taking pills and they don't make any difference. Sometimes I am in despair. Frightened of what's going to happen to me, but I believe you when you say it'll be all right. They won't send me to jail, even if I tell them the truth. That I deliberately killed him. I detested that awful man, Palfreyman. Hands in his pockets and playing pocket billiards, as Polly used to call it. And leering and suggesting I was a hapless old dyke and putting me down and telling me I was a fucking freak, who should never have been recruited. Let alone given all the favours the Feds heaped upon me, when I was young and hopeless and had nowhere to go or to be anything other than a shy cop. Who somehow came back from the brink. And—'

'Shut up,' he said. He'd put a hand over her mouth. 'Don't speak about yourself that way. You don't deserve it. You're a tough cop, but a good woman.'

She said something like under his hand. 'I have to tell you—'

'Don't tell me you're ugly or stupid or a criminal or not worth marrying or some sort of woman that looks like a man and is not smart to look at or worth kissing or shagging or talking to and shouldn't be seen in public. Not capable of walking down the street with a smile on your face without frightening dogs and small children. You're not like that at all. You are really a woman with a good body. Despite some days and weeks and months and perhaps years of despair, you came through. Don't tell me you are not worth loving, you are. And if you really want me to marry you, I will. But not until after a decent interval, which I believe is one year since my wife died. Not that I care what anyone thinks about being married or not married, but I have to think of Muriel. She is taking care of my daughter and my two step-kids and she is a good woman, who would be horrified if I scorned the memory of Robyn, also a good woman. Who tried to be and was worth being a mother and friend and partner and everything else a wife is supposed to be.'

Becker took his hand away, ready to shove it back.

'Understand?' he said.

She blinked again.

'And another thing. You will stop swearing. Children visit this place. I have a daughter and two step-children. Roberta will live here one day. She might own it. I don't want her to pick up your monotonous expletives or whatever you may call them. Saying fuck every two minutes is not very grown-up, is it? Understand?'

She nodded, surprised.

'Nor are you to moan and groan about everything going wrong for you. You are a real misery guts, as Polly said. Remember Polly? In the car going to the safe house in Watson? She said you were a misery guts. Such women are not interesting as wives or any type of woman or man or whatever you like to call yourself. Understand?'

She began to say something.

'What was that?'

'Yes.'

'Now listen,' he said. 'After a decent interval, I will marry you. If you're still interested. Agreed?'

'Yes.'

'In the meantime, you can treat this house as your home. Understand?'

'Yes.'

'All right, do you have any questions?'

She shook her head.

The microwave dinged like a bicycle bell. He took his hand well away.

They sat like that for about fifteen seconds, each looking around at everything except the other. Then she said: 'Yes.'

'Yes, what?'

'I do have a question.'

'What is it?'

'Are you ready to eat, darling?'

Chapter 35

IT WAS ANOTHER fine day. There had been rain, but it had stopped. When they got up and looked outside, mist was hovering over the paddocks. Below the mist was green feed, the first they'd seen for a few months. The cattle looked happy, delighted with such a treat. It was such a good day, a good day for getting away altogether. They were going to climb The Rock. They'd been talking about it for weeks. Chook was so fit she could run up and down it like people in New York who run up and down the Empire State Building.

Climbing The Rock would be much easier, even for a bloke like Becker, who'd lost a lot of condition ever since that bullet had hit his right shoulder in Maroubra, Sydney. The night someone tried to kill him. Even with a bit of hard yacker at the farm, such as repairing the roof on the barn as it was called or fixing fences or rounding up heifers that didn't want to go to the meat works—you had to push or pull or bully or whip them to get them on board a truck. That was not enough. He was steadily putting on weight, so much so Chook was laughing at him, patting his gut and saying, 'You've got to lose weight, fat boy.'

They'd packed a hamper for lunch and young Terry, who was staying with them—it being the last days of the May school holidays—had asked for the Winchester. The Rock was a nature reserve, no shooting allowed.

'We might see something on the way,' he protested. He was determined to get into the Army, even though he was only twelve. And thought the better shot he was the more hope he had, when he turned eighteen.

Becker had been up The Rock when he was a kid, only nine, going up and up into the heavens with his father. But that was a long time ago, when he had young feet and legs and hopes. His mother, Iris, would not climb. She'd sat at the camp site below and sulked until they came down, nearly three hours later. Drinking cups of tea, one after the other, until she was brown in the face.

When Bert came across, they'd finished loading the Nissan.

Carrying the Hollis and he looked worried, as much as Bert could look worried. That kind of man looked worried all the time, being in his seventies now. As rough as bags and having a dirty, furrowed brow. Clothes never washed and hair going every which way. His eyes too. Never looked you straight in the eye.

Even so, you could tell something had happened.

'Blue's gone,' he said.

He meant Blue Two, Blue One having been shot dead by the cattle duffers from down Henty way. Becker was about to close the hatch on the Nissan.

Chook was already seated in the front. Terry holding the Winchester. Becker had told him to give it to him, so it could be stowed in the back too. Terry had said and promised, hand on his heart, he could hold it in the back. To keep it safe, he argued. Becker had told him to hand it over.

'Why?' he'd asked.

'Because I don't want to be shot in the head, just because you couldn't the resist the temptation to play with it.'

'It's not loaded,' the boy had protested.

That was the situation, when Bert spoke.

Becker blinked at him. The morning was rich and refreshing and still golden, not yet clear all the way to the moon. It being in the west, hanging there, upside down like a galah on a phone line on a winter's morning, getting at the dew drops to drink.

'You mean he's run away?'

'Snake got 'im.'

'A snake? This time of the year?'

'Not cold enough yet,' Bert said. 'Must've been sunnin' 'imself. In the long stuff up there.'

'You killed it?'

'Nah, wasn't there. Heard 'im yelp. Yards away at the time, maybe twenty or thirty. Was a tiger b'the look of it.'

'You saw it?'

'Saw 'is tail as 'e went in. Had stripes.'

'In where? Into a log?'

'Yeah.'

'Where's the log?'

Bert didn't answer, looking here and there. Hadn't started scratching yet. Finally, he said: 'Up'n the corner.'

'Whose corner? Yours or mine?'

'Mine,' he said.

'Jesus, Bert, I've told you a dozen bloody times. You've got fallen stuff all over your place. And thistles. No wonder you have snakes.'

'Ah,' Bert said, running a hand through his chaotic hair. 'Leave it to the kookas to clean 'em up.'

'Well, they don't get 'em all, do they? Not full-grown ones. You're sure it was a tiger?'

Bert said: 'Yeah, 'ad bands all right.'

'And where's Blue?'

'Up by the log.'

'Where the snake is?'

Bert nodded.

'How is he?'

'Gone stiff.'

'Nothing you could do for him?'

'Nah, 'ad to sit an' watch 'im.'

'I could've rung for the vet, if you'd come down.'

Bert said nothing, head down. Then, 'Couldn't leave 'im, could I? Good dog like that?'

'Ah, Jesus,' Becker said. 'Everybody out!'

Chook got out. Terry, who was out, smiled and got in.

'What are you doing?' Becker asked.

'Ain't we gonna drive up? To the top?'

'No, we're going to bloody well walk. Give me that rifle!'

That's what they did. Chook stood by the vehicle watching, smiling.

She loved living on a farm, always something happening. Leaned on the vehicle with her arms crossed and legs crossed and watched them setting off. Began to sing to herself: 'Take my hand, I'm a stranger in paradise...'

They walked up the fence.

Had got about half way up, when the first bullet hit. Hit her left shoulder. Spun aroun, reaching for her Glock. Not wearing it. Wasn't even wearing a jacket. Had felt free as the breeze for two months. Got down low, tried to get behind the vehicle. Second bullet hit her in the back, lower right side. One or two ribs up.

She lurched, then fell.

Crawled behind the four-wheel drive, but could see nothing. Someone out in the trees was trying to kill her. Another shot nicked the Nissan, bounced off the spare.

They ran back, Becker, Bert and Terry. They ran like hell, Nutty with them.

'Get him! Get him!' Becker was saying. The stupid dog thought it was a great game. A hundred yards from the Nissan, the fourth shot came.

Missed them, hitting the dirt behind them.

Becker ran to the Nissan. Chook looked reasonably safe, even with two bullets in her. 'I can see him!' She was gasping. 'On the other side of the creek. Behind that big coolabah.'

Another bullet hit the Nissan, low down.

Stones flew up. She flinched, something had hit her on her legs, not a bullet. Shooter obviously trying to bounce a shot under the vehicle. To get at her legs.

'Terry!'

Becker shoved the Winchester at the boy. 'Take this, hide here. Make him keep down.' Another shot hit the Nissan, bounced off the roof.

'I'm all right,' Chook said, but she was not.

He opened a door, a back door. 'Get in,' he said. 'Get down!' He pushed her. She scrambled in, head down.

'Terry? Can you see him?'

'No, I—'

'Get in the house. Pin him down.'

'Okay!'

'Where the hell is Bert?'

'Can't see him.'

'I'm going. I'm gonna take her.'

'I can see Bert. Behind him. Comin' up behind him.'

'Pin him down. Pin him down so he's looking at you. Not at Bert. Understand? I'm going!'

'Yeah, yeah!'

Jumped into the Nissan, started up. Got it rolling around a corner, of the house and away.

Could hear the firing. Regular, not frantic, selective. The boy had got the idea. A good shot, intelligent. Not wasting bullets. Nutty barking in the distance, fading. Becker got the Nissan around the side and into the protection of the house. He pulled out his phone.

'Emergency,' a woman said.

'I want an ambulance at—'

'Wait a moment, please, sir.'

Another pause, another woman: 'Ambulance.'

'I want an ambulance at *Nil Desperandum*. It's a farm about three kilometres short of the Lockhart turnoff on the Sturt highway west of Wagga. My wife, my wife, has been shot in a shoulder and in the back and she's bleeding badly and—'

'Just a moment, sir.'

He waited.

She came back. 'An ambulance is on its way, sir.'

'It's only a few yards past the Kettle's Creek sign. *Nil Desperan—*'

'The driver knows your property.'

'I've got her in a Nissan four-wheel, out front of the house.'

'You've got her in your own vehicle?'

'To get her out of the way. Tell the police.'

'Just a moment.'

Another silence.

He didn't know what to do. Take her in or wait for the ambulance. If he left, he would be leaving the boy. Leaving a twelve-year-old boy to fight off a madman in a tree or behind a tree. Not quite clear. But Bert was there. Bert was somewhere. He had a shotgun. He was mad enough and angry enough to shoot the bastard firing the .22. And Nutty was there.

'The police have been informed,' she said.

'How long? The ambulance? To get here?'

'Estimated time, ten minutes.'

Chook was starting to cry.

'Christ, no!'

'What's that, sir?'

'That's too late. I'm bringing her in!'

He gunned the big vehicle. In a few seconds he was out on the highway.

'What did you say?'

'I'm bringing her in!'

'The ambulance will meet you. Flash your lights when you see—'

'I know, I know!'

'How bad is your wife?'

He called back. 'Chook? Chook?'

'I feel bad, Harry.'

'She's losing blood fast.'

Chook huddled behind the front seats. Collapsed down there. Her breathing bad, moaning. Beginning to cry. Halfway to Wagga he saw the ambulance, flashing everything it had. He flashed back. Slowed down, saw the driver, stopped. Yelled, 'She's going into shock!'

Then kept going. About five kilometres out, he saw the police car. Max Kruger was at the wheel. He slowed again, yelled at him, 'Get to the farm! There's a gunfight there.'

'What?' Max yelled.

But he understood enough. Half way to Wagga Wagga, he met the ambulance, began to slow down, so they could take her. But Anastacia yelled: 'Keep going! I can last that long!' The ambulance turned around, screamed past Becker and led him in. Made the right-hand turn into Docker Street against the lights—and plunged into the hospital.

Becker left her there. Went back immediately. Two police cars were now at the farm. It was all over.

'You have a remarkable son,' Jack Jackson said.

'He's not my son.'

'Then, he should be.'

Terry said: 'That's the bloke with the boar.'

'Which one?'

'The one called Keith.'

An ambulance crew was still working on him, but he looked bad. Too bad to be moved yet. One man was holding up a bottle of blood.

'What about One-Eye?'

'They're looking for him.'

'Where was he?'

'In the lane. Came over and tried to get this one away. Was dragging him, but Nutty went for him. Bert told him to clear off or he'd get one too. He skittled. Must have had a vehicle in the lane. Didn't come out onto the highway. Must've followed the lane back to the Rock road. Probably heading for Henty.'

Jack came back with two other cops. But Max Kruger was not there.

'Gone after him,' Jack said.

'You mean after One-Eye?'

'Must've had someone waiting with a vehicle. Max knows the family. Thinks he knows where to find them. They keep moving around.'

'The bastards,' Becker said.

'How's Anastacia?' Jack said.

'She'll make it.'

'Got there in time, eh?'

'Yeah.'

'Lost much blood?'

'Yeah. But she's a big girl, she can afford to.'

They watched the ambulance crew and the gunman bandaged up tight. Like some dumb animal, he didn't cry. Now and then he said: 'Where's Ron?' Said it over and over. Had nothing else to say.

They lifted him into the ambulance.

The boy was still holding the Winchester. 'I got it right, Harry.'

'Got what right?'

'The action, lever down, lever up, sight up, pull the trigger and—'

The rifle exploded. A bullet hit a tree, bark shattered and fell. Everyone ducked. Jack went for his Smith and Wesson.

'Give me that!' Becker seized the rifle.

'Gosh, I'm sorry.'

'Oh, Jesus, you didn't put the bloody safety on!'

'Ah, gee, I'm sorry!'

'You're as stupid as Forrest Gump.'

'Forrest Gump got into the army.'

'They must have been desperate.'

'Ah, gee!'

'If you're gonna forget the safety every bloody time—'

The boy looked like he was going to cry.

'I'm really sorry,' he said.

Becker looked around. It had been an exciting morning. It was near midday now. Too late to think about The Rock. Maybe another day, when she came out of hospital. If she could walk, then. 'How many shots did you get off?'

'Ah, I was down to the last two in the third clip.'

He reached for the boy's head, mussed his hair.

'You're a good kid,' he said. 'Very brave.'

'Ah, thanks, Harry.'

'What happened to the snake?'

'Bert shot it.'

'He did?'

'Stuck the gun in one end of the log and blasted him out.'

'Just like that?'

'Yeah, that's one for Blue.'

'I suppose so, one for Blue.'

'How's Stacey?'

'She'll pull through,' he said.

He walked with Jackson to his car.

'I told you I was withdrawing charges.'

Jack was offended. 'I told them that.'

'What'd they say?'

'They didn't say anything. You know those deadbeats? They think differently. They thought your dog bit their boy. He lost a leg from the knee down.'

'They never give up, you mean?'

'That's right. Withdrawing charges is a victory for them. Confirms that they are right.'

Jack shot out a hand. They shook. Then he got in a police car.

'So why try to kill Stacey? Instead of me?'

'To make you suffer, I'd say.'

'I'm not so sure.'

Chapter 36

ON THE WAY back to town, he thought: If they wanted revenge for the young bloke's leg, why try to kill Chook? She had nothing to do with that. She hadn't lived at the farm then. Yet it had been a persistent attempt to kill her, not him. The deadbeat with the .22 could have taken a shot at Becker as they'd walked up the hill to look for the tiger snake. Could, with perhaps a lucky shot, have whacked him in a temple, smashed through his brain. After all, the bloke was using .22 longs. Small but nasty. Very high velocity, capable of reaching 1,500 yards. But low impact. One of those could go straight through you without doing much damage. That's what had happened to Chook.

The first shot had hit a shoulder, whacked into a bone. The doctors had got that out. Didn't have to get the second one out. It went in through a lung and out the other side. Nothing vital had been hit. She'd lost blood, but not as much as Becker had thought. Or feared. The holes were small. She was lucky. Or, unlucky, depending upon the way you looked at it. She didn't deserve it. It looked like a deliberate attempt to kill her.

But, whose attempt to kill her? That was the odd thing about it.

Who would pay a couple of whackers and drongos and defectives like the MacKinlays to do it? The young one had persisted in firing, too stupid to look behind him. Didn't seem to know Bert was coming up behind him with the Hollis. And the barking dog was at him persistently, giving him away.

He could have shot the dog, but he didn't.

And another thing. They didn't seem to have an exit plan. How were they going to escape if anything went wrong? They had a truck parked in the lane. An ancient Ford pickup, forty of fifty years old. It could have broken down at any minute. Might not have started, flat battery or flat tire, anything.

Who would employ a pair of incompetents like that?

So thinking, he dropped the boy at his grandmother's house. Then went to the hospital to see Anastacia. She wasn't even in Intensive Care.

She smiled when she saw him.

Her left shoulder was heavily bound. Her back hurt. Tried to move when she saw him, but flinched. Still dopey and still shocked by what had happened. Rigged up for oxygen, a transparent up over her mouth and nose. But she could speak in a wobbly way.

'Hullo,' she said.

He bent down and kissed her on her forehead. She looked groggy and sheepish, as if it were all her fault. A nurse was standing by, holding a small dish with a neat cloth over it.

'How is she?'

'Spitting blood, but that's to be expected.'

'How are you?' he said to Chook.

'Okay,' she said. Tried to smile again, apprehension in her eyes. Blood edging her lips.

'You were very good,' he said. 'Got out of the way fast.'

'Thank you.' Her voice was weak.

'They got him,' he said. 'Some cretin from down south.'

'South?'

'Down Henty way.'

She indicated surprise with her eyes. Why Henty? Or, perhaps farther south. She being a cop, already trying to work it out. Couldn't see what she had to do with cattle rustlers, or duffers.

'Max has gone after his mate,' he said. She nodded almost imperceptibly. 'They'll get him.'

She didn't seem to be worried whether they did or did not, the police.

'It could have been—' she began to say, but choked.

Tried again, but he couldn't make it out. The nurse left them.

He got down low, so he could hear her. So low he could feel her short breath on his cheek.

'What?' he said.

'It could have been—those people in—'

'In Griffith?'

'In Melbourne.'

'Melbourne?'

'Those people, the Donna.'

'*La Donna*? She would hire someone to kill you?'

She tried, it being an effort. 'More likely—'

'The lady's sons?'

'Two,' she said. 'Michele and—Stephane.'

'Why would she do that? Why would they?'

'Because I—'

'You what?'

She was whispering, almost silently. 'I killed the old man.'

'What old man?'

'*Il*—'

'*Il* what?'

'*Il capo*,' she said. It was a struggle.

'Oh, Jesus, no, Chook. No, don't tell me!'

She nodded shakily.

'Strangled him in bed.'

'The *capo*, in Melbourne?'

'*Lo capo dei capi.*'

Becker raised his head, wishing he hadn't heard this.

'Oh, Christ, you should never have done that. I thought you left him to die of natural causes? In a rest home?'

'I helped nature along.'

'Hell, no!'

'He killed Polly. He ordered— He got the fat man to—to send—'

He stood up, thinking: Where was the fat man? She's not dead, so they'll try again. They'll never give up. They paid a bunch of hicks down Henty way to kill her. What a smart cover that was. They select some deadbeat whackers, who have a grudge against himself, Harry Becker.

They pay them to kill the woman, not Becker.

But the police will think it's because of the kid, who'd lost half a leg, because of dog bite. Festered until it had to be cut off. Revenge pure and simple. Soon wrapped up, especially when the cops catch up with them.

If they can't get One-Eye, they'll grab one or two others. Family members. Sure to be a bunch of them. Hicks always had tons of kids, aunts, uncles, old folk. Deadbeats on the dole. Who'll give the same story, that it was revenge. Because they've been told: You talk, you're dead. Because the fat man was still out there, a man named Nekrasoff.

When the police caught up with One-Eye, he did talk. Quite freely, nearly crying. Max Kruger and the local cop in Henty missed them at the run-down squat two miles out of town. But the Henty man knew of a cousin in Victoria, a failed dairy farmer outside Beechworth. He got on the phone to the Beechworth cops. When the Ford chugged to a stop at the farm gate, armed police appeared out of the wattle scrub and thistles. One lone cow watching them, wondering when anyone was ever gonna come and take her milk. Because she was hurting, hurting bad.

Told them to reach for the sky. Then the two New South cops turned up.

One-Eye broke down. Started complaining about never having had a chance. Not since he'd developed a spot in his left eye as a kid. A spot which, over the years, had spread wider and wider and whiter and whiter. Like porcelain.

They asked him a simple question: 'Who paid you?'

He refused to talk for a while, but when they pointed out that attempted murder of a Federal officer could get him fifteen, he gradually opened up.

He was having a quiet beer in the Henty pub one day, when some foreign bloke had sidled up and said, 'We've heard you've been having some trouble, my friend?'

'Yeah?' old One-Eye had said.

'With a certain person not far out of Wagga?'

'Yeah, a bit.'

'A problem, is he?'

'Who are you?' One Eye had said.

'A friend,' the greasy-looking bloke had said.

'Where're you from, then?'

'You don't need to know, my friend.' One-Eye could tell he was from Melbourne, because he was wearing a fancy beige-coloured suit and he smelt of garlic, lots of it. The curious thing about him was that he had a fat gut, which didn't seem to go with his otherwise slight build.

'What're you on about?' he'd said.

'How would you like to earn fifty-thousand dollars?' the stranger had said—very slowly, one syllable after the other. Like a magician waving a wand of words.

He was a fat man, who looked like a Greek or Italian or Turk...

Anastacia was gazing up at him.

'What are you thinking, Harry?'

'The fat man,' he said.

'What about him?'

'He did it.'

'Shot me?'

'Got those two defectives to shoot you.'

'Forget about him,' she said. 'Bend down.'

'What?'

'Bend right down again.' He did so. 'Thank you, husband.'

'Husband?'

'You called me your wife.'

'When?'

'On the phone, in the Nissan. When you were talking to the ambulance people.'

'Did I?'

'Did you mean it?'

'Yes, I did.'

She indicated, lower and lower.

'What is it?'

'Kiss me again.'

He kissed her and left the hospital, thinking he had to tell Jack Jackson: Put a guard on her. They'll try again. He had to do it now, get things organised before someone turned up with a syringe. It was like that last day in Canberra again, the same feeling that no matter what you did, you can never escape. Never get out of Canberra. Never get out of Wagga. Never get out of this untrustworthy world.

He did not see Jackson. Thought better of it.

If he revealed why he feared the Mafia was out to kill her—if he said what had happened in Melbourne—Chook could have been charged with murder. Taking matters into her own hands. Instead, he went home thinking: He'd somehow got involved with another killer. Evelyn had been a killer, and she'd intended to kill again. But events had changed it all. Now he was stuck with Chook, a renegade cop with her own agenda. He seemed to attract women with murder on their minds. But he liked her. He liked her so much he thought he might even get to love her one day.

A few days later, when she was sitting up by her bed quite bright-eyed, he and Muriel went to see her. Muriel was carrying the baby. Chook burst into smiles when she saw Roberta. She was now nine months old.

'Oh, how lovely! Oh, what a darling little girl you are.'

'Would you like to hold her?' Muriel said.

Reluctantly, but she'd told herself Robyn was not coming back and she could not retain the girl forever, bring her up as her own. The little girl was her father's child and, if he wanted to cohabit with a strange woman, who got herself into trouble by shooting people, so be it. He had a father's right.

'Would I? Oh, yes, yes!'

So they passed the baby, now crawling and trying to walk and to talk. Wasn't too proficient yet, but she was trying.

'Hullo, darling?' Anastacia said, holding her with one good arm. Roberta was uncertain. Stared at Anastacia wide-eyed, pretty lips open enough to show two or three teeth. Rich, brown hair piled up in a topknot. Brown hair with a gingery sheen. Smelt as sweet as a rose. Skin as smooth as silk. 'Aren't you the most beautiful little girl?'

The baby was pointing. 'Tay, Tay, Tay,' she said.

'What are you saying?'

'I think she's trying to say Tracey,' Muriel said. 'We told her she was going to see Daddy and Tracey, her new mummy.' It was painful for Muriel to say. But she was a fair woman, no matter what it took.

'Really? Do you want me to be your mummy?'

The girl smiled, nodding.

Anastacia held her to her breast, such as it was.

'Oh, yes,' she said. 'Yes.'

Chapter 37

WHEN SHE CAME out, she was embarrassed because she knew nothing about babies. Never having had a child or an infantile relative or any other kind of child to look after. Or, even been in any house, where there was a child, except the child in the house in the Dandenong Ranges years ago. One of the women there had had a child. It had cried, never had enough milk and care and love and evaluation. It was something that squealed and coughed and shat and went red with rage. Probably colic. Nobody caring a damn about it, not even its own mother. It hadn't been clear which woman was the mother. They took it in turns, the other two. As for herself, Stacey or Chook, she didn't know what to do with a child, when passed to her to hold, while the mother or woman or carer had a smoke. Pot it was. All day long, pot. The place had stunk of it. Anastacia had been a loner most of her life. Even when she had lived with her parents in Melbourne.

She was now on extended sick leave.

It was painful to move. Three wounds, a hole in her left shoulder, another in her lower left side where the bullet had gone in and a third on the right side, where it had come out. One rib was broken, another splintered but not broken. Problems that had to be fixed. After three weeks in hospital, she went into recuperation at the farm: light duties and painful twists and turns and lifts. Her left shoulder needed constant massage and sometimes painkillers.

She thought of resigning from the Federal Police.

That would be hard to do, she knew. Owed it everything, including her own life and dignity and future. If she'd not been in the force in Canberra, she would never have met Harry Becker. Everything had flowed from that. Now, she was offered a child, another woman's child. But she could not look after it and serve as a full-time police officer, a sergeant.

It had been suggested that she return to Canberra permanently, to a desk job, something easy on the ribs and the shoulder. She rejected that idea. Harry would never give up the farm. And she would never give up Harry Becker and his beautiful little girl.

Not so much beautiful to look at, as attractive. You couldn't help looking her.

Gingery brown hair, like her father's. Deep, inquisitive eyes. A brilliant smile when she understood what you wanted. Never grizzled. Seemed to have been born grown-up. A fast learner, full of fun and games. Quick with words. Called her Tacey.

So, she resigned, got out medically unfit. Got a big payout. Had never had so much money. Settled in at *Nil Desperandum*. But, the child. Didn't know how she'd handle a small child. Both physically and vocationally. Just to lift her, hurt like hell. To cuddle her was to make Anastacia wince and frown and grunt. The baby would see it, the hurt in her eyes.

So, they left young Roberta with Muriel and Wendy for the time being.

She would visit them at least once a week, admiring and disbelieving that she was at last a mother. Of a sort, that is. Not yet officially, but soon to be. She and Becker had talked about it, getting married. After waiting a decent period. It being easier now Muriel had signalled her acceptance of the notorious Anastacia Babchuk.

After the second operation, when they put a pin in what was left of her left shoulder joint. Confident enough to show her face in public again, walk along the streets of Wagga with a smile on her face and, eventually, a baby to show to the world. Walk right down Baylis Street, pushing a stroller, little Roberta waving to everyone and every dog and car that went by. The sun in her face, a treat to see.

Chook had a lot of physiotherapy, then took to working out in a gymnasium in Morgan Street, opposite the public pool. Not heavy lifts, of course. Also swimming, awkwardly at first but she soon got into the rhythm of it. Able to keep up with Wendy, the slow rhythm. Wendy was not a fast swimmer but a distance champion. Said she was going to swim down the river all the way to Old Man Creek. Everyone laughed, but she did it.

It was easy. The river flows at about two miles an hour. All you have to do is drift, occasionally stroking. A crowd met her at the Old Man bridge, which meant she had swum or drifted about twenty winding miles. One day, she declared, she was going to swim the English Channel. Never got the opportunity, but that's another story.

One day Chook came out of the gym to Becker waiting in the Nissan, enthusiastic.

'I'm going to buy it,' she said.

He was surprised. 'Buy what?'

'The gym.'

'All of it?'

She laughed. 'No, no, just one-third. One of the partners is leaving.'

'I'll buy it for you,' he said.

She beamed at him. He'd never seen Anastacia beam. She was not the beaming type.

'You will? You'd do that for me? No, you won't. You've done enough. Every girl has to feel she is independent.'

'Do you have enough?'

'More than enough. I got a big payout when I left, remember?'

And that's what happened. She bought a share in a gym. He had to admire her. She had an iron will. Whatever she wanted, she achieved.

She looked happy; she was someone at last.

'You want to get married?' he asked.

'I thought you'd never ask.'

On the second last day of August 1997, Roberta came to the farm. It was her first birthday and this was her first time. Or, her second, because she had been conceived there and had lived there in her mother's belly until that day, a year ago, when the house been blown up and her mother killed. But she herself had been saved.

It was a fine sunny day, not hot and not cool.

Everyone was there. Muriel and Wendy and Terry as well as Nurse Angharad, who drove them out from Wagga. As well as Anika from next door, who brought special treats for the birthday girl. They were having a good time, the baby squealing with delight. She was speaking well now. And walking well enough to get from one knee to another.

'What is your name?' Anika asked her.

She was puzzled, thinking. Looked quickly at everyone, then said. 'Berta!'

'What's your full name?'

'Berta!'

'No, no, that's your short name. What's your long name?'

She thought about that. You could see her mind working. Her eyes closed and then opened.

'Woberta!'

'Well done!' Everyone clapped. They thought she was going to laugh and clap herself, but she did not. She was still thinking.

'Woberta Becker!'

Everyone was stunned.

'Who taught you to say that?'

'Mummy Tacey.'

'Mummy Stacey?'

They all looked at Anastacia.

'She's a very bright girl,' she said. 'Aren't you, darling?'

'Yes!'

'And you are going to grow up and be very smart, aren't you?'

'Yes!'

Three months later, Chook was cleaning the living room when someone knocked at the door. She knew that knock. An authoritative knock, always four sharp knocks, not too loud in case a baby was sleeping. She went to the window, saw the big red pursuit car outside the gate. Opened the front door, about to say, Max? Come in. You're looking for—?

But didn't say it. Too astonished.

Another man was there, very tall, very old and very tired. His was a battered face, not battered by blows but by history. He was not looking directly at her. Was much like old Bert in a way, but taller. Much taller, perhaps six and half feet originally, but a bit bent now. Not making eye-contact, as though he didn't want to see what he'd come to see.

She couldn't believe her eyes.

'Oh, my God,' she said, 'it's you!'

Max was puzzled, smiling as he did. An open-hearted face.

'A surprise, eh?'

'*Bat'ko*?' she said. 'Father?'

'Your dad?'

'Yes.'

'Gee, Stacey, I was coming along, minding my own business and came across him walking.'

'Along the highway?'

'Yeah, saw him about eight kilos back. Stopped, had a look at him. Asked where he was going. Said he was going to Becker.'

'Becker?'

'Yeah, said Becker had a farm. Asked him if he meant Harry Becker, but he didn't seem to be sure.'

'Oh, God, Dad, why are you here?'

The old man didn't answer. Twisted his head, as if looking back at the road he'd walked along, looking for Becker.

'What have you done? Have you left your job? Have you retired?'

'Ah—' he said. It was a deep voice—the kind you would expect to come out of the Red Army Male Choir. Way down in the bass-baritone guts of the world.

'What is it?' she asked again.

He didn't answer.

Max said, 'Reckoned he'd walked from Wagga. Looks like he came up on a train. Got in about eleven and walked around until he found someone who knew about Becker's farm. So he set out to walk. They tried to get him to get on a bus, or get a taxi, but he said he'd walk. They told him it'd be fifteen 'k's', but he shook his head and asked, This way? This way? And set off.'

'Come in,' she said, both pleased and embarrassed. He'd worked in a crematorium. He might yet smell of burnt flesh.

He walked in, cautiously. Max following.

'This is my father,' she said, 'Victor Babchuk.'

'Good day,' Max said.

The old man didn't respond except with a nod of the head. It was an old, wizened head, lined and scarred and blotched with sunspots or age spots of just perhaps the heat of the ovens. His eyes looked as dry as the most parched of paddocks.

'Dad, do you have any luggage?'

The old man didn't seem to understand, so Max said: 'Didn't have any when I picked him up. Might have left it at the station.'

'Where would you like to sit? How are you? Why did you come? Have you lost your job?'

The old man stood aimlessly, bemused.

'Please sit here, Father.' She switched languages. *'Bud' laska, sidayte tut, bat'ko.'*

He sat on the divan, reluctantly. In the middle of it. holding a hat. She'd not seen the hat at first. It was an old-fashioned style of hat, with a high crown and curled up around the brim, with a black band.

Victor Babchuk was a tall man, very tall. Probably taller than Anastacia originally, perhaps six feet six. He would have shrunk a little over the years.

'That's Ukrainian,' she said to Max. 'I don't know much, I never learnt it, but picked up a few—Are you tired?' she asked her father. 'When did you last eat? You must be thirsty?' She repeated it in Ukrainian. 'Oh, this is such a surprise!' she said to Max. Then: 'How did you find us, Father? How long will you be here? What do you wish to do?'

He shrugged, not so much a shrug as a lift of the eyebrows and the eyes. Perhaps he didn't expect anything much, perhaps a glass of water. Or, hopefully, vodka, if they had it.

'You don't know?' She changed that to: *'Vy ne znayete?'*

There was an exchange of words, a few short statements. Then she said to Max: 'He came to say goodbye.'

'Where's he going?'

'Kudy ty ydesh?'

He said something, short and sweet. She gasped.

'To Odessa? You're going back to Odessa? Oh, my God!'

Becker had appeared, holding the baby. Extended a hand and said: 'I'm Harry Becker.' The old man insisted on rising, very correctly. 'And this is my daughter, Roberta.'

'I am Victor,' he said.

'Victor Babchuk,' Stacey said.

The old man nodded.

'You've just arrived? With Max? You must be tired? Would you like to—
Have you eaten? Have you walked far. Would you like to rest for a while?'

Anastacia translated all of this for her father.

'Oh, I am well, I thank you.'

Chook turned to Max. 'Thank you, Max!'

'All part of the service,' he said. And left.

She stepped forward with the baby. 'Harry and I are going to marry. This
is Harry's child, but soon she will be my child too. And your grandchild.'
Then translated as best she could.

He nodded. His eyes flicked to the baby watching him, reaching for
him. He didn't hold out his old hands, but merely observed. How much he
understood of his daughter's speech, was not clear.

Chook found some cold cuts for her father. Then old Victor lay on Terry's
bed, in the room by the back door. Opposite the laundry. And slept. He slept
until six o'clock. The sun had gone down. When he awoke, Anastacia sat with
him, spoke to him. Often, he didn't understand her attempts at Ukrainian.
She'd never learnt it formally and her Australian accent confused him. He'd
decided to go home to the land where he'd been born. Didn't need money.
Had been saving since she'd left home fifteen years ago. Simply wanted to
see her before he left. He'd leave tomorrow, make his way to Sydney in the
morning. She said not to worry about anything. They would look after him.
He insisted, not being the type of man who'd be beholden to anyone, not
even his own daughter.

'Oh, God,' she said to Becker. 'Not that place, not Odessa. The terrible
things he saw there.'

'That was long ago. It won't be the same.'

'It will be for him.'

'Why?'

'He doesn't wish to forget. Still talks about the bodies. Saw people lined up against the wall in the Prospect, saw them shot a dozen at a time, by a special squad, four-hundred Jews. Then they had to burn the bodies. Poured petrol over them. Did it right there against the wall, in the Prospect at the centre of Odessa, the main thoroughfare. Two roads separated by a park. He helped his father to do it. Along with the others. Watched and waited until they were reduced to fat and bones. In a great heap, under the wall. That was the beginning. The Nazi death squads killed more than a hundred-thousand Jews in the Ukraine, at least twenty-nine thousand in Odessa alone. If not in the city, then at Babi Yar.'

Becker didn't know what to say. He had a German name, but was not German. That didn't help. Somehow, he felt responsible.

'He was born there, my father. Mother was born there. He met her there. She had nothing to eat but raw potatoes and scraps out of bins. He had some bread. Someone gave them milk. They lived in the ruins, among the starving and the lonely and the rats. And the endless death. It went on and on. It was a place where you did not die. You did die, but you went on existing after death. It was a place not of infirmity or blissful eternity or suspenseful nothingness. It was four years in a state of everything-ness, to which you do not belong.'

He was holding her hand.

'When is he going?'

'Tomorrow,' he said.

'Does he have a ticket?'

'Yes, he does.'

'Where's his luggage?'

'At the station in Wagga.'

'We'll take him,' he said.

'Take him?'

'To Sydney, if you could stand a drive that long.'

'Oh, oh, I—'

'If that's what he wants to do, we'll do it.'

She smiled. 'You would do that for my father?'

Next day they left Roberta with Muriel, picked up old Victor's luggage from the railway station and drove to Sydney. The aircraft was leaving for Athens at three-thirty. They made it in plenty of time. Sitting four hours in a car was painful for Chook. She wriggled a lot, but never complained. Sat in a rear seat beside her father, all the way, chatting to him. Mostly Ukrainian and holding his hand.

They had a late lunch in a cafe at the airport and then waited with the old man.

He was not communicative. Information had to be dragged out of him. In Athens he would catch a connecting flight to Odessa. Thereafter he had no plans. He was going to die in Odessa, they knew. There was nothing they could do about that. He had decided. Often Anastacia alluded to the past, but his expression didn't change. It had the stony set of history, and you can't change history, even if you have the courage to face up to it. This old man, Victor Babchuk, had the courage. He was going back. To see it all again. No longer in his memory, but see it at the wall in the Alexander Prospect, where the Germans had shot the Jews. And where the Russians had shot his father when they came back, a traitor for helping the Germans.

They watched him walk off through the barrier, where a young woman in uniform checked his ticket and handed it back to him—and smiled quickly as she did hundreds of times a day. But it was a sympathetic smile. Perhaps she'd seen them standing there, staring. People going home. Wide-eyed with regret.

'We should have had him at the farm long ago,' Becker said.

'I should have done a lot more. But he would not allow me.'

'He was an isolated sort of man. I could not get through to him.'

'That's what he wanted to be,' she said.

Chapter 38

THEY WERE MARRIED at *Nil Desperandum* early in December 1997. A reasonably decent time to wait, Anastacia having recovered from the second operation, which had gone well. Everyone was there. Becker had bought his third wife a horse, a beautiful palomino, creamy with blond hair, like her own. The horse's name was *Como el viento*, which in Spanish means: Like the Wind. But was known as *Viento* for short, even though *Viento* is masculine and the horse was a mare. Wendy was fascinated. She'd always wanted to ride a horse. Being an active sort of girl rather than a quiet thinker, she was invited to hop up on top. She was amazed. After that, you couldn't keep her out of the place. So that Becker bought her a filly called Pixie, a dappled grey with a black fringe across her brow. It looked like a pixie cap.

They rode the range together, so to speak. Splashing through the creek, rounding up the cattle. Helped by that fool of a dog, Nutty, who didn't have a clue. He'd run around barking happily, so that often the cattle went the wrong way. Nonetheless, he was possibly the most affectionate Kelpie in Australia at that time.

Anastacia looked good on a horse—triumphant, you might say, often seen rounding up the cattle. Or, cantering along a country lane. Or, at the saleyards, hanging over a fence, raising a finger when the price was right. On the road, she drives the Nissan. As a result, she rarely rides the Harley Davidson. She had wanted to give it to Terry as a birthday present, if he ever reached eighteen. But Becker had talked her out of that, saying he was irresponsible enough without encouraging him to kill himself on the open road.

As for Terry, he couldn't wait to be eighteen so he could get into the Army. So he joined the Boy Scouts. And went mountain climbing and did other mad things like that. Even ran up to the top of The Rock. More than a thousand feet up. It's nigh on impossible to run up The Rock, the track is so rough. In fact, over the last few hundred feet, there is no track. In some spots you had to jump from rock to rock. But he claimed he could do it in an hour and a half. 'Almost,' he'd add. If Terry told you a tale and added 'almost', you knew he was lying. Still, he was an amiable sort of kid. Would do anything for you. Just showing off, Becker used to say. But not to his face.

Chook recovered from her wounds very fast.

It must have been her iron will. The gym was not at all like the those she'd known first in Melbourne and later in Canberra, sweaty places where you pumped iron and did a bit of kick-boxing. It was more like a dance class, full of women who wanted to lose weight. Full of loud music, mainly Latin stuff, salsas and cha-chas! Chook out front, yelling the time at them, getting them psyched up, everyone laughing.

In November of that year, Becker sold twenty-five heifers to the local meat works. He got a good price. Of course, his agent was old Tommy Thomkins, who saw to it that he did. Becker was sorry to see them go. It was like sending off your own children. Robyn would have been tearful. She had loved them and, in some way, they must have loved her. They missed her friendly words, her gentle hand. One day just before Christmas 1997, old Tommy dropped in. He was fully retired now.

'Heard you were doing well,' he said.

'Well enough.'

'How's the new wife going?'

'Good.'

'Pulling her weight, is she?'

'More than her weight.'

Tommy screwed up his face, looking around. Suddenly he didn't look too good.

'Still got some money in the bank?'

'A few dollars.'

'Wouldn't be looking for another investment, would you?'

'Such as?'

'Buying a share in the old firm.'

'You want to sell out?'

'Thought I'd go into a retirement village, but they want four-hundred thousand.'

'Four-hundred? Just to rent a room in a village? Why can't you stay at home?'

Tommy looked uncomfortable. 'Ah, well, I don't want to be a burden.'

'On the family?'

'Can't see why you'd be a burden, Tommy?'

The old man blanched. He was almost eighty now. Didn't meet Becker's eyes.

'Ah, well, you see, it'd be more than just a room.'

'You mean care?'

'Yeah.'

'Medical care?'

'Yeah.'

Becker watched him. Tommy was looking away at the creek and through the trees and across the cow paddock and perhaps on to the foothills, the rolling hills around Wagga Wagga turning purple in the late afternoon sun. The city had been his home most of his life. It was going to be his last.

'Something wrong, Tommy?'

'Yeah, mate, cancer.'

'What kind of cancer?'

'Prostate.'

'Jesus, Tommy, I thought you'd live forever.'

'Ah, yeah, well, so did I, but—'

'When do you need it?'

'Ah, well, they want it by the end of the week. They're holding a bed for me.'

'They'll have it by then.'

'Thanks, mate.' Tommy spoke as though he were ashamed. Quietly, not much more than a whisper. It hurt him to have to ask a favour.

'Which one?'

'Place? Kenilworth.'

'In Turvey Park?'

'That's the one.'

'All right, is it?'

'They have a nurse twenty-four hours and a doctor on call. Not far from the hospital too.'

'You'll be all right, Tommy.'

'Yeah, thanks, mate.'

Tommy Tomkins was still a handsome man, even at seventy-nine. Lean features, small blue eyes, hooked nose, perfectly trimmed moustache, white. Not much hair, though. Long curls at the back, nothing much up top. He was leaning against his car, arms folded, legs crossed. His father, the original Tommy Tompkins, had been a fine horseman. And soldier. He'd ridden in the great cavalry charge at Beersheba back in 1918. Young Tommy hadn't done much riding for many years, but he still had the air of a man who'd just got off a horse.

'I don't know much about business,' Becker said.

'Ah, the son and the girl'd look after you.'

He was referring to his son and granddaughter, Thomasina. 'He has a half share and young Sina has a quarter.'

Becker thought about it. He still had about two and a half million dollars of Evelyn's money, one million of it in Royal Bank shares—and they were paying a good ten per cent at that time. He didn't have to worry about money. The farm didn't yet pay its way, but that didn't matter. He was a man of substance. He'd sell off some of his BHP shares and become of man of business as well. A quarter share in the old established firm of Thos. Thompkins & Son. Half the old families on the land this end of the Riverina dealt with Tommy. People like the Langhornes and McNevins and Bamfords and the Cudlips. People who normally would not shake your hand. Not the hand of a smelly failed cop from Sydney.

'And what do I do?'

'Turn up at board meetings now and then. Otherwise, sit back and watch the money roll in.'

'That all?'

'More or less.'

They shook hands on it. Old Tommy took one last look at the place before he got into his car. 'You know why John Kettle called this place *Nil Desperandum*?'

'No, why?'

'When he arrived in the thirties, he was doing well—too well, as it turned out.' Tommy was referring to the eighteen-thirties. 'Then, suddenly, early in the forties the wool market collapsed.' He meant the English market. 'Settlers like him went broke, desperate. It was so bad they had to boil down their sheep. If that didn't save you, there was always the nearest tree to hang yourself. Or try arsenic.'

'Arsenic?'

'They all had it, for the scabby sheep.'

'Boil them down?'

'For the tallow, the only part of the sheep they could sell. The rest they had to eat or give to the dogs or the blacks.'

'Why tallow?'

'For the illumination. There was nothing else in those days, except a few oil lamps. But John Kettle got through. When his title was finally granted, he'd named the place *Nil Desperandum*.'

'Never give up?'

'Yeah, mate, that's it. If you're on the land, you never give up.' He shot out a hand again. 'So long, son. I'll get Ken Sawyer to draw up a deed. You know him?'

'He's my lawyer too.'

'He's all right.'

'Yeah, I know. So long, Tommy.'

Becker watched him drive away. He was shocked. He was fond of Tommy, a sort of father-figure. A man you could depend upon, no matter what happened. Wagga Wagga would not be the same without him.

Old Bert died in 1998. Becker went over one morning and saw the second Blue sitting on the verandah, looking at him but not moving. Normally, the dog would walk out to meet him as soon as he got his scent. But sat there. The closer Becker came the more the dog looked worried. Put his head down on his paws. His eyes went down at the corners and he looked as though he were going to cry. Or howl, the ways dogs do when they know something is wrong. No sign of Bert. Where is he? The dog wagged his tail, but didn't move. You could see the dog knew, but didn't know any other way to tell you.

Becker tried the door, which was unlocked.

It was dark or darkish in there, although it was mid-morning. Looked in the front room and then the bedroom. The place stank a bit, it always did. Then he went into what would be called a kitchen, if it weren't such a mess. Stuff stacked everywhere, and papers and documents piled on the old deal table. There were two or three rickety chairs, one of them broken, not in the legs but in the backing. A couple of broken spindles. On the floor was Bert, the Hollis lying beside him. Becker kneeled down, had a good look, even rolled Bert over a bit, so he could get a better look.

The old man was lying on his face, one hand out towards the Hollis, the other folded under. No sign of blood.

Must have died of a heart attack. Gone in a minute, the dog outside unable to go to his aid. They really loved each other those two, man and dog. The dog was given a new home, next door. Blue Two proved to be a good with cattle, knew exactly what to do when herding cows. A bigger herd now, Becker having decided to carry stock on both sides of the creek. So, pretty soon, he had eighty Angus in all. Plus, two horses. Even if you're trying to muster them from the saddle with a stockwhip, it's difficult. They never seem to understand where you want them to go. But with a dog does.

They gave him a good funeral, old Bert.

He'd been a bit of bastard at first, almost impossible to talk to. But you couldn't blame him. He hadn't had much schooling. He'd been brought up rough and tough. Gone through hell in New Guinea, but he'd survived. As a kid, he'd walked all the way from Shepparton to Ballarat, with his dead father. At least, dead over the last miles in the back of a utility—back in the old days, when men were walking the roads, looking for work. His father looking for justice, the kind of justice that was all in his head. Because he was mad, mad with self-denial. A real crackpot, if ever you met one. Bert left his rough and scrubby square mile of red-loam country to the Salvation Army. Always grateful to the Salvos, as he called them.

Becker promptly bought it from them, cleared it of the old house and decrepit sheds and water tank and outback dunny and broken fences and fruitless fruit trees. Got the rural fire brigade in to burn it off, the weeds and all the undesirable shrubs and vines and Scotch thistles and paspalum and pumpkin vines and shapeless scrub that had sprung up over the years of neglect. Burnt it right off, rather than use poison. Got the brigade to do the job for a good price. Engaged the fire chief, Hermann Eckhardt, known as Hermie to one and all, a contractor rather than farmer, to plough it twice, then plant it with maize. Finally, he installed a big metal silage bin, so he'd always have feed for his cattle.

If the worst came to the worst, he'd have artesian water connected to the household system. Artesian is usually full of minerals, such as lead, arsenic and uranium. If it were too hard to drink, he'd pump it up to a tank under the roof, then run it down through a purifier. It might smell bad. If it did, he'd install a condenser, so that the steam produced by the boiler was turned into distilled water. Then chilled in the refrigerator, which in turn would be powered by solar panels. So would the whole house. That way, the farm would be drought-proofed—provided the bore held out.

This was the first year of the Millennial drought, as it was to be called.

It lasted eight years.

Shawline Publishing Group Pty Ltd
www.shawlinepublishing.com.au

SHAWLINE
PUBLISHING
GROUP

Milton Keynes UK
Ingram Content Group UK Ltd.
UKHW041226260224
438490UK00004B/103